THE
UNFORTU

Laurie Graham is a former *Daily Telegraph* columnist and contributing editor to *She* magazine. She now lives in Italy, writing fiction and also radio drama scripts. *The Unfortunates* is her seventh novel.

For more information on Laurie Graham's *The Unfortunates* and to download a reading guide visit www.4thestate.com/lauriegraham

'Graham is a writer with a remarkably malleable comic voice' Alex Clark, *Guardian*

'Set in New York, France and England, this witty book is brimming with irony while an understated sadness bubbles just under the surface.' Ann Dunne, *Irish Independent*

'The enchanting tale of a young Poppy Minkel and her spirited attempts to escape her mother's obsession with marrying her off.' *Red*

'Like something out of *Gentlemen Prefer Blondes*. A novel that manages to touch on those things that are near irrevocable, on laughter, and on loss.' Sophie Ratcliffe, *Times Literary Supplement*

Other titles by Laurie Graham

Fiction
The Man for the Job
The Ten O'clock Horses
Perfect Meringues
The Dress Circle
Dog Days, Glenn Miller Nights
The Future Homemakers of America

Non-fiction
The Parent's Survival Guide
The Marriage Survival Guide
Teenagers

THE
UNFORTUNATES

Laurie Graham

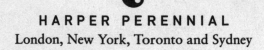

HARPER PERENNIAL
London, New York, Toronto and Sydney

This paperback edition first published in 2003
First published in Great Britain in 2002 by
Fourth Estate
A Division of HarperCollins*Publishers*
77–85 Fulham Palace Road,
London W6 8JB
www.4thestate.com

10 9 8 7 6 5

A catalogue record for this book is available from the British Library

ISBN 1–84115–315–X

Book design by Geoff Green

Typeset by Palimpsest Book Production Limited,
Polmont, Stirlingshire

Printed and bound in Great Britain by
Clays Ltd, St Ives plc

To Joan Fitzgerald

THE
UNFORTUNATES

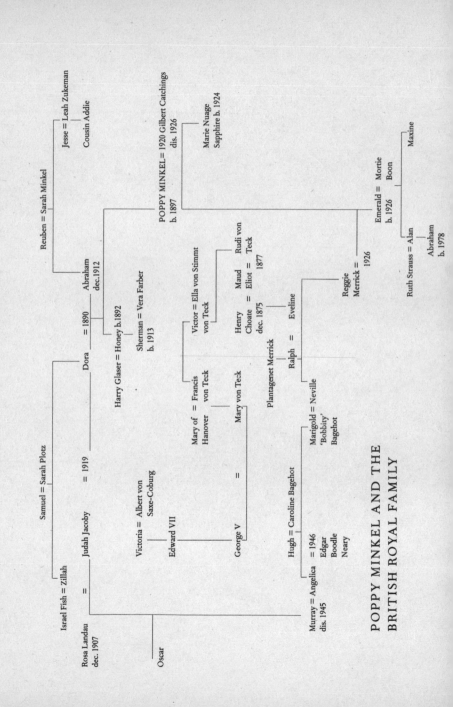

POPPY MINKEL AND THE
BRITISH ROYAL FAMILY

ONE

It was just as well I had ripped off my Ear Correcting Bandages. Had I been bound up in my usual bedtime torture-wear, I would never have heard my mother's screams.

The bandages were part of my preparation for the great husband hunt. I was only fifteen years old, but my mother recognized a difficult case when she saw one. She had taken up the challenge the day after my twelfth birthday and never spared herself since.

'The early bird, Poppy,' she always said, when I complained. 'The early bird.'

And so, assisted by my aunt, she began an all-fronts campaign to catch me a worm.

I was forbidden candy and other waist-thickening substances. I was enrolled for classes in piano, singing and cotillion dancing, and spent an hour every day in a backboard, during which I practiced French pronunciation whilst a series of Irish maids tried to straighten my hair, or at least, defeat its natural wiriness into the kind of soft loose curls preferred by husbands.

On alternate days my neck was painted with Gomper's Patent Skin Whitener, to coax out of it a certain oriental tinge. The label advised using the paste no oftener than once a week. But as my mother said, what did they know? They hadn't seen my neck.

As to my nose, she knew the limits of home improvements. I was to go to a beauty doctor in Cincinnati, as soon as I was sixteen, and have a little cartilage shaved off.

Meanwhile she applied herself to the correction of my protruding ears. She designed an adjustable bandeau to hold them flat against my skull while I slept and had the Irish girl make them up for me in a selection of nightwear colours.

'So you can choose, you see?' Ma explained. 'According to your frame of mind.'

And, gauging my frame of mind all too well, my aunt informed me that some day, when I had grown in wisdom, I would be grateful for their efforts.

The alternative to all this was that I would be left an old maid.

I knew what an old maid was. My cousin Addie was being one up in Duluth, Minnesota, riding around all day with her dogs and not wearing corsets. And I knew what marriage was too. My sister Honey had recently married Harry Glaser and as soon as the marrying was done she had to leave home and put up her hair. As far as I could see she wasn't allowed to play with her dolls anymore, and she had hardly any time for cutting out pretty things for her scrapbook. She had had to go to tea parties all the time, but never appear too eager about cake, and whenever she came to call Ma would make mysterious inquiries.

'Honey,' she'd whisper, 'how are Things? Are you still using the Lysol?'

To avoid the fate that had befallen Honey, I decided on stealthy sabotage rather than outright rebellion. As long as things *appeared* to be satisfactory my mother took them to *be* satisfactory. Surface was her preferred level. Hidden depths were unattractive to her, therefore she behaved as though they did not exist. So, every night, I took off my ear correctors, but only after the house had fallen dark and silent.

Then, that night, someone came to the front door and rang the bell with great persistence. I thought it had to be a stranger. Anyone who knew us knew the hours we kept. They knew our disapproval of night life and lobster suppers and men who rolled home incapable of putting a key neatly in a keyhole.

I heard the Irish slide back the bolt, eventually, and voices. And then, leaning up on my elbow, holding my breath so as not to miss anything, I heard my Ma scream. This signaled excitement. The late visitors were Aunt Fish and Uncle Israel Fish, come straight from the opera, still in their finery, because they had seen newsboys selling a late extra edition with reports of a tragedy at sea. 'At sea' was where my Pa was, sailing home from Europe.

Aunt Fish was my mother's sister and she always seemed as at home in our parlor as she did in her own. By the time I had pulled on my wrapper and run downstairs she had already arranged Ma on a couch and was administering sal volatile.

'Are you sure he sailed, Dora?' she kept asking, but my mother wasn't sure of anything. 'Maybe he didn't sail. Maybe business kept him in London.'

My father had been in Berlin and London, inspecting his subsidiaries.

'Israel will go to the shipping offices,' Aunt Fish said. 'Israel, go to the shipping offices.'

Uncle Israel was stretched out with a cigarette.

'Nothing to be done at this hour,' he said. Aunt Fish turned and looked at him.

He left immediately. And my mother, released from the constraints of being seen by her brother-in-law dressed only in her nightgown, collapsed anew.

'Poppy,' said Aunt Fish, 'don't just stand there. Be a comfort to your mother.' And so while she plagued the Irish for a facecloth soaked in vinegar, and more pillows, and a jug of hot chocolate, I stood by my mother's side and wondered what kind of comforting to do.

I tried stroking her arm, but this appeared to irritate her. I looked at her, with my head set at a compassionate angle, but that didn't please her either. I was altogether relieved when Aunt Fish returned from harassing our help and resumed her post as couch-side comforter.

I said, 'Aunt Fish, is Pa lost at sea?' and Ma resumed her wailing.

'Poppy!' said Aunt Fish. 'Don't you have even an ounce of sense? Your poor mother has received a terrible shock. If you can't be quiet and sensible, then please return to your bed.'

I'm sure it wasn't me that had rung the doorbell in the middle of the night with news of shipwrecks.

'And send the Irish in, to build up the fire,' she shouted after me.

We had stopped bothering with names for our Irish maids. They never stayed long enough to make it worth learning a new one.

'And Poppy,' my mother called weakly, from her couch, 'don't forget to strap down your ears.'

I lay awake, waiting to hear Uncle Israel's return, but eventually I must have dozed, and then it was morning. But it was not like any other morning. Our family was suddenly part of a great drama. The first edition of the *Herald* reported that though Pa's ship had been in a collision, all hands were saved and she was now being towed into Halifax, Nova Scotia.

Aunt Fish returned, having changed into a morning gown, and then Uncle Israel, with news that the White Star Line was chartering a train to take relatives up to Halifax to be reunited with their loved ones.

I said, 'I'll go. Let me go.' This provided my aunt with further reasons to despair of me.

'For heaven's sakes, child!' she sighed, and Uncle Israel winked at me.

'Out of the question, Pops,' he said. 'Too young, you see. But why not write a little note? I'll see he gets it as soon he sets foot on land.'

'There's no need for you to go, Israel,' my mother said. The morning's brighter news had restored her appetite and she was eating a pile of toast and jam. 'I can always send Harry, if it isn't convenient to you.'

'Of course it's convenient,' said Aunt Fish. 'It's Israel's place to go.'

I went to the escritoire and started composing my letter to Pa, but I was still more haunted by the idea that he might have drowned than I was uplifted by the prospect that he was safe. I had no sooner written the words 'Please, never go away again' than I burst into inappropriate and inconsiderate tears and was sent to my room.

Soon after, my sister arrived with her husband. Honey came up to my room and lay on my bed beside me.

'Don't cry, Pops,' she said. 'Pa's safe. And you don't want to get swollen eyes.'

I said, 'Why did he have to go across an ocean, anyhow?'

'Why, because that's what men do,' she said.

I said, 'Would you allow Harry?'

'Allow?' she said. 'It isn't my place to allow. Besides, I know everything Harry does is for the very best.'

I had often suspected that marrying had caused a softening of Honey's brain.

Uncle Israel left that afternoon on the special train to Halifax. And Harry went downtown, first to his broker with instructions to buy stock in the Marconi wireless company whose wonderful shipboard radio had helped save so many lives and bring comforting news to the waiting families. Then he went to the White Star offices to inquire when the passengers might be expected back in New York.

Honey and I were pasting scraps, just like old times, when Harry walked in, looking smaller and flatter and grayer than usual. He scratched his head.

'It's gone,' he said. 'The *Titanic* has sunk, with heavy losses. A boat called the *Carpathia* is bringing the survivors home.'

It was eight o'clock. Up in Massachusetts Uncle Israel's train was stopped, directed into a siding and reversed. There had been, he was told, a change of plan.

My cheeks were hot from the fire, but something deathly cold touched me. My mother fainted onto a couch. My sister uttered a terrible little cry. And Harry studied the pattern on the parlor rug.

'Marconi stock closed up one hundred and twenty points,' he said, to no one in particular.

TWO

My Grandpa Minkel and his brother Meyer arrived in Great Portage, Minnesota, in 1851 intending to set up as fur traders, but they were too late. The beaver pelt business was finished. They stayed on though and changed their plans and did well enough trading in lumber to build a fine house on top of a hill in Duluth. From Grandpa Minkel's house you could see clear to Wisconsin. So they said.

Meyer and his wife were never blessed with children. This was somehow due to the accidental firing of a Winchester '73, but I was never allowed to know the details. So when Grandpa headed south, looking to buy a spread and turn farmer, he left behind one of his own boys, Jesse, as a kind of second-hand son. Gave him away near enough, though he was a grown man and might well have had plans of his own. Grandpa took his other boy, Abe, to Iowa to be a mustard farmer. And that was my Pa.

Uncle Jesse stayed where he was put, married one of the Zukeman girls and had a number of obedient children, plus Cousin Addie, the one who refused to knuckle down to marriage. Grandpa Minkel grew so much mustard he had to buy a factory. Grandma Minkel told him he should make mustard that had a fine flavor but a short life, and she was right. Folks just had to keep coming back for more and Minkel's Mighty Fine Mustard did so well Grandma and Grandpa had to send Pa to New York City, to invest the profits and keep his finger on the quickening pulse of finance.

My mother's people were Plotzes. They sold feathers and goose down, in Cedar Rapids. She married Pa in 1890 and came with him to New York soon after, in a delicate condition with my sister Honey. Ma took to her new life as if to the city born. She sent directly for her sister Zillah and fixed her up with Israel Fish, and from then on a veil fell over the Iowa period of their lives. Cedar Rapids had been a mere accident of birth, and was never discussed. As far as Ma and Aunt Fish were concerned everything from the Hudson shore to the Pacific Ocean was nothing but a social wilderness.

Minkel's Mighty Fine Mustard was to be found on every discerning table and the profits were invested in railroads and mining, and the consequence was Honey and I were mustard heiresses, more or less.

Pa, though, kept his finger on more than the pulse of finance, and was often absent from his own table, indulging, as I had overheard discussed by my mother and Aunt Fish, in 'a man's needs'. I understood these to be cigars and blintzes, two things that were not permitted at home. For these comforts Pa went elsewhere. We lived on West 76th Street. My mother bore the impediment of this address as bravely as she could. Pa and Uncle Israel Fish assured her that before too long New York society would abandon their houses on Fifth Avenue and follow her there.

'We're setting a trend, Dora,' Pa used to say.

But my mother didn't want to set trends. On the steep climb to good society, novelty was one of those hazards that could pitch us all back down where we'd started. Her plan was to keep us as unremarkable as possible. Correct and unremarkable. Let no Minkel be a protruding nail. I don't think Pa ever appreciated what a close watch Ma kept over our reputation and standing. And no matter how much she protested, he bought that rose pink low-stoop house and encouraged the architect to add as many turrets and finials as could be accommodated.

My aunt, who still lived safely within visiting distance of The Right People, should the call ever come, said, 'Never fear, Dora. Marriage may be a sacred institution, but if Abe tries to drag you any further into the wilderness, you may depend on having a home with us.'

On evenings when Pa was home, a fire was lit in the library and I was allowed to sit in there with him and look at the things on the shelves of the vitrine. He had a beaver skull, and a rock of fool's gold, and an Ojibway Indian necklace, and a little silk cap, brought by Grandpa Minkel from Germany. There was a rubber plant, and a stuffed osprey, and books. I was allowed to take them down off the shelf and read them, as long as I sat in a good light and didn't scowl or screw up my eyes. Careless reading can cause the setting in of ugly, permanent facial lines. For this reason my mother never risked opening a book.

When the lamps and the fire were lit and Pa and I sat, cozily turning the pages, it was the best of times. I hated to hear him clear his throat and take out his watch. It meant my time was nearly up and he was preparing to go out into the night.

'Pa,' I'd say, 'don't go for a blintz tonight.'

But he'd snap shut his watch case and go anyhow. I wasn't altogether sure what a blintz was, but I knew Pa's favorite kind was cherry, and I liked the sound of that. I knew, too, that for the best blintzes you had to go to Delancey Street, a dangerous place teeming with something Ma called 'the element'. I worried that one of those nights Pa wouldn't come home. Murdered by 'the element', and all for a cherry blintz.

THREE

It was Tuesday night when Harry brought the news. There was no sleep. Honey cried until she made herself sick. Aunt Fish said she had always doubted the flotation principle. Harry steadied himself with a hot buttered rum, advising us against plunging into despair before the list of survivors had been published. And the Irish, who could hardly keep her eyes open, was kept from her bed, letting out the side seams on Ma's mourning wear. Unaccountably, every gown had shrunk in the years since Grandpa Minkel's passing.

Wednesday, there was still no news and Ma was on her second bottle of Tilden's Extract, a tonic she usually only resorted to in order to face the rigors of giving a dinner. By Thursday our house was in a permanent state of receiving. Mrs Schwab and Mrs Lesser called, and the Misses Stone and Mrs Teller. Maids came with soup. And Uncle Israel drove down to Broadway three times in search of information and came back with none.

Aunt Fish was exasperated with him. 'Go back, Israel,' she said, 'and stay there until they tell you something.'

My poor uncle. Sometimes he seemed to be as much of a disappointment to my aunt as I was. Once again, it was Harry who delivered the goods. He called by telephone, a device my mother had never wanted in the house because of the extra work it would heap upon her. She refused to answer it, and Honey would never do anything Ma wouldn't do, so I was the one to take the call.

'Poppy!' Ma chided. She was at a loss to know what to do with me. Two whole days had passed without my hair being straightened or my slouch corrected, but she was too distracted to insist. And now there I was, crossing the room at an unseemly pace, snatching up the hated telephone and chewing my fingernails.

'Tonight,' Harry said. He was breathless. 'The *Carpathia*'s expected tonight.'

Aunt Fish loosened Ma's collar.

'Bear up now, Dora,' she said. 'Israel will represent you. There's sure to be a crowd and it'll take a man of Israel's standing to get to the head of the queue.'

'Harry will go,' was all Ma would say. 'Harry will go.'

Harry didn't realize he had a passenger in the back of his automobile. I waited until he turned onto Columbus before I emerged from under the pile of blankets Ma and Honey had had brought out. They seemed to imagine Pa might still be wet from the sinking.

'What the hell are you doing there?' he said. 'Get out! Get out at once!'

'Make me,' I challenged him.

'Oh please, Poppy,' he whined. 'You're going to get me into hot water.'

For all his talk of turning around and taking me home, he carried right on driving. He knew who'd win if it came to a fight. Harry's trouble was he didn't have any backbone.

I said, 'When Pa steps off that boat I want to be sure the first thing he sees is my face.'

'There you go,' he said. 'Getting your hopes up. Well don't come crying to me. I never invited you along.'

Around 32nd Street we began to see people. Hundreds of them hurrying down to the Cunard pier. Harry parked the Simplex and we joined the crowds. There was thunder rolling in over the Palisades and the *Carpathia* was on her way up the Hudson, with tugs and skiffs and anything else that would float swarming round her and blasts of magnesium light flashing from the newsmen's cameras. She was making slow progress, and then word came up she had paused, down by Pier 32, so that certain items could be taken off. Lifeboats. Property of the White Star Line.

Harry whispered, 'They'll fetch a pretty penny, as curios.'

But they didn't. As I heard years later, they were picked clean by human vultures before anyone could start the bidding, and the name *Titanic* was rubbed off them with emery paper and that was the end of that.

Slowly the *Carpathia* came home. Some people had cards bearing the name of the ones they were hoping to see. I wished I had thought to make a card. They held them up, praying for a wave or a smile, but nobody at the rail was smiling or waving.

It was half past eight by the time they began to warp her in, and then the thunderstorm broke. We waited another hour, in the rain, until she was moored and the gangplank was lowered, and lists of survivors were finally posted. That was when I got separated from Harry.

There was such a crush I could scarcely breathe and I was wet to the skin.

'Please,' I asked the man in front of me, 'can you see if Minkel is there?'

But he gave me an elbow in the ribs and I never saw him again. A woman said she'd find out for me if I gave her a dollar, but I didn't have a dollar. And so I just found a place to lean, against the customs shed, figuring the best thing was to stand still and allow Pa to spot me easily.

Then a Cunard porter noticed me.

'Are you all right, Miss?' he said. 'Is it First Class you're looking for?'

I said, 'Mr Abraham Minkel. I can't pay you though. I don't come into my money until I'm twenty-one. But my father will tip you.'

He touched his cap and disappeared, and I didn't expect to see him again. A sense of service was a thing of the past, as Ma and Aunt Fish often remarked, and everyone expected something in their grubby hand before they'd stir themselves.

And so I waited, shivering, wondering at the uselessness of Harry Glaser, trying to draw up a balance sheet of my standing at home. I believed my crimes of disobedience, ingratitude and impropriety might just be offset by the triumph of being the one to bring home Pa.

The ladies from First Class began to file into the echoing shed. There were children, too. Some were crying, most were silent, and the ladies still had on their hats. 'How odd,' I thought. 'A sinking must be a good deal gentler than I imagined.' And then this happened. I saw a face I knew.

The very moment I looked at her, she sensed it and looked back at me, quite directly. Then she turned her head away and disappeared into the crowd. I was still puzzling how an Irish, dismissed without references, could have sailed first-class and in such Parisian style, when the Cunard boy reappeared beside me.

'Miss,' he said, 'I'm afraid to say I couldn't find a Mr Abraham Minkel listed, but Mrs Minkel is there, alive and well. You should be seeing her any moment now.'

But the women had all disembarked. The men filed through next, but my Pa was not amongst them. They all had downcast eyes, and a hurried step, and somewhere in the crowd I heard somebody hiss. Being a survivor isn't necessarily a happy condition, I realized later. There would always be the question, hanging in the air, too awful to ask, 'And how were you so fortunate? What other poor soul paid for your life with his? Or hers?' If you were an able-bodied man, it would have been better form to perish nobly.

'Not spotted her yet, Miss?' the porter asked. 'Well, that's a mystery.'

He was now taking more interest in my case than I liked. He was like a stray dog, eagerly padding along at my side, on the strength of one brief expression of gratitude.

I said, 'It's not a mystery. It was a cruel mistake. There was no *Mrs* Minkel. Only my Pa, but he's not here. Is there another boat? Are there more following on?'

He looked away.

'I don't think so, Miss,' he whispered. 'I don't think so at all.'

People milled around us, plucking at him, wanting his attention. 'My Pa's lost,' I said. I knew it.

And he was glad enough then to make his getaway.

A woman said, 'There's to be a service of thanksgiving. Right away.'

What did I care? Thanksgiving for what?

'Not just thanksgiving,' she said, reading my expression. 'To pray for the ones that were lost as well. A prayer is never wasted.'

The third-class passengers had been directed to another shed, and a group of them were leaving, and some first-class ladies, too, walking to the nearest church.

Over the heads of a hundred people I thought I saw the feather trim of the Irish's hat, and I decided at that moment to add another item to the list of my transgressions. I abandoned all thoughts of Harry Glaser and followed the throng, walking as quickly as I could so as to catch up, trying to remember whether I had ever known her name.

We had had any number of Marys, several Annes and a Videlma Teresa who broke, against stiff competition, all previous records for brevity of employment with us, but on the whole, their names disappeared. They were, to a girl, impertinent, uncouth and given to 'carrying on' so that Ma often predicted her death would be certified as 'caused by Irish'.

I had never been in a church before. Ma and Aunt Fish had formulated a plan for their concerted rise in New York society, and a key decision had been to keep a low profile *vis-à-vis* God.

'Religion gives rise to intemperate opinions, Dora,' Aunt Fish advised, 'and a hostess does well to keep those from her table.'

So we avoided any association with God as carefully as we avoided cold drafts, and, with regard to this, nothing could have made Ma happier than Honey's choice of Harry Glaser as a husband.

'A good thing about Harry,' I had often heard her say, 'is that he doesn't go in for religion.'

I knew therefore, as we came to the doors of St Peter's Episcopalian church, to expect dangerous excesses inside, and I resolved to stay in command of myself. I kept my eyes downcast for five minutes at least, for fear of coming face to face with this God who was too controversial to have to dinner.

All around me grown men wept and crumbled, and candles were lit, and a song was sung, in poor cracked voices, for those in peril on the sea.

'Too late now for that,' I thought, aching for the smell of my Pa's hair tonic. But I liked being there, close to people who had been saved from the dark and deep. I liked how determined they had been to walk to 20th Street and pray when they might have gone home directly and been cosseted with warm milk and cake.

She was kneeling, across the other side of the church, busy with some Irish hocus-pocus. I kept her in my sights and moved a couple of times, to get nearer to her, squeezing past people who complained and people who were too lost in their sorrow to notice. I had remembered her name.

When the singing and praying was over I moved quickly, to be sure of blocking her path as she made to leave.

'Nellie,' I said, 'is it you?'

She gave me a stubborn look I recognized, but her face colored. She may have been dressed by Mr Worth, but she still had the look of a maid caught trying on her mistress's gown.

I said, 'My Pa was on the *Titanic*. Did you see him, by any chance?'

Still she resisted me, and I felt my chance slipping away, to know the worst, or to find new hope.

'Please, Nellie,' I begged. 'Can you tell me anything at all?'

Her pertness dissolved.

'I'm so sorry, Miss Poppy,' she said. 'I'm so sorry for your loss. He went back for my muff. I begged him not to, but he would go . . .'

We stood face to face but at cross purposes, and people flowed around us, away, out of the church and back into life.

'. . . it was my Persian broadtail muff,' she said, 'and it was an awful cold night.'

I said, 'So you did see him? Were you close to him? Did he say anything?'

'He said "Go to the boat station, Nellie. I'll come to you there."'

Then her tears started.

'He lived and died a gentleman,' she said. 'Whatever people may say, there were no irregularities between us. I was there by way of secretary to him.'

I said, 'How could you be? Mr Levi was his secretary. And anyway, can you read?'

'I can,' she said. 'Well. I was more of an assistant. A personal assistant. There was no one could take away his headaches the way I could. And that's how things stood. I'd swear to it on the good book.'

They always said that when they were lying. Next thing she'd be asking for wages still owed.

I said, 'Where do you live? Where are you going?'

'To my sister,' she said. 'Or maybe to my cousin.'

The slipperiness of the Irish. How right my mother was.

It was a long walk home. Three miles, I now know, but then I had no idea of distance or time. My shoes rubbed holes in my stockings and my toes were pinched and sore, but I pressed on as fast as I could. I knew the streets were full of robbers and murderers and women who drank sherry wine.

It wasn't exactly fear kept me hurrying along. Now my Pa had died, dead seemed an easy thing to be. Still, I wasn't sure I'd be as brave as he had been. 'Go to the boat station, Nellie.' When the moment came, I might squawk, or not quite die, and lie in agony in the gutter.

I knew, too, I'd be the subject of a full inquiry at home, and I preferred to face it as soon as possible. There was no predicting what grief would make of Ma. She might forgive all, in a fit of tenderness, or she might turn on me, like a wounded beast. In any event, it has always been my nature to take whatever I have coming to me as quickly as possible.

As I passed the New Theater, nearly home, I heard an automobile chugging toward me and I knew it was a search party in the shape of Harry Glaser. He all but threw me into the car. I didn't think he had it in him.

'You damned fool,' was all he could say. 'You goddamned fool!'

I said, 'You were the one abandoned me. I waited for you. And does Honey know you use language?'

'Don't we have hard enough times ahead of us with your Ma,' he said, 'without you disappearing and putting me in a bad odor? What's your game?'

I said, 'I lost you in the crowd, that's all. Why are you so afraid of Ma? What did she say? What's my punishment?'

'Consider yourself mighty lucky,' he said. 'So far you haven't been missed, but you're not home and dry yet. You've still got to get back into the house and into your bed, and I suppose you'll be expecting my help? You're a brat, no two ways.'

'Harry,' I said, 'a porter told me there was a Minkel on the list of survivors. Did you see that?'

'No,' he said. 'I definitely did not, and neither did you if you know what's good for you. Anyway, it was clearly a clerical error.'

A lamp was burning in the parlor, but it was only Uncle Israel Fish, smoking a last cigarette. He appeared in the doorway as I tiptoed up the stairs but seemed not to notice me. We only see what we expect to see, I suppose. It was another lesson for me, and I had learned so many in just one day. I listed them as I lay in bed, too tired for sleep.

1. My Pa was not indestructible.
2. Personal assistants got Persian lamb muffs and trips to Europe.
3. I was blessed with powers of invisibility.
4. Harry Glaser was a half-wit, my sister married him, therefore I would be expected to marry a half-wit, therefore I would not marry.

I got up, lit a candle, and one by one I committed to its flame my ear-correcting bandeaux. First the pink one, then the apricot, then the eau-de-Nil. They created an interesting and rather satisfying smell.

FOUR

I t was Aunt Fish who came into my room next morning. She was wearing her black bombazine.

'Poppy,' she said, gravely, 'a terrible sadness has come to this house, so you must now make great efforts to be a good girl, for your dear mother's sake.'

I said, 'I'm sure I always do try to be good.'

'There is all the difference in the world between trying and succeeding,' she said, 'and quibbling with me is not a promising way to begin.'

I said, 'I know Pa is drowned, Aunt Fish. I know Ma is a poor widow now.'

She leapt up and knotted the ends of her shawl in despair.

'That is precisely the kind of heartless remark good girls do not make,' she said. 'Your duty is to spare your mother from harsh reminders.'

I got up and put on my wrapper. Aunt Fish was looking at my ruined stockings and muddied shoes.

I said, 'Am I to pretend then that Pa isn't drowned? Am I to pretend he may come back some day?'

'You are to wash your face and show respect,' she said. 'You are to go to your mother, and try to persuade her to sip a little peptonized milk, to keep up her strength. And you are never ever to speak of drownings, or steam ships or . . . oceans. How worn out your shoes are, Poppy. I'd suggest a new pair, but you'll be going out so seldom now it hardly seems worth the expense.'

And with those words, Aunt Fish raised the curtain on a whole new period of my life.

Ma was propped up with extra pillows. Her night table was cluttered with various bottled remedies, her little helpers. I could see she had been crying. I suppose she could see I had, too. She patted the bed beside her.

'What a blessing I have you, Poppy,' she said. 'I see now, this was all meant to be. If you had been as favored with beauty as Honey you'd soon make a good match and then what would I do, left all alone in the world?'

I opened my mouth to say I didn't think Honey was all *that* favored with beauty, but Ma was getting into her stride.

'But it's so clear to me now,' she continued. 'I was given a beauty for the consolation her children will bring me, and I was given a plain one for companionship in my old age. How wise Nature is!'

I said, 'Does this mean I don't have to go to Cincinnati for a new nose?'

'The nose is cancelled,' she said. 'And the singing lessons and the French and the cotillions. There's no sense in exerting ourselves in that direction anymore.'

The husband hunt had been called off. Still, I had rather enjoyed my singing lessons.

I said, 'Shouldn't you like me to be able to sing for you sometimes, Ma?'

'Not at all,' she said. 'I should like you to read to me sometimes from the *Home Journal*. And mend stockings.'

She tried to stroke my hair, but her fingers caught in it. Standing in the rain had given it a particularly vicious kink.

'We'll just live quietly now,' she said. 'No more dinners.'

Dinners had always been a trial to her, as she clambered the foothills of society. She had once committed the solecism of following a *potage crème* with creams of veal *en dariole*. It was only the dessert, a Prune Shape, produced by Reilly, our cook, in a moment of whimsy, as a substitute for the Almond Shape that had been ordered, which saved Ma from the social ruin of presiding over a completely beige meal.

As far as I know she never descended to the kitchen. Her negotiations with Reilly were conducted entirely through a speaking tube that connected the parlor to the scullery. The temperature of their exchanges rose as the dinner hour drew near, and neither party ever seemed to understand that they could not only hear and be heard. They could also be overheard.

'Reilly has been nipping at the brandy,' was one of Ma's favorite asides.

Reilly herself was fond of the prefix 'fecken'', as in, 'I'll give her fecken' *fricandeau* of sweetbreads, all right.'

I took this to be a quaint usage from Reilly's home country and sometimes repeated it, in imitation of her. I had no idea what it meant, and neither did Ma, so no harm was done.

On the day of a dinner, Ma required an extra dose of Tilden's, for her nerves. The day after a dinner, her shades were kept tightly closed and she took nothing stronger than seltzer water. That Pa's death meant an end to all this was no cause of regret to me.

I said, 'What about the backboard? Do I still have to wear that?'

'Good posture is always an asset,' she said, 'even in a homely girl.'

I sensed, though, that this was the moment to strike as many bargains as possible, and I was just about to sue for a ceasefire in the war against my protruding ears, when Aunt Fish appeared in the doorway. In her hand were the ashes of my corrective nightwear bandeaux.

'Dora!' she said. 'I have had the candle removed from Poppy's vanity table. I fear she is not yet to be trusted with unguarded flames.'

FIVE

L ike Great Uncle Meyer, Aunt and Uncle Fish had not been blessed with children of their own, and perhaps they had expected Ma and Pa to follow Grandpa Minkel's example and hand over their spare. At any rate, Aunt Fish seemed to believe she had some lien over me and the bigger I grew, the more forthcoming she was with her advice and opinions.

On the subject of molding and polishing Honey, she had deferred to my mother. Clearly she, the elder sister, understood better than Aunt Fish, a younger and childless person, how to raise a daughter, especially a daughter as perfectly pink and golden as Honey. But my aunt sensed the moment would come when her talents for, as she put it, 'the handling of more difficult cases' would be gratefully received. If Aunt Fish ever had a career, it was me.

After Pa's death she deemed her normal daily visits to be inadequate and she moved into our house for an indefinite period, to spare Ma the burden of household decisions and make good my deficiencies as a tower of strength. Ma suggested that this might be a great inconvenience to Uncle Israel, but he insisted that nothing could be more convenient to him. He would dine at his club, he said, and be occupied until late every night going through Pa's complicated business affairs with Mr Levi, ensuring everything was in order.

Complicated was a word that filled Ma with terror.

'Are they not all in order, Israel?' she asked him, handkerchief at the ready.

'Nothing to worry about, Dora,' he said. 'I'm just going through things to make sure. Abe would have done the same for me.'

I said, 'Are we ruined, Uncle Israel? Am I still a mustard heiress?'

'Poppy!' Aunt Fish said. 'That is a thing to have said *about* one. One should not say it of oneself!'

'Never fear, Pops,' Uncle said, 'you'll come into a handsome amount.'

Ma said, 'Not that you'll have any need of it, since you will always have a home here and be provided for. You might think, Poppy, when you are of age, of making donations and helping with good works.'

'There'll certainly be plenty for that,' Uncle said. 'The Education Alliance is doing fine work with the immigrants. And The Daughters of Jacob. Both very worthy causes.'

Aunt Fish said, 'Dora didn't mean *that* kind of cause, Israel. One has to be careful in selecting one's charities. They reflect on one so. Poppy might do better sending money to the little black babies in Africa.'

I'm sure it's very easy to spend someone else's inheritance. I didn't bother to tell them I intended spending mine on silk harem pants and a gasoline-powered automobile and cake.

So Uncle dined at the Harmonie Club every night and Aunt Fish moved in with us and began nursing my mother through a carefully planned convalescence. At first, no callers were received. Ma stayed in her room and toyed with a little calf's-foot jelly. I was allowed to brush her hair for fifteen minutes each day, and sometimes Honey came and read to her from *Fashion Notes*.

The name Minkel had only appeared in the first list of survivors published in *The New York Times*. By the time the next edition went to press, the phantom Mrs Minkel had disappeared and Ma seemed to be none the wiser. Harry Glaser had done something useful for once in his life.

By the middle of May, Ma had progressed to a small, baked fillet of sole with bread and butter fingers, followed by vermicelli pudding or perhaps an orange custard, by way of variety, and she felt able to receive Mrs Lesser and Mrs Schwab, and eventually the Misses Stone.

Mrs Schwab was herself a widow and understood what was appropriate, but Mrs Lesser was unpredictable. Sometimes she simply reported on the refreshments and gossip at her latest crush – she was very keen to be known for her afternoon teas – but sometimes she would canter off into more dangerous territory. Would there ever be a funeral for Pa, she would suddenly wonder out loud. If not, could there be a funeral monument? And if there could, what form should it take?

One of my duties was to anticipate this kind of conversational turn and head off Mrs Lesser at the pass, but sometimes my attention wandered and before I knew it Aunt Fish would be fanning Ma and tutting at me and suggesting to Mrs Lesser that she had already given us more than enough of her valuable time.

The thing was, I had questions myself, most of them far more macabre than Mrs Lesser's. I knew, for instance, that the bodies of drowned persons were often hooked out of the East River and the Hudson, but I suspected things worked differently in an ocean. Still, sometimes I imagined Pa's poor body, slowly finding its way to Pier 32. And other times I imagined he had never boarded that accursed boat. That he was still in London, inspecting his subsidiaries, and Irish Nellie had been, as usual, telling whoppers.

None of these ideas could ever be aired, of course. They were merely evidence of the unhealthy state of my mind and I knew better than to draw that kind of attention to myself. Apart from my sleeplessness and loss of appetite, daily life had become easier with Pa gone. Since April eighteenth my hair had been left *au naturel*. This alone gave me such a fierce appearance, I doubt even Aunt Fish would have dared to suggest resuming the applications of neck-whitener. We had reached a kind of accommodation. No one troubled me with beauty regimes, and I troubled no one with my questions. Then the Misses Stone came to call.

'It occurs to us,' one of them began, 'we might be of assistance,

23

at this sad time, in the . . . disposal of . . . unhappy reminders.'

The Misses Stone were collecting unwanted clothes for their
Immigrant Aid Fund. It had never crossed my mind that Pa's
things wouldn't hang forever in their closets. I visited them every
day and buried my face in the cloth of his coats, to smell his cologne.
The possibility that the Misses Stone might bundle them away and
give them to strangers hit me much harder than the news of the
sinking. I sprang from my chair while Ma and Aunt Fish still sat,
pudding-faced, absorbing the request.

'We have only happy, treasured reminders of my dear father and
there are no plans to dispose of any of them' was what I intended
to say. But it came out as 'They're mine, you hateful crows! Pa's
things are mine! And no one else shall ever take them.'

They were unnerved by the sight of me, I know. Even diminished
by grief, there was enough of me to make two of the birdlike Misses
Stone, and then there was my hair, which weeks of neglect had turned
from a deformity into an instrument of terror. They fluttered toward
the door under cover of Aunt Fish's bosom.

'Unhinged by our loss,' I heard her whisper. 'Perhaps, when a
little more time has passed . . .' and the Misses Stone made little
gobbling noises of sympathy.

Ma was looking at me in amazement.

'Don't let them take his things,' I yelled at her. 'Don't let anyone
take them. I miss Pa. I have to have the smell of him.'

'Oh Poppy,' was all she said. 'Oh Poppy . . .'

'Well!' Aunt Fish said, when she returned from seeing off the
Misses Stone. 'That was a fine display you made of yourself.'

Ma struggled to her feet. I realize now she was only forty-two
and not at all the old lady she seemed. She put out her arms and
held me stiffly to her jet stomacher.

'Oh Poppy,' she said, 'how stricken you are. I think perhaps
one of my powders . . .'

She turned to Aunt Fish, who was all for smacking me, I
dare say.

'Zillah,' she said, 'I think poor Poppy needs a powder. Or perhaps some of my special drops?'

'Hmm,' said Aunt Fish. 'And time alone, in her room, to compose herself and consider what embarrassment she has caused.'

I said, 'I'm sure it wasn't me who came begging for a dead man's clothes. I'm sure we are not the ones who should feel embarrassed.'

Ma released me from our awkward embrace.

'They are crows, Aunt Fish,' I cried, as I fled the room. 'They are crows and you are a gull for allowing them.'

I hid for an hour inside Pa's closet, comforted a little by its smells but anxious, too, that they might be fading. When I returned to my room, a small bottle had appeared on my night table. Pryce's Soothing Extract of Hemp, recommended for cases of nervous excitement.

SIX

All through June and July our household was run by Aunt Fish, and then she stayed on through the worst of the August heatwave because we had an electric fan and she did not, and she feared she might expire without it. Uncle Israel struggled on without her, quite weary I suppose of having to dine out every night and drink champagne and play cards with other poor bachelors.

The days hung dead and hopeless. We visited no one, we had nothing to refresh our conversations, and every exchange was hobbled by unmentionable subjects. Water, travel, Europe, mustard, Iowa, money, joy, happiness, unhappiness; these were the main taboos. But to those I added my own secret list: Irish secretaries, gowns by Mr Worth, death by drowning and ghosts.

I was employed in a series of sewing assignments, trimming handkerchiefs with black ribbon, and turning slightly worn sheets sides to middle, a pointless exercise made all the more absurd by the fact that I had ten thumbs. In the privacy of my room, when I made clothes for my dolls and stitched them with my preferred left hand, I sewed very well indeed, but in the parlor, of course, only the use of the correct hand was permitted.

'How awkward you look, Poppy,' Ma said. 'But you must persevere.'

While I stitched, Ma and Aunt Fish conversed. In the morning, dinner was discussed, and the social events none of us would be attending. Just once a week my aunt would tear herself away from us to attend the opera.

'It gives me no pleasure, Dora,' she always said, 'but a box cannot go to waste.'

Otherwise the evenings were spent considering next day's luncheon and reviewing our health, two not unconnected subjects.

'An omelette *is* very binding,' Aunt Fish would bid.

'But celery is invigorating,' Ma would counter-bid.

My only release from this was that once a week I was allowed to visit Honey. She and Harry had a red-brick on West 74th Street with a bay window high above the street that made it lighter and more cheerful than home. The serviceable, dark plum chintz had been picked out on Ma's advice, and I now recognize, recalling the abundance of valances and frilled portières, other signs of her hand. If society abhorred a naked door frame, who was she to argue?

Still, I loved to visit there and play Chinese checkers and try on Honey's new hats, and she enjoyed my being there. Sometimes, without Ma around, or Harry, she could be quite gay.

But in the fall of 1912 something changed. On my weekly visit there was no gaiety. All afternoon Honey just sat in her cushioned rocker and sucked peppermints. And the next week, and the next. It was December before I found out why. A baby was coming to live with Honey and Harry.

This news made me very happy. I had often wished to have a brother or a puppy and Honey's baby seemed to promise a good alternative.

'Where is it coming from?' I asked, and Honey turned scarlet.

'A little star fell from heaven,' Ma said, 'and has come to rest under her heart.'

I had noticed that the area beneath and around Honey's heart had expanded recently, but I'd attributed this to the quantity of violet creams she ate.

'And then what?' I asked.

'The stork will bring it from a special baby garden,' Aunt Fish cut in.

27

'Yes,' said Ma, abandoning her story about the star, 'and give it to the nurse and she'll place it in the cradle.'

I was confused. So next time I was down in the kitchen, looking for company and cookies, I asked the Irish. We had a rosy-cheeked one at that time, quite pretty.

'I wonder where Honey's baby will come from?' I said, drawing on the oilcloth with my wetted finger.

The Irish put down the silver cloth.

'How old are you, Poppy?' she asked.

I was just fifteen.

'Well,' she said, 'you know you get your monthly health . . . ?'

Reilly slammed down a tureen in front of her.

'Wash out your mouth and get on with your work,' she said.

The Irish grinned at me and polished on in silence until Reilly disappeared into the pantry. Then she leaned across the table.

''Tis very simple,' she whispered. 'Mr Harry had his way with her and put a bun in her oven and now she'll blow up and up till her time comes and then she'll be brought to bed of it and scream and scream and drop it like a sow-pig, and then there'll be a grand pink little baby.'

I ran to my room and tried to compose myself before luncheon. I vowed, on my next visit to West 74th Street, to tell Honey what I'd learned. She seemed so calm, languid even, I couldn't believe she understood what a terrible fate awaited her.

'Harry will do it,' Ma always said. 'Leave it to Harry.'

Leave it to Harry indeed. I might have guessed *he* had something to do with it.

My sister was brought to bed of a baby boy on May 28, 1913. Three weeks before, she had taken up residence in her old room, so Ma and Aunt Fish could keep watch for the stork, so I supposed. In the event, things turned out much as the Irish had said they would, with Harry being sent away and Honey screaming, and a nurse arriving who drank quantities of tea, and finally a doctor in a top hat, with something in his bag that put a stop to all the yelling.

I was allowed to see my nephew when he was two hours old,

and then it devolved to me to start breaking the news to Ma that he would not be named Abe, for his dear departed grandpa.

'How well he suits "Sherman",' I said. Honey had suggested this as an opening.

'Sherman?' Ma said. '*Sherman?* As usual you are quite mistaken, Poppy. In this family we do not name our children after . . . hotels.'

'Not after the hotel, Ma,' Harry tittered, when he was finally admitted to see his wife and child. 'Sherman, as in General William Tecumseh Sherman.' And he attempted to sing 'While We Were Marching Through Georgia', as though that explained everything.

Ma was quiet for a while.

'It seems to me,' she said, returning to the battlefield, 'that if you wish to name my grandson for a public figure, it should be for our new president. Abraham Woodrow Glaser sounds very well.'

''Fraid not, Ma,' Harry said. 'Can't tar the boy with a Democrat brush. His name will be Sherman Ulysses, and that's my final word on it.'

Ma's knuckles whitened round her handkerchief.

'Tell you what though,' he said, backtracking a little at the prospect of tears. 'Tell you what. If the next one's a girl, we'll name her Dora, for you.'

From what I had seen and heard that day, I doubted there would be a next one. I planned to consult the Irish again and see whether such things could be prevented.

Meanwhile ugly little Sherman Ulysses Glaser cried and slept and cried some more, and eventually I was allowed to cradle him.

'I'm your maiden aunt Poppy,' I told him, and he curled his little fingers around my thumb. Honey had three weeks lying-in before she took him home to West 74th Street, and Ma didn't waste a moment of it.

'Abraham,' she kept whispering to him as he slept. 'Grandma's special little Abraham.'

Down in the kitchen I heard talk.

'Is Mrs Honey's baby to be cut?' the Irish asked me.

'Why?' I asked, and she and Reilly exchanged annoying little smiles. I took the question straight to Ma, who was sitting with Aunt Fish and Honey and Harry's mother, the senior Mrs Glaser.

'Poppy!' Ma said. 'Not in the parlor!'

I had to wait until the company had left. Then I was taken to Ma's bedroom to have it explained that some baby boys underwent a *procedure*, but the Minkels and the Glasers were unanimous in judging it quite unnecessary.

'It's just an old-fashioned *racial* thing,' Honey said, 'and we are civilized New Yorkers.'

I said, 'I wish you could stay here, Honey. I'd help you with Sherman Ulysses and we could make dolls' clothes and have fun.'

'I'm a mother now, Pops,' she said. 'I don't have time for fun.'

So the party was over. Honey took Sherman home, and time slowed down again, crawling past me while I read to Ma from *Collier's Weekly*, and danced imaginary cotillions, but very quietly, so as not to tire her.

Mrs Schwab visited, and Mrs Lesser, and even the Misses Stone returned. They had forgiven me my hysterical outburst and after I turned sixteen they seemed more inclined to take me seriously. They knew better than to mention the distribution of second-hand clothes, but some of their projects, their work amongst 'the element', sounded adventurous and exciting. They raised money for the settlement houses where the Russian Hebrews could be washed and fed and trained out of their rude oriental ways. They arranged classes where the unfortunates could learn hygiene and gymnastics. They sent them to summer camp.

I said, 'Gymnastics and summer camp! I'm sure I shouldn't mind being an unfortunate.'

The Misses Stone laughed.

'No, Poppy,' one of them said, 'you wouldn't say so if you saw how people lived. Workers and donations are what we need. Perhaps some day, when you're not so much needed at home?'

'I hope,' Ma sighed, 'some day I may feel strong enough to spare Poppy for a few hours.'

Her true intention was that I should never set foot anywhere near such dangerous territory, but I wore away her resolve with the daily drip, drip, drip of my requests. It took many months. Then suddenly, one summer morning, she threw down her needlepoint and said, 'I see you are determined to break my heart, Poppy, so go and be done with it.'

Two days later I was taken by trolley-car to the Bowery, and then, with a Miss Stone on either side of me for safety, I was swept into the tumult of Delancey Street, the very place where Pa had enjoyed his cherry blintzes.

I tried to tell the Misses Stone about this exciting coincidence, and they smiled, but I wasn't at all sure they could even hear me. I had never in my life encountered so much noise or seen so many people. Then we turned onto Orchard Street and the buildings and the noise of the stinking, shouting unfortunates pressed in on me even closer.

There were dead ducks and chickens hanging from hooks, and women with dirty hands selling eggs from handcarts, and pickle barrels, and shop signs in foreign squiggles, and small boys carrying piles of unfinished garments higher than themselves, and ragged girls playing potsy on the sidewalk.

'Why is everyone shouting?' I shouted.

'Because they're happy to be here.' That was the best explanation the Misses Stone could offer.

I said, 'I'm sure abroad must be a very terrible place if Orchard Street makes them happy.'

We went to The Daughters of Jacob Center where the element could learn to dress like Americans and raise healthy children. And then to the Edgie Library where they could study our language.

'You see, Poppy,' they said, 'how much needs doing?'

I said, 'I don't come into my money until I'm twenty-one

and I don't know how much there'll be because Pa had compli-cated affairs.'

But the Misses Stone said it wasn't only money they needed but helpers, and why didn't I try sitting, just for five minutes, and helping someone with their English reading.

A small girl stood in front of me with a primer in her hands, trying to stare me down. I turned to tell the Stones I probably wouldn't be very good at it, but they were hurrying away to inspect another class, and the staring girl was still waiting with her book.

I said, 'The first thing you should learn is not to stare, especially not at your elders and betters.'

She was pale as wax, and skinny.

'What's your name?' she said. She spoke perfect English.

I said, 'And if you're going to read to me you had better start immediately because I have to go home very soon.'

I sat on a stool and she stood beside me, a little too close for my liking, and read. She was pretty good.

I said, 'You can read. You don't need good works doing for you.'

She grinned.

I said, 'Have you been to summer camp?'

She shook her head.

I said, 'How about gymnastics?'

'Yes,' she said. 'I did do that, but now I can't be spared. I have to help make garters. We get one cent a piece. My name's Malka but I like Lily better. What do you think?'

I didn't really know what gymnastics were. As I had never been allowed them I surmised they were something desirable.

'How old are you?' she asked. She was one impertinent child.

'And how were the gymnastics?' I asked, feeling my way.

'They were fun,' she said. 'Are you married? I like your coat. Want to see how I can turn a somersault?' And she just flipped over, like a toy monkey. She went over so fast, I couldn't see how she did it. This attracted the attention of the other little monkeys, who all left off their studying and gathered around me, fingering the fabric of my coat.

I looked around for someone to rescue me, but minutes passed before a Miss Stone appeared.

'I knew it,' she said. 'You've made some friends already. They're quite fascinated by you.'

I said, 'I think I have to go home now. I think I'm needed there.'

'But you've made such a hit,' she said. 'It's because you're a younger person, I expect. Do stay a little longer.'

I had to insist most firmly that I be home no later than four.

The girl called Malka shouted after me as we left the room.

'Hey, Miss No Name,' she called. 'You have pretty hair.'

It was a measure of everyone else's poor opinion of my looks that a compliment from an unwashed unfortunate went straight to my head.

'That child reads well,' I said. 'How does she come to be here?'

'The Lelchucks?' she said. 'They had to run from the Russians. Would you like to meet the rest of the family?'

I was torn. On the one hand I felt uneasily far from home. The loudness and smell of the place exceeded anything I could have imagined. But on the other hand I had a Miss Stone either side of me, greatly experienced in the ways of the 'element', and anyway, wasn't I always longing to escape from the monotony of the parlor? I decided I would rather like to see where Malka Lelchuck lived.

We turned onto Stanton Street, where the buildings seemed still taller and darker, and every fire escape was cluttered with boxes and furniture. The entrance to Malka's house was unlit and dirty, and as we climbed two flights of stairs people pushed past us.

I said, 'These unfortunates seem to have a great many callers.'

The thinner Miss Stone laughed. 'No, Poppy,' she said, 'these are their neighbors. The Lelchucks have only two rooms.'

Then I began to understand why they were called unfortunates. They had to share their buildings with strangers.

The door was open. The Misses Stone went in and beckoned me to follow, but I peered in from the threshold. Mrs Lelchuck kept her head bowed, too shy to speak, or perhaps too tired. She and four girls were busy around a table, finishing garters. There was a smell of frying, and vinegar, and other unknown things. My head swam.

There was something in the scene I recognized. Tedium, possibly. Finishing garters looked like very boring work. But there was something else I noticed, though I couldn't name it. I think I now know it was the simple concord of a family working together. At any rate this, combined with the information that Malka Lelchuck had learned gymnastics, suggested to me that these so-called unfortunates were a good deal better off than I. Furthermore, I could not stop toying with the novelty of a compliment. Someone thought I had pretty hair. The unfortunates had looked at me with wonder and admiration. I passed the trolley ride home aflame with self-glory.

By dinner time the surprise of becoming an intrepid doer of good works *and* a beauty had so drained me I was unable to give an account of myself.

'I feared as much,' Ma said. 'You have caught a disease and now we shall all pay for your recklessness.'

That night I dreamed of pickles that turned somersaults and ducks with no feathers and when I woke next morning I had a circle of itching red weals around each ankle. I had brought home with me from Stanton Street a deputation of fleas. Ma had the house dismantled. The floors were scrubbed with brown soap. Small dishes of camphor were burned in every room. And every surface was dabbed with kerosene until an inevitable encounter between a naked flame and kerosene fumes deprived Reilly of her eyebrows, and consequently us of our cook.

As the Irish had been dismissed just days before for ferrying quantities of canned goods out of our pantry and home to her mother, carrying them away under her skirts, the final reckoning was that we were reduced to one housemaid, one parlor maid and a person who came in weekly to do mending and alterations. We faced social ruin and starvation, and all because of my headstrong expedition down amongst 'the element'.

'I hope,' Ma said, 'you are quite satisfied.'

But I wasn't. On reflection, from the safe haven of West 76th Street, I decided I wanted more expeditions. I wanted to ride on trolley-cars, and maybe even on the elevated railway. I wanted to do good works amongst grateful people who admired my hair. I wanted to taste a cherry blintz.

But further visits to Delancey Street were unthinkable for a while. I was in trouble, and my disgrace was intensified by our having to dine every night with Aunt Fish and Uncle Israel until the first in a series of unsatisfactory replacements for Reilly began her duties. Even then it was many weeks before I sensed any let-up in my aunt's watchful disapproval. In fact it wasn't until November and the occasion of my seventeenth birthday that I felt I had finally been forgiven.

'Getting to be quite the young lady, Pops,' said Uncle Israel.

He and Aunt Fish gave me a sketch book and a metal box with little blocks of paint.

'Watercolors. An elegant and suitable occupation for you, Poppy,' explained Aunt Fish.

'How kind,' said Ma, 'and how timely, now that you will be settling down to your duties at home.'

I heard a door slam shut on my career as a brave and beautiful benefactress.

From Ma I received a new writing case, and from Baby Sherman Ulysses a framed photograph. My best gifts though were from Honey who, in addition to a dreary manicure set, brought me a bag of scraps from her dressmaker, a bag with pieces of pale green crêpe de Chine and red taffeta and blue satin.

I hugged her.

'Well,' she said, 'you are old enough now to stop chewing your nails, so I thought I'd encourage you. It's time you took more care in your toilette.'

I said, 'Why? We're not looking for a husband anymore.'

Honey said that neat nails were an asset to anyone and Ma and Aunt Fish couldn't have agreed with her more.

In a roundabout way I even received a gift from Reilly, who

returned, on November fourteenth, and offered to give us just one more chance, thereby saving me from further nightly inspections at Aunt Fish's dinner table.

I used my birthday scraps to make dolls' clothes, as Honey had intended, and when the scraps were all gone, I used my paints to plan what I should like to make next. Shiny, slippery dresses, and pantaloons with beads and tassels, and big, bright coats that trailed behind like folded butterfly wings and flashed a lining of shot orange silk.

Ma said, 'Wasting paint again, Poppy? How I should love you to make me a painting of trees and clouds. Just a small one. I'm sure there is no necessity to splash the paint about so.'

I was allowed to resume my weekly visits to Honey's house, too, once we could be certain fleas were the only bad thing I'd brought home from Stanton Street. I'd go for a whole afternoon, and look through Honey's closets and try on her hats and shawls and bang about until I woke Sherman Ulysses. He always seemed very pleased to see me, and he was quite advanced, for a Glaser.

'Honey,' I said one time, 'you know how I have to stay with Ma now and be her help and comfort? Well, what will I do when Ma is dead?'

'Gracious, Pops,' she said, 'that won't be for years. Thirty years maybe.'

'No, but still,' I said, 'what will I do then?'

'You'll live with me and Harry,' she said.

That was the day I decided to write to Cousin Addie in Duluth.

'Dear Cousin Addie,' I wrote.

I am your Uncle Abe Minkel's girl. We have never met, but I am an old maid like you. I hope we can be correspondents. What are your dolls' names? I make very good dolls' clothes which I could send you some time. I would certainly be willing to visit Duluth some day.

I never mailed it. Before I could work out a secret way to discover her address and to receive her replies without interference from Ma, I was distracted by new thrills and skirmishes. A war had begun in Europe.

SEVEN

resident Wilson told us that the United States of America must be seen to be impartial in thought, word and deed, but the Prussians cared nothing for that, so we were preparing for invasion. Quantities of canned goods were brought in and a lock, to which only Ma held a key, was fitted to the pantry door. This reawakened Reilly's dormant desire to flounce out and leave us in the lurch again, and threats were exchanged. Only the news, flashed to us from Harry's office, that a German submarine had been sighted in Long Island Sound, pulled Reilly back into line.

'Well?' Ma said, with the confidence of a player who is holding a royal flush. 'The Hun is at the door. Are you staying or leaving?'

Reilly returned below stairs, but as long as Ma kept up the locked pantry regime, Reilly exacted her own small satisfactions.

'Asparagus tips, if it's not too much trouble.' Her voice would erupt from the speaking tube, like an Upper Bay foghorn, and quite destroy the gentility of Ma's parlor.

It turned out there had been no submarine. But something else was menacing us, as I should have guessed from conversations between Ma and Honey which always ended abruptly as I came into the room. Then a meeting was convened, for Sunday afternoon. Honey and Harry were to attend and the Aunt and Uncle Israel Fishes, and tea and seed cake would be served.

I said, 'I'll take Sherman Ulysses for a walk in his bassinet.'

Seed cake was my least favorite.

'No, Poppy,' Ma said. 'This concerns even you.'

We were assembled to discuss the question of German connections.

Harry said, 'Weiner, Ittelman, Schwab, they've all stopped speaking German, even behind closed doors.'

Ma said, 'I'm sure I wouldn't know German if I heard it. Abe never used it. Nor his father.'

I said, 'Are we Germans, then?'

'Of course not, you foolish girl,' Ma and Aunt Fish chorused.

'It's a question of appearances,' Harry went on. He stood up and stroked his moustaches and rocked on his heels as he spoke. I suppose this helped him to feel less of a nonentity.

'We all know we're not Germans,' he said. 'We certainly don't behave like Germans. But we have to face facts. Every name tells a story and as patriotic Americans we'd be fools not to free ourselves of any taint. A change of name. That's all it takes. We're changing to Grace. A good old American name.'

'Don't see the need,' Uncle Israel said. 'I recall when your father changed from Glassman to Glaser. Seems to me that was change enough.'

'You're wrong, Israel,' Harry said. 'You'd be surprised what little things folk pick up on. I have to do this, for my boy's sake.'

Aunt Fish agreed with Harry and had quite set her heart on becoming a Fairbanks, but Uncle Israel would have none of it.

'Question,' he challenged her. 'What is a herring? What is a carp? What is a turbot? I'll tell you. They are fish. F-I-S-H. A good plain American word. I rest my case.'

Meanwhile Ma was eyeing me nervously. As well she might.

'We were thinking of Mink,' she said, 'but as Harry pointed out, even Mink has a *ring* to it. So I have settled upon Minton. A very elegant, English name that will serve us well. Poppy Minton! How pretty it sounds. I believe it suits you better than Minkel any day.'

I allowed her to keep talking until I was sure I understood her meaning. Then I upended tea and seed cake all over her and the Turkish rug.

'Good,' Harry continued, as though an overturned tea tray was nothing remarkable, 'so that's settled. And you'll be interested to hear I've just acquired a little jobbing printers, so your cards and so forth can be changed at advantageous rates.'

'I'm not changing my name,' I screamed. 'I shall always be a Minkel. Always, always. I'd rather be a German than a Minton.'

It fell to Aunt Fish to slap my face and express loud regrets that I had returned from my afternoon amongst the wild Asiatics of Stanton Street rebellious as well as lousy.

'Now, now! Nothing's decided yet, Pops,' Uncle Israel called after me as I ran from the room. But it was. Harry had already made moves to change his name to Grace, and wherever Harry led, Ma would follow.

I hid in Pa's closet and wept. Down in the parlor another part of him was being taken from me, and it seemed – perhaps it was the crying affecting my sinuses – but it seemed that his clothes hardly smelled of him anymore.

'If they do it, Pa,' I whispered into his gray worsted, 'I shall change it back to Minkel the moment I'm of age.'

I did too. And though Honey may have gone to her grave a Grace instead of a Glaser, to this day I address my correspondence with Sherman Ulysses to Mr S. U. Glaser. He complains and says it causes confusion and inconvenience to the staff of the Pelican Bay Retirement Home, but I tell him, the money he's paying he's entitled to discommode a few people. They're all foreigners anyhow.

Nineteen fourteen turned into nineteen fifteen. The Misses Stone continued their work trying to uplift the unfortunate Hebrews, Uncle Israel Fish joined a relief committee and Harry, correctly anticipating a trend for changing disadvantageous names, bought two more printing firms.

In May the Germans sank the *Lusitania* with the loss of one hundred and twenty-eight American lives, and Ma and Aunt Fish reviewed their invasion precautions. There was an evacuation plan, involving dollars stuffed inside corsets and a secret address in Cedar Rapids. Iowa was apparently to be given a second chance. Priority of travel was awarded to Honey and to Sherman Ulysses, carrier of the blood of Abe Minkel, if not of his name, and they would be accompanied by Ma. I was to bring up the rear with Aunt Fish. This didn't bother me. Much as I longed to escape the monotony of West 76th Street, a Hun invasion sounded too exciting a prospect to miss.

In the event, the closest Ma and Honey came to running for port was when the Atlantic Fleet was anchored in the Hudson and German agents were caught planning to blow up the guests at a Grand Naval Ball that was to be held on 72nd Street.

Defeated by the concept of traveling light and traveling fast, Ma was so unable to decide which hats to leave behind that the moment passed. The Germans were deported. The fleet, having danced till dawn, sailed safely away. And I was left, untangling the silks in Ma's embroidery basket, wondering what an invasion might feel like.

I redrafted my letter to Cousin Addie, hoping to capture her interest with the news that I had been as close as four blocks to the barbarian invaders. I obtained her address and a postage stamp from Ma's writing table, and I dropped it in a mailbox on the way to my weekly visit with Sherman Ulysses. As to how I would explain the arrival of Cousin Addie's reply, I felt that Providence would inspire me when the moment came. All that talk of war made audacity seem the order of the day.

EIGHT

I followed the war as best I could using my old school atlas. Honey and I had enjoyed a brief exposure to education at the Convent of the Blessed Redeemer. We both started late, due to measles, whooping cough and Ma's conviction that paper harbored disease and all books were written by socialists, and I finished early, almost immediately after Honey graduated, due to scarlatina and the nuns' inability to warm to me once my blonde and sainted sister had left.

'We pray you may find somewhere more suitable,' Sister Diotisalvi wrote to my parents, and Pa said, 'Let her go to the Levison School.' But the Levison was on the East Side. I'd have had to cross Central Park every day, a journey Ma and Aunt Fish equated with finding the Northwest Passage. Worse still, the Levison was getting a reputation for turning out bookish and disputatious students. One of the Schwab girls had attended for just one year and had emerged so deformed, so stripped of delicacy, that Mrs Schwab had had to search as far afield as Winnipeg, Canada, to find her a husband.

So I was not enrolled there, nor anywhere else. From the age of thirteen I had been tutored at home. By which I mean I received erratic visits from teachers of French, piano and dancing, and Ma taught me the correct way to serve tea. Of the Balkans, or Belgium, or Kaiser Wilhelm, I knew nothing. But I was a fast study, and Ma depended entirely upon me to explain about the Eastern Front.

'All this rampaging around is most unsettling, I'm sure,' she said.

'If only people would be polite and stay in their own countries. Prussians and Russians and Macedonians. It's all too hectic.'

I was a little confused myself whether the brave Russians who had taken on the Hun were the same ones who had cruelly chased Malka Lelchuck from her home, and I should have liked to ask the Misses Stone about it, but they never called anymore. They were too busy with war work.

Then the Ballet Russe came to the Century Theater and as a reward for recent good behavior I was invited to join Aunt Fish and Uncle Israel to see the opening performance of *Petrushka*. Preparations began immediately after breakfast when Honey arrived with her burnt-orange Directoire gown and a chocolate-brown velveteen evening coat.

Burnt orange, it turned out, was not my color, but with a little help from Ma's seed pearl choker and a dab of cream rouge my skin was coaxed out of a tendency to mealiness. The shoe problem was not so easily solved. Honey's tapestry evening slippers were size 4. My feet were size 7.

The Irish was assigned to do the best she could with a can of boot black and my battered day shoes.

'No one will see,' Ma said, 'if you are careful to take small steps.'

After luncheon I was excused all further duties and sent to my room with instructions to double my dose of Pryce's Soothing Extract of Hemp and lie still with my eyes closed.

'Attending a ballet is a very draining business,' Ma advised me. 'You must conserve yourself, otherwise you will be no use to me tomorrow and then what shall I do?'

At six I was collected by Uncle Israel's driver. We no longer had one of our own. After Pa's death Ma had given him notice.

'After all,' she said, 'we shall hardly be going anywhere.'

Ma had plenty of money, but she seemed always to derive pleasure from small economies.

'Remember, Poppy,' Ma called after me as I bounded downstairs to the front door, 'small steps.'

We ate an early supper of clear soup and epigrams of mutton, and I was supplied with an extra precautionary napkin, to be tied under my chin.

'It would be a tragedy,' Aunt Fish said, 'if Honey's beautiful gown was ruined, when she has been generous enough to lend it.'

It wasn't all that beautiful a gown.

Uncle Israel asked, 'What is it again we're going to see?'

'It will come to me momentarily,' Aunt Fish said, 'though why you ask I cannot fathom. I see you are quite determined to dislike it, whatever it's called.'

I suppose musical comedies were more to Uncle Israel's taste. I suppose he took along the evening paper as a fall-back in case of boredom.

I had never dreamed how wonderful a theater might be. The carpets were thicker and deeper, the chandeliers were vaster and sparklier than anything I had imagined. And there were marble staircases curving either side of a palm garden. I should have liked to practice majestic sweeping on those stairs.

But most exciting of all was the frenzy of the orchestra preparing to play and the roar of the audience. Aunt Fish was examining every face in the grand tier, and occasionally she would flutter her hand.

'The Elmore Ferbers are here,' she observed, 'in spite of the talk. How brave she looks.'

Uncle Israel looked up from his paper and rolled his eyes.

'And I spy Mrs Root,' she pressed on, 'with a person who may be her sister from Buffalo. What a serviceable gown that twilled silk has turned out to be. I declare I must have seen it a hundred times.'

The lights went down.

'Now, Poppy,' she whispered, patting my hand, 'we need only stay for the first act. And do sit up nicely. With good posture and Honey's lovely gown I believe you look rather pretty this evening.'

The curtain went up. The stage appeared to be covered with snow, and crowds of people were walking about, just like they were in a real town. There were candy stalls and a merry-go-round and a puppet theater, and everyone seemed happy, except for Petrushka who looked sad and the Ballerina who looked plain dumb. Petrushka wore beautiful blue boots and red satin trousers, but the clothes I liked best were the Wicked Moor's. He wore gold trousers and a bright green jacket and his hat was made of twisted yellow and violet silk.

Uncle Israel didn't care for the music.

'Darned racket,' he said, and he took out his newspaper again, even though it was far too dark for him to read.

Aunt Fish kept wondering aloud why they hadn't been able to find a dancer who could point his toes.

I said, 'I think he's meant to be dancing that way.'

'Meant to?' she said. 'Of course he isn't meant to. Ballet is danced with pointed toes, as I would have expected you to know. And I'm sure one pays enough to see correct technique.'

I was anxious that the combination of rackety music and incorrect feet might provoke an early exit, so I fairly begged Aunt Fish to be allowed to stay to the end. This made a sickening spectacle, I dare say, but it worked. I believe she was so astonished by my fawning she quite forgot about leaving the theater early. So the Moor killed Petrushka, the curtain came down, and far below us the livelier element of audience divided, two-thirds whistling and stamping, one-third booing.

With the house lights up, and the prospect of a second supper drawing near, Uncle Israel became cheerful again.

'Nine-thirty and our duty is done,' he said. 'Now that's what I call a decent show.'

I said, 'I should like to see it all again.'

'Well, don't look at me,' he said. 'I've swallowed my dose. Bring your sister. Bring your mother.'

Aunt Fish gave him a warning tap with her fan.

'Dora would find the stairs far too taxing,' she said. 'And I don't know that anything so *progressive* would suit Honey. Besides, it seemed to me a rather silly story. How much more satisfactory it would have been if someone had married the dainty little doll.'

But I was glad Petrushka never got the Ballerina. It was bad enough he always had to go to his poky room and couldn't wander around and buy gingerbread and just please himself, without having a prissy girlfriend, too. He was better off dead.

Uncle Israel said why didn't he treat us all to steak tartare at Luchow's, but Aunt Fish said she thought we'd had quite enough stimulation for one evening. I didn't care. I was ready to go home and dream about bright blue boots and turbans made of yellow and violet silk. It seemed to me I had discovered an elegant answer to the question of my mutinous hair.

NINE

By the beginning of 1917 President Wilson had taken about as much as he could from the Hun, and even Reilly, who never had a good word to say about the British and believed they intended to take over the world, even she was preparing herself for all-out war. She kept a heavy poker by her bed, in case of a night-time invasion, and was working, in her spare time, on a type of cambric nosebag filled with crushed charcoal biscuits, which she hoped would protect her from phosgene gas. After she had made one for herself and one for the Irish she began work on a miniature one for Sherman Ulysses.

I ran upstairs to report this act of kindness, but it cut no ice with Ma.

'Little wonder,' she said, 'that we are expected to eat our chicken still pink at the bone, when the help amuse themselves all day with handicrafts.'

I said, 'When the war comes . . .' but she would never let me get any further. She was of the firm belief that talking about a thing could bring it on, and that, therefore, the best policy was to look on the bright side. She even planned a season of gay afternoon teas, her first social foray since Pa's death.

'Teas,' she said, 'are quite suitable for a widow, and not nearly so draining as dinners.'

When war did come, in April, she said, 'Poppy, you have been humming this past hour and smiling to yourself like a loon. I fail to account for your happiness. I'm sure war is a most inconvenient thing.'

It wasn't quite happiness I felt, but a little bubble of excitement. Whatever her shortcomings, my mother was deeply patriotic, so it seemed possible that my country's need of me might outweigh her own claim on my time. I was, after all, nearly twenty years old.

I said, 'Ma, I should really like to do something for the war effort.' Nursing was what I had in mind. I liked the crisp femininity of the uniform. I hoped I might be sent to the Western Front and have a handsome blinded officer fall in love with my voice.

'How proud your father would have been,' she whispered, and her eyes quite shone.

The very next day Miss Ruby was sent for. She was an unfortunate person who had lost her money through unwise investments and so was forced to do mending and alterations for good families. After a brief discussion with Ma, Miss Ruby provided me with a basket of sludge-brown wool and a lesson in turning heels. I was to be a knitter of socks for the American Expeditionary Force.

I confided in Honey my hopes that I might have been sent to the front line.

'There are many important ways to serve,' she said. 'I shall be very glad of your help at my War Orphans Craft Bazaar, for instance.'

I said, 'But I wanted to go to France.'

'And what use would you be to anyone there?' she asked.

I reminded her that I had studied French for four years, but she laughed.

'Looking into French books doesn't signify anything, you goose,' she said. 'Minnie Schwab went to Paris and she found they spoke something quite unintelligible. Besides, if you went away who would take care of Ma?'

I said, 'She has Reilly. Or she could stay with you.'

'Isn't that a rather selfish scheme, Poppy,' she said, 'to think of uprooting her from her own home?'

Somehow, at the age of nearly twenty, I managed to be both useless and indispensable. My country didn't need me, my mother couldn't spare me, and the French would not be able to understand me. I knitted socks in such a fury of frustration, Miss Ruby could barely keep me supplied with yarn.

We suffered almost immediate casualties. Our parlor maid and housemaid had conspired to inconvenience us by leaving together to work in a factory. Then Sherman Ulysses' day nurse volunteered for the signal corps, and Ma, in the spirit of sharing during a time of national emergency, offered Honey the use of our Irish. Honey wasn't sure. She and Harry wished their son to be cared for by a person of the highest caliber, someone who would truly understand the ways of an exceptional four year old. My nephew was exceptional in a number of ways. His speech was still immature and when he failed to make himself understood he would lie on the floor and hold his breath until he erupted into a howling rage. 'Num num,' he'd sob piteously, 'num num.' And all around him would try to guess, with the utmost urgency, what he was trying to convey. Also, though he knew perfectly well how to sit nicely on extra cushions and use his spoon and pusher and drink neatly from a cup, he did not always choose to do so.

'I don't know, Ma,' Honey said. 'Does your Irish know anything about children?'

'Of course she does,' Ma said. 'The Irish are never fewer than thirteen to a family.'

Still Honey dithered, driving Ma to become unusually testy with her.

'I must remind you, Honey,' she said, 'that war requires sacrifice. And if I am prepared to make my sacrifice you might be gracious enough to accept it.'

All of this turned out to have been futile because when the Irish was sent for, to be given new orders, she had her coat on, ready to go to Westchester County and be a wartime fruit picker and leave us in the lurch.

Ma was beside herself, but the Irish was fearless.

''Tis to free up the men, d'you see ma'am?' she said. I studied her as she said it, and often rehearsed to myself later how she had told this to Ma, as cool as you like, and then simply walked out of the door.

It took a week for Ma and Honey to regroup and decide there was a simple choice. Either Reilly had to be seconded to the part-time care of Sherman Ulysses or Honey must suffer a total collapse. Reilly was called upstairs.

She said it was bad enough managing without a girl to help her downstairs, without having to run to another house and play nursemaid. She said she couldn't see the justice of being asked to do the work of three for the wages of one, and not very generous wages at that. She said she thought herself quite unsuitable for the care of a small child on account of an ungovernable temper.

'Then you must learn to master it, Reilly,' Ma said. 'Think of it as your war effort.'

Two things occurred to me. The first was that Reilly had a newly defiant look about her. I sensed she would only endure this latest imposition for as long as it took her to make other arrangements. The second was that when she disappeared I might well acquire a new set of shackles. I might have to learn to cook and clean. I might have to endure the flailing feet and slimy top lip of Sherman Ulysses in full spate.

TEN

No one paid afternoon calls anymore. Mrs Lesser and Mrs Schwab were busy meeting troop trains with coffee and cigarettes, one of the Misses Stone was driving for the Motor Corps, and the other was speaking at Liberty Loan rallies when she could spare time from helping the unfortunates. As for Aunt Fish, she had become the very paragon of a committee woman.

Monday was Milk for Polish Babies, Tuesday was the Maimed Soldier Fund, Wednesday was Trench Comfort Packets and Thursdays she alternated French Orphans with Plows for Serbia. The Blue Cross Association were anxious to capture her for their Suffering Horses and Disabled Army Dogs Committee, but Ma counseled against taking on any more.

'You will prostrate yourself, Zillah,' she said, 'and however deserving the cause, you may be sure it's not worth paying for it with your health. Besides, think of Israel. When a man comes home to an empty hearth every night . . .'

But Uncle Israel was busy, too, with his War Relief Clearing House and I believe he found, as I did, that my aunt was improved by war. It distracted her with practical problems and filled her address book with new acquaintances.

'Mrs Elphick,' she reported, 'proposed that we add sewing machines to the list, and Mrs Bayliss seconded the proposal.'

Ma played with the fringed edge of the tablecloth and yawned.

'And then Miss Landau suggested . . .' Miss Landau now featured prominently in Aunt Fish's conversation.

'Such a genuine person,' Aunt Fish would prattle. 'Quite tireless, and so generous with her time. And helping to raise her nephews, too, since her sister was so cruelly taken. They were Philadelphia Landaus, I believe, and her sister was married to Jacoby the furrier. Only thirty-five when . . .' Here Aunt Fish would lower her voice. '. . . it was an obstruction of the internal parts, and she might have been saved if only she had given in sooner to the pain.'

'Yes,' Ma would reply, 'I believe you told me a dozen times already. Fatigue must be making you forgetful.'

It was the tireless and genuine Miss Landau who lured Aunt Fish through the door of something called the B'nai Brith Sisterhood, and soon afterwards, onto its war relief committee.

'Don't look at me that way, Dora,' Aunt Fish said.

'I begin to wonder,' Ma said, 'why you troubled arguing with Israel about names, if you're now willing to associate so freely with racial factions.'

Uncle Israel had refused to become a Fairbanks, but my aunt had had her cards changed anyway. Harry had given her a special price.

I said, 'Is B'nai Brith German then?'

Aunt Fish laughed. 'No, Poppy,' she said. 'It's just a silly old name.'

With Reilly dispatched to look after Sherman Ulysses every day between the hours of ten and three, Ma had taken upon herself responsibility for preparing luncheon. This led to a series of mishaps with knives, hot pans, gravy browning and corn starch and to a consequent shortage of anything edible between breakfast and dinner. I was hungry, all the time, and I had sore elbows caused, Ma decided, by immoderate knitting.

I said, 'Perhaps now I could do something else for the war?'

'Yes,' she said. 'Perhaps you could. You have really applied yourself most commendably to socks, so I believe you have earned a change.'

I was so buoyed by the prospect of being sent to France at last, to patrol my wards by lamplight, and adjust the pillows for dashing lieutenants, that I stole two slices of cake and allowed myself to be caught with the second piece jammed sideways in my mouth. Ma had in her hand the official Red Cross list of required items.

'Hot-water bottle covers,' she said. 'I dare say they are quite easy to make. Or warming wristlets. And Poppy, you might bear in mind that like charity, the war effort begins at home. Reilly is with us so little now we have given her to Honey, and cake doesn't grow on trees.'

But Reilly and Sherman Ulysses' reign of mutual torture was almost at an end. In September Sherman announced, 'Shernum kicked fat Yiley, ha ha', and Reilly announced she was going to New Jersey to make hand grenades and not to bother keeping her position open.

Ma replied stiffly that she hadn't intended to, and then went to lie down with a vinegar compress, while Reilly packed up her few poor things.

I felt something in me change. A page turned, or a cloud passed. I couldn't quite say. But sitting alone in the parlor, waiting to hear Reilly's footsteps on the back stairs, everything seemed to be shifting and stirring, and I liked it. I heard her door close and then the thunk of her valise on the stairs.

I stationed myself in the stairhall and smoothed down my skirt. She paused a moment when she saw me blocking her way, but then she came on down and took the hand I offered her.

I said, 'I wish you well, Reilly. I'm proud to think you'll be doing such important work.'

'You get board and lodging,' she said. 'And a day off every week. And it's only a bus ride into Atlantic City.'

I suppose she thought I might ask her to change her mind.

She said, 'I can't stay cooking for two and nursemaiding a child that's never been corrected. There's a war on.'

We shook hands.

I said, 'I shall soon be doing war work myself.'

I had no idea where those words sprang from. Perhaps it was the thought of knitting wristlets.

As soon as Reilly was gone, I put on my cloth jacket and took the elevated railway all the way to Exchange Place. Uncle Israel was most surprised to see me, but not a bad kind of surprised.

'Someone give you a bang on the head, Pops?'

Uncle Israel always deemed himself something of a humorist.

I said, 'It's a turban. I designed it myself. Uncle, I want to do some proper war work.'

I explained that our Irish had gone fruit-picking and Reilly was on her way to a munitions town and everyone in the world seemed to have something to do except me.

'I guess you heard about your cousin Addie?' he said. 'I guess that's what's brought this on?'

I always loved my Uncle Israel but that day even he seemed condescending. I couldn't endure any more. I banged my fist on his desk and he jumped a mile in the air.

'Nothing has brought it on,' I shouted, 'except a war. A great big war where everyone else is doing good works and having fun but I'm not allowed. I'm a grown-up but I'm still obliged to stay home with Ma. It's not fair!'

Simeon the secretary put his head round the door, ready to eject me I dare say or bring in a glass of restorative brandy, or place his skinny body between Uncle Israel and any physical danger. Uncle waved him away.

He was quiet for a moment, weighing up, I suppose, where his loyalties lay. I gave him a little help. I said, 'Even Aunt Fish is doing a hundred different things so I'm sure it wouldn't hurt for me to make myself useful.'

'Pops,' he said. 'If you want to do your bit you won't find me standing in your way. Not at all. Your Pa would have been proud.'

I said, 'That's what Ma said about the socks. But I'm through with knitting.'

'Quite right,' he said, 'quite right. Well, I wonder what I can do to help?'

How banging on a person's desk can make them change their tune.

I said, 'I need you to ask someone. You know lots of people. Tell them I'm a very good worker and I'm available to start immediately. And I know French. And I'm not afraid of blood.'

I didn't think I was afraid of blood.

Uncle Fish stood up and put on his top hat.

'This calls for some thought,' he said, 'and thinking calls for lunch.'

So he offered me his arm, and Simeon stood back as I swept by him, in case of continuing fireworks. We went to Child's restaurant for corned beef hash and fried eggs.

I asked about Cousin Addie. Cousin Addie, he told me, was quite the talk of Duluth. She had tried to join the marines, but when she realized all they were offering was work as a stenographer, she had used strong language to the recruiting sergeant and then gone directly to the bank to organize her own war work.

She had bought four large gasoline-powered vehicles for a mobile hospital and was having them shipped to France at her own expense. Better yet, she was going with them. I was hurt that Cousin Addie hadn't thought to invite me along. Especially as I'd written her a letter and explained we were made of the same stuff. Her mobile hospital was going to have an operating theater, with its own lighting generator and a laundry and a disinfection unit, and it was all in trucks that could be driven to forward positions. Uncle Israel said she wouldn't see change out of twelve thousand dollars.

I asked him if I had twelve thousand dollars.

'Not yet,' he said. 'Have some peach pie. Girls like pie.'

But I was eager to be off to the Red Cross. It seemed to me that once they realized I was kin to Addie Minkel of Duluth I'd be on the next boat to France.

I said, 'Uncle, how long would you say it might take a person to learn to drive a truck?'

'Pops,' he said, 'I'm going to introduce you to Max Brickner's wife at Surgical Dressings. I can't be party to anything that might lead to getting shelled or sunk, so don't ask me. As it is, I have the feeling I'm never going to hear the end of this from your Ma. And anything that incommodes Dora has a habit of turning right round and incommoding me.'

Red Cross headquarters was all comings and goings. Telephones rang, vehicles arrived and left, and Isabel Brickner's hair had worked loose from its pins.

'Of course I can use you,' she said. 'Why don't you answer that telephone?'

I took a message about surgical scrubs while Mrs Brickner searched for shipment manifests and sent an avalanche of papers onto the floor. Uncle Israel looked on, smiling.

'Looks like you could do with a filing clerk, Isabel,' he said, 'and Poppy's a good little tidier-up.'

Mrs Brickner straightened up and looked at me.

I didn't even allow her time to open her mouth.

'No I'm not,' I said. 'I'm a hopeless tidier. But I'm strong and healthy and I want to do something for the boys at the front.'

'Do you, Poppy?' she said. 'Then take off your coat, roll up your sleeves, and report to Room 19.'

And so I began the next stage of my war effort. I sat at a long table with a dozen other girls, rolling cotton bandages and singing songs.

> Tramp, tramp, tramp, the boys are marching
> I spy the Kaiser at the door
> But we'll get a lemon pie and squash it in his eye
> Then there won't be a Kaiser anymore

It was after five o'clock by the time I finished my turn at the Red Cross and boarded a trolley-car to go home and face Ma. The sun was still shining and I felt full of energy. Some of the girls said it was boring work but I thought it was the greatest fun. You were allowed to make coffee and talk, about anything at all, even beaux. And, anyway, I felt certain this was only the beginning.

As I had explained to the other girls, as a mustard heiress I would soon be coming into my fortune, and then I'd be able to buy a surgical flotilla like Cousin Addie and go to the Western Front and save lives. After I told them that they were much more welcoming. As soon as I walked into the room I'd see them smile. Hot Stuff, they called me, because of Minkel's Mighty Fine Mustard.

I walked the last ten blocks, composing myself for Ma, and when I looked down 70th Street I could see camouflaged transports moving slowly down the Hudson toward the open sea. I was, I had decided, now effectively head of our household. Pa was gone, Honey had her own establishment, our help had all left us and Ma was advanced in years and enjoyed very poor health. I bounded up the front steps, ready to take on the world.

Ma didn't answer when I called out, but I found her in the library, sitting in Pa's old chair with a duster in her hand. It was the first time I had ever known her enter that room.

'So many trinkets,' she said. 'I'm sure I don't know why he was so particular about them.'

I said, 'Ma, I have found a position with the Red Cross and I have to go there as often as I possibly can to do essential work, but I promise that I'll take care of the dusting, and I'll leave you a luncheon tray, and be home in time to make dinner for us. And if some day you are very indisposed, I might be spared from my work, just until Honey can come to sit with you, for we all have to make sacrifices you know.'

'There will be no need for a luncheon tray,' was her first response.

I said, 'It came to me, after Reilly said she was needed for the munitions, that I had to volunteer, too. Uncle Israel took me along and they were so grateful to have me they begged me to start right away.'

'How industrious you've been,' Ma said. 'And Israel, too. And how convenient, for it so happens I've decided to answer my country's call, too. We shall both be modern working women, and in the evening we shall eat sandwiches.'

I said, 'Ma, what ever kind of work can you do?'

It seemed most capricious of her to rise from her sick bed and become modern on the very day of my own triumph.

'I shall make jam,' she said. 'I have joined,' she announced, 'the National Campaign for the Elimination of Waste. Let me see no more crusts left on the side of your plate, Poppy. Let me see no more cake toyed with, on account of dryness.'

I am sure I had never toyed with cake in my life.

Still, suddenly Ma and I had full and important lives. We talked all evening about household economies we might make as part of our war effort. I even steered our conversation round to the expedience of riding in public trolley-cars.

'Only be sure to wear your gloves,' Ma said, 'and to wash your hands at the very first opportunity. Minnie Schwab rode on the elevated railway, you may remember, and immediately became ill with a hacking cough.'

'What a pity,' I crowed, 'that Honey can manage nothing more demanding than her Widows and Orphans Bazaar.'

'Now, Poppy,' Ma said. 'Honey doesn't have your sturdiness. As long as she remembers to take her elixir, though, she manages very well. And she can hardly be reproached for finding wars difficult. She's a married woman. She has a husband to fear for.'

But Harry was having an awfully good war. A patchy lung kept him away from any military engagements. His steel investments were doing well. Also his holdings in oil and rubber. He had bought a house in Palm Beach, Florida, and parcels of land bordering on three of Long Island's most up-and-coming golf courses. He had even been elected to the Wall Street Racquet Club.

'If he has any sense,' Uncle Israel had said when he heard that news, 'he'll be polite enough not to insist on playing.'

We dined on sardines on toast and after dinner I tried to show Ma how to turn a heel. We had, after all, baskets full of yarn, and we were in a fever of thrift and industry. But I made an awkward teacher. Within an hour Ma had abandoned knitting and was thinking of embroidering handkerchiefs.

I said, 'I think our boys may do well enough with plain ones. How can you be sure of embroidering the right initials?'

'Why, I shall do a selection, of course,' Ma said. 'As long as my eyesight holds up.'

Emptied of staff our house seemed suddenly vast and vulnerable. With Reilly gone it now fell to me to protect the Minkel fortress and I was doing the rounds, securing all the doors and windows for the night, when I heard the telephone ring. It was the hour for Aunt Fish's daily report on her committees.

I raced upstairs to take the call but arrived in the parlor to discover that Ma had picked up the hated gadget and answered it herself.

'I am quite well, thank you Zillah,' she said. 'Answering the telephone is now part of my war work. To spare poor Poppy. She's practically running the Red Cross bandage effort, you know? They had her there till half past four this afternoon and us without so much as an Irish. But we are determined to manage. One must do what one can for the duration. And I shall fill the solitary hours with needlework. I am embroidering for victory!'

ELEVEN

My new friends at the Red Cross took me for younger than twenty, especially as I didn't have a beau as yet. As I explained to them, I hadn't even had my debut, what with Pa's passing and my being needed as a companion and helpmeet to Ma. I didn't feel deprived. I remembered Honey's debut. Her head had filled up with names of dance partners and designs of gowns, and ever after that she hadn't been much company anymore. It had all cost a mountain of money and the result of it was she married Harry Glaser, so it seemed to me we hadn't had such a good return on our investment.

Sometimes at the depot boy drivers passed our way, picking up consignments of dressings and hospital garments, and certain girls, like Junie Mack and Ethel Yeo, always called them in and made them laugh and blush. Of course, they were all boys who weren't fit to fight so I wouldn't have considered actually walking out with any of them, but they interested me nonetheless. Boys were an entirely new variety of person and I enjoyed learning about them.

Ethel and Junie liked boys who'd take them hootchy-kootchy dancing and buy them cocktail drinks. They liked to be squeezed, too, and kissed.

'Hey, handsome,' they'd call. 'Are there any more at home like you?'

If Mrs Max Brickner was around or any of the older ladies, they kept their voices down. Otherwise we were a very jolly room, and I joined in with the laughter even if I didn't always quite understand the joke. There was a blond boy with an eyepatch who was around for a while.

'Hey, good-looking,' Junie used to shout to him. 'Have you met Hot Stuff, here? Her folks are big in mustard, but she sure could use a little sausage.' And we all laughed when the boy turned pink.

'Keep your eye out for her, anyway,' she'd shout after him, and Ethel would scream.

Ethel and Junie taught me a lot of things. How to smoke a cigarette without choking and how to dance the tango. I didn't accompany them to dance halls, of course, because after I finished my turn on bandages I had to hurry home to Ma, but just knowing about that side of life gave me more confidence.

I was even able to pass along to Honey advice Ethel had given me about avoiding the getting of a baby. Sherman Ulysses was now large and boisterous for his age and I felt sure she wouldn't care to double her troubles.

'After Harry squeezes you,' I told her, 'be sure to stand up directly and jump up and down and if possible douche thoroughly.'

'Poppy!' she said. 'What kind of company are you keeping? You mustn't talk about such things. Please don't oblige me to speak to Ma about this.'

But Ma and I were now great allies. The only time we spent together was in the evening, by which time we were too tired for warfare of a personal nature. Ma would report from the vegetable canning front and I would give her selected anecdotes from surgical dressings. Of my tea-break tango lessons I said nothing.

'Ethel Yeo?' she'd ponder. 'Yeo. Where did you say her people are from?'

'All that is a thing of the past,' I'd explain to her. 'No one cares what your name is or where you came from, just as long as you're doing your share. Everything's changing, Ma.'

'Oh dear,' she'd say. 'I do hope it doesn't change too much.'

But she herself was continuing to change. One of the Misses Stone had explained to her about war bonds, and she had made a decision to invest without consulting either Harry or Uncle Israel.

'I'll only be lending the money, Poppy,' she said. 'It's to feed a soldier and help beat back the Hun. And it will repay me at three and a half percent guaranteed, tax free.'

Aunt Fish was shocked until she learned that no less a person than the prudent Miss Yetta Landau had herself invested fifty thousand dollars in Liberty Bonds.

'One's money is quite safe,' Aunt Fish allowed, 'and as Yetta rightly says, better we fill the war chest this way or we shall be taxed and taxed until we are wrung dry. Dora, I should very much like you to know Yetta. Perhaps the B'nai Brith Charity Bazaar would be the time for you to meet.'

Ma pleaded pressure of Comfort Packet handkerchiefs to embroider, but Aunt Fish would have none of it.

'It will take you out of yourself,' she insisted. 'A person can be too much in their own company. Solitary needlework can leave one prey to thoughts.'

'Very well,' Ma said, amazing us with her decisiveness. 'I'll be happy to attend your bazaar. But have no fears, Zillah. I have never been prey to thoughts. What about Poppy? Is she invited?'

'Poppy may come, too,' Aunt Fish said, looking at me menacingly over Ma's head, 'though I'm sure she must have a hundred other things she would sooner do.'

It was all the same to me. Whatever my aunt's reasons for not wanting me along, they were nothing to the benefits of staying home alone. I could try out, in a looking-glass, the effect of shortening my skirts. I could dance a silent tango and imagine what it might be to be squeezed by a man. I could so load a slice of bread with jam that it would take two hands to lift it to my mouth.

'How soon is the bazaar?' I asked. 'How charming for Ma to have an event to look forward to.'

Aunt Fish continued to eye me. 'Whatever you are up to,' her look said, 'you don't fool me.'

'Likewise, I'm sure,' I shot back to her, without a word being spoken.

'Yetta Landau has raised single-handed the money for two ice machines to be sent to the front,' Ma hurried to tell me upon her return. 'Few people realize how essential ice is for the field hospitals, or would think it worth their attention, but she cares nothing about the popularity of her causes. Indeed the less they are known, the harder she works at them. And then there are her family responsibilities. It is no exaggeration to say she has raised her sister's family as if it were her own. How many aunts would do as much as Dear Yetta has done?'

Miss Landau had become Dear Yetta on the strength of two hours' acquaintance. Not only had Ma freshened up her gray lawn and attended the B'nai Brith Sisterhood Combined War Charities Craft Bazaar, but she had also circulated. Cards had been exchanged, some from as far afield as East 92nd Street, and visits were presaged. Visits appropriate to a period of national austerity, of course.

I heard the door creaking open on Ma's narrow life and I was glad. The pace of her days quickened and filled with Thrift Drive rallies and fund-raising teas. Weeks passed without our boys receiving monogrammed handkerchiefs or any vegetables getting canned. And when I came home from bandage rolling she was no longer inclined to listen to my news. She wanted me to listen to hers.

Yetta Landau was sister-in-law to Judah Jacoby, and Mr Jacoby had been ten years a widower, left with two sons to raise.

'It was Oscar's bar mitzvah,' Ma started on the first of many tellings of the story. Oscar was the elder Jacoby son. I had no idea what a bar mitzvah was.

'It's a special kind of birthday,' Ma said, hurrying on.

'How special?' I asked. Since Pa's death my own birthdays had become the occasion of muted, utilitarian giving.

'Special for boys,' she said. 'Now, please don't interrupt. Mrs Jacoby had not been feeling well but no one suspected she was mortally ill. It was only when she was missed during dinner and found collapsed in her boudoir that the gravity of the situation was realized. By the time she was seen at St Luke's Hospital it was too late. She had suffered a fatal torsion of the insides.'

Ma refused to tell me how they knew what had killed her if it was inside, or to explain why boys had special birthdays. Only that Oscar Jacoby was now twenty-three years old and had just completed basic training at Camp Funston.

I asked Honey if she knew about bar mitzvahs.

'It's a Jewish thing,' she said. 'They have to go to the temple and read an old scroll and then they get gifts and money and a dinner.'

I asked her how she knew.

'Because Harry did it,' she said. 'But Sherman Ulysses won't. We've progressed beyond that.'

Giving up dinners and gifts didn't sound like progress to me.

I said, 'Is Harry Jewish then?'

'Poppy!' she said. 'What kind of a question is that?'

I had no idea whether it was a stupid question or merely an embarrassing one, so I took it to a person who already knew the extent of my stupidity and lack of savoir faire. I left home an hour earlier than usual and stayed on the trolley-car as far as Uncle Israel's office.

'Don't tell me the Red Cross have run out of work for you,' he said when he saw me. Simeon had left Uncle's door open when he showed me in and was hovering just outside, remembering my earlier show of spirit, no doubt.

'No,' I said, 'but I have something to ask you and if you don't mind I prefer not to do it with that person eavesdropping.'

'Pops!' he said. 'Simeon is my right-hand man.'

Still, he sent him away and closed the door.

'Now,' he said, 'what is it? Are you sure I'm the person to ask? Mightn't Honey be more suitable? Or your aunt?'

'Uncle Israel,' I began, 'I want to know if Harry Glaser Grace is Jewish.'

'Ah,' he said. 'I see. Well, I suppose it all depends what you mean by . . .'

'I don't know what I mean by it,' I said. There was a little tremor of frustration in my voice. 'I'm not even sure what Jewish is.'

He lit a cigarette.

'Let me see,' he said. 'Shall we begin with Moses? No. Let's begin with Abraham.'

So my uncle told me a story about people who lived in tents and sacrificed sheep and listened to the Word of God. It was a rather long story. By the time he mentioned the Free Synagogue on West 68th Street the urgency had gone out of my question. Harry had many faults but I was certain he'd be too scared to sacrifice a sheep.

I said, 'Honey says Oscar Jacoby had a bar mitzvah party because he's Jewish?'

'Yes,' Uncle Israel replied.

'And Honey says Harry had one too. Does that mean he used to be Jewish?'

'Yes,' he said.

'So you can stop being Jewish? Like biting your nails?'

'Yes and no,' he said, and got up and walked around behind his desk. I suppose he knew what was coming next.

'Are we Jewish?' I whispered. 'Am I?'

I suppose I had actually worked out the answer already.

Uncle Israel weighed something invisible, first in one hand, then in the other, then sighed deeply.

'In a manner of speaking,' he said. 'But it's really not a thing to get bothered about. These days . . .'

I said, 'Oh I'm not bothered about it. Do you know, I always thought it would be nice to be something, apart from just an heiress. Like Junie Mack is Scotch and Mrs Lesser's kitchen maid was albino. And now it turns out I am something. What fun.'

'Well,' he said, 'my advice is not to make too much of this. No need to make, what shall we say . . . a *feature* of it. One needs to rub along in society. And in business. There are degrees of Jewishness. Yes. It's really a question of degree. How are the bandages going?'

'Very well,' I told him. 'It does me very nicely until I come into my money and can buy a hospital to take to Flanders.'

Something occurred to me.

I said, 'Is Cousin Addie Jewish too? I suppose she must be.'

'Yes,' he said, 'I suppose she must.'

I gave Uncle Israel a most affectionate kiss.

'Thank you so much,' I said. 'I knew you were the person to ask.'

'Pops,' he said, as I was leaving. 'Another word of advice. I wouldn't trouble your Ma with this Jewish business.'

'Why?' I said. 'Doesn't she know?'

TWELVE

Uncle Israel need not have worried about Ma. She knew all about our Jewishness but had simply never gotten around to discussing it.

'It wasn't the fashion,' she said. 'And one was always so busy. Running a house. Raising one's children to be good Americans. Your Pa and I were agreed that those were the important things.'

I said, 'So you're not vexed at my mentioning it?'

'Not at all,' she said. 'Indeed I was only saying to Dear Yetta, when this war is over and we are not all so occupied I should very much like to attend Temple Emanu-El. They say the chandeliers are quite exquisite.'

Yetta Landau and her adopted family now featured as much in Ma's conversation as they did in Aunt Fish's. As far as I was aware neither my mother nor my aunt had ever met Mr Jacoby and his sons, but they were discussed with proprietorial familiarity.

'How Murray must miss his brother now he is gone for a soldier,' Ma would observe.

'Oscar will break hearts,' Aunt Fish would predict, 'with his father's looks and his aunt's sweet manner.'

I cannot say for sure which occurred first; the idea that the sweet and handsome Oscar Jacoby might be the one destined to give me my first squeeze, or the suspicion that Ma and Aunt Fish were hatching a scheme. I only know it began to happen that whenever I walked into the parlor their excited voices would fall silent. Also, that I revealed Oscar's name to my friends in bandaging.

'We're Jewish, you see,' I told them.

'You don't say!' Ethel laughed.

They wondered why he hadn't given me a ring before he left with the American Expeditionary Force.

'We want to test our love first,' I explained.

'Uh-oh,' Junie said. 'First you get the ring. Then you test the love.' I could have kicked myself. I had a pink tourmaline at home that would have served. It had been Grandma Plotz's. Honey got the brilliant-cut sapphire because she was the eldest, and I got the tourmaline.

Next the Red Cross girls wanted to see Oscar's picture. I played for time, day after day pretending I had forgotten to slip it into my pocketbook.

'I should have thought,' said a person called Mrs Considine, 'you would carry him next to your heart.'

'Yes,' said Ethel, throwing down the gauntlet. 'Seems pretty odd to me. No ring. No picture.'

That night I set to work. I carved up an old photograph from Honey's debut year, took from it the head and shoulders of John Willard Strunck, and fitted it to my gold locket. John Willard Strunck once danced a cotillion with my sister but he had subsequently died of thin blood and dead men tell no tales.

At the Red Cross next day everyone huddled around admiring my beau.

'He's cute,' Junie said. 'Real blond and wholesome looking, for a Hebrew.'

'Does he write often?' Mrs Considine wanted to know. She said she got letters from her son all the time. That woman was trouble.

I pleaded Oscar's slow passage across the Atlantic Ocean while I considered what to do next. I had no idea how often a soldier might write to his sweetheart. Nor did I know what kind of things he'd tell me. How often he would fight the Hun, or whether I should allow him to be wounded. I thought perhaps a minor wound, about three months into his tour of duty. Something large enough to excite admiration, but too small to warrant repatriation.

I had a slight unease, which I pushed repeatedly to the back of my mind, that I might be playing with Oscar Jacoby's real fate. What if I said he was wounded and then fact followed fiction? What if he became a famous war hero? How would I explain not being at his side when he returned in triumph? And what if he was killed? What if he sensed that somewhere his courage was being talked up, and he ran blindly into battle, anxious to live up to his reputation?

I began to have a nightmare in which Aunt Fish and Mrs Considine were playing trumpets and a bandaged man forced me to dance the tango. His bandages kept unwinding and getting under my feet. Sometimes underneath the bandages I seemed to see John Willard Strunck and sometimes there was no one under there at all.

I was relieved when someone from the Women's Bureau telephoned Mrs Brickner and asked for the loan of a bright and willing person who understood French.

'Looks like I'm on my way to join Cousin Addie,' I said, as I waved Ethel and Junie goodbye.

'Heck,' Junie said, 'wouldn't it be the wildest thing if they sent you the same place they sent your beau? I sure hope he's behaving himself.'

'You take care now, Hot Stuff,' Ethel called. 'Don't you go getting shot or anything.'

'So far as I am aware,' Mrs Considine said, 'enemy fire has not reached No. 5 Depot.'

And so it turned out. It wasn't the front I was bound for at all, but Front Street, where a fissure had appeared in American–French relations, caused by badly judged shipments of nightwear.

A large perspiring woman handed me two pages of close-written mystery. 'Please translate,' she said. 'I have boxes here waiting to be filled and shipped.'

I'm sure I might have made shorter work of it had she not stood over me, wheezing and dabbing her brow.

'It seems to be about pajamas?' I ventured.

'Well I know that,' she snapped back.

I threw her morsels of information as best I could.

'They require larger sizes. No. They require no large sizes. They want small sizes, and medium. And they prefer blue cotton. Not stripes.'

Gradually she stopped perspiring and treated me with the respect due to an interpreter.

'What a gift to be able to puzzle out such gibberish,' she said. 'Do they mention nightshirts at all?'

By the time I had wrung all the meaning I could from the French requisition she had quite taken to me.

'If only I could hold onto you,' she said. And I permitted her to do so for the remainder of the day, helping to finish up packing twelve hundred pairs of leatherette bedroom slippers and making a start on pajamas and convalescence suits.

It was gratifying to know that I'd helped ensure that the more capacious sizes of hospital wear went to our fine American boys instead of being wasted on small Frenchmen. And it was good to make new acquaintances and hear new stories, especially from one sweet girl who read us her husband's latest letter. He was with the 212th Field Artillery but she didn't know exactly where. A soldier was not allowed to say.

On the trolley-car home I began composing Oscar's letter. 'My own little girl,' it began. I was hoping that Ma might have had another fatiguing day preserving root vegetables. I hoped she would favor an early night so I would be left in peace to practice styles of handwriting.

The house was silent. The more I called for Ma the more she didn't reply, and all I found were jack cheese sandwiches, cut on the diagonal and left under a dainty chain-stitched cloth. I had been abandoned.

I called Honey, but Harry answered and before I could tell him Ma was missing he said, 'Ah, Poppy. Just the person I need. Could you possibly run over and give us a hand? Our help's doing war work, you know, and it's all getting rather too much for Honey.'

I said, 'Why can't you help? I've just put in a day's war work myself.'

'Oh be a sport, Poppy,' he begged me. 'Just an hour. Honey's been caring for Sherman Ulysses all day but she's just had to go and lie down. You have no idea how taxing it all is, and there's no sign of dinner.'

But I had a very good idea. I could hear my nephew playing his drum, right up close to the telephone. Still, Honey never did have much vigor.

I said, 'I can't help you. I have to send out a search party for Ma. Why don't you get dinner at your club?'

'I intend to,' he said, 'just as soon as Honey rallies enough to put the boy to bed. Seeing as his aunt isn't willing to put herself out a little.'

I replaced the handset on its cradle. That was the beauty of telephone conversations. One click and you could disconnect Harry.

I tried Aunt Fish next, but there was no reply. Neither were the Misses Stone at home, and Mrs Schwab had not yet succumbed to the vulgar intrusion of a telephone in her house. I resorted to calling Mrs Lesser, who adored the telephone and stayed by it every moment she wasn't at Penn Station pouring coffee for doughboys in transit.

'How right you are to worry,' she said. 'One hears such horrors. Have you checked the kitchen stairs? She might so easily have missed her footing.'

We discussed other possibilities. Murder. Kidnap. I believe she was quite disappointed when I mentioned the sandwiches.

'Then her absence seems to have been anticipated,' she said, 'and I must ask you not to occupy the line any further. I expect a call from my sister in Nyack momentarily.'

Ma appeared at the unwontedly late hour of half past seven and interrupted me just as I had decided to stop pacing the floor and exploit such rare solitude. When Ma was at home she never found it convenient for me to sing or lie stretched on the hearthrug.

'Where have you been?' I yelled. 'I was all but ready to look for you in the morgue.'

She had the dull flush of a person who had been drinking sherry wine.

'Poppy,' she said, 'I told you last night and again this morning, I was invited to Dear Yetta's crush for starving Polish babies. How inattentive you have become.'

I'm sure I would not have forgotten such a thing. Had I been told, I'm sure I might have hurried home sooner from Depot No. 5 and accompanied Ma myself, to the house Yetta Landau shared with her brother-in-law, to the very home and hearth of my secret sweetheart, Oscar Jacoby.

Ma and Aunt Fish had been driven home in Mr Jacoby's Studebaker automobile, but I was unable to find out much more than that. For a woman who had crossed Central Park twice in one day and partaken of intoxicating drink, Ma had surprisingly little to say for herself. She could give me no account of the people she had met, or the style of the Jacoby house, and when I asked whether she might arrange a little affair of her own, whether Miss Landau and her family might pay us a return visit, she only gave a contented sigh.

'I think,' she said, 'I may take a powder and retire.'

She climbed the stairs, listing gently to starboard.

'Please be sure to dock all the laws,' she called, and disappeared into her boudoir.

My appetite restored by the knowledge that I wasn't an orphan after all, I wolfed down the sandwiches and set to work on creating a love letter from my soldier on the Western Front.

'My own little girl,' I began.

Well here I am in Flanders' field, killing the Boche and having a dandy time. I get off about six every night and I sure wish you were here with me so we could go out dancing. The eats here are pretty good. Still, I can't wait till we have whipped the Hun and I can return to your loving arms. I know a girl like

you won't lack for gentlemen admirers, but I hope you can find
it in your heart to wait for your devoted sweetheart, Oscar.

I wrote it first in a selection of styles until I hit upon a hand
that looked manly. Then I made a fair copy on onionskin paper
and jumped on it a while. By the time I was finished it had the
appearance of having come to me through fire and flood, and for
good measure, I slept with it under my pillow that night.

Oscar Jacoby was beginning to take on flesh.

He was good fun, I decided, with just the right amount of
seriousness. He was a first-rate dancer, and he had cool hands, not
clammy and pink like Harry's. And he'd take a girl to supper and
allow her to choose anything she liked, even two kinds of dessert.
He wouldn't give her a baby and leave her at home with it banging
its drum.

Ethel Yeo gave me a sly smile when I showed them my letter
next day. I turned away and when I looked again, she was still
smirking at me.

'As a matter of fact,' I said, 'my Ma dined with his people only
last night.'

'Yeah?' she said. 'And what division did you say he's with?'

Hellfire and damnation if I just couldn't remember whether I'd
said he was with the 26th or the 28th. I pretended I hadn't heard
her. I excused myself and went to pay a call.

'Never mind, Hot Stuff,' she whispered, next time she came near
me. 'I'll be able to ask him myself, won't I? When he comes home
from the war?'

THIRTEEN

In March 1918 the Bolsheviks surrendered to the Hun and Uncle Israel Fish took me to the theater to see Harry Lauder. Mr Lauder was a Scotchman. He wore a skirt and sang songs I couldn't understand, but Uncle Israel seemed to enjoy them very much indeed. After the show we went to the Waldorf for champagne wine and oyster soup, and he said it would be a good time to have a little talk about my impending inheritance.

'You'll get a monthly allowance,' he said, but he wouldn't say how much. 'Don't want you running wild with it, Pops,' he said. 'And you'll have a nice spread of stockholdings, keeping your money working for you.'

I said, 'Will I be richer than Honey?'

'What kind of a question is that?' he said. 'Harry's made some smart investments for Honey. I'm not party to the details, of course, but Harry has a head on his shoulders. He has a nose for the coming thing.'

I remarked that I didn't want Harry's nose anywhere near my investments.

'Never fear,' Uncle said, 'I'll be managing your fund, and you'll find me a more conservative investor than these young bloods. Stay liquid, that's what I always advise. You won't catch me buying big houses in Oyster Bay.'

That was Harry's latest thing. He foresaw a need for convalescent homes on Long Island once we had won the war.

I said, 'But when shall I be old enough to manage my own fund?'

I believe Uncle Israel looked a little hurt.

'Well, of course,' he said, 'I shan't be around forever. And when you marry . . .'

I said, 'But I'm not allowed to marry. I have to stay home and take care of Ma.'

'Who told you such a thing?' he said. 'Of course you'll marry. And then your husband will advise you on your investments. But no hurry. I'm good for a few years yet.'

He ordered a rack of lamb with *pommes de terre boulanger*. It was news indeed to me that I was no longer expected to remain an old maid. I thought this over as we ate, Uncle making short work of the ribs while I concentrated on the potatoes. They were the best I had ever tasted.

The champagne wine had made me feel a little fizzy, but I was suddenly awake enough to see a connection between my secretly restored eligibility and the abrupt silences that fell whenever I walked in on Ma and Aunt Fish. They were matchmaking.

'Uncle Israel,' I said, 'did you ever meet Mr Jacoby?'

He choked a little on a piece of meat and turned quite purple before he was able to catch his breath and order a glass of brandy. He dabbed at his eyes with his napkin.

'Judah Jacoby?' he said, eventually. 'Yes, I know him. I remember his father, too. Of course, they were just importers when they started, but they're in everything now. Everything from the pelt to the finished garment. Fine quality and square dealings. That's Jacoby.'

I said, 'His wife died, you know, and her sister helped him raise his sons?'

'Oh yes,' he said. 'I hear all about it, never fear.'

I said, 'And Oscar Jacoby is gone for a soldier. Do you happen to know which lot he's with?'

'No idea,' he said. 'Though I'm sure I've been told. I leave my superiors to keep up with that side of things.'

And he gave me a funny greasy smile. My heart was racing.

I said, 'Uncle Israel, Ma and Aunt Fish are always laughing and whispering when they come home from the Jacobys' but they don't tell me anything. Do you suppose . . . ?'

'Pops,' he said. He leaned across the table and patted my hand. 'I have learned not to suppose anything. Who can possibly fathom what Dora and Zillah find amusing? Perhaps they're matchmaking. Perhaps they're just enjoying their war. Now, who's for charlotte russe?'

I went home with a warm, fluffy feeling inside my tummy. Ma was already in bed, but her light was still burning so I went into her and gave her a kind of hug that was not customary in our family.

'Oh Ma,' I said, 'I'm so happy.'

'Poppy,' she said, 'I do believe you're tight. Did Israel explain everything? About your money?'

'He did,' I said. 'He explained everything.'

Alone in my room I tried on Grandma Plotz's tourmaline ring, then I lay down and counted my blessings.

1. By November I would be a mustard heiress and Uncle Israel would keep me liquid. Whatever that meant.
2. Destiny was conspiring with my mother and my aunt to unite me with none other than the very beau of my choice, Oscar Jacoby.
3. I was Jewish, to just the right degree.

FOURTEEN

Toward the end of July Mrs Considine received a Western Union telegram informing her that her son had been killed during the Battle of the Marne. I didn't know him, of course, and I never much liked Mrs Considine but, still, I did feel sad for her, him being her only boy and now he wouldn't be coming home. He had been a bugler, which sounded like a safe kind of soldier to be, so when I heard I became anxious about Oscar who was probably doing far more dangerous things.

A night nurse and a tutor were engaged for my nephew Sherman Ulysses and they accompanied my sister Honey when she went away to Long Island for her health. She had seen a number of doctors but every one of them gave her different advice and none of it helped. She tried sitz baths. She ate charcoal biscuits till her teeth turned black. And she had her magnetic fields adjusted by a person from Brooklyn who only ate nuts and berries.

It was my belief that Honey's problems were the result of lying too much on her couch, but Ma believed quite the opposite.

'Now she can really rest,' I heard her say to Aunt Fish, after Honey had left for her convalescence, 'because she won't have Harry bothering her.'

As Honey faded, so I bloomed. I was much happier in my work because I could almost count in days when I would come into my money and be able to buy a field hospital and take it to France and be talked about, like Cousin Addie. Also, Ethel Yeo, who had become a thorn in my flesh always inquiring after Oscar and trying to catch me out, had left to become a manicurist at the Prince George Hotel. Junie Mack was gone, too, having caught a baby from a soldier, and although I missed her, this left me more at liberty to talk to any good-looking boys who passed through the depot. I had no intention of being unfaithful, but I welcomed the chance to gauge my powers of enchantment. I wanted to learn to spoon, so that when Oscar came home from the war I should be word perfect. I allowed one boy to walk me to the trolley-car and light my cigarette and everything seemed to be most satisfactory, but he never offered again nor was even especially friendly when he saw me.

Then an older man called Albert began to make love to me. He was thirty-two and couldn't go to war because he had rickety legs, but in every other respect he was a handsome devil.

He took me to Riker's for an ice-cream soda and asked me all about my fortune. Everything was going along just fine until he tried to put his arm around my waist. I told him to keep his distance. I told him I had no wish to catch a baby just when I was about to go to war, and the people standing nearby seemed to find this amusing.

I said, 'I'm sure I don't know what any of you find so droll. I'm one of the mustard Minkels and I'm going to buy a hospital and take it to France.'

This made them laugh all the more.

I said, 'And I'd sure like to know why all of you are leaning on this counter, drinking sarsaparilla when you might be volunteering.'

That quietened them. I held my head high and made my exit, but I heard that Albert say, 'Crazy kike.'

Of course, I hadn't meant it about *him* not volunteering. I knew he was too old and crippled. It made me realize, though, how easily I might have gone the way of Junie Mack. Men seemed to believe treating a girl to an ice-cream soda entitled them to certain liberties.

Ma, meanwhile, was forever leaving off her knitting to go to any charity bazaar Yetta Landau might recommend, and sometimes to lectures on subjects relevant to the war effort. These, I know, she found as draining as she had once found the giving of dinners, but she tried to bear up and listen attentively, because she knew this would earn her Miss Landau's respect.

'As Dear Yetta says,' Ma would report, rubbing her temples to ease her aching brain, 'education is our hope and insurance against another war.'

Harry said he believed a safer bet was to shell the Hun until they came out with their hands raised.

'President Wilson,' Ma said, 'has laid down Fourteen Points for peace.'

'What are they Ma?' I asked.

'Poppy!' she said. 'There are fourteen of them! He has also devised Four Ends and Five Particulars, but I'm sure he doesn't expect us all to have them by heart. And then there are all these new countries one has to know about. Montedonia. And Maccnegro. It was all so much easier when there was just America and the rest of the world and one didn't have to concern oneself with the little places. Aha! I have remembered one of President Wilson's Points. Serbia must have a corridor to the sea!'

She produced this with a flourish.

'I say, Dora,' Harry said. 'I'm impressed!'

Ma blushed.

'Well,' she said, 'it may have been one of his Particulars, or perhaps one of his Ends, but anyway, there you have it.'

'Never would have taken you for a bluestocking,' he said. 'Abe wouldn't know you.'

'What do you mean?' she asked, sharper suddenly.

'No. Nothing,' he said, retreating as usual. 'Nothing at all.'

I didn't care for the way Harry was laughing at Ma. I knew she was doing all this for me, raising our stock with Miss Landau, paving the way to Oscar becoming my beau. I was proud of her and I told her so.

'Why thank you, Poppy,' she said. 'I must say, sometimes I quite surprise myself.'

We sat for a while, after Harry left us, basking quietly in mutual contentment.

'It occurs to me,' Ma said, after a while, 'that you might accompany me to Madame Paderewski's lecture next week. It would broaden your education. Madame Paderewski is very desirous of Polish independence, you know?'

'Will Miss Landau be there?' I asked.

I cared nothing about the Polish. They might have their independence without bothering me over it. But I was avid to get any member of Oscar's family in my sights. And so I fell in with Ma's suggestion and hurried up to my room. I had only five days in which to prepare myself, and I wanted to strike the right note, or rather, a pleasing chord of spirited patriotism, savoir faire and unusual beauty. I decided I would leave off my turban, which Ma found worryingly foreign, and make a feature of my hair.

There was standing room only in the Fairway Hall. The Germans and Mr Lenin, Madame Paderewski explained, were picking over the remains of the Polish nation, but a committee had been formed, in Paris, to call a halt to this. Committees had really become quite the thing since the war started. Before that I don't believe I had ever heard the word.

The Polish National Committee were getting up an army, and Madame Paderewski showed us on a large hanging map the places she said belonged in a united Poland. Silesia and Galicia. Poznania.

'More countries to remember,' Ma shuddered.

President Wilson, it seemed, was a true friend of the Polish nationalists, and one of his Fourteen Points was – here Ma dug me in the ribs – that an independent Poland must have a corridor to the sea.

'Didn't I tell you so?' Ma whispered.

I said, 'No. You said Serbia.'

'Why, Poppy,' Aunt Fish interrupted, a shade contemptuously, '*everyone* needs a corridor.'

Yetta Landau had been identified for me as an earnest-looking woman in a boater hat and a high-collared shirtwaist. She was sitting some distance from us, so Ma and Aunt Fish could do no more than smile and flutter their hands until the lecture ended and the donation buckets had been passed around and we were free to circulate.

Miss Landau shook my hand and hoped that I would do what I could for Poland.

'Poppy is with the Red Cross, of course,' Ma said. 'In bandages.'

'Important work,' Miss Landau replied, 'but we all have to ask ourselves what more we can do.'

She had a dry mouth that crackled when she spoke, and slightly gamy breath.

I said, 'I shall be of age in November. Then I'm going to do something really important.'

'Indeed?' Ma said. 'This is the first I heard of it.'

I said, 'I'm going to buy trucks, like my cousin Addie, and drive them to the Western Front.'

Ma looked quite stunned. Miss Landau was studying my hair. I had allowed it full rein, and wound through it a twist of satin ribbons in lemon and raspberry. What could not be subdued should be emphasized, I had decided.

'Don't vex yourself, Dora,' my aunt said. 'Money for madcap schemes will not be forthcoming. I shall speak to Israel about it as soon I get home.'

I opened my mouth to protest, but over my shoulder Aunt Fish had spied another means of silencing me.

'Mr Jacoby!' she cried. 'We had no idea you were here with Dear Yetta. What a pleasure!'

He had separated himself from the crowd and was heading toward us, smiling a little. Judah Jacoby, the real live father of the boy I dreamed about.

I turned scarlet, and Ma and Aunt Fish, in sympathy with me perhaps, glowed pinkly.

'This is Dora's girl,' Miss Landau told him. 'Seems to have her head screwed on, even if it is trimmed up like a circus pony.'

Mr Jacoby took my hand and bowed. Then he did the same to Aunt Fish and Ma. He was a small, soft, silver-haired man. His skin was buttery and his eyes were dark. He was, in fact, not at all what I had planned him to be. And Oscar had his father's looks. Aunt Fish had said so.

'Which lot is your son with, sir?' I asked him, trying to retrieve something of the Oscar I had created. 'I heard he volunteered.'

Mr Jacoby seemed pleased by my interest.

'He's with the 27th,' he said. 'In France, as far as we know.'

'I pray he'll come back to you safe and well,' I said and I caught sight of Ma and Aunt Fish exchanging saccharine smiles, which faded as I declared, 'I'll be over there myself before long. I'm going to buy a field hospital, you see.'

'Well now,' he said, 'I'm sure you're doing sterling work on the home front, and taking care of your dear mother, too. Your father would be proud.'

I said, 'Did you know my Pa?'

'No,' he said, 'I didn't. But if I had a daughter . . .'

And mawkishness returned to Aunt Fish's face.

Later, at home, I took one last look at the picture in my locket, then dropped it into a drawer. Before I fell asleep I counted four reasons why I had no further need of it.

1. It couldn't look anything like Oscar Jacoby.
2. Ethel Yeo and Junie Mack were no longer around pestering me to see it.
3. It was an uncomfortable reminder of my shackled, girlish life.
4. The face of John Willard Strunck had not stood the test of repeated examination. In fact, it was now as clear as day he had been nothing but a weak-mouthed sap.

FIFTEEN

The afternoon of November seventh I was at the Red Cross helping to pack boxes of dressings when suddenly we heard car horns tooting and one of our drivers ran in to tell us the war was over. Mrs Brickner closed up the depot immediately and we all poured out onto Fifth Avenue, along with just about everyone else in the city. Tickertape rained down on us from the offices above, and tugboats in the East River were honking their sirens, and everyone was smiling, even me, though it did cross my mind that peace might have snatched away my chance for an adventure. But I smiled anyway and danced on a snakeline, and kissed at least four soldier boys before I lost count, and by morning the news had changed. We were still at war, after all.

Then, on the eleventh, before we had cleared away breakfast, and long before the polite hour for making calls, the telephone rang. It was Harry.

'The Boche surrendered,' he said. 'The city's going crazy. Listen.'

At the end of the telephone line I could hear church bells ringing out. But outside, on 76th Street, it looked like any other day.

I said, 'It's probably another mistake.'

Ma said, 'Well, Harry is usually right about things.'

'That has not been my experience,' I said. 'I shall go to work anyway.'

'You might look a little more delighted,' Ma said. 'I'm sure the ending of the war is a most welcome thing. We shall all be able to get help again, and hold dinners and not have to attend educative talks and make jam. Hardship has really grown very tiresome.'

I said, 'I thought we were managing rather well without help. Besides, Reilly won't want her old position.'

'Just as well,' Ma said, 'because she will not be offered it. She will have forgotten everything I ever taught her, and bomb-making is sure to have made her more temperamental. There will be plenty of other fish in the sea. Harry told me so.'

Harry had explained to Ma how all those girls would be thrown out of work when the boys came home, and be grateful to take anything.

'Low wages, Dora,' he'd said. 'Like I told Honey, you'll be able to afford a hundred maids.'

I said, 'But Ma, you never liked to throw dinners anyway, so why begin again?'

'The point of throwing a dinner is not enjoyment,' she said. 'How little you understand of society, Poppy.'

'It doesn't matter, Ma,' I snapped, 'I understand silliness when I hear it. The war made you get up from your couch and learn to light the gas range and know where Macedonia is. Haven't you had a much finer time of it? How can you think of going back to the way things were?'

'Because the way things were was the correct way,' she said, 'and that is surely why we went to war. To preserve civilized life. Well, the barbarian is vanquished, so now I think I may at least be allowed to engage a parlor maid. I fail to account for your peevishness, Poppy. One would almost think you were displeased the war has ended.'

I left Ma on the telephone with Aunt Fish, discussing armistice trimmings for their gowns, and rode a crowded trolley-car down to the depot. It was closed, of course. Fifth Avenue was packed with people singing and dancing and blowing whistles. Bells rang and firecrackers exploded. Drivers tooted their horns, though they knew they'd be going nowhere fast, and they didn't seem to care. All day I stayed out, tagging along, following the press of the crowd. Once or twice someone linked their arm in mine and we jigged for a while. More than once or twice I was kissed, but I didn't feel a thrill.

I only felt flat. I wished the war could have lasted just a little while longer, so I might have done something spunky. I wished I wasn't always outside, looking in. I wished I had a friend.

I was cold in my cloth coat. The light was fading as I made my way uptown, pushing through the crowds. The numbers still were growing and so was their loudness and gaiety, and outside the Public Library I became entangled in a rabble of girls and soldiers singing doughboy songs. I caught one of them by the shoulder as I tried to squeeze past her and she turned a moment and looked at me. It was Irish Nellie.

She fell on me with kisses.

'Is it you, Miss Poppy?' she screamed. 'Is it you? Isn't it a grand party?'

She took me in her arms and peered at me in the twilight. She had the smell of liquor on her breath.

'Is it you, Miss? Do you know me now?'

I had known her at once. The last time, that night at the Cunard pier, it had been harder to place her, with her Paris gown and her powdered nose, but this time she was just plain Nellie again.

I nodded, too cold to speak.

'Look at you,' she said, rubbing my arms and my cheeks. 'You're starved. Here, take a nip.' She put a little flask to my lips and forced me to swallow the nastiest thing I ever had tasted. It was to take me a while to cultivate a taste for hooch.

'What happened to your gown?' was all I managed to say. She looked down at her skirt and then back at me, puzzled. But I hadn't meant *that* gown. I meant the plum and silver velvet fourreau, trimmed with a satin bias and stained with the salt water that had drowned my Pa.

Suddenly she understood.

'Got good money for it,' she shouted in my ear. 'Do you think Stouffer's is open?'

She pushed me ahead of her and we turned onto 42nd Street.

Away from the noise and press of the crowd we were awkward with one another.

'I've been working for the Red Cross,' I told her. 'I would have been going to France any day, but now this peace has come along.'

'Ah well,' she said, 'they'll likely have another war presently and you'll get your chance. Do you have a sweetheart over there?'

'Yes,' I said. 'I expect we'll be married as soon as he comes home.'

I was quite surprised to hear myself say this.

'Listen to you,' Nellie said. 'Aren't you quite the lady now. And I remember you when you were all the while playing with your dollies.'

We found a booth in Stouffer's and Nellie advised me to have an egg-flip, the same as her.

'It'll fortify you,' she said. 'You look so pinched.'

I asked her what she had been doing.

'Dispensing comfort and cheer,' she said, and laughed.

'Oh, like Mrs Schwab,' I said, 'at the railroad station, with coffee and cigarettes.'

'Yes,' she said. 'That kind of thing. I see they gave up on your hair. All those hours they had me trying to prevail over it, and you squawking and wriggling. Do you remember? And Mrs Fish threatening you with a dose of vermifuge if you didn't sit still? The old witch.'

Ma had always depended on Aunt Fish to tell her when it was time to send an Irish packing, so I guessed Nellie had disappeared after one of her household reviews.

I asked her why she was let go.

'Don't recall,' she said. 'Don't recall and don't care.'

But her face said something different, and so, I suppose, did mine.

'Ah, Poppy,' she said, 'don't rake over old troubles. Leave the dead in peace.'

'I only wondered,' I said, feeling my way, still not quite sure what it was I was wondering.

She had two more fortifying egg-flips brought.

'I get the night terrors still,' she said. 'About climbing into the little boat. I was afraid I'd be tipped out and it was an awful long way down to the water. I was all for staying. I thought they'd fix up the hole and we'd be all right, but he said I must get in line for a place in a boat, to be on the safe side, and he'd be back directly with blankets and my muff. And that was the last I saw of him. They lowered our boat with places to spare and he was left behind. He was a darling man, your daddy. Oftentimes I've wished I'd just stayed with him and saved myself these hard times and sorrows.'

I said, 'I don't believe you were his secretary, Nellie, nor his personal assistant. I believe you were an adventuress.'

'I was not,' she said, quite indignant. 'I was his sweetie pie.'

'I see,' was all I could say. It had never occurred to me that old people had such things.

'Well, you've no need to look so disapproving,' she said. 'Aren't I pretty enough to have been his cutie?'

As a matter of fact I didn't think she was so pretty anymore. Her skin had grown coarse. But that wasn't what was troubling me. I sensed I had come upon some kind of iceberg, too, and was bound to collide with it, just like Pa's ship.

I said, 'I didn't know he had a sweetie pie.'

'Of course he did,' she said. 'They all do.'

I asked her whether her pa had one.

She laughed again. 'I mean all the *gentlemen* have them,' she said. 'It's just a natural thing. They have their wives for the one side of the business and their cuties for the other and that way everyone is suited.'

I said, 'Does my Uncle Israel have one?'

'Sure to have,' she said, 'if he has breath in his body.'

'And Harry?' The extent of this iceberg was becoming horribly clear.

'Harry?' she said. 'Is he your beau?'

'No,' I said. 'Harry who's married to my sister.'

'Oh *him*,' she laughed. 'He probably has a string of them.'

I hated Nellie for knowing something about Pa that I hadn't

known, and yet I wanted to stay there with her. In the six years since he was lost, she was the first person to speak of him, freely and happily. The egg-flips were my undoing. I began to cry.

'I miss him so,' I whispered. 'I can't remember his face anymore, or his smell. I tried to keep his smell locked in his closet, but it faded away.'

This touched off her tears and we sat opposite each other, sobbing into our empty glasses.

'You were always his favorite,' she said. 'He always spoke of you. And now look at you, all grown-up and engaged to a soldier boy. Well, he's watching over you, never fear.'

I had heard of heaven, of course, but I had no more idea what it might be like than I did of Iowa. Nellie though seemed quite familiar with the place.

'He's up there all right,' she said. 'I know your kind don't believe in it but sure the good ones get sent there anyway.'

She painted the grotesque picture of a platform, high above the clouds, from which dead people could look down on the living and, if they chose to, guide them away from harm. She was quite unable, though, to explain why no one in heaven, Grandpa Minkel for instance, had prevented Pa from sailing on a ship that would sink. But then, she was only an Irish. Also, I believe she was tight.

She kissed me over and over when we parted.

'I'm so glad I bumped into you, Poppy,' she kept saying. 'And I wish you long life with your sweetheart when he comes home. Long life and a house full of babies.'

I hurried away from her. She had disturbed me with the idea that Pa, from his vantage point in heaven, might have seen me stealing cake in a time of national austerity and passing off John Willard Strunck as my fiancé. Also, she had revealed certain unsavory facts about husbands. I decided, there and then, I would not marry Oscar Jacoby, no matter how much he begged me.

SIXTEEN

On my twenty-first birthday I received a tortoiseshell vanity set from Ma, a garnet bracelet from Harry and Honey, and from Aunt Fish an introduction to a good corsetière. Uncle Israel took me to lunch at Sherry's and explained to me about my money. I was to have a monthly allowance of one hundred dollars, to be reviewed after I had proven my steadiness and thrift, and I might apply to him for approval of occasional larger expenses.

This certainly wasn't the liberation I had expected, but as I had only a hazy idea of what one hundred dollars might buy, I acceded, for the time being. He slid across the table an envelope containing fifty dollars in crisp new bills.

'Just a little something to start you off,' he said. 'But take care now, Pops. There'll be folk who only cultivate you for your money and you must learn to recognize them.'

I rather liked the idea of being cultivated, for whatever reason. I liked the feel of the cash in my hand, too.

I said, 'On Armistice night I met Irish Nellie, that was saved from the *Titanic*. She said she was Pa's sweetie pie. She said all gentlemen have one . . .'

Uncle Israel had a spoonful of coffee parfait stopped stock still, halfway to his mouth.

'. . . even you probably. Do you?'

'I do not,' he said.

'Don't you want one?' I asked. 'Nellie said any gentleman can get one, as long as he has life in his body, and it quite suits the wives because then husbands don't come home every night expecting conversation.'

He pushed his dish away from him.

'Nellie said Harry probably has a string of them,' I continued. 'Do you think so? Honey does find conversation awfully tiring.'

'Poppy,' he said, 'this person is precisely the kind I was warning you against, and may I say, this is not polite talk for a young lady. What else did this person say? Did she ask for money? Did she name names?'

Uncle Israel appeared to have lost his appetite, though I couldn't see I was to blame. If he chose not to have a sweetie that was his affair. As to Harry, I had already decided I was going to question him myself.

On the way home I went to Macy's in Herald Square. I ordered a Singer sewing machine and spent thirty dollars on Vinolia vanishing cream, fruit cake, flesh-tone stockings and a garter belt, scent, a Kolinsky fur collar for my winter coat, and a selection of hatpins which I gave to Ma.

'But I already have hatpins,' she said. 'What possessed you to buy me more? Such extravagance. A small tablet of cucumber toilet soap would have been most acceptable.'

I was a little hurt by her criticism. I had had fifty dollars to dispose of and I'm sure I had done the very best I could. I'm sure, had they been given by anyone else she'd have said, 'One can never have too many hatpins.'

At the beginning of December Honey sent word that she felt strong enough to return to New York.

'She will stay with us,' Ma said, 'until I'm satisfied as to her recovery. A month at least, I think. How cozy we shall be!'

We had just engaged, at great expense to Ma's nerves, a new maid-of-all-work, a foreign girl with rudimentary English. She was put to work scrubbing and airing the room that had once been mine, before Honey's marriage, but it was soon decided that it was incurably damp and cheerless and quite unsuitable for a convalescent.

'She must have your room,' Ma decided. 'It was once hers anyway, so she'll feel quite at home there, and you always did well enough in the damp room. You are lucky, Poppy, to have been blessed with a strong constitution.'

Harry was to bring Honey and Sherman Ulysses home in his Packard. As soon as I heard this, I went to 74th Street and made my demands.

'I have to learn to drive an automobile,' I told him, 'so it may as well be you that shows me how. Then I shall be able to drive us all from Oyster Bay.'

He sniggered.

'Drive from Oyster Bay!' he said. 'You fool! You can't just jump behind the wheel.'

He soon came round to my way of thinking.

'Do you know what I heard about you, Harry?' I said. 'I heard you have popsies. I wonder whether Honey knows? I believe I may discuss it with her. I have a feeling she has no idea what a considerate husband she has.'

'Just get into the car,' he whined, 'and pay close attention to what I do. It's a great deal harder than it looks, as you're about to find.'

But it wasn't, of course. It was amazing what an ill-founded reputation Harry had for knowing about things.

I studied what he did for a while and then, after we were over the Queensborough Bridge, I resumed my questions about popsies until he caved in and allowed me to take the wheel myself. There was nothing to it.

The nurse and the tutor were dispatched to bring Sherman home by railroad, which still left three of us to squeeze in beside Honey's luggage.

'Driving!' Honey cried. 'How modern you've become. And as thin as a pencil, too, with all that rushing around I suppose, fighting wars. Or have you been slenderizing? I shall have to learn your secret, Poppy. I eat next to nothing but I never seem to reduce.'

When they heard about my driving, Ma and Aunt Fish were amazed and anxious in equal measure. On the one hand Yetta

Landau drove, so driving was, by association, a Good Thing. On the other hand, she brought to it a carefulness I could never hope to emulate. I was famously untidy and erratic. What if I had untidily steered the Packard over a precipice and killed us all?'

'Ma,' Honey said, 'I don't believe Poppy took us anywhere near a precipice. She doesn't even waver when she's having her cigarette lit. As a matter of fact, I found her to be a more soothing driver than Harry. Now tell me about the Jacobys. I want to hear all the news.'

But she was hushed, with significant looks from Ma and Aunt Fish, and then Sherman Ulysses arrived, in the care of his nurse, and caused a change of topic. I didn't care. I was feeling proud and excited about my ability to drive a car all the way to Oyster Bay and back, and, anyway, I was accustomed to the whispers and secret smiles connected with the name of Jacoby. I knew what was going on.

My nephew had certainly grown some, and that good sea air had given him a fund of energy. He shot through the door, bumped against the credenza and tumbled up stairs to the parlor with his bootlaces flying.

'Now, Shermy,' Honey said, 'shake hands nicely with Grandma and Aunt Poppy. He's learned to shake hands, you know?'

But Sherman Ulysses' hands were busy investigating the face on one of Ma's china shepherdesses, picking at it with a fat little finger.

'Hey, Sherman!' Harry bent low, holding out his own hand. 'Come and show us how it's done.'

But Sherman blew a raspberry in his daddy's face and fell back, very pleased with himself, against Ma's chair. Harry laughed.

'That's my boy!' he said. 'Want to fight? Eh? Eh?' He put up two silly fists.

'Harry!' Honey warned. 'Please don't get him overwrought.'

It was too late, of course. Sherman was already beside himself with fatigue and excitement and uncurbed bumptiousness. I observed him. I knew that the sight of a small child, close kin, should arouse tenderness in me but I felt nothing, and he himself sensed there was someone in the room he had failed to enrapture. His eyes kept returning to meet mine.

'I think,' said Ma, 'he might like a nice glass of buttermilk. Poppy? And a cookie?' But Sherman was smart enough to know I was not his friend. He clung to Ma's skirts and I fumed within, refusing to coax him. A grandchild, no matter how unlovely, was apparently to be fussed and petted and fed on buttermilk and cookies, but *I* had never enjoyed any of these privileges. My grandparents had lingered in Iowa, stubbornly declining ever to come to New York City and adore me. They had given me nothing, except a tourmaline ring and a pile of money.

Ma took Sherman down to the kitchen herself and I remained in the parlor with Harry and Honey, until I grew tired of the way Harry prowled around, picking up vases and bowls, examining them as though he were in a shop. I went in search of a little soothing buttermilk for myself and found Sherman and Ma in the top stairhall, standing in front of the twin oil paintings of Pa and Ma.

'And this is your Grandpa Abraham,' Ma was whispering. 'Shouldn't you like to be named Abraham, same as your grandpa? Isn't it a very fine name?' And Sherman Ulysses was nodding solemnly, chipping away with his pointed little teeth at one of my favorite brown sugar cookies.

So Honey began her convalescence, in my bedroom, and we dropped into a new regime. She slept till eleven and then a breakfast tray was taken in to her. Every afternoon, Sherman was brought by his nurse for an hour of caresses. And twice a week Harry came to dine. A perfunctory affair, this. As soon as the savory was cleared he always had to rush away to a card game.

'Just as well,' Ma would say. 'I believe Honey may have overreached herself today.'

I was hardly at home. There was still work to be done at the Red Cross.

'The guns are silent, but the battle goes on,' Mrs Brickner had said. 'So many devastated lives. So many orphans and widows and poor crippled heroes.'

There were victory parades, too, with bands playing and our soldier boys marching up Fifth Avenue. At Madison Square there was a victory arch, made of plaster, and further uptown a curtain of sparkling glass beads suspended from two white pillars. I always looked out for Irish Nellie, having in mind to quiz her on certain things, such as her travels in Europe, and the habits of married men. But I never saw her.

Honey was still with us in January, although beginning to dress a little earlier in the day. I petitioned Uncle Israel for enough money to buy an automobile, and while he hesitated I made short work of my monthly allowance, buying quantities of fabric which I turned into experimental gowns.

I had let slide Aunt Fish's offer of a set of bespoke support garments, and created for myself a system of layered tubes that fell loosely from the shoulder seams and made me feel tall and strong and rather beautiful. Ma referred to them as my *robes*, and hoped aloud that the craze would soon pass. Honey judged the line interesting but the colors too shrill. I enjoyed this compliment and repaid it by making her a three-layer muslin in matronly shades of gray, blue and indigo. She loved it. She declared all her set would want one, though I wasn't aware she had a set anymore, and I began to feel that at least my sister no longer saw me as a child.

Then I came home one day to find her pink and agitated and ready for a quarrel. Whiling away the long hours, she had been rooting around in my drawers and unearthed John Willard Strunck. She was waiting for me, swinging the locket on its chain, trying to look more injured than triumphant.

'What can you have been thinking of?' she began.

Having no explanation I cared to share with her, I remained silent. She reeled at the damage I had done to a treasured photograph, shed crocodile tears over a departed one-time cotillion partner, and scorned my need of someone else's beau. All the while I stared her out. It was only her threat to bring the matter to Ma that roused me to defend myself.

'He was never your beau,' I said. 'He danced with you because Pa knew Dr Strunck and you quite despised him. I remember it, Honey. You found his chin weak. And since he is dead don't you think he deserves to have his picture in someone's locket, instead of moldering in albums you had quite forgotten? I did it first because I've been so pursued by boys this last year and needed to fend them off . . .'

Honey snorted.

'. . . but now I'm rather proud to have it. I'm sure even a person with a weak chin would like to be remembered and carried in a locket.'

'You were so proud of it,' she said, 'you dropped it amongst your hair pins and tangled ribbons. How slovenly you are, Poppy. Sly and slovenly.'

'You should go home,' I said, evenly. 'You should go and attend to your own affairs. Before Harry spends any more of your fortune taking showgirls to supper.'

'How dare you,' she said. 'Harry does no such thing!'

But she telephoned for the car to fetch her, packed away her sleeping powders, her Tilden's Extract and her tonic wine, and was gone within the hour.

Ma was quite put out when she returned from a bazaar and found her gone.

'I fail to account for her urgency,' she said. 'Can you account for it, Poppy?'

I reclaimed my room that night and flushed John Willard Strunck down the water closet, may he rest in peace.

SEVENTEEN

It took a crisis to reconcile me with my sister. One afternoon early in the New Year Uncle Israel returned to his office and suffered a seizure.

It occurred to me that he might die, and then that any of us might die. In a funk over the fragility of life, I went to 74th Street and begged Honey that we be friends again.

'Of course we're friends, you noodle,' she said. 'How could we not be?'

I apologized for what I had hinted about Harry.

'Well,' Honey said, 'let's say no more about it. What matters now is Uncle Israel.'

He blamed the episode on a rogue clam in his lunchtime chowder, his doctor blamed it on his having eaten too many good, sweet clams and the attack left him with a strangely lopsided face. It also temporarily loosened his grip on my money. Weakened by bed rest and health lectures from Aunt Fish he agreed to transfer to my personal account enough funds for the purchase of a Pierce-Arrow cloth-top roadster. This brought me more pleasure than I had believed possible. Driving Harry's Packard had been all very well and good, but behind the steering wheel of my own car anything seemed possible.

I had in mind to visit Duluth, Minnesota, and see whether Cousin Addie was home from the war, also Blue Grass, Iowa, to inspect my mustard roots. I had in mind to drive sheer across the United States of America till I came to the end of the road, but I figured to do it with a companion of some kind. A dog perhaps, or a beau. And until that was settled I contented myself with driving around the city.

'How restless you are,' Ma observed. A fine remark from a person who was out playing canasta at least four times a week. And I came home one day to find her in a fever of excitement.

'The most wonderful thing,' she said. 'Oscar Jacoby's regiment will be home in time for Passover. There's to be a Seder, Poppy. Dear Yetta is making a Seder, and we are invited.'

Oscar's name was the only thing in this announcement that signified anything to me. Though I had decided I wouldn't marry him, I was theoretically willing to be pursued and courted, and I was certainly curious to see him. Of Passovers and Seders, I knew nothing.

Ma brushed aside my queries.

'Passover!' she insisted. 'You know! *Passover!* The Bible. Egypt. Dinner. Good gracious, Poppy, you exhaust me with your questions. Well, ask your uncle. He will explain it to you, and be sure to pay close attention. A Seder is a most particular dinner.'

This became more and more evident as Ma and Aunt Fish went for fittings for their new gowns, and I was put under pressure to order something for myself.

I already had one of my own new designs under construction, a loose calf-length skirt in black and crimson surah and a matching Slav shirt fastened across one shoulder with a line of frogging and Chinese balls.

'We have seen such a suitable pink voile, haven't we Dora?' Aunt Fish began.

But I resisted. If Oscar Jacoby chose to fall in love with me he would do so understanding that I was a girl who wore crimson. And the fact that I had recommended secret applications of Gomper's Patent Skin Whitener was neither here nor there. I was doing it for myself.

Simeon visited Uncle Israel for an hour every day, Monday to Friday, with a digest of who was buying and who was selling, what was up and what was down. He also, I learned, on a day when our visits coincided, brought certain items into the house under cover of papers for signing. Knishes. And cheesecake. Aunt Fish had imposed a strict regime on Uncle after his seizure, but as I had heard her say to Ma, she was baffled.

'Nothing seems to help,' she said. 'He has nothing but clear broth and a cigarette for luncheon yet he doesn't reduce an inch.'

I saw a difference in him, though. His body might not have shrunk, but his spirit had, and the palsy on one side of his face made him look sad even when he was smiling.

'I have to learn about Passover,' I told him. 'Ma seems to think I'll let her down in front of the Jacobys.'

He said, 'I haven't been to a Seder since I was . . .'

He wasn't coming to this one either. Aunt Fish had overridden the doctor's verdict that it would do him good to go out and circulate.

'It's the dribbling,' I'd heard my aunt confiding to Ma. 'At home I can remind him to mop, but how should we go on at a party?'

'We used to have such Seders,' Uncle said. 'When I was a boy. Such . . . We were slaves, in the land of . . . And the Angel of Death passed over us. Smote the . . . and passed over us. My mother. Oh, we used to have such Seders.'

I said, 'Uncle, does this mean we've decided to be Jewish again?'

He smiled.

'There was always a . . .' he began, and then stopped, looking around him for the missing word. This happened a lot after the seizure. His speech was slower than before and often, by the time he was ready to use a word, it seemed to have fluttered out of reach.

I said, 'What was there always?'

'Hmm,' he said. 'I'll think of it.'

I peeled him an apple and quartered it.

'A stranger,' he said, 'that's what there always was. You had to have a stranger at your table, to share your blessings. Because if you don't share them, they're not really blessings. It was a good time to be a stranger. You could have had ten dinners.'

I couldn't imagine such a thing. You might get a murderer or a robber in your house, or a smelly unfortunate. Unless it was someone who came with a letter of introduction, in which case I suppose he might not count as a stranger. When Ma and Pa gave dinners there had always been people like Mr and Mrs Teller and Dr and Mrs Strunck, so you knew where you stood. You knew what you would talk about. I could see that a stranger might make things more interesting.

I said, 'We'll be the strangers at the Jacobys'. I guess that's why we were asked.'

'No,' he said, 'I don't think so. I think you're asked because . . .'

He never did remember why.

'My mother,' he said, 'used to make such . . . Such knaidlach.'

I wiped the dribble from his chin. I had noticed that Uncle Israel remembered things from long ago much better than things from right now.

'Dear Yetta has quite advanced ideas, you know?' Ma warned me proudly, as we climbed to the Jacobys' front door. 'She has introduced some very modern furnishing trends.'

Aunt Fish puffed and panted behind us. I had noticed, that very afternoon, how Ma and her sister appeared to have changed places. Ma was now the one who had energy and took the lead.

I attributed Ma's particular friskiness that day to my presence. She was excited at the prospect of showing me off to her new friends, and with good reason. I had topped off my crimson Slav outfit with a Cossack hat in black astrakhan, and on the recommendation of the beautician at Elizabeth Arden I was wearing scarlet lip color. Oscar Jacoby was going to be stunned, and she knew it.

The Jacobys lived in a dull row house on East 69th Street. It wasn't pretty like ours, with patterns in the brickwork or limestone tracery. Outside it had nothing to distinguish it from its neighbor. Inside, though, it was quite different from anything I'd ever seen. There were no rugs or tassels or doodads. There was very little furniture and the few chairs and couches they did have were covered in pale slipcovers. And everything was painted ivory. It was a house that seemed full of light and air and the thought crossed my mind that if Oscar's wooing should turn out to be irresistible I should be very happy to be mistress of it some day.

Mr Jacoby and Miss Landau were waiting for us in the parlor, with an elderly couple called Roth, both deaf, and a young Landau cousin from St Louis who wore eyeglasses and a little silk cap, just like the one in Pa's vitrine. Of Oscar and his brother there was no sign.

Mrs Roth examined me with a hatchet face and remarked loudly to her husband that there was an undressed person in the room and he should avert his eyes. I saw Aunt Fish give Ma one of her didn't-I-say-as-much looks, until Yetta Landau stepped forward to defend me.

'Young women have earned themselves a new style,' she declared, 'and a wonderful style it is too. So free and healthy.'

'Well said, Yetta.' Judah Jacoby added his seal of approval to the length of my skirt.

'And Poppy makes up her own designs,' Miss Landau continued, chastening my aunt still more. 'If I were a few years younger I might be commissioning her new look for myself.'

Mr Jacoby laughed and said she should do it anyway. They made a very jolly pair. I wondered why he had never married her, since she had famously been such a mother to his children.

Suddenly, something bumped against the outside of the parlor door, there was the sound of a scuffle and then the high clear voice of a child.

'But you have to,' it cried. 'You *have* to. We made it specially for you and now you're being beastly. I'm telling. I'm telling Auntsie.'

The door burst open and a thin boy stood before us.

'Auntsie,' he said, 'Oscar's being beastly about the Seder. He says he won't come. He says he doesn't have to. But he does have to, doesn't he?'

'Murray,' Miss Landau sighed, 'first you must say how-de-do and *gut yomtov* to our company. To Mr and Mrs Roth, and Mrs Fish, and Mrs Minton and Miss Minton, and Cousin Landau.'

'How-de-do and *gut yomtov*,' he gabbled, not looking at any of us. 'Now will you please tell Oscar?'

But Miss Landau allowed no cutting of corners. He was made to shake each of us by the hand.

'My name's Poppy Minkel,' I said, when he reached me. 'Minkel. Not Minton.'

I took Murray Jacoby for about nine years old, but he was twelve and just a slow developer. He still is.

Miss Landau went in search of Oscar, with Murray close at her side eager to see justice done, while the rest of us went in to dinner.

The table was set with a fine white cloth and candles. In the center was a dish, exactly as Uncle Israel had said there would be, with a bone and an egg and parsley and other things. Mr Roth brought out a silk cap from his pocket, too, and clapped it to the back of his head and Mrs Roth made him change seats twice, so that he'd have to sit neither next to nor opposite an undressed person.

Aunt Fish was admiring the stemware and Ma was nervously eyeing the little back-to-front book left in front of each placement, like a child's picture book, but with strange Hebrew writing facing the English words. We Jewish people must be very clever indeed it seemed to me, if we could make any sense of such an unusual way of writing.

'Aha!' said Mr Jacoby, 'here he is.'

Yetta Landau came into the dining room, and behind her, allowing himself to be pushed along by the boy Murray, who was beaming from ear to ear, came Oscar. Not tall, not husky. He had the same darkness around the eyes that his father had, and the same smooth skin. He bowed inattentively and took the seat next to mine, Murray sat opposite, Miss Landau went to the place at Judah Jacoby's right hand. Ma was at his left hand, in a seat of honor, smiling inanely at everything and nothing. She always did this when her composure was threatened and I knew, from the way she kept fingering it, that the little Hebrew book was troubling her.

One seat remained empty, next to the boy Murray.

'Well now,' said Mr Jacoby, and he got to his feet.

'But are we all here?' Ma asked. I believe she hoped that if she spoke out with a confident air on inconsequential matters, she would be saved from anything more onerous, like knowing what to do with the ceremonial parsley, or how to say the squiggly foreign words. If ever Ma saw a difficult subject advancing on her, she would divert it with a remark about the weather, and this was a technique that had served her well. But that evening I sensed her nervous twittering might be the undoing of her.

I decided, mainly out of benevolence, to keep watch over her. I knew I was looking astonishingly good and I was sitting right beside a most satisfactory suitor. I was at peace with the world, but in particular I was at peace with my mother, who had dragged herself back into society and taxed herself with lectures and even reopened the difficult subject of Jewishness all in the interests of my future happiness.

'I think, Ma,' I said pleasantly, 'the empty chair is for Elijah.'

She promptly grabbed the rope I had thrown her and hanged herself with it.

'Of course,' she said. 'Elijah. Well, there was a great deal of traffic on Park Avenue. We were almost delayed ourselves. Does he have far to come?'

The boy Murray guffawed into his hand, Mr Jacoby chewed the inside of his cheek and I blushed, for Ma, for myself, and for poor Uncle Israel who had taught me what he could about Seders and then had to stay home lest he dribble and disgrace us all.

Miss Landau lit the candles.

'Well now,' Mr Jacoby said again. He poured wine into the cup in front of him and then I heard, for the first time in my life, the sound of those strange Hebrew letters.

He took the big matzo crackers and broke one of them in two.

One piece he wrapped in a napkin and Miss Landau took it away. The rest he held up, showing them to us.

'This is the bread of affliction,' he said.

And so the Seder began.

EIGHTEEN

More of the thick red wine was poured and then the boy Murray did his party piece, pronouncing the Hebrew words and looking very pleased with himself.

'Now in English,' Mr Jacoby said, 'so that everyone understands.'

'Why is this night different from all other nights?' Murray recited. 'Why on this night do we eat only unleavened bread? Why on this night do we eat only bitter herbs? Why on this night do we dip our herbs twice? Why on this night must we all recline?'

'And who cares?' Oscar said, quietly.

'Oscar!' Miss Landau warned.

'Because if God hadn't brought us out of Egypt,' Mr Jacoby said, 'we'd still be slaves.'

Ma nodded solemnly, as though she had never heard a wiser answer.

'God didn't bring us out of Egypt,' Oscar said. His hand was trembling, so the piece of onyx in his cuff link drummed against the rim of his plate. 'Pharaoh chased us out.'

Everyone was looking at him, except Aunt Fish, who was examining the silver.

'We'd be there yet,' he said. 'If some Pharaoh hadn't chased us out we'd still be sitting there, playing the tragic card.'

The cousin from St Louis prepared to speak. He took off his eyeglasses first. Perhaps he could hear that cuff link rattling too.

He said, 'You're not suggesting slavery is an agreeable condition?'

'I'm saying it's an easy habit,' Oscar snapped back, 'human nature being what it is. Once you've got a slave and kept him down a while, you don't have to worry about him striking out for freedom. He might mutter a bit, but that's as far as he'll go. You can pretty much depend on him to sit on his haunches and eat his rations.'

Cousin Landau fingered his eyeglasses some more.

'You've come back from this war a cynic,' he said.

'It's remarkable I've come back at all,' Oscar replied. 'Well, if we must have this Seder why don't we get on with it?'

So Mr Jacoby told the story about the striking down of firstborns. Camels and asses and wicked Egyptians, but only boy firstborns, and not Jewish ones, because God watches out for his own. Then he dipped his finger in his glass and dripped wine, drop by drop, and Murray called out all the different plagues that had beset the people of Egypt.

'Blood, frogs, lice,' he shouted. 'Wild beasts, pestilence, boils, hail, locusts, darkness at noon.' It was obvious he was enjoying this part.

The evening dragged on. Everything was explained with a story. The matzo crackers, the horseradish, the lamb shank. It was seven o'clock and there was still no sign of dinner. My stomach rumbled so loud even the deaf Roths seemed to notice it, and I believe I saw Aunt Fish suppressing a yawn.

At long last Miss Landau took away the Seder dish, and their Irish brought in soup with dumplings. Ma, who had been visibly shocked by Murray's joyful shouting of the words 'frogs' and 'boils', was restored by her first spoonful of soup and became quite gay.

'And shall you be going into the family business,' she asked Oscar, 'now you're back from your adventures?'

I had been wondering the very same thing myself. The House of Jacoby was especially known for its minks, and I could imagine the pleasure of wandering between long racks of deep furs, free to take my pick.

'Adventures?' he said. 'Is that what you think?'

Ma quite missed his tone and continued smiling.

'But surely,' said the cousin, 'war is a kind of adventure. Isn't there a need in every man to run a noble risk? I wish I could have been there.'

'You may have your chance yet,' Oscar said. 'There'll be another war, and the saps who went this time won't go again. Next war, they'll take even you, cousin, and then you can run your noble risk.'

'Another war?' I said. 'Do you really think so? Do you think it'll come soon?'

He didn't even look at me.

'Not all that soon,' he said. 'Not until people have had time to forget. But it'll happen.'

'Well, I shan't go,' the boy Murray piped up.

Ma ventured back into the conversation. She said, 'But I understood it was the war to end all wars. How very unsettling to think we may have another one.'

'How so?' Oscar said. His cuff link had begun to rattle again. 'Didn't you describe it as an adventure? And Cousin Landau here thinks it makes men nobler. He'd like to find out if he has what it takes.'

He pushed back his chair and rose to his feet.

'Well, I'm sure he does. Blood, brains . . . anything that's easily spilled . . .'

The dumplings in my soup suddenly lost their appeal.

'Guts. Lights. Skin and bone. That's what soldier boys are made of.'

I watched him leave the room, pale but sweating.

Murray had finished his soup.

'Shall I go after him, Auntsie?' he said. 'Is he allowed a tray in his room?'

'Oscar is . . .' Mr Jacoby seemed at a loss.

'What has happened?' Mr Roth shouted.

'Eat your soup,' Mrs Roth shouted back.

'Oscar is suffering from exhaustion of the nerves,' Miss Landau explained, 'and it might have been better after all, Murray, if we had not insisted on his being here tonight. Now he's been rude to our guests, a thing he never would have done before.'

She said it kindly enough. Murray considered for a moment.

'Oh, yes, he would,' he murmured. 'Sometimes he would have been even ruder.'

It had been a shocking performance from Oscar. He had been sarcastic and surly. He had mocked his cousin, affected not to notice my dress, and he had said disgusting unrepeatable words. He seemed not to give a damn about anything. I fell deeply and crazily in love.

A boned lamb roast followed, and a strawberry sherbet, and gradually the mood lightened. There was talk of going to Saratoga to see the trotting races. And even the boy Murray deigned to be interested in my own plan to drive across America.

'But where will you stop for luncheon?' he asked, scraping the very last traces of sherbet from his sundae dish.

When dinner was finished, the Seder dish was brought back in, and the broken pieces of matzo cracker, and more wine was poured.

'Is it time yet?' Murray asked his father. But there were more prayers and blessings to sit through before he finally got the signal to leave the table and open the door for Elijah. We all stood, and drank, but Elijah didn't appear and neither did Oscar. He was in his room, I decided, pacing the floor, wondering whether he had ruined his chances with me.

Then Miss Landau and Murray and Mr Jacoby finished off with a song, and we withdrew, ladies and gentlemen all together, to take coffee in the drawing room.

*   *   *

As I drove Aunt Fish home I strained to hear what she and Ma were whispering, but neither of them ever seemed to finish a sentence.

'I have every confidence . . . ,' Ma began.

'Of course, the important point to be decided . . . ,' Aunt Fish interrupted.

I did manage to catch 'June might be very suitable . . .' and then a motorized bus passed by and drowned the rest of Ma's words.

I gave up trying to hear, and in my mind's eye began designing my trousseau. Oscar and I would be a very modern couple. We'd probably live in a new apartment building until we inherited the Jacoby house, and might even dispense with servants. Since the war it was becoming quite the trend to manage with help who just came in as required. It was a very satisfactory arrangement. Backstairs girls had always seemed to create more problems than they solved, and cooks were positively hazardous, always so hot and cross and liable to boil over.

Oscar and I would dine at the Plaza, and for breakfast I'd make French toast. The silk pajamas I planned to hand-paint would be both chic and practical in the kitchen. Then I would need car coats for our honeymoon drive to California, a roomy batwing in lined wool, a lightweight one in natural linen. For the wedding ceremony I envisioned a slender collarless tube of dove gray crêpe de Chine with a single gardenia pinned to the shoulder. Or, if we had to delay until the fall, the same dress but worn with a short cape trimmed with silver mink. I decided we wouldn't have children but when we went to Paris, France, for our first anniversary we might adopt two pretty French dogs, a boy one and a girl one.

When we arrived at West 73rd Street I suggested we might go in and say goodnight to Uncle Israel.

'I expect he'd like to hear all about our evening,' I said.

'No, Poppy,' Aunt Fish replied, looking over my shoulder and smiling at Ma in a rather flagrant way. 'I believe you should go home directly and share a soothing tisane with your mother.'

I wanted no tisane. I wanted to go to bed and be alone with my racing thoughts. But Ma insisted. The help was required to put down her novelette and prepare a tray and I was required to accompany Ma to her room and await the arrival of the tasteless brew.

Ma sighed contentedly. 'Now wasn't that a most congenial evening?' she said. 'And so interesting. You know, the Jewish parts weren't at all difficult to follow. And they were over soon enough.'

She tossed her hat onto a chair. Tossed it. And then she did something else I had never seen before. She twirled.

'Well?' she said. 'Don't just stand there. Unhook me at the back and tell me what you think.'

I grinned. She grinned back.

'You've guessed?' she said.

'Yes, Ma,' I said. 'Of course I've guessed. And I'm very happy.'

'Oh Poppy, are you?' she said. Shorter than me by a head, she took me in her arms and looked up at me, full of tenderness. 'Dearest Poppy,' she said, 'you can't imagine what it means to hear you say that. I've quite dreaded the moment of telling you.'

'But you must know it's what I want too,' I said.

A person may stand so close to the obvious that it becomes invisible to her. Ma's smile wobbled and a few happy tears spilled down her cheeks.

'What a darling daughter you are,' she cried, 'so generous and gracious. Judah predicted you wouldn't stand in my way, and I should have known. It was just . . . well . . . you were always such a girl for your Pa.'

The help made a clumsy entrance with a tea tray and banged about a great deal. This interruption allowed me enough time to grasp that my conversation with Ma had veered away from its expected route, and to understand, with horrible clarity, why. If good help had been easier to come by, if we had managed to employ someone who could efficiently and pleasantly deliver a tea tray, say goodnight and leave, it all might have happened too quickly for me to master my tongue and save myself from making the most humiliating mistake.

Finally we were alone again.

'You were such a girl for your Pa,' she resumed, 'but it has been seven years. And Judah is a good man. I hope some day, after we are married, you may even grow to think of him as a kind of father.'

Ma made herself comfortable on her day bed, sipped her tea and between sips smiled to herself in a gratingly smug manner. She had robbed me of my dreams but didn't even know it. My mother was to be married and it didn't seem to have occurred to her that it was my turn.

I immediately began chipping away at her happiness.

'Oscar was very rude to you at dinner,' I said, succeeding in sounding casual.

'Oh, but Oscar has neurasthenia,' she said proudly, 'brought on by the war. The doctors say he needs a great deal of rest. And I'm sure dinners don't improve anyone's nerves. I quite disagreed with Yetta when she forced him to attend this evening, and I shall tell her so.'

I said, 'How strange, though, that Miss Landau and Mr Jacoby never married. They seem so suited. I dare say she is quite like her sister. I dare say she reminds Mr Jacoby of his first wife.'

'How little you know,' Ma said. 'Yetta is not at all the marrying kind. She is far too full of opinions to make a man happy. Of course, she has been a tower of strength to them. But she lacks . . . well . . . A husband, you know, likes a certain softness in a wife, a certain fragility. This is something you should bear in mind, too, Poppy. I have noticed a rather defiant tendency in you and if I have noticed it you may be sure it will discourage any suitors.'

I said, 'But you told me I wasn't to have any suitors. After Pa was drowned you said I was to stay with you and be an old maid.'

Ma brushed away this objection as though it were a small fly.

I said, 'So now I'm not needed anymore as a companion, I suppose I may please myself? Take a husband or not take a husband.'

'But this is precisely my point,' Ma said, surfacing a little from her golden haze. 'It's not for you to *take* a husband. It is for a husband to . . . choose you. And you are only twenty-one. There is hope for you yet.'

'Where shall you live?' I asked.

'Why, in Judah's house,' she said. 'Where else?'

'And will Miss Landau stay on?'

'Naturally,' she said. 'I shall take on the general running of the house, but Yetta will still be needed. As I told her, I only know about the raising of girls. Boys are a mystery to me. Although, of course, as a real mother one notices errors that a maiden aunt might not. I'm sure she will welcome the benefit of my advice. The boy Murray, for instance. Your aunt and I detect a certain impudence about him. It was probably considered comical in the younger child and not corrected. Well anyway, time enough for that.'

In an instant I warmed to Murray Jacoby. Like me, he had lost a parent. Like me, he was charged with impudence. And like me, he was considered a candidate for one of Ma and Aunt Fish's programs of improvement. I vowed to stand by him in any way I could.

I said, 'I shall stay on here, of course.'

'Oh no!' Ma said. 'That would be quite unsuitable. And besides, I shall want your help redesigning my rooms. They are a little too plain for my taste, and you have such a good eye for color. What fun we shall have.'

The wedding was to take place in June or July. Ahead of me stretched weeks and weeks of disappointment and hurt and crushing, unendurable shame.

'Ma,' I said, 'I'm so tired I can hardly keep my eyes open. May I be excused?'

'Why, how selfish I am,' she said. 'Off to bed now. We both need our beauty sleep! And in the morning we'll call Honey. This calls for an urgent tea party. Goodnight darling. Come and give your Ma a kiss . . .'

She offered me her silly self-satisfied face.

'You may kiss the bride,' she simpered.

I forced myself to brush my lips across her soft old-lady skin and she was waiting for me, ready with one final sharpened knife to plunge into my heart.

'Poppy,' she whispered, 'I should very much like you to design my gown. Goodnight dearest. And sweet dreams.'

NINETEEN

On Sunday, July 6, 1919, Ma was married to Judah Jacoby. A minister came to the Jacoby house on East 69th Street and the marrying was done in the ivory parlor, where Ma had already begun to make her mark. Little by little our home had been emptied of porcelain garniture and Venetian doilies. They had been ferried across Central Park in discreet packages and reappeared, looking every bit the overdressed guests, to clutter Miss Landau's tables.

A parasol lamp had sprung up, purchased from W. & J. Sloane's and delivered one afternoon when Ma had been sure of having the Jacoby place to herself. And the mantel was now festooned. The mantel and the mirror above the mantel and the piano, too, all draped in Spanish shawls. Mr Jacoby, I remember thinking, had better not fall asleep in his armchair when Ma was in a fit of home-making. He might wake up swagged in fringed silk.

I found myself unable to call Mr Jacoby anything but Mr Jacoby. When the nuptials were announced he had taken me to one side.

'I do hope, Poppy,' he'd said, taking my hand tentatively in his, 'that you will find a place for me in your heart, if not as a father, perhaps as an uncle? Or at least as a friend.'

But I had the only uncle I wanted, and I failed to see how an old man could be my friend. A friend was someone you met at Horn and Hardart for pie and coffee. A friend was someone you could talk to about lingerie and beaux. And besides, I was uncomfortable with the way he had taken to calling Ma 'Dorabel'.

I designed for Ma a slender sheath dress in hortensia blue silk, with a vermilion side-slashed kimono coat lined in the same blue. I prepared detailed colored drawings and made up a toile so she could try the shape and see how trim it made her appear, but she wavered, and the next I knew she had been to A. T. Stewart's with Aunt Fish and picked out a serviceable two-piece in fawn.

'I'm sorry to disappoint you,' she said, 'but I decided your design was altogether too progressive, didn't we Zillah?'

Aunt Fish had very strong opinions on all aspects of a marrying. The room should be decorated with calla lilies. The groom should be at least three years older than the bride, and taller. Brisket should be served.

'I believe Honey might wear your design,' Ma said, trying to mollify me. But Honey had lost interest in fashion. Honey had lost interest in pretty much everything. Even with a full complement of servants and Sherman enrolled at the Jauncey Day School for Boys, she still found it taxing to do much more than leaf through *Town Topics*.

We were a small wedding party. Harry was away, buying property on Bay Shore, Long Island, Uncle Israel excused himself because of the difficulties of climbing to an East Side front stoop. Also because the tendency to dribble had persisted. And Oscar was in a veterans' convalescent home in the Catskill Mountains, suffering from black moods.

But four men were needed to hold the corners of the chuppah. It had to be men. So the deaf Mr Roth had been prevailed upon, and two valued employees from the firm of Jacoby, a Mr Klot who was the senior pelt grader, and a Greek called Basil.

'A genius,' Mr Jacoby said. 'This man can make a garment out of nothing but mink tails.'

I saw Aunt Fish later, examining the jacket that was Ma's wedding gift, looking for the joins.

With Murray they had four to hold the poles of the canopy and the marrying was done with Sherman Ulysses stretched out on the rug, gently drumming his feet. He wasn't throwing a tantrum exactly.

It was simply that Honey had asked him to stand up nicely, so he felt obliged, I suppose, to do the opposite. It was a listless kind of disobedience.

The brisket was served with potato salad and pickles, and throughout the meal a jar of Minkel's Mighty Fine Mustard sat on the table. Pa's ghostly presence. He would not have minded, I had decided. Ma had accepted her widowing and if she had gained new happiness, it wasn't because she had gone looking for it. Judah Jacoby thought her price was above rubies. He stood up and said as much before the fresh raspberries were served.

'Her candle goeth not out by night,' he said.

'She eateth not the bread of idleness,' he said.

'She points with her knife,' added Murray. He was sitting directly opposite me. Whoever else heard it, Ma was not one of them. She sat in Yetta Landau's old place, flushed and mawkish and deaf to everything except her husband's compliments.

At five o'clock the newly weds left for three days in Sea Bright and after we had waved them off and Honey's driver had collected her, with Sherman and Aunt Fish, I found myself alone momentarily with Murray Jacoby.

I said, 'You're not obliged to like your new mother, but you'd better be civil to her or she'll make you sorry.'

'I already have a mother,' he said. 'She just went away for a while.'

I said, 'Your mother's dead, you booby, the same as my Pa, and now we have to be family.'

He narrowed his eyes.

'No,' he insisted. 'She just went away for a while.'

He was a thin, sissy-looking kid. His ears stood out like jug handles and his eyeglasses had thick pebble lenses.

I said, 'How old are you?'

'Twelve,' he said.

I said, 'Do you go to school?'

'Of course I do,' he said. 'I go to Schiff's. Which school do you go to?'

I said, 'I'm twenty-one. I don't have to go to school. I can do anything I please. Or go anywhere I please. Why does Oscar have black moods?'

He shrugged.

'What,' he said, 'can you go even to Manitoba?'

And then Miss Landau came and found us.

'Are you really set on staying alone in that house, Poppy?' she said. 'You know room could easily be made for you here. And I'm sure Murray would be glad of your company.'

I said, 'It isn't *that* house. It's *my* house and I don't want to leave it anymore than you'd want to leave here.'

Out on the stoop, she lowered her voice.

'Oh, but I shall leave here,' she said. 'As soon as Dora and Judah return I shall go to Peekamoose, to care for Oscar.'

'Is he very sick?' I asked. A little ember of hope glowed for a moment. A nurse's uniform was so very flattering.

'It's a kind of melancholy,' she said. 'There's a deal of it about, since the war. I hope you're going to do something useful, Poppy. You have every advantage in life.'

The boy Murray reappeared.

'Auntsie,' he said, 'I shouldn't be glad of her company. I shouldn't be glad of it at all.'

'And anyway,' he shouted, as I slid behind the wheel of my roadster, 'your mother *does* point with her knife.'

Then he ran inside his house.

TWENTY

I was alone for the first time in my life, and I liked it. Yetta Landau's words stayed with me and I began to think about my future. My decision was that I would become a more interesting person. I gave the help notice, closed up my house and on October first I moved into a three-room suite at the Belleclaire Hotel.

'Well,' Ma said, 'I see you are determined to drag the family name into the gutter.'

I said, 'Which name would that be, Ma? Minkel, or Minton, or Jacoby?'

'You know quite well what I mean,' she replied. 'Why must you always be so contrary? Living on a . . . rented shelf, when there are proper houses at your disposal, at good addresses.'

I said, 'You used to say West 76th Street was a ruinous address. You begged Pa not to take us there. I remember.'

'No,' she said. 'You are mistaken, as usual. On West 76th Street one was safe beneath one's own roof, but who knows who may be hiding under the roof of a hotel. French persons. Theatrical types.'

Mr Jacoby suggested I was old enough to choose my own roof. He had found a way of contradicting Ma without offending her, something I don't believe Pa ever achieved.

'I'm afraid you don't know Poppy,' she sighed. 'She has always craved excitement and danger. Did I ever tell you, Judah, how she begged to be allowed to go and minister to the unfortunates? It was the Misses Stone who put it into her head.'

'Yes,' he said, 'you did tell me.'

'They encouraged her most unfairly,' she went on anyway, never afraid of repeating herself, 'and I was placed in an impossible position. If I stood firm, I was frustrating her wishes and making my child unhappy. A torment no mother can endure. And if I allowed her to have her way, I was placing her in every kind of danger . . .'

'But surely, Dorabel,' he said, 'she was in safe hands and doing good works. And she came home unharmed.'

Ma ignored this.

'. . . and as I feared,' she said, 'she came home overwrought and impudent and infested. Covered with crawling, biting . . . creatures. We might all have died of some terrible fever, had I not had the help fumigate the house from top to bottom. And did I ever hear a word of apology or regret? I did not. And now, when I might hope for her to have grown in wisdom, she is moving into . . . Trust me, Judah, Poppy will never rest until she's living in the midst of scandal and mayhem.'

The boy Murray had overheard enough to be interested.

'Are there murderers in your hotel?' he asked.

'Not yet,' I said. And he gave me an artful smile. There was something about my stepbrother I was taking to.

The Belleclaire was just around the corner from the house I grew up in, but it might have been in a different country. There was a wonderful elevator to whisk me to my top floor suite. There was light and space. And it didn't matter that there was no kitchen because I could dine in the hotel restaurant every evening and choose whatever I pleased. I could skip the soup and have two desserts. No one could prevent it.

I decided on a witty, interesting look for my rooms. I had my decorator cover the walls with bone-white huckaback. I had Muller's pick me out fifteen yards of books on assorted subjects. And I purchased a bottle of gin, a bottle of vermouth and a jar of cocktail onions, so that when I had acquired some friends I should be able to invite them up, to drink Gibsons and admire my view of the Hudson River. All I brought with me from West 76th Street were the piano, though I never played it anymore, and the contents of Pa's vitrine: the fool's gold, the beaver skull, the Ojibway Indian necklace, Grandpa Minkel's little silk *kippah*, as I now knew it was called. The stuffed osprey never made it to the Belleclaire. The moment I tried to move it, it crumbled away to dust.

Recalling the company I had enjoyed at the Red Cross depot, it seemed to me the best way for me to find new friends was to get a job of work, so I applied for a post at the Fair Lady Company, hand-finishing high-class lingerie.

They didn't mind at all that I sewed with my left hand and I believe I would soon have risen to a senior position there, but the other finishers made my life impossible, sniggering when I wore my black Mexican pearls, complaining when I took a day off to drive my sister to one of her houses in Oyster Bay.

I asked the finishing room supervisor how a person was expected to lead any sort of life if she might not take a day off when she pleased. She replied that from that moment on I might take off all the days I liked, and to close the door behind me on my way out.

I began to see how small-mindedness held back the working classes. I began to understand why they always looked so glum. And but for a chance encounter, I might well have given up my project to join the masses and make new friends.

I went out for a spin one morning, called in at an amusing new milliner's on Madison Avenue and recognized a face I hadn't seen in about ten years. Bernadette Kearney.

'Minkel!' she screamed. 'Is it really you?'

She was trying on a felt cloche decorated with five fat cherries dangling on stalks.

'Whatever happened to you?' she asked. 'Could your Daddy not pay the fees?'

The last time I'd seen her was the day I was hurried away from the Convent of the Blessed Redeemer covered in scarlatina and Ma decided I had had enough education. I never went back.

The Kearneys were not the usual kind of Irish. They were the kind who themselves employed Irish below stairs. The Kearneys had feet that were accustomed to shoes and a father who was an attorney at City Hall. They were Irish in the size of the family though. There was a Kearney girl in every class at Blessed Redeemer and I knew there were brothers, too. Dozens of them.

I said, 'What do you mean? My Pa could have bought the whole convent. I was kept at home, that's all. I hated that place anyway.'

'Love your hair,' she said. 'Crazy.'

I had had it bobbed and hennaed.

I said, 'Are you married?' She had turned out pretty.

'Managed to avoid it so far,' she laughed. 'Keep them wanting, that's my motto. Keep them on the run. How about you?'

'Same as you,' I said, wondering whether there was any more mileage to be had out of Oscar Jacoby. I decided there was not.

We went for layer cake at Child's. Bernie – she preferred not to be called Bernadette anymore – loved to talk. She had lost a brother, Ambrose, in the Battle of the Marne, and a sister, Celia, from the influenza, and her mother was bearing up as best she could but her father was a broken man. During the war she had worked as a stenographer at the New York bureau of the National Food Administration and after office hours she had seen a good deal of military action.

'Nothing below second lieutenant,' she said. 'I have my standards.'

I said, 'I was thinking I might learn stenography myself, and typewriting.'

'Don't do it, Minkel,' she said. 'It's a short cut to insanity. And anyway, why would you? Aren't you busy enough spending your money?'

As I explained, my mustard millions were all well and good, but I felt the need to get out more and mix with different types of people.

'I was at home so much,' I said, 'just being there for Ma. I never had the chance to go around with a crowd. Honey did, but all that ended after we lost Pa. I'd like to have a place to go where there are other girls, you know, maybe of a lower class, but we'd be able to have a lark? Like I did sometimes at home, when we had a nice Irish. Sorry. I didn't mean all Irish are of the lower class.'

'I'm not Irish,' she said. 'I'm American. Well anyhow, there'll be no larks if you're a stenographer. You'll just be "taking a letter Miss Minkel!" Why don't I see if I can get you a start at the Keynote. Can you do the grizzly bear?'

Bernie was working as a taxi-dancer at the Keynote dance hall on Seventh Avenue.

'Only a dime a dance,' she said, 'but you never know who you'll meet. A lonely guy can find all kinds of ways to show his appreciation.'

'I'm not sure,' I said. I didn't like to tell her the only dances I knew were the tango and the two-step.

'Yes,' she said, 'I see what you mean. You'd have to loosen up a little before they'd look at you at the Keynote. How about shop work? My sister Ursula does that and she meets all kinds of people. Of course, she's on her feet all day. Minkel, did you never think of doing anything with your eyebrows?'

And so Bernie plucked my eyebrows for me and I got a job selling neckties in Macy's department store. Most days I went with Ursula Kearney to the Woolworth lunch counter, and sometimes Bernie would join us. She was right. I did meet all types and I found I had a special knack for dealing with ladies of advanced years who ventured in, looking to buy a gift for someone. I was more nervous around gentlemen customers, not being accustomed to such casual contact with the opposite sex, but gradually I grew more confident. Gradually I became able to look a gentleman directly in the eye and advise him on his choice of neckwear. Eventually I didn't even shrink from handling a customer's collar and helping him tie a perfect knot. Which was how I met Gilbert Catchings.

TWENTY-ONE

H e must have tried out a dozen different spotted silks and still couldn't decide.

'Cutting a figure's a damned puzzling business,' he said. 'What time do you get off? We could go someplace. Get a little something.'

Gil Catchings was a tall, broad-shouldered johnny, strong-looking considering how an asthmatical chest had prevented him from going for a soldier in the Great War. He had lion mane hair and the palest blue eyes I ever saw. I thought he meant to take me to Woolworth for meat loaf and a soda, but that wasn't his plan at all. We went to the Knickerbocker Hotel and drank a number of dry martini cocktails.

'Those are some pearls for a shop girl,' he said.

I never saw anything wrong with wearing good jewelry to work. I never encountered any envy or thievery, even when I wore my diamond pin. And pearls improve with wear, so I always figured it was a crime to leave them lying in a drawer at home.

He said, 'You somebody's cutie?'

I said, 'I'm a mustard heiress. I buy my own pearls.'

He whistled.

'Well, that's just dandy,' he said. 'So you're just playing at being a shop girl? You're like Marie Antoinette. And you don't have a fiancé or anything like that? Because I have every respect for another man's property. I don't care for complications.'

He touched my knee.

We went upstairs and he paid a chambermaid for the key to a room.

'Half an hour,' she said.

He laughed. He said, 'Is it cheaper for less?'

It was an ugly room. The rug smelled stale. But I had my first squeeze from Gil, without going through all the worries of introducing him to Ma and wondering what to wear when he took me on our first date and all that. We were doing things the modern way.

Gil took off his necktie and stuffed it in his pocket, and afterwards, when he went to put it back on, he put his hand in the other pocket and pulled out one of the spotted silks from Macy's.

'Well, will you look at that!' he said. 'It must have dropped in there while I was busy admiring your lips.'

He thought it all a tremendous lark.

I was only fifteen minutes late getting back to my post, but I was called in by the supervisor and dismissed. She didn't give me the chance to explain myself, and just as well because I'm not sure what I could have said.

I wasn't sorry. I had still had no lunch, my head was spinning, and I felt in need of washing and changing my clothes. I was also eager to talk things over with Bernie. Ursula said she had talked of getting her hair finger waved, so I might try looking for her at Regine's Salon.

'Not sticking at the job, Poppy?' she said. Ursula always was a goody-two-shoes.

I said, 'The hours are discommoding me. And anyway, I'm probably getting married.'

That silenced her.

I found Bernie just finishing up at Regine's. Can't say I cared for her new look.

I said, 'Let's go get cake and tea. I think I just lost my virginity.'

The *styliste* gave me a pretty cool stare considering I hadn't been addressing her.

Bernie said, 'Want to wait till I'm out of this chair?' She turned to the girl. 'Cancel my manicure,' she said. 'Something came up.'

It was a raw afternoon. We ran in arm in arm, too cold to talk until we were snug and warm at a corner table in Sadie's. Then I told all.

'On your first date!' she said. 'My, aren't you the fast one! Was it wonderful?'

I wasn't sure what kind of wonderful it was meant to be.

I said, 'I haven't been too modern, have I?'

'No, no,' she said. But I wasn't convinced she was being candid with me. 'Did you really go all the way?'

That was just the problem. I had pieced together certain facts given me by the Irish, after I discovered my sister was with child, but I still wasn't absolutely sure what 'all the way' involved. I hesitated.

She said, 'Poppy, did you lie on a bed?'

We had lain on a bed.

She lowered her voice. 'And did you take off your bloomers?'

Gil had partially removed my bloomers but then lost patience.

'Did it hurt?' she asked.

'Not at the time,' I said, 'but I'm feeling awful sore now, and I have a hole in my stockings.'

She dipped a macaroon in her tea.

'I think you went all the way,' she decided. 'Did he tell you he loved you?'

'Yes,' I lied.

'And is he real handsome? And rich?'

'Oh yes,' I said. 'And he wears a scrumptious cologne.'

I didn't tell her he had stolen a necktie from Macy's.

'Gracious, Poppy,' she said, 'now you're a woman of the world. When do I meet him? Is he taking you out dancing tonight? Oh do bring him to the Keynote. I can't wait to see him.'

But Gil hadn't offered to take me dancing, or anything else that night. He had told me to expect him at the Belleclaire the next afternoon at three o'clock.

Bernie frowned. 'That's not so good. No dancing, no dinner. I'd hate to think he was two-timing you. Are you sure he's not married or anything?'

This hadn't occurred to me. But he hadn't *seemed* married.

I said, 'Oh no. And he was most particular to find out whether I had another beau.'

'That's irrelevant,' she interrupted. 'It's his situation I'd like to know about. Where does he live?'

And there she had me, because in our haste Gil had forgotten to tell me his address.

'Washington Square,' I said. It seemed like the kind of place he might live.

'Hmm,' she said. 'Well, when he turns up tomorrow, *if* he turns up tomorrow, you're to tell him you expect dinner, and dancing at the Keynote, and flowers and new stockings, and his card, so we know what number Washington Square. And you mustn't let him go all the way every time because men soon take these things for granted. And when you do, be sure to douche. You did douche?'

'Oh yes,' I said.

Bernie finished the macaroons. I had lost my appetite, even though I had gone without lunch.

'I wonder,' she said, 'if I went back to Regine's now, whether they'd do my nails after all?'

I went home and searched along my fifteen yards of books for something that might explain about douching, but I found nothing but dry old stories. So I took a scented bath, put on one of my new little skirts that swung as I walked, and went downstairs for grilled turbot and blueberry pie.

TWENTY-TWO

Gil was thirty-five minutes late for our appointment, but as soon as he walked in, raccoon collar coat slung round his shoulders, I felt he was worth the wait. His face was icy cold and smooth when I kissed it. He had no beard to speak of.

Bernie had instructed me there was to be no more squeezing and carrying on until certain matters were clarified, such as when he would be taking me to dinner and where, but he would have his way and that second time I was left in little doubt that we had gone as far as it was possible to go. I even found it a little thrilling myself.

'Poppy,' he said afterwards, gazing at my bookshelves, 'you're not an intellectual, I hope. I'm something of one myself, but I don't find it agreeable in a girl.'

I was pretty sure I wasn't an intellectual. I had lost my taste for looking at books the day I lost my Pa.

I said, 'No, I'm modern and fun-loving and rich.'

He chuckled. 'You're a caution,' he said. 'Just how rich are you?'

I mixed us a Gibson kind of cocktail, except that I had omitted to have ice sent up, or to buy glasses, so we had to drink it out of teacups, and then I settled down to tell him all about Grandpa Minkel, and the factories in Blue Grass, Iowa, churning out all that ballpark mustard and money.

He said, 'Is that right? And do you have to go out there, inspect your mustard fields, count your money once in a while?'

I had not really thought much about the mustard fields. All I knew was, Minkel's Mighty Fine got turned into money and then it was sent to banks and railroad companies and steel mills where it was turned into even more money. Finally it got sent to Uncle Israel, who had explained all this, and then he passed it along to me and Honey, and some to Ma too, I suppose, although she had her new husband paying for her gowns.

I said, 'No, I never was there. I haven't started my traveling yet. And we were never allowed when we were children. My Aunt Fish reckoned it was best to stay away from Iowa if you wanted to go up in New York society.'

'Ask me,' he said, 'you can't have much higher to climb. If the dollar is king, you must be a princess at least.'

Ever after that he called me Princess.

I said, 'Can we go dancing?'

'We can do anything you choose,' he said. So I chose for us to go to Sherry's for supper and then onto the Keynote to see Bernie and learn how to do the chicken-flip.

I said, 'I want you to meet my friend Bernie. She's Irish, but not the unfortunate kind.'

I snuggled against him, reveling in the wonder and completeness of him. I'd known men were different to women, and now I really understood. With Gil I experienced the same pleasant shock as the first time I touched a frog.

I said, 'Tell me about your folks. Are you terribly rich, too?'

'No,' he said, sipping on his gin, 'I'm just a poor struggling poet.'

I remarked that he wore very good shoes, for a pauper. They were a gift, he said, from a kind widow woman whose husband had died leaving unworn shoes of the exact same size as Gil's feet.

'What luck,' I said.

'Yes,' he said. 'Once in a while fortune smiles on me.'

I said, 'Did you bring me a book of your poems? Did you write a poem about me yet?'

He sighed. 'If only it were that simple, Princess,' he said. 'You don't just sit down and write a poem. And as for bringing out books, that's a costly business.'

I said, 'Well, when we're married you'll have enough money to bring out a hundred books. Recite me one of your poems. Recite me your best one.'

'There you go again,' he said, sliding off the bed and buttoning up his pants. 'My poems are not really the kind for reciting. They're more for reading quietly and thinking on and absorbing into your heart and soul.'

I said, 'And will you bring me some? When you come calling for me tonight?'

'Sure,' he said. 'About this dinner. Are we talking about real fancy prices?'

He looked so pained, I could have kicked myself for putting him in such a humiliating position.

I said, 'We don't have to go to Sherry's. Why don't you take me to your favorite. I'd like that.'

'No, no,' he said. 'I'm sure I'll love Sherry's. I'm just a little out of funds this week.'

'Then it's my treat,' I said. 'And I won't hear another word about it. Where exactly is your house? Can I come and see it tomorrow?'

My telephone rang. It was the doorman.

He said, 'Miss Minkel, I have a young gentleman down here, says he's your brother.'

I made him wait while I pulled down my camisole. Sometimes I understood why Ma had resisted the telephone for so long.

I said, 'I don't have a brother.'

'Madam,' he said, 'I'm sorry to insist but this young person is asking for you most particular and I should prefer not to have him thronging my lobby.'

Then I heard Murray's voice crying, 'I *am* her brother. I am.'

This was quite maddening. His visit was uninvited and ill-timed, and he had also placed me in the position of having to explain myself to a doorman.

I gestured to Gil to pass me my bloomers.

I said, 'Perhaps you meant to announce my stepbrother, which is quite a different matter.'

'Of course, Miss Minkel,' he said. 'It'll be your stepbrother then. I'm sorry for any misunderstanding.'

'You may send him up,' I said, 'but not immediately. In five minutes' time. I'm momentarily unable to receive company.'

Gil said, 'I'll slip away down the stairs.'

He had his coat on already.

I said, 'But we haven't made our plans for this evening. Shall you pick me up in your motor or shall we take a taxicab?'

'A cab,' he said. He was on the point of leaving without even giving me a farewell embrace. I straightened the coverlet on the bed and checked in the looking-glass that I wasn't in disarray.

I said, 'Why the hurry? Murray's just a silly boy, but you may as well meet him. Darling, I want us to know absolutely everything about each other.'

I had been longing to try out the word 'darling', and when I did, I loved the sound of it.

'Tonight,' I said. 'Shall we say seven o'clock? Darling, do you have a tuxedo?'

He said he did have a tuxedo, given him by a kind friend who had given up the high life and who, most conveniently, was the same size.

Then Murray commenced hammering on the door and wouldn't stop until I opened it. He appeared not to notice Gil. He walked right in, eyes red from crying, and handed me a small potted plant. It had dark, glossy leaves.

'It's a lemon tree,' he said. 'It's for you.'

I said, 'You should have called ahead. You can't just turn up and expect it to be convenient.'

His face fell.

'Don't you like your lemon tree?' he said.

I said, 'Now, Murray, please say how-de-do to Mr Gilbert Catchings.'

'How-de-do,' he said. 'Poppy, that Dorabel says I have to go to the B'nai Brith program every day, but I don't, do I? Auntsie never made me.'

Murray was on school vacation and Ma was keen for him to be profitably occupied and not mooning around, being disagreeable and preventing her from playing canasta.

I said, 'You mustn't call her That Dorabel. You have to call her Step-Ma. She's your new mother so you'd better get along with her.'

Gil was edging out of the room.

'Seven, then,' he said.

'Seven,' I said. 'And don't forget those poems.'

I turned my attention to Murray. He was wiping his nose on his sleeve.

'I don't want a new mother,' he sobbed. 'What will Momma say when she comes back?'

I said, 'Now stop that! You know she's not coming back. She's been dead even longer than my Pa.'

He punched me, hard as he could, which wasn't very hard at all.

'You're a liar,' he said. 'A rotten liar. She's coming back just as soon as her pains get better.'

Poor Murray. When she died, he had been too young for the facts, and by the time he was old enough, everyone else had picked themselves up and ceased talking about it.

I said, 'Was your Momma beautiful?'

'Oh yes,' he said. 'Very beautiful.'

I said, 'Can I see her picture?'

But he didn't have one. Not next to his heart, nor even on his night table at home.

I said, 'You should have a picture. Ask your daddy to give you one. I have a picture of my dead Pa. Would you care to see it?'

He quieted down while I brought out the silver gelatin print. It had been a portrait of Ma and Pa, but I had cut Ma off in a fit of pique one time.

'See?' I said. 'That was my Pa. But he died, so now I just have his picture to look at.'

He said, 'But how do you know he died? Did you see him with his eyes closed?'

So I told him about the sinking of the *Titanic*, and then I told him what I had heard about the death of his mother.

I said, 'A person doesn't stay away all those years. Not if they love you. Not if there's any way for them to come back. I know it's hard, but there it is. We're in the same fix, Murray, except I have a picture to look at.'

He listened to me intently and I stopped feeling mad at him for interrupting my afternoon of love. He had been waiting ten years for his Momma to appear and no one had done him the kindness of taking him to her graveside or showing him a portrait.

I said, 'Now why don't you want to go to the B'nai Brith vacation program? I'm sure they do exciting things.'

He said he didn't like the other boys. He said he didn't like folk dancing.

I said, 'There must be other activities. What about learning Hebrew? I wish I could have learned Hebrew.'

'You're a girl,' he said. 'And anyway, I already know Hebrew. We have to visit a matzo factory.'

I said, 'And if you stay at home what will you do all day?' I suspected this was the kind of thing a mother might say. And although Ma had previously been a great believer in staying aimlessly at home, avoiding the stimulation of novelties, she appeared to have revised her opinion since gaining a son.

Murray shrugged. He was looking a good deal less tragic than when he arrived.

I said, 'Would you care to come out driving?'

It had occurred to me I could take him with me on my first visit to Washington Square. If Bernie was right about a beau needing to be kept in a state of anticipation, I had to find a way of reining in Gil's ardor, and arriving with Murray at my side seemed as good a way as any.

'Where shall we go?' he asked.

I said, 'To visit Gilbert Catchings. We'll go tomorrow.'

He said, 'Is Gilbert Catchings a reprobate?'

He had heard Ma expressing the opinion that the Belleclaire attracted deviationists, reprobates and showgirls.

I said, 'No. As a matter of fact he's my fiancé, but we haven't yet made our announcement, so you must be sure not to breathe a word of this to your Step-Ma.'

I rather relished the idea of Murray hurrying home to ruin Ma's evening with his loose lips.

I said, 'What made you think this is a lemon tree?'

'I know it is,' he said. 'I grew it. From a pip.'

That boy had been allowed to get away with way too many untruths.

TWENTY-THREE

The Keynote dance hall was the greatest lark. You could dance as close as you liked and until midnight. I remarked to Gil that I wouldn't mind applying for a position there myself, like Bernie, but he made it clear he didn't care for the idea of his sweetheart dancing with other men and I found the pleasure of being so fiercely protected outweighed the irritation of being overruled. It was just what I had hoped for from Oscar Jacoby, before he had had to go away to the country for fresh air and basket weaving.

After the Keynote closed we went onto the Hootsy Tootsy Club for drinks with maraschino cherries. Bernie came along, too, with her last fare of the evening, a captain recently discharged from the 339th, one of our Polar Bear Boys who had risked his life in the fight for Russia. He had a fresh, friendly face. His name was George and he was from Kalamazoo, Michigan, and I don't believe he ever had drunk Manhattan cocktails before.

Bernie said, 'George here was in a place called Archangel. Did you ever hear such a pretty name for a town?'

'Nothing pretty about it,' he said. 'We had thirty degrees below. What are the arrangements for paying for these refreshments?'

Gil said, 'Consider them paid for.'

Bernie was wearing her soldier boy like he was an Oak-leaf Cluster, angling the conversation around to battalions and regiments and such, asking Gil which bit of the fray he had gotten into, even though I had told her about his asthma.

'Couldn't persuade them to take me,' he said. 'My state of health

133

obliged me to stay behind and take charge of a factory. We supplied uniforms to the military.'

Bernie said, 'Your state of health looks pretty fine to me.' She said it in a light, flirtatious manner, but it could have been differently received. I noticed her friend George kept adjusting his cuffs. I dare say he was hoping Gil wasn't going to take offense. I dare say he'd had his fill of fighting.

He needn't have worried. Gil did no more than turn round Bernie's implication and return it as a compliment to George.

'Not as fine as your friend's here,' he said. 'And thank God for men like George, or we'd all be living under the Prussian heel.'

'Yes, well,' George said, still fussing with his cuffs, 'it made a man of me.'

Bernie had her arm around his shoulder. 'George is thinking to stay on in New York,' she said. 'He's thinking to set up as a mortician. Isn't that wild?'

Gil said, 'Never be out of work there, George! Morticians! Always the last people to let you down!'

He made us all laugh. Over the months we often went out drinking after Bernie finished at the Keynote. Most times she was with some new face, and whoever it was, Gil could get along with him.

It turned out Gil didn't live on Washington Square exactly. He was in Minetta Lane, which was off Macdougal Street, which was off Washington Square. He shared a low redbrick with a number of other poets and pamphleteers. I discovered this when I kept my promise to my stepbrother Murray to take him out driving and spare him from having to go to B'nai Brith and dance with scarves and other boys. I collected him from East 69th Street and was disappointed to find Ma in a good humor with me. Murray had omitted to tell her about my drinking gin and being engaged to be married.

'How considerate of you, Poppy,' she said, and then she whispered, loud enough for Murray to hear, 'Boys are *so* difficult.'

I quizzed him as we drove downtown. 'Where did you tell Ma we were going?'

'To visit your nice friend,' he fawned, 'and not be underfoot at home and an encumbrance.'

Gil's house smelled of sourness and he seemed not to have completed his toilette although it was quite two o'clock in the afternoon. Poets, of course, can become so abstracted that they forget to shave. He already had company when we arrived, sitting in all the mess and confusion. An artist called Casella who had paint under his nails, and an anarchist called Frederick who had brought a gift of bourbon whiskey.

I said, 'What a muddle. Didn't the help come?'

They all laughed. They seemed quite as fascinated by me as I was by them.

I said, 'Now Gil, you really have no reason not to show me some of your verses.'

I could see a quantity of notebooks and loose leaves of paper covered with scribbling. Mr Casella was all for a poetry reading, too, and Murray, who was in a most obliging mood. Only Frederick appeared bored by the prospect of being entertained. I have often found this to be the case with anarchists.

Gil began.

'Here's one I wrote yesterday,' he said.

> Winter Poppy Blooms
> You cut the mustard for me
> My Westside Princess

I waited for more but that was all it amounted to. He said it was an ancient Japanese style of poetry called haiku and quite the rage with those in the know. 'Seventeen syllables,' he explained. 'Five in the first line, seven in the second line, five in the third line. Here's another one.'

> Homecoming doughboys
> Purple hearts on Fifth Avenue
> Soot blackened branches

Mr Casella nodded solemnly and I did, too, because Gil did recite most affectingly, but as I pointed out, if people paid for verses by the line, a haiku was never going to pay the rent. This caused the anarchist to stop being bored and roar with laughter.

Then Murray piped up.

'That's not seventeen,' he said. 'That one has eighteen.'

And so an argument ensued between my stepbrother and my intended, as to the number of syllables in the word 'purple'.

I said, 'I fail to see that it matters. Let's go out for pastries.'

I was a little concerned for the safety of my new Packard. It had attracted a deal of attention when I parked it in Minetta Lane, and keen as I was to meet artists and revolutionaries, I didn't want my property ruined by envious vagabonds.

Mr Casella, who had a hungry look about him, was all in favor of pastries and so was Murray, but first he wanted another verse, looking to catch Gil out, I suppose.

'Okey-dokey,' Gil said, and he composed one right there and then.

> Thin boy, gloved, hatted
> Counting syllables and cakes
> Is this haiku too?

It didn't rhyme, of course, which in my opinion is the very least a poem should do, and it led to a discussion on the number of syllables in 'syllable' but I was impressed by the way Gil could just conjure things out of his head, and I was gratified to see him getting along so well with Murray. They were destined to become kin, after all.

We drove to Rivington Street, in the neighborhood of Orchard and Delancey and the unfortunates. Even the anarchist was persuaded to ride with us, and I treated everyone to apricot *ruggelach*. I asked Mr Casella how much he charged for portraits, having in mind that Gil and I might get our likenesses painted before the wedding, but he explained to me he wasn't that kind of artist. He was something called a vanguardist, and vanguardists regarded portrait-painting as outmoded.

Frederick agreed with him. 'Portraits!' he scoffed. 'Nothing but a bourgeois conceit. What about the *real* people? Where are *their* portraits?'

I couldn't answer him. I said, 'I'm sure anyone might like to have their portrait painted.'

But I took note of what was being said, especially the word 'bourgeois' which was used frequently. Minetta Lane people seemed to have a fund of unusual ideas. They felt sorry for the unfortunates, but they didn't wish them to get rich, because they regarded wealth as another kind of misfortune. As for the in-betweens, the little people who had jobs of work and were neither tragically rich nor tragically poor, they seemed to despise them above all. I wasn't sure I understood the figuring behind this, but I did feel instinctively that if I couldn't be rich, I'd sooner be poor than a dreary in-between.

Having already promised myself to become a more interesting person, I now saw how this might occur. With the help of Gil and his friends I could easily acquire a set of new opinions.

'Well?' I said to Murray, as I drove him home. 'Isn't Gil a handsome and fascinating creature?'

'He's all right,' Murray replied. 'His house is rather smelly though. Shall we have to live there, after you're married?'

I said, 'Certainly not. We shall live somewhere amusing and have the help put lavender in the linen press. And anyway, you shan't live with us. You'll stay in your own house until you're old enough to find a wife.'

'I'm nearly fourteen,' he said. 'I may just run away.'

He fell silent for a while. I felt sorry for him, facing the prospect of another dinner with Ma and the uxorious Mr Jacoby, but there was little I could do. Gil and I were going to the Blue Ribbon Grill for ribs and dancing.

'Your Step-Ma is really very fond of you,' I lied. 'And if you'll promise to try and get along with her, I'll take you out for a spin again soon.'

'Listen to this,' he said.

Eating chicken soup
Step-Ma Dorabel sounds like
Draining bath water.

He counted off the syllables on his fingers.
'Seventeen!' he said. 'It's a haiku!'

TWENTY-FOUR

At midnight on January 16, 1920, the selling of alcoholic beverages became prohibited, thanks to the efforts of Representative Volstead who wished to prevent the unfortunates from spending all their money on intoxicating liquor and beating their wives and failing to be reliable employees. Gil and I began that last evening at the Waldorf-Astoria but they soon ran out of liquor so we made our way to the Park Avenue. The snow was getting blown about in flurries and people were in a somber mood considering we were meant to be having a party. When midnight came, I even saw men weep.

I said, 'Now whatever shall we do?'

I had laid in a quantity of gin and rye whiskey for consumption at home, but that wasn't going to last forever. Gil replied that nothing on earth would keep Manhattan dry.

'Ways and means, Princess,' he said. 'You ask Harry if I'm not right.'

My brother-in-law Harry had taken to Gil, after an inauspicious start when he had been sent by Ma and Aunt Fish to investigate the Catchings family and prove Gil's unsuitability as a husband. Here is how it all came about.

Returning home from his second visit with me to Minetta Lane, Murray disturbed the concord of the Jacoby dinner table by calling his father a bourgeois pig.

Questions were asked, I was summoned to give an account of the company we had been keeping, and Ma greeted my announcement about marrying Gil with a fit of palpitations so severe that Aunt Fish had to be sent for, with her bottle of Tilden's Extract.

'Poppy,' Aunt Fish said to me, 'why is it that just when a person thinks they may be allowed to enjoy a peaceful old age, you find new ways to trouble them.'

'It's not a question of my age, Zillah,' Ma interrupted, surfacing from her attack of the vapors. 'I'm sure I have never felt more vigorous. It was the shock that felled me. I'm almost resigned to Poppy ruining her life, but that she would expose Judah's boy to such low company . . .'

'You must be resigned to nothing,' Aunt Fish instructed her. 'If Poppy has taken up with penniless idlers we must act without delay.'

I said, 'Gil isn't an idler. He writes poetry and looks into ways of changing society. Anyway, I have enough money for both of us.'

My aunt turned pale.

'This proposed union,' she said. 'Have letters been exchanged?'

'No,' I said. 'Only verses.'

She made me feel like a child again with her interrogations. Mr Jacoby had absented himself from the room as soon as Aunt Fish arrived. Throughout my life I have observed that whenever a strong emotional tide starts running, men discover urgent business in another part of the house.

Murray, though, had stayed for the spectacle. He had not yet learned manly ways. He knew if he sat quietly no one would notice him in his ringside seat, waiting for blood and teeth to fly.

'But did you sign anything?' she asked. 'Anything at all?'

'Only my account at the Hootsy Tootsy Club,' I replied. I hadn't intended to play Aunt Fish's game and answer her questions. I had planned to laugh at her bourgeois anxieties and goad her with her powerlessness, but it all went wrong.

'Who are his people?' she wanted to know.

I said, 'I believe he's an orphan.'

Gil had always refused to discuss family. I took this to be because he had none, or because he was embarrassed by their penury.

'A likely story,' she said. 'We must have this investigated, Dora, without delay. And who are his set? Whose teas have you been attending?'

I mentioned Frederick the anarchist, and Casella the painter, and a women's righter called Anne.

'Well, these are certainly not people we know,' she interrupted, 'and you surely realize a girl cannot marry into the unknown? You must marry someone like Leopold Adler.'

Leopold was one of the banking Adlers. He had hairy knuckles and his lips were always wet.

I said, 'But Leopold Adler is already engaged.'

Aunt Fish said, 'I give his name merely by way of an example. When, and *if* you marry, it will be to someone known to us. This is why I always kept such a particular watch over you when you were growing up. But, of course, recent events have distracted me. That terrible war. And then your uncle. Perhaps I'm a little to blame in all this. Perhaps I didn't do all I could to prepare you.'

I was aware of the boy Murray watching me.

'Well, Aunt,' I said, 'your preparations left me somewhat confused. First I was told I was marriageable, but only if my hair could be subdued and the yellowness bleached out of my neck. Then I was redirected to become an old maid and stay at home with my poor widowed Ma. Then, just as suddenly, I was released from that obligation and sent out into the world to try my luck, which is what I was doing when I met Gil Catchings.'

'Marriage has nothing to do with luck,' she said, ignoring my other points. Then she had another alarming thought.

'Poppy,' she said, 'have you been . . . alone with this person?'

I hesitated, measuring just how much I wished to scandalize her, and into the silence rushed Murray, eager to help.

'Of course you have!' he cried. 'Remember? The day I came to your apartment and the doorman made me count to three hundred before I came up and you'd been drinking gin on the bed?'

Ma let out a muted yelp.

'We shall need a lawyer and a doctor,' Aunt Fish murmured. 'If only Israel would hurry up and recover. Perhaps Judah . . .'

'Oh no,' Ma said. 'This is not at all the kind of thing Judah would undertake. Harry will do it. Send for Harry.'

Harry traveled a great deal in those days, seeing to his diverse business interests, but as soon as he returned from Havana, Cuba, he was to investigate the background of Gilbert Catchings and devise a means of keeping his hands off my millions.

'In the meanwhile,' my aunt said, 'Poppy must be kept here, under close supervision.'

'I'm not sure . . .' Ma began. It turned very much to my advantage that her new husband's tranquility took precedence over everything else.

'To forestall an elopement, Dora!' Aunt Fish whispered frantically. 'Until Israel can talk plainly with her.'

I said, 'I shall visit Uncle Israel tomorrow. It'll be my pleasure. And tonight I shall sleep in my own home. There's no question of an elopement. When I marry Gil you shall all be there to see it.'

The truth was, I'd have eloped in a heartbeat, but he was in no great hurry.

Murray accompanied me down to where my roadster was parked.

'Poppy,' he said, 'I do hope they won't prevent us from helling around with Gil.'

I said, 'If you repeat words like "bourgeois pig" they most certainly will, so we shall have to lie low for a while. But after Gil and I are married you'll be welcome to come to our house and hell around as much as you like.'

'Thank you,' he said solemnly. 'And Poppy? I don't think your neck is too yellow at all. I'd say it's pretty much exactly the right color for a neck.'

TWENTY-FIVE

M oves were made to keep my money safe inside the New Amsterdam National Bank while Harry established sound reasons to have Gil run out of town, and I was sent for by Uncle Israel. He had been instructed by Aunt Fish to give me a stern talking to, although I don't believe he ever was capable of that, even before his health failed.

He had never made a complete recovery from his first seizure and over the next few years suffered a number of relapses that left him weak and lopsided. His working days were reduced to working mornings, and then only when he was judged strong enough to ride downtown to his office. This adjudication, made by Aunt Fish, seemed to have more to do with her condition than his.

When the cask of benevolence was overflowing she kept him at home and fed him on dainties encased in aspic, a substance she believed to be fortifying, soothing and not far short of plain miraculous. Then, after a heavy run on her stores of compassion, she would find herself with nothing left to give and declare him sufficiently fortified and soothed to go to the office and do a little of whatever it was he did.

'Your poor uncle wishes to see you,' she told me.

'Your poor aunt wishes me to see you,' he told me.

I said, 'Uncle, I'm of age. I can marry Gil Catchings and there's nothing anybody can do to prevent it.'

'Don't be so sure,' he said. 'Now why don't you get off your high horse and tell me about him.'

I told him about Gil's pale blue eyes and lion hair.

'But what is his situation?' he kept asking. 'Didn't I warn you, Pops, when you came into your money, against flatterers and adventurers?'

I said, 'Gil's not a flatterer. He truly cares for me. Why he never leaves off kissing me.'

'I don't care to discuss that,' Uncle said, pulling on his cigarette. 'I leave that side of your education to your aunt, though why you weren't better guided by your mother, I fail to understand. What I need to know is, have you given this rake money? Have you signed anything over to him or entered into any kind of binding agreement?'

I assured him Gil had never asked me for a cent. Of course, he never needed to because I always offered it anyway.

I said, 'You seem to be fading away, Uncle. Are you sure your doctor knows his business?' I thought I'd change the subject before he asked to examine my checkbook. And he was fading. Though his memory was improved and his ability to hold a thought and express himself, he wasn't the same man.

'I put it down to fewer good dinners,' he said. 'I don't recall the last time I enjoyed a late supper at the Harmonie Club.'

I said, 'You know champagne wine isn't so easy for any of us to come by these days? President Wilson has prohibited it for our own good. Twenty-five dollars a quart, if you can get it.'

'Next thing he'll be prohibiting cigars,' he said. 'Well, I make my own drinking arrangements. No one tells me what's good for me.'

Sadly this was not true. As far back as my memory stretched he had been taking orders from Aunt Fish.

'And if you've developed the taste for good liquor,' he continued, 'you'd better start making your own arrangements, too. Talk to Harry.'

This was my family's preferred method of dealing with problems. Uncle Israel may have been recognized as nominal head of Minkel interests, but it was a mere courtesy, accorded him so he could then delegate. So Harry was deputed to warn off my fiancé and keep us all supplied with liquor, and Aunt Fish to test my knowledge of carnal relations. She, in turn, ceded the opening moments of this inquisition to my mother, who asked me nervously whether any unchaperoned embraces had occurred.

'Dora!' Aunt Fish cried. 'Everything about this affair has been unchaperoned. That is precisely the problem.'

Poor Aunt. She didn't want to do the dirty work herself, but she knew in her heart no one else could be trusted to do it properly.

I said, 'We go dancing.'

The word 'dancing' would, I knew, conjure for Ma a polite two-step. So far so good.

'Have you . . . spooned?' she trembled.

I smiled coyly. 'Sometimes,' I said, 'when I'm driving him home.'

Ma and Aunt Fish agreed that this was a very great danger with driving, but there were powerful arguments against depriving me of my motor. They were often very glad of me to run errands. Ma knew more hazardous terrain lay ahead. She seemed reluctant to proceed, and so just sat, hoping to bring me to heel with a look of hurt and disappointment.

'The main point is, Dora,' my aunt prompted, 'has there been any . . . romping?'

'Yes,' Ma said, bracing herself. 'That is the question.'

And there my own courage failed me and I grew devious. I abandoned my plan to announce the loss of my maidenhood, and played a tricky caviling game.

Romping? Wasn't that what puppy dogs did in Central Park, or little children in the first fall of snow? Gil and I had certainly not done that. Our encounters had been earnest, resolute.

'No,' I said, 'no romping.'

Ma softened. Her ordeal was over.

'There!' she cried. 'I knew Poppy had more sense. No romping. And neither must there be, Poppy. That is a privilege of the marriage bed.'

This hinted at something unspeakable involving Judah Jacoby. I made a move to leave, before Ma grew even more indiscreet, but my aunt wasn't finished with me.

'Nevertheless,' she said, 'we cannot ignore certain things the boy mentioned. A gin bottle. A disturbed coverlet. Exactly the kind of looseness one associates with living in an hotel. She must leave the Belleclaire, Dora. Perhaps she should live with Honey. Or with me. This is not a burden I look for at my time of life, but something must be done.'

Faced with the devil, I opted for the deep blue sea.

'I have in mind to stay with Honey for a while,' I said. 'She gets so lonesome when Harry's traveling and entertaining his floozies.'

My plan was to go directly to Gil and invite him to marry me without further delay.

'Poppy!' Ma said. 'I'm sure Harry is a very considerate husband.'

'Indeed,' agreed Aunt Fish. 'And don't think to distract us by defaming others. It would profit you to study on your sister's marriage, Poppy, and follow her good example.'

So it was settled that Honey should be put in charge of my moral hygiene and living arrangements, until a suitable match could be made and I could be married out of harm's way. Meanwhile her considerate husband tracked down Gil's family to Scranton, Pennsylvania, where it turned out they weren't paupers at all but the owners of two garment factories.

'Tell me the worst, Harry,' Ma said, when he returned. 'I am braced for it.'

'No need,' he said. 'Couple of nice little outfits they've got up there. The kind of thing it'd be good to get into, in the event of another war. Uniforms. Kit bags. Catchings himself doesn't have a fortune, of course, but then, neither did I. He's going to be a self-made man. Nothing wrong with that.'

Aunt Fish took up the cudgel Ma was on the point of dropping.

'But Harry,' she said, 'are the Catchings the kind of people one would visit?'

'Don't see why not, Zillah,' he said. 'But Scranton's a fair old way to go for tea.'

To tell the truth, I felt let down. I had been looking to elope with as much money as I could stuff inside my bust bodice, start life anew as a revolutionary and create a great *scandale*. Instead I had to make do with the pleasure of seeing my mother and my aunt sheathe their claws and prepare to be kissed on the hand by my fiancé.

Gil and I were married at City Hall on March 10, 1920.

I wore one of my own originations in peppermint shantung, and a silver fox jacket with full sleeves and a johnny collar, a gift from my stepfather. He had offered me the run of Jacoby Furriers. I could have picked out the finest mink in the showroom, but then I would have felt certain obligations to him, such as to spare my mother any further shocks and anxieties. I could have had the silver fox hat, too, but I declined. Give in to one inducement and you may find yourself considered bought. Besides, I had had my hair styled *à la garçonne* and I had no wish to hide it.

Since becoming Mrs Judah Jacoby, Ma had succumbed to a light form of Jewishness and she would have liked to see me married under a chuppah, but Gil wasn't made of the right stuff. I heard her remark that Gil might pretend to be Jewish and who would know the difference, but Mr J replied that *he* would know and anyway it would be a bad show to start off a marriage with a fraud. So it was arranged that we would go to City Hall and afterwards to the Elysée for lunch.

Two days before the ceremony, I bought myself a platinum wedding band from Tiffany and I received some words of sisterly advice from Honey.

'Well,' she said, 'are you ready for married life?'

I said, 'If you're talking about squeezes and thrills I already know about all that. What I'd like to know is, how do you stop a person staying out all night with showgirls?'

I wanted to believe Gil would stay true to me, but I had heard so many warnings. It appeared that men could never get enough candy, until they moved into the candy store, upon which they developed a taste for saltines instead.

My sister stared at me.

I said, 'Do you and Harry still spoon?'

She said, 'Poppy, you have developed an ugly, modern way of talking.'

I said, 'And I've seen changes in you, too. You never smile anymore or act gay.'

I held back from remarking that Harry seemed to spend his nights out of town attending to business, except when Honey was away, taking Sherman to the shore or getting her magnetic fields corrected. Then you could guarantee Harry would be back in town. They were like the little figures on Aunt Fish's weather house. If one was out the other was in.

I said, 'When did it stop being like it was before you were married? Does Harry thrill you anymore?'

I wasn't convinced she understood me.

I said, 'It seems to me men get their thrills faster than we do. Sometimes I haven't even started getting mine . . .'

'Poppy!' she gasped. 'Have you really . . . *given* yourself to Gilbert Catchings?'

'What if I have?' I said. I loved to see her so scandalized. I was looking forward to a scene. But she refused to make one. Didn't have the energy for it, I suppose. She just looked sad and shook her head.

'I fear I've let you down,' she said. 'There are things a girl might expect to be told by an older sister, but I've been so busy since Sherman Ulysses came along, and now you've gone and grown up without correct guidance. You've been led astray by a bounder and, of course, he's only done it for your money.'

I said, 'Don't think of trying to stop the wedding. We'll elope and then you'll never see me again.'

'Stop the wedding?' she cried. 'On the contrary. The sooner you're married to him the sooner you'll be safe from shame and dishonor. Uncle Israel has mounted a guard on your fortune. The only other thing we can hope for is that Mr Catchings is clean and careful. Would you say he is?'

I thought I would. It was hardly Gil's fault he lived in such disorder. He had no help at all at Minetta Lane.

The day before the wedding Mrs Catchings came by railroad from Scranton and took accommodations in the Louis, a hotel that had been the scene of a shooting. There was really nothing more I could do to break Ma's heart.

Only seven guests witnessed our ceremony and that included Simeon from Uncle Israel's office. Uncle Israel insisted no one could push his invalid carriage as smoothly as Simeon. Pressure of business prevented Harry and Mr Jacoby from attending. Sherman Ulysses was in school, Bernie overslept and Yetta Landau remained in the country keeping watch over Oscar and his dark thoughts. Gil gave me a kiss and a red rose and Murray presented us with a piece of card.

'I wrote you a haiku,' he grinned.

> Wedding March. Here Comes
> The Bride. I Hope We Get Shrimp
> At This March Wedding.

Mrs Catchings and Murray rode with us to the Elysée. The way it turned out was that Gil sat behind with his mother. I heard her ask him if we were Hebrews.

'Not enough to bother about,' he whispered.

We did have shrimp. Then Bernie turned up in duck-egg taffeta with a dropped waist and annoyed Honey by mistaking her for Ma, and Ma by mistaking her for Mrs Catchings. I guess she had had a late night that morning. We followed the shrimp with steaks and peach melba and a little rye in hip flasks provided by Harry, and Uncle Israel hardly dribbled at all. I believe he enjoyed the occasion in spite of the fact I was ruining my life, and I'm glad he did because it was probably the last time he went to a restaurant and smoked a cigar.

Gil and I prepared to drive away to our new life. We had taken a five-room apartment in the Ansonia building and intended creating a love nest there until we were ready to sail to our honeymoon in Paris, France.

My mother-in-law instructed me to call her Elizabeth and to visit with her sometime. I acceded to her first request and ignored the second. Wherever Pennsylvania was, I had no desire to see it.

Uncle Israel squeezed my hand, Aunt Fish gave me a begrudging kiss and Honey looked at me quite tenderly. 'My little sister!' she said. Then Ma took me stiffly in her arms and stretched up close to my ear.

'Remember, Poppy,' she whispered. 'Always use the Lysol after any . . . romping.'

We emerged from the Elysée to face the first problem of our marriage. Murray was in the front passenger seat of the Packard, quite convinced he would be joining us at the Ansonia, for our wedding night, and for the rest of his life.

It took a good deal of cajoling, followed by violent tugging, threatening and hauling to remove him to the sidewalk.

'But I like you,' he sobbed.

He cried for the rest of the day, so I was told.

'That boy is way too sissified,' Gil said as he climbed into the seat unwillingly vacated by Murray.

I kept to myself the thought that my stepbrother had just been dealt another unkind blow. He had lost his mother, he had effectively lost his brother and, as a consequence, his Auntsie, and now he had gone and lost me. I owed him nothing, of course. And I had never said he could live with us. It had never even been discussed. That was the problem and that was the reason something settled on my chest like a stone. Gil said it was very likely the second helping of shrimp, but I knew it was to do with Murray. I knew the kind of plans and ideas that can run unchecked in the mind of a lonely, longing child.

TWENTY-SIX

The Ansonia Hotel occupied a whole Broadway block between 73rd and 74th Streets. It stood seventeen stories high with corner towers and copper lanterns. It had a chop house and a Child's restaurant and a swimming pool, and the apartment walls were three feet thick which meant we were protected from fire and also from anyone overhearing our fights.

Married life was hard on Gil. I had taken him uptown, away from his friends, and although he shopped a good deal, time hung heavy for him. All the other men I had known, my Pa, my uncle, Mr Jacoby, even Harry, seemed obliged to go to the office most days, or to inspect their subsidiaries, but Gil had neither an office to go to nor subsidiaries to inspect, and he was having a tough time of it composing his haiku verses. In fact, it appeared to me that Murray dashed them off more easily than Gil did and it was my tactless remarking on this that first provoked him to strike me. It was a glancing blow that left no lingering mark on my face, but the surprise of it caused me to lose my balance, fall against a chair and bruise my arm. This was an inconvenience to me. I had a new set of coral bracelets I'd intended to wear to the Hootsy Tootsy Club, but I was forced to change my plans until the bruise had faded.

Gil was broken-hearted over what had occurred.

'I haven't been sleeping well, Princess,' he said. 'I'm so fatigued I'm just not myself.'

I had already observed that the people in life who appear the most weary are the ones who are least active, so after we had made our peace I suggested to Gil he might take some kind of position, perhaps in one of the family concerns. I was sure something could be found for him at Uncle Israel's office.

'Don't know that I'm cut out for sitting behind a desk,' he said.

I said, 'Or Judah Jacoby might find you something. You could go to the fur market for him. Ma would like it if he could stay home more and play cards.'

'I'll give it some thought,' he said. But he continued to languish. While I was always up and about by ten o'clock, hurrying to Elizabeth Arden to get my nails done, then onto lunch with Bernie, Gil remained in bed, awaiting inspiration, or sat around in the lobby, hoping to say how-de-do to our neighbor Mr Babe Ruth.

Gil didn't especially follow the sport of baseball, but he did love to think of all that mustard getting consumed every time the Yankees played a game.

I stayed away from Murray for a while, to allow him to get over his disappointment. Then, two weeks after the wedding I drove across to Schiff's Academy, parked outside and waited for him to emerge from afternoon school.

He made a big performance of putting his nose in the air and disregarding me, but I drove alongside him calling to him that I missed him, until he relented and climbed in beside me.

'Does this mean I'm coming to live with you?' he said.

I said, 'No. Honeymooners don't have boys living with them. But you can visit us. Hell around a little.'

Murray was far too young for helling around, but he liked it when I pretended he was my peer.

'I suppose soon a baby will appear,' he said gloomily. 'That's generally what happens.'

I took him to the Tip Toe for cake and he told me there was brighter news from the country. Oscar's spirits had lifted and if the improvement was sustained he might return to the city.

'And what will he do?' I asked. I saw a threat to the prospect of Gil's joining the Jacoby enterprise.

'Perhaps he'll be an anarchist,' he suggested. 'We could introduce him to Frederick. He could tell him how it's done.'

I said, 'I don't believe anarchy is a paid job of work. Does Oscar have an allowance?'

Murray didn't know what an allowance was. This was congruent with what I knew of his father. Judah Jacoby believed everyone needed a job of work, even if they were rich as Croesus.

I said, 'Should you have preferred it if I'd married Oscar instead of Gil?'

'Oscar?' he said. 'Hardly. Anyway, Oscar doesn't care for girls. Step-Ma Dorabel says Gil keeps bad company. I think that's rather fun, don't you? I never knew bad people before.'

I said, 'They're not bad people. They're interesting.'

'That's what I told her!' he cried. 'But she said it amounted to the same thing. People who were just wishing to get dragged off to jail. I must say, Poppy, you're looking pretty peaky since you got married.'

It was true. The air in our new suite seemed stale and going out dancing and drinking wasn't so much fun since Gil was there before my eyes every minute of the day. He hardly ever visited Minetta Lane anymore since his friends there called him a poodle.

The first time I canceled lunch with Bernie she came round to the Ansonia post-haste. Gil was out, selecting new shirts.

'When did you last have your monthly visitor?' she asked. I suppose growing up in a house full of sisters she was accustomed to that kind of discussion, but I was not.

I said, 'I don't know. It's not a thing I pay attention to.'

'Well, you should,' she said, 'or how else are you going to know if you've fallen?'

She sat me down and explained in quite shocking detail the workings of a woman's body. Then she asked me certain questions, and from my replies she deduced that I had begun to have a baby. If it had been left to me I would simply have lain down and wept but Bernie insisted there was no time to be lost. She poured me a large measure of our precious prohibited gin and told me I better start jumping off a stepladder.

Of course, we didn't possess a stepladder, so I just drank a second tumbler of gin and jumped repeatedly off a Windsor chair until I turned my ankle. The baby, though, showed no sign of leaving. I had thought Harry's special gin might be cut with water, and this confirmed my suspicions. When Gil returned he found me on the couch, stone cold sober with a pregnancy and a severe sprain.

'Don't worry, Princess,' he said. 'I know a person who can take care of things.'

And indeed he did. Gil knew an *accoucheuse* who made house calls. She came the very next day, and again a few months later when the same misfortune had befallen me. On her second visit she presented me with a package of Trojan prophylactics and advised me to persuade Gil to try them.

'They're the latest thing,' she said. 'I don't generally talk myself out of future business, but you're a nice young woman. Some day you'll start wanting to keep one of these babies, and I'd hate for you to have any difficulties. Hygiene procedures can have consequences, you understand?'

I neither understood nor cared. I was more concerned to keep Gil happy until we arrived in Europe, a place he felt sure would be conducive to finding himself. Our passage was booked for early October on the *Berengaria*. Then my dear Uncle Israel passed away in his sleep and we were forced to change our plans.

My aunt was desolated by her loss. Uncle's lopsided dribbling and his occasional forgetfulness had brought a new fire to their marriage. Aunt Fish enjoyed nothing better than a patently hopeless case to nag and bully, and suddenly she had none. Had I not married and removed myself safely beyond her reach I have no doubt she would have renewed her efforts with me.

She turned first to Ma for comfort, but there was little on offer.

Ma, who had leaned so heavily on her sister at the time of her own bereavement, was busy attending to her new marriage. Perhaps, like me, she was concerned to keep her husband out of the clutches of chorines with delicate upturned noses, though she really had no cause for anxiety. Judah Jacoby was a carpet slipper man. He was also a man who liked regularity, and opening one's home to a grief-stricken shrew is a sure recipe for chaos.

Prayers were said at East 69th Street and light refreshments provided. Seven days of this was recommended by the *rebbe*, but Ma deemed three days to be ample. As it was, a quite enormous quantity of brisket was consumed. Mrs Schwab came, and the Misses Stone, and even Mrs Lesser. Her bunions now kept her at home, but she never allowed them to keep her from a good funeral. By special request to the head of Schiff's Academy, Murray was given extra math which confined him to his room longer than usual each evening, until the practicalities of death had been dealt with. Uncle Israel was laid to rest in Pinelawns, Brooklyn, in a section with a good class of person.

'Well now,' Ma began, that evening, 'what are we to do about your aunt?'

I said, 'What is there to do? She'll be lonely for a while and then perhaps she'll find another husband, like you did.'

'I was strong enough to bear such a blow,' she said. 'But Zillah is quite different. And older than I was, too. I was blessed with the resilience of youth.'

This wasn't at all my recollection, but Ma insisted that she had only permitted Aunt Fish to move in with us after Pa's death and take over the daily running of the house so as not to offend her.

'But circumstances are different now, Poppy,' she continued. 'I can't go to her, and she cannot possibly come to me.'

'Why not?' I asked. The Jacoby house was certainly large enough.

'Because it would discommode Judah,' she said, 'and furthermore Oscar may soon be coming home. I cannot be expected to run a hospital.'

Ma made the presence of a bereaved sister and a delicate stepson sound like the challenge Miss Nightingale had faced at Scutari.

'I believe,' she continued, 'she might benefit from the company of younger people. And now you'll be staying on, now you have come to your senses about the risk of traveling on oceans . . .'

I saw, clearer than ever, that my plans would never count for anything. When it suited them my family would always regard me as a kind of above-stairs Irish. Expected to be available on a moment's notice to pick up unpleasant chores, otherwise to be silent and invisible, and never ever to be trusted with the good silver.

I said, 'But we won't be staying on. It seems to me Honey is the one you must turn to here. Aunt Fish always did favor her, and Honey gets lonely with Harry traveling so much.'

In my eagerness to offload my aunt I almost added that she might do us all a service and make a project of Sherman Ulysses, but at the last moment common sense persuaded me this would do nothing to strengthen my case. For one thing, in our family anything connected with Honey was held to be flawless. And in particular, Ma would not have welcomed the suggestion that Sherman Ulysses, her own special little Abe, was a suitable candidate for improvement. I held my tongue. Honey was informed that Aunt Fish would be moving in with her until she recovered her spirits, and Ma and I both prepared to resume our married lives.

I did sit with my aunt one evening though. She had invited me to select a small keepsake of my uncle.

I said, 'I should like his top hat. And perhaps his silk scarf, if it smells of his cigars.'

'That's two things, Poppy,' she said. But she let me have them.

'You may as well,' she said. 'They're no use to me. Just silly reminders.'

I said, 'But you will keep some things? You won't let the Misses Stone take everything?'

'I have my memories,' she said. 'So many happy memories.'

It was the nicest thing I ever heard her say.

I said, 'What's the best one?'

'Oh,' she said, folding his silk scarf and wrapping it in tissue paper, 'the first time I saw him. He was everything I'd dreamed of.'

I said, 'That's how I feel about Gil.'

'Indeed?' she said. 'But you have a very long way to go. Twenty-seven years, we had. Twenty-seven happy years.'

This made me feel a good deal better about our little problems. My recollection was that my aunt and uncle had never agreed on anything. If that counted as twenty-seven happy years, clearly Gil and I had nothing to worry about.

Nevertheless, I soon made two unpleasant discoveries. One was that Gil was running through money a deal faster than I expected him to, having sunk funds into a radical pamphlet called *Zero* and settled a regular allowance on Mr Casella the painter. The other was that one of my uncle's final and mischievous acts had been to place my fortune in the trust of two comparative strangers: my stepfather, Judah Jacoby, and Simeon, a mere employee and pusher of invalid carriages. It was insufferable, and I had to endure it until I was thirty years of age.

'We could go to law,' Gil suggested. 'Get it overturned. Prove the old guy was deranged.'

Honey said, 'I fail to see why it matters, as long as your money is safeguarded. Harry takes care of mine and I'm sure I prefer it that way.'

Gil and I booked a spring passage to Cherbourg on a Cunarder called the *Aquitania*, sister ship to the *Berengaria*, and we whiled away the weeks till our departure buying traveling clothes and finding new places to hell around. Some were just addresses we had from Harry, ordinary brownstones where you had to know the special word before you were allowed inside to the party. Some were miles away on Lenox, almost out of town, full of darkies playing wild music. We were getting the reputation of being real adventurers.

Honey said, 'You will be careful, won't you? Be sure always to sleep in your life-vest. And when you get to Paris, you must let it be known you are Americans. That way you'll be treated with greater respect. They may think twice before murdering you in your beds.'

'Honey!' Ma cried. 'Don't give into such terrible thoughts. We must think of gay, pleasant subjects.'

'Yes,' said my aunt. 'We must decide who will do the flowers for Poppy's stateroom and who should cater the farewell. It may be the last palatable meal she'll taste for a very long time.'

Honey said, 'I wonder why dangerous things always fascinated you so? You always were a terror for seeing how close to the fire you could put your hand.'

I said, 'Paris is only a little dangerous. Don't forget, I did war work. I'm accustomed to dealing with the French, and it is *the* place to be, you know? Everyone in Paris is interesting.'

'Are they?' she said. 'How very tiring that must be.'

She took me to one side.

'I do admire your pluck, Poppy,' she said. 'I shall miss you dreadfully. But when you come home, perhaps you'll have had your fill of danger and stimulation. Perhaps you'll have a baby? Then we can be real sisters again and have heaps to talk about.'

I explained that we used prophylactics to prevent the inconvenience of babies.

'But a baby isn't an inconvenience!' she said. 'A baby is a dear, smiling angel.'

A picture of Sherman Ulysses' angry red face flashed across my mind.

'How I should love to have another baby,' she said. 'A little girl baby, with big green eyes.'

Gil and I had left open the date of our return passage. I was looking forward to being in a place where no one knew me or remembered my youthful gaffes. I was genuinely unsure whether I would ever want to go back. But I didn't articulate this. I kept things light and vague, to spare the feelings of people like Honey, and Murray.

I took Murray to Hegeman's for a final egg cream.

'I wish I could go to Paris, France,' he sighed. 'I wish I didn't have to go to Bethel.'

It had been decided that Oscar was better suited to the Catskills than he was to city life, and once a month Murray traveled to Bethel to spend the weekend with him. Oscar was teaching himself to repair furniture. He apparently had a great liking for woodland and lakes and silence, so it was just as well we had never married.

I said, 'I expect you have adventures up there, in the forests?'

'No,' he said. 'I get rashes and sneezing fits. What shall you do in Paris?'

'Go to parties,' I said. 'Meet artists and writers and stay out all night.'

He whistled. 'Won't you get pretty tired?' he said.

I taught him a new toast I had invented, based on the name of one of my favorite dancing clubs and we drank each other's good health.

'Tinkety Tonk,' I said.

'Tonkety Tink,' he replied. He had a line of soda on his top lip and the faintest beginnings of a mustache. My stepbrother was growing up.

TWENTY-SEVEN

We arrived in Paris, France, on the last day of April 1921. I was wearing a suit of flamingo pink jersey, made to one of my own designs, and two-tone spectators and a Milan straw toque with a russet cockade. The sun flickered through the lime trees as we rode away from the railroad station, and I liked the smell of our driver's cigarette so much, I begged one from him for myself. I was feeling most contented.

I said, 'Maybe we'll never go back. Maybe we'll just stay here and be interesting Parisians. That would teach them all a lesson.'

Every sea mile the *Aquitania* had put between me and my interfering family had raised my spirits. But Gil was subdued. I didn't work out till later he was anxious about not speaking French, which didn't matter in the least, of course, because he had me by his side to take charge of things, and, anyhow, I have found wherever you travel in the world, bellhops and others of that type understand the American language.

We took a suite at the Crillon, but it wasn't the place to meet amusing and modern people. It was full of old folk who talked in whispers. I soon realized we'd have to make other arrangements.

After three days of clinging to my side and breaking a looking-glass in a fit of cabin fever, Gil finally got up the nerve to search out a bar recommended by Frederick the anarchist as a place to meet advanced and amusing people. It was way across the river in a neighborhood called Montparnasse, right by the place the boat-train had deposited us, and somehow, I don't know how for I don't believe

Frederick had ever been to Paris himself, he was right. Every seat in the Café Dingo was occupied by somebody droll or outrageous or just plain brilliant.

Pretty soon we had the makings of our very own set.

I rented us a furnished house in the rue Vavin and the day we moved out of the Crillon, I gave the manager an overdue reminder of his place. In the running of a hotel there is sure to be wear and tear, and a departing guest should not be troubled with inventories and housekeeping details and insolent remarks. I'm sure I have always settled my accounts.

I had decided we would live simply in the rue Vavin, with just one maid and an outdoors man to bring in ice and wood and coal and to keep our motor polished. I had purchased a new Citroën in the hope Gil would be persuaded to learn how to drive, but he showed no such inclination. As for myself, I found the irregularities of Parisian streets most inconvenient and often I preferred to hire a taxicab. In those days you were pretty much guaranteed to get an interesting chauffeur. A Galician duke or some such, who had fallen on unfortunate times. It was quite the vogue to go to Paris after you had been ruined, like Stassy, who was my business assistant, until she turned on the hand that had fed her.

Stassy was practically a princess, but she was living in just one room with cardboard walls and a kettle until I saved her from destitution. I was introduced to her by Nancy Lord, who lunched with me one day wearing the most extraordinary mohair garment that consisted of one sleeve and two long scarf-like drapeable flaps.

Nancy said, 'Isn't it fun? A little Russian woman made it for me. Shall I put you on to her?'

Unlike my mother, I had never shrunk from mingling with the poor and sometimes I pretended to be poor myself, restricting myself to ten dollars a day and dining on nothing but potato salad. Stassy was very poor indeed. The Bolsheviks had taken everything she owned and she had run away from them through Persia and Greece and all kinds of places before she came to Paris.

I put her at her ease by telling her I adored travel myself. Then she admired the origination I was wearing and asked to see how it was assembled. I purchased two of her knitted neckties for Gil and before we knew it we were chattering away like old friends. I had the feeling Nancy was a tiny bit piqued.

I said to Stassy, 'Let's go into business. You make fabulous things. I make fabulous things. Let's sell them.'

'I already tried,' she said. 'The shops won't take them. Only crazy people buy my things.'

'Then we'll open our own shop,' I said. 'For crazy people.'

I'm sure Stassy didn't believe it was possible.

I said, 'Trust me. All things are possible.'

'Oh yes,' she said, 'I know all things are possible. But still. A shop?'

The winter of 1921 we worked all hours. While Gil was busy establishing himself with a damned smart bunch of intellectuals at the Dingo, I was creating two- and three-piece layered ensembles in soft jersey lined with silk, and Stassy was knitting. She was some knitter.

I rented a small shop in St Sulpice and had it painted a delicate shade of eau-de-Nil. I named it Coquelicot, which is the French way of saying Poppy, and by the end of the first month word had gotten around. All we had left were a few of Stassy's ties, plus four girls, two knitting and two sewing, as fast as we could show them how.

By the summer anyone who was anyone was wearing Coquelicot and I was becoming quite bored with it. I didn't even have time to play tennis. Stassy, though, wanted to do nothing but work. She was excited, I suppose, at the prospect of being rich again, although she never used the money she was making to buy amusing things. All she did was count it. I have often observed how tiresomely obsessed paupers are with hoarding money.

She wore her own designs, which saved her from being thin and plain, and the bones of her face shone through in a rather enviable way. All she ever drank was black tea, and if I sent out for pastries, she could never be tempted. Gil called her the Skull and Crossbones.

He'd say, 'What is it with you two, playing at shop? Is there something going on? She one of these sapphics?'

There were any number of unusual living arrangements going on in Paris at that time, but not involving Stassy. The only person I ever saw her kiss was the picture of Jesus she had on her wall. And she'd never come to our parties, no matter how fabulous they promised to be.

In that first year we saw a good deal of people like Felix Swain and Jack Barty, as well as the Dingo crowd, and Nancy and Orville Lord. If Orville and Gil hadn't fallen out over those silly allegations of money owed I dare say Nancy and I would have remained friends. It was too ridiculous. Why would Gil have needed to borrow money? But, as I explained to Stassy, we had all drunk enormous quantities of Taittinger that night, and that always made Orville rather fast on the draw.

She said, 'You were supposed to be here this morning. You were supposed to show the girl how you wanted the cloth cut.'

Stassy could be terribly priggish about champagne.

I said, 'Well I'm here now, though I could hardly lift my head off the pillow. But if you're going to be disagreeable I may just turn around and go away again.'

'Go away then,' she said. 'How much for you to go away?'

And that was what she said each time we quarreled. She nagged me about keeping regular hours. She nagged me about keeping regular accounts. And she tortured me for new designs.

'They are bored with your tubes now,' she said. 'They want to see something new.'

She quite failed to understand how busy I was. My flying lessons alone devoured whole days.

Meanwhile, letters kept arriving, inquiring as to the date of our return to New York.

'You must certainly be tired of honeymooning by now . . .' Ma wrote.

'Aunt Fish is bearing up, but will greatly benefit from your return . . .' my sister hinted. 'She has always taken such an interest in you and feels your absence greatly.'

'I don't believe I shall ever see you again . . .' mourned my stepbrother, Murray. 'I grew you a hyacinth in a dark cupboard but you weren't back in time to see it.'

As I explained in a letter to be circulated to all of them, we had no reason for a hasty return. Contrary to Stassy's opinions, *le tout Paris* was still enchanted by my tubes, and Gil was preparing to write an important novel. What I could never have explained to them was how much lighter and easier I was in myself, knowing there were no aunts or mothers or Schwabs or Lessers awaiting my downfall.

From my earliest recollection, from Honey's ninth birthday party which I had not been allowed to attend because of the certainty of my wetting my drawers or eating too much cake, I had managed to be simultaneously excluded and yet still occupy center stage. As long as I was tangled in the threads laid down by Ma and Aunt Fish, I was too big, too clumsy, too *unusual* either to ignore or to approve. Paris had ended this confusion. There it was impossible to be *too* anything.

I had met a number of amusing English pansies, including Humphrey Choate, with whom I played tennis. I had acquired an adorable bulldog called Beluga. And Gil and I were becoming famed for our smashes. We'd start late, with plenty of good champagne, and serve scrambled eggs for breakfast, with truffles as often as not. People could always depend on something of interest occurring. Tiny Kaminski often accessorized with animals. Once she brought along a pig, in a diaper. Then she had acquired a cheetah, but she had to give it to a circus when it became too boisterous, and the next time she came to us she simply brought along Jack Barty on a leash. It was so amusing.

It was also *chez nous* that Ava Hornblower abandoned Moo Greenaway and seduced Jane Speke. Feelings ran very high and so did Moo, who went up into the *mansarde*, and threatened to throw herself from our maid's window. And whatever Nancy Lord may claim, it was *we* who erected a boxing ring in our salon so that Chip Angus and Desmond McGrath could settle their differences in accordance with Queensberry Rules, and it was in *my* house that Badgirl Duprée first wore her transparent gown.

And my family expected me to return to dreary old New York!

It was rumored that my Cousin Addie had also declined to return to the United States after peace broke out and had stayed on in Paris. I welcomed this information. Cousin Addie promised to be the type of kin who would add to my standing as an interesting person. She had been a trailblazer, after all.

I made inquiries and discovered her next door to an abattoir in the shadow of the Salpêtrière hospital. She was wearing a sack suit and smoking black cigarettes and wasn't pretty at all.

I said, 'I'm Abe Minkel's girl. We're cousins. Just fancy we both come to be living in Paris, France.'

'Just fancy,' she said.

I told her how Gil and I were creating a salon where wild and shocking events might occur and invited her to attend our next costume party.

'Cousin Poppy,' she said, 'I'm here to work. I've already seen a lifetime's worth of wild and shocking.'

I believe she was acting superior with me on account of being older and having gone to war.

I said, 'I know about the ambulances you bought. I wanted to do the very same myself, but I hadn't come into my money and my uncle wouldn't permit it. I was needed at home, too. My Ma was a delicate widow. But I did roll bandages and avert a crisis with my French interpreting.'

'I'm glad to hear it,' she said. 'Well, the work goes on.'

She had a lecturing tone about her that reminded me of Yetta Landau.

I told her about Coquelicot, lest she think I didn't understand the meaning of work.

I said, 'And what line are you in now?'

She took me through her malodorous little house to a workroom, and there I saw a sight that made me jump out of my skin. Men's faces lined up on a shelf, ghostly gray. They were made out of plaster. Two women were at work. One was molding thin sheet copper to a plaster form, making a metal mask in its likeness. The other was painting a mask with oils, turning it the very color of a person's skin.

I said, 'Are these for *bals masqués*?'

'No,' she said. 'These are for life.'

Then she showed me photographs of the men they were being made for. Soldier boys who had lost their faces. No jaw. No nose. A mouth that gaped open right up to the ear. I believe she was trying to shock me. I believe she was testing what kind of stuff I was made of. To tell the truth, I was disappointed in Cousin Addie. She wasn't at all friendly. She hadn't even offered me a chair, or a glass of wine.

I said, 'Do you need a donation?'

'If you want to,' she said, 'but I wasn't soliciting funds. I'd be happier if I knew I'd given you something to think about. And pass the thought along to your salon. What happens to a man when you take away his face? It's an excellent subject for discussion.'

I didn't care for her tone or her suggestion that our friends didn't talk about the aftermath of war. They talked about it often. It was the reason Gil had decided to reject rationalism, as he announced to me only the day before.

'Where did rationalism lead?' he'd asked. 'I'll tell you. It led to the trenches. Therefore, I reject it.'

Of course, Cousin Addie didn't know Gil. Also, she was from Minnesota. And it didn't escape my notice, Beluga hadn't warmed to her either.

TWENTY-EIGHT

By the fall of 1923 I was flying my own two-seater pumpkin-orange Oriole out to Bois de Vincennes to see the trotting races. I could always depend on the company of Humpy Choate, and people at the racetrack would gather to watch me land my plane, eager to see my latest aviatrix ensemble.

Humpy was rather elegant, with the droll English way of speaking. He never shouted or got excited, except toward the end of a closely run race, and he always remembered to hold the door. Gil didn't care for Humpy. He declared him to be both a fairy and a seducer of wives, and I could never make him see the inconsistency of these accusations. He'd just fly into a rage whenever I tried. Rages were something that plagued Gil. Also a tendency to melancholia whenever he drank red wine. It should have been a simple matter of just not drinking the stuff, God knows there was choice enough of liquor, but oftentimes he was so wrapped up in planning a better world, he'd forget and then next day I'd be expected to endure his remaining in bed, silent and unsociable.

Apart from this, and Stassy's constant pestering me, life was pretty sweet.

'If you don't want to work anymore,' Stassy'd say, 'let me take it. I'll pay you. Some now, some later.'

And she'd start grubbing banknotes out of her pocketbook.

But I didn't see why I should. Coquelicot was *my* name. And I did still like coming up with originations and picking out the fabrics. I just didn't want to do it every day of my life.

Then, during October, I became aware of a certain familiar indisposition, feeling too tired and nauseated to go anywhere or do anything. I lay in bed one morning, considering whether to confide in Nancy Lord and ask her for the name of a hygienist, or sail home to New York and take care of things there.

I turned to look at Gil who was asleep beside me, recovering from the effects of red wine, and I don't know what happened, maybe he just looked so cute curled up there, dribbling a little from the corner of his mouth, anyhow, I got to thinking it might not be so bad to get a little baby. He'd look just like Gil, and he could go everywhere with me. I'd design him an adorable flying suit and teach him French words and we'd have such fun.

Ignoring my queasiness, I got up immediately, dressed and took a taxicab to Samaritaine. It was a fresh and wonderful day.

I asked my driver if he was a grand duke.

'Not very grand,' he laughed. Those Russians were always so cheerful about being dispossessed, I was inclined to think they couldn't ever have possessed very much in the first place.

I said, 'See the color of the sky? That's the shade of blue I'm looking for. I'm going to make my baby boy a silk flying suit.'

'Beautiful!' he said. 'What is his name?'

I said, 'Oh he isn't born yet. But I'll probably call him Abraham Gilbert, for his grandpa and his daddy.'

He turned and looked at me.

'Well, many years,' he said. 'God grant him many years.'

Beluga always found shopping quite prostrating, so I allowed him to ride all the way home in Abraham Gilbert's new bassinet. He sat there, surrounded by packages, causing passers-by to smile, and I began to appreciate how just the sight of a bassinet improves the mood of people. I was eager to show Gil the layettes and nightdresses and squirrel fur coverlets I had bought, but by the time we got home he had defeated the melancholia enough to go out and face another evening of revolutionizing. I laid out all my purchases on the bed, had the maid bring me my dinner on a tray and waited. I heard midnight. After that I guess I must have fallen asleep, and Beluga didn't stir himself either, being accustomed to the sound of Gil's footsteps.

The first I knew, the lights were blazing and Gil was yelling, 'What in tarnation is all this stuff? You branching out into the nursery business?'

I said, 'Yes, I am, sweetheart, and so are you. We're going to have a little baby and he'll be named Abraham Gilbert Catchings.'

'Not me,' he said. 'I don't want any baby, and neither do you if you have a lick of sense. You'll have to take this nonsense back to the store. Tell them you made a mistake.'

I loved Gil and I hated to discommode him, but something had taken hold of me that day. The grand duke taxi driver had thought a baby was a good idea and the shop girls at Samaritaine had thought it was the best possible idea.

Gil said, 'You been forgetting to douche?'

Sometimes there were too many things to remember.

I said, 'You just need time to get accustomed to the idea. My brother-in-law Harry was the same at the start.'

This was a lie. Harry had been more than happy for Honey to have a baby. He had picked out names and considerately dined at his club in the evenings instead of going home and making conversational demands of my sister. But I wanted to reassure Gil. I could see the taint of red wine on his teeth again, and I didn't want to provoke another fit of depression. His hand moved so fast I never saw it. It caught me under my jaw and sent me flying back into the display of matinée coats. Beluga growled a little.

'Get it fixed,' he said. His face was right up close to mine. 'It's the easiest thing in the world.'

I had already decided I wouldn't get it fixed and the excitement kept me awake long after I thought Gil had fallen asleep. Suddenly he spoke.

He said, 'How can you be sure it's a boy?'

I said, 'I just know.'

My jaw was still stinging. Sometimes, when a person drinks

red wine, they find it hard to stay in command of themselves.

I wrote to my sister informing her she would presently become an
aunt but I asked her not to tell Ma the news until I felt strong enough
to face an inquisition. Honey, of course, never could keep a secret.
Toward the end of November I received a letter from Ma.

'My dearest Poppy,' she wrote.

How odd that I should hear your important news at second hand.
I suppose Paris has made you forget your New York manners.

I hope this finds you in good health. How strange it feels
to know that my little Poppy is now a 'complete' woman.
I recommend you to leave off those elastic girdles of which
you young people are so fond, and to take extra milk,
eggs and butter in your meals, for a strong baby, and a
sugar sandwich every afternoon, for energy. The sooner you
return and enter the care of a good New York doctor the
less racked with worry I shall be. In the meanwhile be most
vigilant against hot baths, overflavored foods, and the raising
of your arms above your head, which is a well-known cause
of infant strangulation.

Your aunt sends her good wishes.

Please let us know the name of your boat and the date of its
arrival. Judah insists our help must be sent to your apartment
to air it and prepare it. I know you will remember to write
and thank him for his generosity, though how I am expected
to spare both girls for the hours and hours it will surely take
I can't imagine. It would be altogether more satisfactory if the
lease was terminated. Harry can see to it. You have a home
here with us until you can find a more suitable address for
the raising of my grandchild.

By the way, I have advised Judah against sharing the news

with your stepbrother. At seventeen it is better for a boy not to have his attention drawn to such things and Murray is, in any event, quite put out by the duration of your honeymoon.

Your ever-loving Ma

PS: Will your husband sail with you? Perhaps you should keep on that place after all. Bachelor quarters are always useful while a woman needs her rest. Please advise.

It had never crossed my mind that I would return to New York. Babies were born every day in Paris and I saw no reason mine shouldn't be one of them. I was in the habit of calling him my baby. Gil had gradually acquiesced to the idea of having a child and had even kept his promise that in future he would take only white drinks. He had resumed calling me 'Princess' and then, as my condition became more visible, 'Lady-in-waiting'. He worked hard preparing to write his novel and going to happenings and debating with Romanians at the Café Dingo.

Letters plowed slowly back and forth across the Atlantic Ocean. I declined to return to New York for my confinement. Ma regretted that motherhood had done nothing to improve either my sense of correctness or duty. I announced that I had secured the services of a good French nurse. Ma wondered how early in the long hours of agonizing travail I should regret throwing myself on the mercy of an ignorant foreigner. I offered to visit with Abraham Gilbert as soon I felt strong enough for the voyage. Ma questioned whether she would live long enough to see the day.

It was Honey who broke the deadlock.

'I am coming to be at your side,' she wrote. 'Sherman Ulysses has to go to the Tilton School in Connecticut, to be gotten ready for a good college, which will leave Aunt Fish and me far too much in each other's company. I believe the time has now come for her to return to her own house, and your greater need of me in Paris will surely make her recognize this.'

But Honey's decision only made Aunt Fish recognize that she

was, to quote her, a burdensome old widow whom no one should be expected to care for.

'STAND FIRM,' I wired Honey. 'COME SOONEST.'

I should have adored to fly my sister from Cherbourg to Paris, but by the time she arrived, in May, I could no longer fit into the cockpit of the Oriole. I took the train to meet her and was glad I'd done so when I saw how Honey's own girth had expanded in the three years since I left. And then there was her luggage to consider. As well as ten boxes of gowns and hats she had brought with her a trunk of her favorite violet creams, an oil painting of Sherman Ulysses and a traveling water closet.

'Poppy!' she cried when she saw me. 'I have decided to enjoy travel. Sailing the ocean wasn't half as frightening as I expected, and I met the most fascinating person, a doctor who has the very remedy for my slow digestion. An elixir of cayenne, to burn away unwanted tissues. I purchased a supply for each of us. I remember how sluggish the system can be after a confinement.'

I had obtained a suite for her at the Lutèce, but she was inclined to go to the Prince de Galles instead because that was where the digestion doctor had said he would be staying.

'In case I mislay the regime he wrote out for me. I think it would be better. Don't you think it would be better?'

Everything was unloaded from the taxicab before we ascertained that no Dr Laslo was registered at the Prince de Galles, nor even expected.

Honey insisted that there must be another hotel of the same name and that I clearly didn't know Paris as well as I claimed. So we had our first fight and I left her on the sidewalk outside the Lutèce. The time had come for my family to learn I would no longer be derided and discounted and pulled from pillar to post, and my sister was in the advance party.

She settled into the Lutèce well enough once she had had her picture of Sherman Ulysses hung, but she continued to make inquiries after her doctor, calling the Prince de Galles at least once a day, especially after the cayenne mixture disagreed with her. She never did track him down.

I said, 'Well anyhow, you do appear to be reducing.'

'I am,' she said. 'I'm reducing away to a shadow, but that's because I've been unable to move away from my . . . comfort closet . . . long enough to enjoy the smallest bite of anything.'

After two weeks she moved into rue Vavin, to be with me in my hour of need. Honey found our house very pretty, with its gray shutters and muslin drapes, but she was shocked by our modern ways. We had no fixed hours, nor any idea who might turn up. Badgirl Duprée looking for a loan. Felix Swain looking for a game of cards. Some hungry intellectual with nowhere to sleep. Then, sometimes Gil would be gone all night.

'Is it showgirls?' Honey asked.

I believe she would have been pleased to hear that it was.

I said, 'Gil does his best thinking at night. He's going to write a novel you know?'

'Oh dear,' she said.

The evening my pains began, we were At Home to some of the Café Dingo crowd. I had been restless all day, taking Beluga for two long walks in the Luxembourg Gardens, and then sipping nothing but consommé for dinner. Honey watched me like a hawk. I only dared to rub my back a little because she seemed absorbed in the laying out of baby clothes, but she noticed anyway, out of the corner of her eye.

'Aha!' she said. And she was so delighted at the thought of being able to shoo away all those philosophers and Romanians she almost ran downstairs.

Our outdoors man was sent to fetch the nurse while Honey tried to bathe my brow and persuade me into bed. I refused both. I was in torment, and the only thing I could think to do was walk up and down rapidly until it was all over. Having evicted the intellectuals, Honey's next campaign was against Beluga, but no matter how many times she dragged him from under the bed, he found his way back.

'We'll see what the nurse has to say about this,' she said.

I found time between birth pangs to tell her the nurse wasn't getting paid to express opinions about dogs.

Hostilities between us didn't really cease until the nurse arrived and provided us with a new mutual enemy. The nurse demanded coffee and complained about the height of the bed and cleared my hairbrushes and scent bottles off the vanity in a most careless manner. I feared for Beluga if he should be discovered.

I wanted the outdoors man dispatched to find Gil, who had misunderstood the situation and run away with his friends when Honey ended the party so abruptly, but Honey said it would be better if he just stayed away and did some of his best thinking.

'This isn't a time for husbands,' she said. 'This is a time when a girl wants her mother. And as Ma couldn't be here . . .'

If I could have loved anyone in that hour of grinding, gnawing agony, it would have been my sister, for sparing me the bedside attentions of my mother and probably my aunt, too.

'Will Abraham Gilbert be having a little . . . procedure?' she asked.

It had never occurred to me.

'I don't think so,' I said. 'How Jewish are we being these days?'

But before I could hear her answer, I was swept away on another searing wave. I believed I was about to die.

At six o'clock in the morning I was delivered of a baby girl. She was the color of a skinned rabbit and not much bigger. I never did work out how such a small tenant could have made me balloon out so wide.

At seven o'clock Gil came home. The child was wrapped up and taken out for him to see, and when he put his head around the door to show me he was pleased enough with the outcome, his teeth bore the tell-tale stain of red wine.

'It's a girl,' I told him.

'I know,' he said. 'Suits me.'

'Therefore,' I said, 'she can't be named Abraham Gilbert.'

'She can be named any damn name we choose,' he said. 'I'll give it some thought. Have to get some sleep now though, Princess. It's been a long night.'

Later that day I received two dozen pink roses from Humpy Choate.

We did not name her Abraham Gilbert. The nurse informed us she would have to have the name of a good holy saint or burn in hell forever more, Gil wished to choose a name by the revolutionary method of sticking a pin into the page of a book, and I really couldn't have cared. She was a peevish, florid creature with a tiny tight mouth that alternately mewed for milk and then rejected it.

At the end of the first week she was still nameless and I was so sick with milk fever that Honey quite took over the whole business of the nursery.

'She is so delicious,' Honey crooned. I believe she was trying to prompt me into agreeing. 'So delicious. What a darling baby girl. How blest you are, Poppy.'

Finally she was named Marie Nuages Sapphire. Marie after one of the top saints, Nuages after the word Gil hit upon with his pin, and Sapphire after my favorite type of gem.

Before long she was only ever referred to as Sapphire, and news of her arrival brought about a miraculous recovery in Aunt Fish's spirits. Dolls were purchased, and embroidered Swiss night gowns. Ma confessed herself moved to tears. Judah Jacoby went to the temple and prayed the *mi sheberah* for her. And my stepbrother Murray was inspired to write one of his haiku verses.

> Dear Sapphire, they say
> Your little face is awfully
> Red. But don't be blue.

Come August, when Honey sailed back to New York, it seemed only right and fitting that Sapphire should go with her. My sister had been with her night and day, enduring her discontented bleating, fathoming her strange ways. And she had always longed for a daughter.

I said to Gil, 'It seems cruel to separate her from the child now.'

'Whatever you think, Princess,' he said.

TWENTY-NINE

As soon as I felt refreshed enough to renew my interest in Coquelicot, I designed a set of garments for infants, and I named it my Sapphire collection. Stassy, needless to say, was most put out. She had been ruling the roost during my indisposition, filling the spaces vacated by my designs with her own new line in knitted skirts. She was developing ambitions above her station and beyond her pocket.

'Why are you here?' she said. 'You have your baby. Let this be my baby.'

I said, 'No, this is *my* baby, too. It was my idea. And I can afford as many different babies as I like.'

'Then we have to have new rules,' she said. 'We have to have a contract.'

I corrected her. I reminded her how I had found her living in penury and could easily send her back there.

'May God forgive you,' she said.

The cheek of it! I'm sure I had no need of forgiveness and even if I did, I certainly wouldn't go to some Russian unfortunate's God for it.

'I'll pray for you, Poppy,' she said.

I said, 'Don't you dare. I make my own arrangements.'

She gathered up an armful of her neckties and skirts and banged the door so hard as she left the glass cracked. The shop girl burst into tears and ran after her. I didn't care. I sold a tiny apricot batiste dress and a white seersucker playsuit with bloomers, just that first day, and I enjoyed myself. It was like being back at Macy's without any impertinent floorwalkers interfering with my comings and goings.

The only thing was, being around all those darling little costumes that bore her name made me have a few melancholy thoughts about my own Sapphire. Honey wrote me every week how she was thriving and getting quite doted upon by Ma and Aunt Fish, and I knew in New York she was growing up surrounded by the finest of everything, but I wondered whether she would even know who I was.

I said to Gil, 'Do you suppose we made a mistake? What if Honey gets too attached to her?'

'She's our kid,' he said. 'We can take her back any time we like.'

I said, 'Maybe she could be here some of the time and there some of the time. Maybe I should tell Honey to bring her back for a while.'

'Well,' he said, 'right now wouldn't be the best of times. I'm going to require peace and quiet, you understand?'

Gil was on the very point of writing his novel, having suffered a setback when he lost his notebook containing months of work. He had placed it on a shelf at the Dingo while he took an aperitif and when he went to retrieve it, it was gone, stolen no doubt by some envious scribbler.

It seemed like everyone we knew was busy with an origination of some kind. Sudka and Blin had gotten up a new movement to create a better world. They had written a manifesto and even invented a language that everyone would be able to understand, and if they had not been so plagued by schisms and defections I believe their names might be more widely remembered today.

Hannelore Ettl was creating collages out of macaroni. Oca was doing experimentations with pianola rolls. Frotti and Schiuma were staging *événements* at which the audience was required to provide its own entertainment. In those days we hardly knew a single person who wasn't droll or just downright outré.

I asked Gil how soon his book would be written and what it

would be called. He said it was to be titled *Nothing* and would have a black cover and a blank title-page, but as to how long it would take to complete, it was impossible to say. I believe his downfall may have been his perfectionism. Other people may be able to dash off a masterwork, but Gil required a great deal of time to arrange his work table and tap his fount of inspiration.

Our falling out came about after he had spent an afternoon pacing the floor and chewing on his pencil and I wondered out loud whether he was quite cut out for the writing life. He said the greatest genius on God's earth couldn't be expected to work if he was constantly interrupted by the sound of people breathing and dogs moving about and scratching themselves.

I observed that we only had one small bulldog, who hardly ever scratched, and the only person breathing was me, Wednesday being the help's day off.

I said, 'Why don't you give it up? You don't have to write a book. Gracious Gil, I wouldn't be surprised if books aren't about to become passé. Why not invent something else and be in the vanguard? Or just do nothing, like Humpy. I have enough money for the both of us.'

'Sure,' he said. 'You and your money. I'm sick of it. How can I create when I'm shackled to a fortune?'

He had that mean, hard look in his eyes I had seen before. I loved him though, and I truly wanted to make him happy.

I said, 'Can't you pretend to be poor?'

He said, 'See? You just have no idea. An artist has to suffer.'

I said, 'But you do seem to be suffering. Isn't being rich the right kind of suffering?'

He took a step toward me with his hand raised and my darling Beluga bared his teeth. Gil stopped in his tracks.

'I've a mind to kill you both,' he said. 'I hate you enough.'

I scooped up Beluga under my arm and ran. Humpy wasn't home, but his *bonne* allowed me to wait until he returned. As soon as he walked in I burst into tears.

'He raised his hand to me,' I said. 'He intended striking me.'

'The cad,' Humpy said. 'That's really very bad form.'

I said, 'He's so disagreeable these days. Maybe I should leave him alone until this book is written. It seems to be a very tricky business.'

'Jolly tricky, I imagine,' Humpy agreed. 'Shall we have a little something?'

We drank vermouth on the rocks.

I said, 'I suppose I could go to New York and see our baby.'

'I suppose you could,' he said. 'Or you could fly me down to Cap Ferrat. That might be fun.'

And that's what we did. Humpy gave up his bed so that I should have a good night's sleep and next morning, before Gil had time to regret his harshness and come looking for me, Humpy and I, with Beluga between us in his Hermès collar and his special little motoring goggles, flew south, to where someone called Flicky Manners was having a house party.

Flicky was a most amusing English person who didn't at all stand on ceremony or get anxious about the kind of things that always perplexed Ma, such as whether to risk an aspic dish in hot weather, or what to do if the conversation inadvertently turned to politics. I question whether Flicky ever knew exactly who was staying in her house at any given time. It was she who introduced me to the idea of allowing the sun to bronze my skin and of going without stockings. It was she who introduced me to Reggie.

THIRTY

Reggie Merrick was a darling English boy from a top drawer family and he put me in mind of Gil, with his fair hair worn a little long, and his blue eyes. But he had none of Gil's changefulness or spleen. He was happy to play tennis for as long as he had someone to play with and then he was just as happy to swim, or play tug-of-war with Beluga.

At Flicky's there was always something going on. People arriving. People motoring over to Monte Carlo. Every afternoon the help brought out bicycling machines to the terrace and an exercise tea was held, for those who were keen to slenderize. And often there were parties and masquerades. One evening we were instructed to attend dressed as paupers, and jellied eels were served. Reggie and Humpy wore enormous flat caps and sang a comic song called 'Ilkley Moor', which those who understood the language of English unfortunates found most amusing. That summer was full of laughter.

I wrote to Gil and expressed the hope that he was profiting from his solitude. I never alluded to our angry parting. I guessed that when the season ended and I returned to Paris, it would be as though nothing bad had ever passed between us. But in the meanwhile I was finding life most congenial. My skin had turned a deliciously nutty shade of brown which looked very well against my white-silk day pajamas. I loved the hot, flowery smell of the hills behind Flicky's house. I loved the way the English talked without moving their lips.

Humpy and Reggie were practically cousins, Reggie's Ma being a Choate of some kind, and they knew each other from school, too. They were the greatest of friends, except for a few days after Humpy fell in love with a boy who delivered melons for the kitchen and gave him a quite lavish pearl stickpin as a token of his ardor. Reggie hated waste.

Most often the three of us would lark around all day, but once in a while Flicky would commandeer Humpy to go with her into Nice to meet new arrivals, and then Reggie and I would keep each other company. He trained Beluga to sit with a caramel balanced on his nose until given the command to eat it. He taught me a domino game called Muggins, and I taught him the charleston.

Then, one August night, we tiptoed away from a very boisterous game of Up Jenkins and climbed down to the sea for a dip. He took my hand, to steady me for the final jump down onto the shore, and as I landed I kissed him, on the mouth.

'I say, old thing,' he whispered. And then we romped and I discovered a completely different, slippery, wriggly kind of thrill than I had ever known with Gil.

By the time Humpy and I returned to Paris, in September of 1925, I was deeply troubled. I was in love with Reggie Merrick, but he was going back to his English life, far too much the gentleman to steal another man's wife.

'Better to keep a straight bat, old thing,' he said.

I knew he adored me and I longed to go with him to Melton Mowbray, England, to start a new life.

I said, 'You know we belong together. And Gil won't stand in our way. I'm sure he's happier without me anyway.'

'No,' he said, 'it would be terribly bad form. I'm sure your husband has missed you most dreadfully. Chin up, old sausage. After all, didn't we have the greatest fun?'

My philosophy has always been that when you're having fun you should continue to have fun. But Reggie's outlook was different. He seemed to think that fun and happiness came in small portions and had to be paid for. We had had our month of ecstasy and now he was going to pay for his by putting on a tweed suit and looking into farming. My penalty was to return to Gil. I thought my heart would break. And what I didn't dare tell Reggie was, I had reasons to suspect our romping had created consequences.

I was silent throughout our flight to Paris and Humpy chose to disguise my silence with a particularly irritating hum. Finally, as we drove in from the airdrome, he said, 'You're awfully pensive today, Poppy. Feeling anxious about the homecoming? Probably nothing to worry about. Probably all blown over by now. Definitely, I should say.'

I said, 'But I don't want to come home. I want to go to England and marry Reggie. I'm having his baby, you see.'

It was Humpy's turn for silence.

Eventually he said, 'Gracious. How on earth did that happen?'

We were bowling down through Ménilmontant, getting closer by the second to the life I was expected to resume with Gil.

I said, 'You won't tell Reggie, will you?'

'Not a word, cross my heart,' he said, obtusely missing my point.

I said, 'Because I'm just going to have to brave this out all alone. Whatever happens I should hate any sense of duty to drag Reggie into this mess.'

'Quite right,' he said, agreeing with unnecessary conviction.

I parked the motor outside Humpy's place.

'Well, that was fun,' he said. 'Good old Flicky.' He seemed to have quite forgotten the tragedy of my situation.

I said, 'Of course, there are ways and means. Reggie's child may never see the light of day. Maybe Reggie will never have a child and never know he might have had one.'

'Oh, I don't think the outlook is quite as bleak as that,' he said. 'I believe one of the Burton girls is pretty keen on him. They'll probably get hitched some day and keep the line going.'

The house was empty. Gil was out. The maid had left because her wage hadn't been paid. Beluga padded around remembering old smells, reclaiming his territory, while I lay on my bed and cried, for Reggie, and for my own unfortunate position.

Humpy proved to be correct about Gil. When he came home and found me returned, there were no recriminations, nor even any probing questions. He assumed I'd been enjoying innocent pleasures, and was in an amiable enough mood himself. He had profited from my absence, discovering in solitude that he didn't wish to write a book after all. Instead he was collaborating with Hannelore Ettl on a series of paradoxical *objets*, such as a smoothing iron made from down-filled silk. Their next project was to be a set of fire irons sculpted from ice.

We rubbed along amicably and Gil was too absorbed in his own new enthusiasms to notice that my thoughts were elsewhere. I opened up Coquelicot, but couldn't stand the sight of the infant garments. I played tennis with Humpy but I was sluggish. I had lost the desire to win and the sight of him, composing himself for his second service, brought me painful reminders of Reggie.

Six weeks after my homecoming I broached to Gil the possibility I was having another baby.

'Well, Princess,' he said, with an evenness I couldn't read, 'I guess we both know what has to be done.'

I agreed with him and in spite of the oncoming winter I booked the next stateroom I could get on a sailing to New York. I omitted to tell Gil what *I* meant by 'doing what had to be done'.

I closed Coquelicot, had my hair tinted a stunning shade of red and had a final lunch with Nancy Lord.

I said, 'Gil beats me, you know?'

'Does he?' she said. 'What a bore. Why don't you have an affair? I've found that very uplifting.'

I said, 'Why? Does Orville beat you?'

'Good God, no!' she said. 'But I still find affairs uplifting. How about Martinez? He's available.'

How she disgusted me, offering me her discards.

'Or Ava Hornblower?' she said. 'I believe she's on the loose again. Did you ever try anything like that, Poppy? It might be fun.'

'I'm going to New York,' I told her. 'To see our little girl. So if you could keep an eye on Gil . . .'

'I see,' she said. 'Oh, I *see*! Well . . . God, darling! Should I borrow Chip Angus' boxing gloves?'

That wasn't at all what I had meant.

I lay wide awake beside him that last night, while he slept peacefully. He had no idea. He thought I was just getting out of his hair for a month or two, going away to fix my little problem. And I hadn't resolved how he was going to find out. Whether I was going tell him, straight out, or leave him to come to a gradual realization. I couldn't even decide how cut up he was going to be. There was never any telling with Gil.

THIRTY-ONE

Beluga and I were so sick during the crossing I prayed we might sink. Unable to lift my head from the pillow, I imagined Pa waiting for me down at the bottom of the ocean, smiling, arms open. If we sank, my troubles would be over. But eventually we came safely into port and I was so gaunt from *mal de mer* neither Ma nor Aunt Fish noticed my true condition.

I received the warmest welcome of my life. As well as my mother and aunt, I spied Honey waiting for me, with a handsome young man at her side, tall and dark. It was my stepbrother Murray, and in his arms he was carrying a small girl with a quantity of wiry hair. My baby Sapphire.

Ma wept and crushed me to her bosom for the longest time, and I believe I saw Aunt Fish wipe away a tear as well. Sapphire was too shy to look me in the eye. 'Say how-de-do to Mommy Poppy,' Honey coaxed her, but she buried her face in Murray's collar, and he kept his own eyes downcast, too. Pleased as he must have been at my return, he felt obliged to punish me a little first, for staying away so long. Also, he was now eighteen years old. I dare say he couldn't decide whether to resume being an annoying stepbrother or to play the young swell.

I said, 'I'm so exhausted. I'll go directly to the Ansonia.'

'Now Poppy,' Ma said. 'You cannot possibly expect to raise a child in *that* building . . .'

'And anyway,' Honey interrupted, 'you must stay with us, to give Sapphire time to get accustomed to you. And we thought you should go to 69th Street for tonight. You and Ma'll have so much jawing to do.'

'No,' I said. I intended making a firm start with them.

'Poppy,' Murray said, 'you don't have the Ansonia anymore. It's been vacated.'

I saw something pass between my mother and my sister. The briefest look. They had been scheming no doubt, since the moment they heard I was sailing back into their clutches.

'So,' I said. 'The interfering has started again.'

Murray gave me quite a shocking glare.

'Why don't we discuss this later,' he said. 'Because you must surely be raring to spend some time with Sapphire.'

He drove Ma and Aunt Fish back to the Jacoby house with my luggage, leaving Honey's driver to follow on with me and my sister and my daughter, who had been prised free of Murray only to clamp herself just as fast around Honey's neck. She seemed to be an oversensitive child. It occurred to me too much pandering had been going on.

I said, 'Who closed up my apartment?'

Honey said, 'Gracious, Poppy, you only just stepped off the boat and already you're picking fights.'

I said, 'How dare some person get rid of my home.'

'Well, first of all,' she said, 'it was hardly a home. It was more of a perch, and a pretty slovenly perch at that. Secondly, you have given the very clear impression nothing would persuade you ever to live in New York again.'

Sapphire had ventured to peep at me with one pale blue Catchings eye.

'Thirdly,' Honey went on, with unusual energy, 'if you have finally decided to reclaim this innocent lambkin and be a mother to her, you must realize that the Ansonia is an unsuitable place to do it.'

I didn't care for her use of the words 'reclaim' or 'lambkin'. Still, I had no idea what I'd do with the child, now I'd seen her.

I said, 'I don't intend rushing in and dragging her from your arms. I want what's best for Sapphire, you understand?'

'I would hope so,' she said.

I said, 'I see how fond of her you've grown. And, of course, I'll have a mountain of affairs to attend to. Including, it now appears, finding us a new home. I don't see any need to uproot her immediately. Do you?'

Honey's face softened somewhat.

'I'm glad to see you're being sensible,' she said. 'Now, you sly puss, why didn't you write and tell me you're expecting another happy event?'

I asked her how she knew, but she couldn't explain. She said it was a knack she had.

'Is Gil following on?' she asked.

I said, 'Well, that's the thing. There are a few complications.'

'Is it showgirls?' she said.

Marie Nuages Sapphire was now daring to examine me closely, staring and staring at me, with no sign of a loving smile.

I said, 'I guess this isn't the time to go into it. Does she still drink from a feeding bottle?'

'Heavens, no,' she said. 'She sits up nice and dainty and drinks from a cup. She's such a darling child. She never kicks or bites or does any of those things Shermy used to do. Hope for another girl, Pops. Hope for another little angel.'

Several weeks passed before I felt able to tell Honey I hoped I was carrying a boy. An heir for the Merricks of Melton Mowbray, England, who so far had no sign of one.

She held her head in both hands, as though it was about to fall off.

'I knew,' she said eventually, 'no good would come of Paris.'

'It wasn't Paris,' I told her, determined not to be dampened. 'It was St-Jean-Cap-Ferrat.'

'You realize,' she said, 'this will kill Ma. And the rest of us will be dragged through the gutter. Adultery. Divorce. A child born out of wedlock. I question your fitness, Poppy. I question your moral fitness ever to have charge of Sapphire. I abdicate all responsibility for persuading her to warm to you or call you Mommy. Harry will have to deal with you. Harry and Judah will have to decide what's to be done.'

I was twenty-eight years old and being spoken to like a naughty child, threatened with the censure of a pair of milquetoasts who weren't even my flesh and blood.

'I'll decide,' I warned her. 'It seems to me this family should make up its mind. It did all it could to prevent my marrying Gil, so it would be very contrary of it to oppose my divorcing him. And Ma may survive the blow better than you think, when she hears she's to have a grandson who'll be related to the King of England.'

I overstated the case slightly, the royal connection being to Queen Mary through Reggie's mother's stepfather, but I knew it would be enough. Ma was never rigorous with details. As for ruining the family, Harry seemed to be taking the lead in that himself. When I asked after Honey's rose-colored pearls that always looked so well on her when she wore dark blue she told me Harry had needed them.

I said, 'You mean he sold them?'

'No,' she said. 'It's for something called deficit financing. I'm sure I'll get them back soon.'

With the cat out of the bag I no longer had any reason to wait. I took a suite at the Whitell, consulted the firm of Klein, Klein and Hubert about obtaining a divorce and mailed letters to Gil and to Reggie. Then I called Bernie Kearney and begged her to meet me for lunch.

'Jeez, Minkel,' she screamed when she saw me, 'look at you! You've gone and turned all Pareesian.'

I'm sure my style and chic had nothing to do with Paris and everything to do with my own sure touch, but I received this as the compliment Bernie intended it to be. She didn't condemn me for leaving my husband either, nor for romping with another.

'Gil was cute,' she said, 'but there was always that other side to him.'

I said, 'What other side?'

'Oh, you know,' she said. 'The changeable side.'

How full of wisdom friends are after the event.

'Tell me about your new sweetheart,' she said, and she listened, enthralled.

'But what are you doing here?' she said. 'Sounds like Reggie is sitting there in his castle just pining for you.'

I said, 'Well, first I have to go to Nevada to get my divorce. Then I have to find myself a good doctor to deliver me of this child. Also I have Sapphire to attend to.'

Bernie didn't know about Sapphire. This appeared to scandalize her more than anything else I'd told her.

She said, 'You mean you gave her away?'

I said, 'Hardly. Honey is my sister, and it's only a temporary arrangement.'

'Even so,' she said. 'How could you be parted from her? Does she know you? Does she call you Mammy?'

She didn't, of course. She was aged one and a half years, and my reappearance in her life had hardly registered. Attempts had been made to train her to call my sister Mommy Honey and me Mommy Poppy, but the best she could manage in her lisping infant way was 'Mop'. I settled for that.

Bernie had grown more sedate. She was wearing her hair in a chignon, with Spanish combs, and she had a cabochon amethyst on her third finger. Her new beau was a banker called Wendell Tite, and they were engaged to be married.

'I'll soon be catching up to you,' she said. 'I'll soon have a whole nursery full of little Tites. Of course, mine won't be royal. Isn't it a caution, how Gil always called you Princess, and now you're practically going to be one?'

It was so good to see her. In Paris I'd missed having a friend. Stassy had been too foreign, and Nancy couldn't be depended on. Humpy was all right, but there were certain things one could never discuss with a boy. Not even if he was a fairy.

THIRTY-TWO

As I had predicted, I was able to divert much of Ma's distress over my modern condition, with the prospect that she would soon be connected by marriage to Queen Mary of England. I obtained a newspaper photograph of the Queen and King George visiting English unfortunates in their hovels, and Ma studied it assiduously.

'Tell me again, Poppy,' she'd say. 'How many times removed is Mr Merrick?'

The challenge of raining on my parade revived Aunt Fish's spirits.

'I question whether Queen Mary is in possession of the facts,' she said. 'Consider, Dora. Can a person who is between husbands, and between them in a regrettable condition, can such a person be a fitting ornament to a royal family? Are there no English roses available? I'm sure there are. And another point is this, why hasn't Mr Merrick a noble title? I'd be circumspect, Dora, about raising people's expectations. How foolish you're going to appear when Poppy doesn't become a Highness.'

'Don't throw up so many puzzles, Zillah,' Ma said. 'I had just begun to understand it all, and now you've confused me.'

I said, 'Reggie doesn't have to marry an English rose. Why Queen Mary herself is German.'

This silenced both of them. Ma examined the photograph again and Aunt Fish considered her position. Then Honey arrived with my child. I was meant to be spending an hour with her each morning, to be increased to two hours when she had taken to me enough to stop howling the instant she saw my face.

'An important development,' Ma cried, as soon as Honey entered the room. 'Queen Mary is German, so I'm sure she'll be very happy to have Poppy.'

'I believe,' Honey said, 'Sapphire may be getting a head cold.'

Honey hated to talk about the new life that awaited me in England.

I said, 'Ma, is that a German card you're suddenly playing? I thought we had removed all those from the pack. Don't I recall your changing our name to Minton?'

'I did it for the best,' she said. 'I did everything for the best. Have you mentioned . . . Germanness . . . to Mr Merrick?'

'Another point,' Aunt Fish resumed, 'is how this will place Sapphire. Can the child of a person from Pennsylvania possibly be *accommodated* by nobility?'

'Of course she can,' Ma said. 'All that has to be done is to remove that person from the record. Harry will know how. Harry will see to it.'

Harry seemed to have gathered around him an army of people he referred to as his 'difficulty adjusters'. It was hard to conceive of that half-wit having any kind of power, but it still caused me a momentary chill to hear talk of removing Gil from the record, and from Ma's innocent lips, too.

I said, 'Well, I never mentioned Germanness, because I never think of myself as having any, and Reggie knows about Gil and Sapphire. Our love is going to conquer all. And my being a Hebrew doesn't bother him either.'

Honey said, 'You told him a thing like that?'

'It just came up,' I said. 'Our friend Humpy Choate mentioned it. He knows pretty much everything there is to know about me. And anyway, as Humpy said, lots of English have mixed blood. Over there you see inexplicable features in the very best families.'

'There!' Ma said. 'So everything is quite in order. Harry will see about the Catchings man, and as soon as ever possible Poppy will sail for England and marry Mr Merrick. Then I shall face the perils of the ocean myself to be there when Queen Mary asks to meet Poppy's people. And you must come with me, Zillah, because I doubt that Judah can be spared from business to make such a long trip.'

'And in the meanwhile,' my aunt concluded, 'it would be better if Poppy went away to Nevada, until her time comes, lest gossip undo all our good work.'

I was excused my hour with Sapphire as she was feverish and Honey and Ma were united in wishing to avoid any harm to my unborn child, a scion of the blood royal. Instead I borrowed Ma's driver and took my stepbrother Murray to Delancey Street for a blintz.

'If you don't mind being seen with an ungainly and fallen woman,' I said.

'No,' he said. 'I'll think of it as an act of charity.'

Judah Jacoby had very strong ideas about good works and insisted that his boys followed his lead. He gave away one-tenth of everything he made.

'One-tenth!' I remembered my aunt flinching. 'And you may be sure the people he gives it to have no idea of its value.'

'But it doesn't end there,' Ma had whispered. 'He says one-tenth is his duty. He says giving only counts when it goes beyond duty.'

'I think he has been misinformed,' Aunt Fish had said. 'If people were obliged to give away their money like that, Israel would have known about it. This is probably an idea got up by Yetta. I sense her hand in this. But you must put a stop to it, Dora. You are the mistress of this house now.'

But Ma had put a stop to nothing. Judah gave and gave, and he preferred to do it secretly.

'Now Dorabel,' he said, when she objected to his hospital donations. 'Are you going barefoot? Are we starving?'

'Then they might at least name a wing for us,' she complained.

'No,' he said, 'a secret gift is doubly blessed.'

His ideas had implications for Oscar and Murray, too. They didn't have fortunes, nor even proper allowances. They were supposed to support themselves, unless ill health prevented it, and give what little they had to worthy projects.

I said, 'So, Murray Jacoby, what's to become of you?'

'What's to become of *me*?' he laughed. 'That's pretty rich. Well, I'm meant to be enrolling at the School of Commerce, Accounts and Finance, but actually I'd rather be a gardener.'

I said, 'And how do you go about that?'

'Don't know,' he said. 'I suppose one runs away to the country. Oscar and Auntsie have a garden.'

I thought it sounded rather boring. When I wanted flowers I just called up Fleischmann's and they delivered.

I said, 'And do you have a sweetheart yet?'

'No,' he said, flushing and immediately changing the subject.

'Let's talk about Sapphire,' he said. 'And Gil. What's to become of them? I feel pretty sorry for them in all this.'

I said, 'Gil has his new friends in Paris and his paradoxical art. And Sapphire has Honey and Ma and everyone else treasuring her. I'm sure she has no reason to be pitied. I think perhaps you *do* have a sweetheart.'

'Sapphire doesn't understand who you are,' he said. 'It's all too complicated for her. She needs to be at home with you, not just seeing you now and then. I think you must make more of an effort, Poppy.'

'Well,' I said, 'I thought we were here to enjoy a blintz and be friends, but I see you've been sent to lecture me. Did my Ma put you up to this?'

'No,' he said. He had really turned out rather well. More filled out than Oscar, more open-faced. If he didn't already have a sweetheart it wouldn't be long before he did.

'Are you really going to take her to England?' he asked.

'I expect so,' I said. 'That's where Reggie's home is, you see? In the city of Melton Mowbray. Do you still write those little verses?'

'When the spirit moves me,' he said. He looked glum.

I said, 'Don't be so downhearted. You'll be able to visit us, you know?'

'Yes,' he said. 'When I'm not being an accountant. What will you call your new baby?'

'Abraham Reginald Murray,' I said, and at long last brought a smile to his face.

We dropped him just by Washington Square where he was supposed to be making inquiries about enrolling in New York University. Then I had the driver take me to a cablegram office.

'STILL NO NEWS REGGIE,' I wired Humpy. 'ADVISE SOONEST.'

THIRTY-THREE

Reggie's daughter was born on February 18, 1926. After ten hours of torment composed of childbirth pangs and the alternating attendance of my mother, my sister and my aunt, I gave in and was admitted to Mount Sinai Hospital.

'God knows you may as well,' Ma said. 'Judah has poured enough money into the place.'

I had heard nothing from Gil, nor from Reggie, a point Aunt Fish never failed to bring up at least once a day. I had tried to seed the idea that this was due to his natural English reserve. This succeeded with Ma, but fell on stony ground with my aunt.

'I begin to wonder,' Aunt Fish said, in a whisper that could have been heard the other side of Madison Avenue, 'whether Mr Merrick isn't one of Poppy's imaginings.'

For once Ma defended me. She was relishing the thought of my illustrious future and spent a good deal of time considering what names would be suitable for a minor princess.

'Protocol prevents him from being here, Zillah,' she said, 'until Poppy has been to Nevada and Harry has dealt with . . . that other business. *Then* Mr Merrick will come. Do you know, I believe Dora would do very well. Princess Dora.'

But with every day that passed and still nothing from Reggie, I felt something in me withering away. Humpy's letters arrived regularly, but they were no help.

'Has Reggie received my news?' I wrote. 'Perhaps my letter went astray. Have you mentioned it to him?'

'Not as such,' Humpy replied.

'Well, please do mention it to him,' I sent back immediately, 'in the clearest possible terms.'

'Poppy, I hope you're not going to create an unpleasant flap,' came Humpy's reply three weeks later. 'The thing is, Reggie has been in Africa, deciding whether to go into tobacco. I dare say he'll have come home to a mountain of correspondence.'

I named the child Emerald Merrick Minkel and resigned myself to a life of misery. To the tedium of motherhood, and the shame of being abandoned, and Aunt Fish's insufferable triumph. Then, the day before I was due to leave for Reno, Nevada, to end my marriage to Gil Catchings, I received a cablegram.

'Gosh,' it said. 'Meet You Southampton. Never Fear.'

How different the world can look, from one moment to the next. Those six words filled me with energy. I immediately began a design for my disembarkation outfit.

Honey was crestfallen at my news.

'You can't think of sailing so soon,' she said, 'with a tiny baby, and Sapphire not even accustomed to you yet. And what if Mr Merrick has decided to go into tobacco? Africa is quite unsuitable for women and children.'

'You're right,' I said. 'I had wondered how to broach this, but now you've spared my blushes. I think Emerald and Sapphire might do better waiting here till I can send for them. I hate to put upon you again, Honey . . .'

'Not at all,' she said. 'It's the least I can offer, and besides, you know, I've grown so attached to the both of them. If it should turn out that Africa is on the cards, you can depend on me to keep them safe till your return. What an adventurer you are, Poppy!'

I could almost have believed my sister was in a hurry to see me go.

My final week in New York was a whirlwind of shopping and visiting and closing up my trunks. Only one or two small black clouds invaded my patch of blue sky.

First, Bernie declined to lunch with me.

'I can't believe you're leaving two darling waifs behind,' she said. 'Whatever happened to your heart?'

She had become so old-fashioned and sentimental since taking up with Wendell Tite.

Then a farewell luncheon was arranged, to be held at the Jacoby house. My preference was for Sherry's to cater a champagne send-off in my stateroom, but Ma said it would be unsuitable to be so ostentatious, given recent events. I believe she was merely parroting what Judah had said.

The whole family had gathered to bid me bon voyage, even Harry. I was hardly through the door before he began quizzing me on the financial provisions I was making for my daughters to be lodged in his house.

'Harry!' Honey said gently. 'You promised!'

'I'm merely trying to place this on a business footing,' he said. 'You'll find it's for the best.'

I said, 'Name your price, Harry. I know better than to expect anything for nothing from you. Go on! I'll write you a check.'

'Don't Harry, please!' Honey begged. 'Aren't we family? And didn't we always intend having a little sister for Shermy? I'm sure we should be paying Poppy for the pleasure of having these little lamby-pies around.'

On hearing the word lamby-pies, Harry stormed out onto the front stoop for a cigarette.

'Pay no heed, Pops,' Honey said. 'He's just in a bad humor since that uppity Union Club stiffed him. Between you and me, he has just adored having Sapphire around. He'd be heartbroken to see her go.'

I took her word for it.

Downstairs Honey's day nurse spooned glop into the babies, whilst upstairs we had Russian salad and roast chicken and port wine mold. Ma and Aunt Fish spent the meal surmising whether they would require tiaras when the summons came to meet Queen Mary.

Judah said, 'Why not invite her here and save yourself all this worry and expense?'

'Invite her here?' Ma squeaked. 'Queen Mary of England? What a silly idea. Every drape and chair cover would have to be replaced. And we'd need a new tea service. I doubt it would represent any kind of saving, Judah.'

Murray had not once looked my way or spoken to me.

I said, 'And why are you so cross with me? You may as well spit it out.'

He finished spooning up his jello before he answered. Then his eyes flashed.

'Cross?' he said. 'Not me. I'm plain disgusted with you.'

Silence fell.

'Know something, Poppy?' he said. 'You pay more attention to the whereabouts of your vanity case than you do to your children.'

Ma looked to Judah to rein Murray in but Judah was making a great business of dabbing at the corners of his mouth with his napkin and checking his pocket watch.

Aunt Fish was usually reticent with her opinions when Judah was around, but she spoke up.

'You are too young to understand,' she began – a sure way to sour things still further. 'Poppy's situation is delicate and complicated.'

'Yes,' Honey chimed in. 'And how would you feel, Murray, if she dragged Sapphire and Emerald off to Africa and they died of a fever or got eaten by tigers?'

I said, 'What is it to you anyway? They're my children . . .'

'And Mr Merrick's,' Ma interrupted. Ma was anxious for us all to become a seamless whole with the Merricks as soon as possible, before questions were asked in certain royal quarters.

'*Your* children?' Murray snorted. 'Do they know they're *your* children? I very much doubt it. Honey's been the only mother Sapphire knows. And now you're doing the same to Emerald. You're selfish, Poppy. You're really quite breathtakingly selfish.'

He pushed back his chair and left the room. Honey reached over and patted my hand, but it didn't help. I was meant to be the guest of honor. Everyone was meant to be nice to me.

'Well,' said Judah and Harry in unison, getting to their feet and putting on their business faces.

Judah shook my hand.

'Safe landing, Poppy,' he said. 'And a swift return. You have responsibilities now.'

'Hear, hear,' Harry said, but then he pecked me on the cheek because he knew there'd be trouble from Honey if he didn't.

Tea was brought in, and the babies, but Murray didn't return.

I said, 'I know why he's sulking. He hoped I'd stay on. He wanted me to go and bury myself somewhere like Long Island and play house and have a garden.'

Honey said, 'He's a very attentive uncle, you know? I know Shermy would be just the same if he weren't away at school, but I really must commend Murray. He picked out Emerald's rocking horse all by himself.'

'A gift more suitable for a boy, of course,' said Aunt Fish. 'It will have to be closely supervised.'

But Honey would hear nothing against my stepbrother.

'He even composed her one of his little verses,' she said. 'Did I read it to you, Ma? I have it here in my pocketbook.'

She took it out.

'GREEN,' she read.

> Uncle Murray never
> Knew, emeralds can be pink
> Too. Uncle Murray's green.

'Time that boy settled to something useful,' Ma said. 'Like adding up figures. And sparing his father.'

THIRTY-FOUR

We were quite the toast of the *Mauretania* on that sailing to Southampton, England. A thousand men fell in love with me and no one could resist my darling Beluga, but we encouraged no one. We lived rather quietly, always taking a novelette with us into the lounges, and turning in early, to get our beauty sleep.

The crossing was smooth and I felt on top of the world, until we stood off Southampton and the tugs began taking us in. Then my heart began playing the fool and my knees turned to water and I thought I might be going to have a seizure, like Uncle Israel. I'd have taken myself below to the infirmary if I'd felt strong enough to push against the flow of passengers. Everybody was headed upstairs, to line the rail and wave to their loved ones.

I medicated myself with a small scotch and soda and tried on my *chapeau* a hundred different angles. But no matter what I did, I still didn't feel I looked right. My prince awaited me and I wanted to be perfect for him. The problem was, I didn't know what his idea of 'perfect' might be.

It was Beluga who picked him out in the crowd. He pulled on his leash, yelping for joy, and scrabbled across the shiny floor, to be the first to receive a kiss from Reggie. Beluga was often a help to me at difficult moments.

Reggie was younger and paler than I remembered him. His hair was cut shorter. And he was shyer, too. We were finally face to face, but it wasn't how I'd dreamed it would be. I wanted a passionate embrace, of the kind that were going on all around us. I wanted him to tell me how completely ravishing I looked. But all he did was talk about the train schedule and the kind of weather we might expect.

'Well,' he said eventually, 'where have the babies got to? Is there a nursemaid?'

I had omitted to let him know the arrangements I had made for Emerald and Sapphire. I figured it would be an easier subject to discuss once I had him safely in my arms.

'They'll follow on later,' I said. 'When we've had time to prepare a place for them.'

And as soon as I said it, he relaxed. I suppose he had been anxious about having to start right away playing the father, making admiring remarks and not discriminating against another man's child.

I said, 'I thought it might be easier this way.'

'Yes,' he said. 'You're right. It's all been rather a bolt from the blue, frankly. Got back from Nyasaland and well . . .'

I said, 'I thought you'd abandoned me.'

'Hardly, old thing,' he said, and slipped his arm through mine. 'Merricks don't welsh.'

I saved the photographs until the boat-train picked up speed and there was nothing interesting to look at anymore. Just sky and fields, fields and sky.

I showed him Emerald first.

'I say!' he said. 'I say!'

Then I showed him Sapphire posed alongside Emerald's bassinet.

'I say!' he said again. 'A foal at foot *and* a two year old. Well, why not? Ample nursery quarters back at HQ. Ample.'

I said, 'Will you really take them both? Just like that?'

'Of course,' he said. 'The only thing I wonder about . . . your husband?'

'Ex-husband, Reggie,' I said.

'But about the child,' he said. 'He'll want a say in certain things. Visits, possibly? Governesses. And is he very very furious? About us?'

I had heard nothing from Gil.

I said, 'Think of Gil Catchings as dead. He may as well be.'

'Extraordinary,' he said. 'Well, oddly enough I was thinking it might be best to describe you as a widow. Would you mind awfully? It's just that some of the modern conveniences are not quite . . . usual yet in Melton Mowbray. Divorce and so forth.'

I said, 'But what about Emerald? Is she allowed to be your child?'

'Oh absolutely!' he said. 'Merricks have often sired children out of wedlock. The ninth baronet married the nursery maid after he was widowered, and no one could ever see any difference between the ones born before and the ones born afterwards. They were like peas in a pod. And he was highly respected. He was my grandfather, you know? He was Master of the Belvoir until he was seventy-nine.'

I wasn't to see my new home immediately. We were to stay at a small Belgravia hotel until we could be married by special license. Then I was to be sprung on the Merrick family. A foreign person, with two children and difficult hair.

I suppose Reggie and I had had our honeymoon at Cap Ferrat, without even realizing it. What had seemed easy on a moonlit beach, came less readily between damp English sheets, but he was tender enough with me, and when I cried, from relief and fatigue, he fetched me a monogrammed handkerchief.

'Chin up, old sausage,' he said. 'I'd say it's all going to be rather fun.'

I asked if we were going to Africa.

'I think not,' he said. 'I looked into tobacco. And coffee. Coffee does have its attractions, but there's Neville to consider.'

Neville was his brother.

'He lorst an arm in Mesopotamia and has been pretty middling ever since.'

'Lorst' was Reggie and Humpy's way of saying 'lost'. In

England many different languages are spoken and very few of them are intelligible to Americans. I resolved then to study hard and learn Reggie's native dialect.

I said, 'So we'll stay in England and help Neville?'

'I think so,' he said. 'Don't you think so?'

I was nervous of asking what kind of help we'd be giving Neville. Reggie took it quite for granted that I understood what he meant. Still, I had learned from my dealings with Stassy, better to get things on a clear footing right from the start.

'And what does Neville do?' I asked.

'Runs the estate,' he replied. Which left me none the wiser.

I said, 'My Ma's most eager to meet the Queen.'

He laughed. 'No one *meets* the Queen, Poppy,' he said. 'Possibly not even the King.'

'Good,' I said. 'That will discourage Ma from visiting us.'

'But she'd be most welcome,' he said. 'A girl needs a mother around. At certain times.'

'Gel' was how he said 'girl'. I was getting the hang of things already. I have always been blessed with a keen mind.

Humpy came from Paris to be a witness to our marriage and it was he who explained the Merricks to me.

'Neville's the eldest,' he said, 'so he inherited. That makes him Sir Neville. He's a baronet, you see?'

I said, 'Like the one who married the nursery maid?'

'Precisely,' he said.

I said, 'So what does that make Reggie?'

'Reggie's just Reggie,' he said.

I said, 'So I shan't be a ladyship?'

'No,' he said, 'not as such. Not unless Neville goes to his reward. Which he may do. He had a pretty bad war, you know?'

Reggie had been too young for the war. He was a child really.

Sir Neville, minus one arm, was married to Bobbity.

Humpy said, 'She's been awfully good for Neville.'

I said, 'Is she a ladyship?'

'Well,' he said, 'she is Lady Merrick, but I wouldn't labor the point. Bobbity certainly doesn't.'

This was very hard to comprehend. It would be like owning very fabulous diamonds and leaving them in the bank vault.

'And where does the Queen come in?' I asked.

'The Queen?' Humpy seemed to be overlooking their special connections. I began to suspect that the English were far too casual about things.

'Oh *that*!' he said. 'Well, Reggie and Neville's mother was a Choate. Perhaps she was my aunt. I don't remember. The Choates were very numerous. So *she* had a stepfather and *he* was related to the Herzog von Teck who was practically almost a total Hun, although he did have a place in Kensington. Not that it signifies anything now. We're all English these days.'

'So complicated,' I said. 'But I will master it.'

'I shouldn't bother,' Humpy said. 'Once you're there it won't seem at all important.'

I said, 'Now tell about Melton Mowbray. Is it like Paris? Or Cap Ferrat?'

A little smile played around his lips as he lit a cigarette.

'The first thing you must learn,' he said, 'is how to say it. Not Mow-Bray. Merbrey. Meltun Merbrey.'

I tried it a little.

'But is it fun?' I asked.

'Well,' he said. 'Some people think so. I saw Gil, did I mention?'

I said, 'Did he ask after me?'

'Not as such,' Humpy replied. 'He called me a home-wrecking little queer.'

Gil always had trouble with logic. All I could learn was that my automobile had been sold, and that Hannelore Ettl had moved into my adorable little house, in order that she and Gil could collaborate more closely on their paradoxes.

'Oh, and Nancy Lord is learning to fly,' he said. 'She's quite plaguing me about taking me down to Flicky's next summer, to see what she can pick up. See what you've done, Poppy? You've started a trend.'

Nancy Lord never had an original idea in her life.

'I shan't go though,' Humpy said. 'I've heard she's not terribly bright at flying.'

Reggie and I were married at the Caxton Hall, with Humpy Choate and a clerk from our hotel as witnesses and a ring from a used-ring store. Afterwards we went to a chop house, with divine glass ceilings, and had a wedding breakfast of broiled beefsteaks and treacle sponge, and then to a matinée at the Lyric Theatre, before we began our journey home.

We left Humpy in a cab at St Pancras railroad station. I'd loved having him around. It had brought back memories of our golden summer.

He shook Reggie's hand and kissed me on both cheeks.

'All the best, my dear,' he whispered.

I said, 'You will come to visit? To Meltun Merbrey?'

'Not bloody likely!' he laughed. And off he drove.

I was wearing one of my new asymmetric hemlines, in Egyptian red, with a coiled asp bracelet above my elbow, and stockings trimmed along the seam with tiny rhinestones, and Beluga had a quilted jacket in the same shade of red. It was a cold evening, the railway car was unheated, and the long journey preyed on my nerves and made me tremble. When we changed trains, at Leicester, Leicestershire, my darling new husband wired ahead so we could be met with blankets.

Reggie's family home was Kneilthorpe Hall, pronounced Niltrup, in the Vale of Belvoir, pronounced Beaver. It was a pretty house built of pinky-golden stone and stood on so much land you couldn't see the neighbors, who were Bobbity Merrick's people, the Bagehots, pronounced Bajuts.

We were expected. A car had been sent to meet our train. And yet somehow we were not expected. No one greeted us at the door and Bobbity, my new sister-in-law, only came running when she heard the sound of a dog in distress. Beluga had been set upon by a small terrier.

I attributed her failure to welcome me correctly and her staring long and hard at my wedding ring to the fact that the asymmetric hemline had not yet arrived in the Vale of Belvoir. She herself was dressed for some kind of menial work and in her hand she was brandishing a large steaming fork.

'Snapper!' she shouted. 'At ease!'

And the terrier withdrew, still grumbling under its breath.

'Boiling tripes for the doggies,' she said. 'I suppose you're hungry?'

It was Beluga she was addressing.

'He's an interesting little chap,' she said, crouching down to inspect him. 'Carrying too much weight, but bags of character. Better get him out of this foolish garment, though. My boys will think he's a rag doll.'

Reggie was walking up and down with his hands in his pockets.

'Bobbity,' he said. 'The most extraordinary thing. Poppy and I got hitched.'

'Reggie!' she said. 'You're far too young. Go and tell Merrick. He's in the Smoking Rum, brooding.'

'Rum' was the Merrick way of saying 'room'.

The pattern on the stairhall rug was quite worn away. Bobbity's hands and face were ruddy, like an old Irish. And although Kneilthorpe was capacious, it had neither turrets, nor suits of armor, nor priceless tapestries. I was relieved Ma and Aunt Fish weren't there to see the castle I had promised them.

An old, old version of Reggie appeared. An empty sleeve hung at his side. It was Sir Neville, who had gone to Mesopotamia and left behind an arm.

I wondered whether I should drop a curtsy, but my frozen knees, tangled in Beluga's leash, wouldn't co-operate and, in any event, formality seemed not to be the order of the day. Reggie didn't bow to his brother, nor even introduce me properly. I had been prepared to have my hand kissed, but no such thing occurred.

And though Bobbity did call her husband by his last name, I felt it was probably a strange English mark of affection rather than a point of protocol.

I decided almost immediately that I liked my new family, and those first instincts turned out to be right. Merricks never flapped over anything, or collapsed onto couches or threatened to write new codicils. And if they ever complained to Reggie about his marrying me, I certainly never heard about it. They accepted my foreignness and my sudden appearance, and eventually even the news that there were two small girls in New York, waiting to complete the picture.

'Poppy is a very good friend of Humpy Choate,' Reggie told them over a late supper of sharp cheese and dark beer.

'Humpy!' they both laughed. As though that explained everything. The only moment of discord I remember that evening was when Reggie mentioned I was in possession of a fortune.

'Steady on,' Sir Neville warned him. And the subject was never touched on again. I had no idea about Reggie's money. I believe he may not have had much, but, anyway, there was very little to spend it on in Melton Mowbray, England.

Supper was served on trays which we balanced on our knees. Bobbity provided me with a knubbly hand-knitted garment to wear over my Egyptian red, and an outdoors man was sent up with my luggage.

'I shall put you in the Acorn Rum,' Bobbity said. 'It's drectly across from Reggie's old rum. And Bullyboy had better be put in the Boot Rum. Give my boys time to decide about him.'

She refused ever to call Beluga anything but Bullyboy. The girl who brought me a dish of oatmeal next morning, a kind of local Irish, told me he had howled and whined all night, bereft of my company and the comfort of my eiderdown, but he soon recovered. Within a week he became convinced he was an English terrier.

He frolicked in mud and ate unspeakable things brought by

a butcher's boy and boiled in a cauldron, and the only time I ever tried to coax him back into his Hermès collar, for Murray's wedding, he sank his teeth deep into the ball of my thumb.

THIRTY-FIVE

The daily routine at Kneilthorpe was unlike anything I'd ever known. Sir Neville visited farms, of which there seemed a great number, and looked at milk yields, which always seemed satisfactory but never satisfactory enough to cheer him, and Reggie tagged along behind.

'Thank goodness he met you, Poppy,' Bobbity often said to me. 'Otherwise we'd have lorst him to Africa.'

Bobbity's days centered around horses and dogs. She was in a perpetual state of letting them out or bringing them in. It was a sadness to her, I know, that I would never be persuaded closer to a horse than observing it from inside the morning-room windows. A horse, to my mind, lacked all the advantages of a roadster or an airplane, and was equipped with an arsenal of dangerous features such as whimsy and temperament.

Bobbity, though, seemed to have been born to the saddle. Out of it she was bulky and ponderous. Even in the hip-skimming gunmetal chiffon tube I created for her to wear to the Quorn Hunt Ball, she had the look of a retreating rhinoceros. But on horseback she was transformed.

'Bobbity's an odd name,' I observed one day.

'Got it because I mastered the rising trot so young,' she explained. 'I'm Marigold on paper. Funny, we're both flowers.'

Bobbity's younger sister was a flower, too. Angelica Bagehot. She became my friend, though having a friend in Meltun Merbrey was nothing like New York or Paris. There was nowhere to get a manicure or shop for scent. There were no lunch counters where you could sit on high stools and gossip. But sometimes, at breakfast, Bobbity would say, 'Angelica may heck over today' and I could look forward to a little girlish company.

Hecking was when you rode your horse along the metaled road, as distinct from riding crorse-country. Within six months I was quite fluent in English.

I settled as best I could into the position of junior mistress of Kneilthorpe. I overcame the cold by spending a great deal of the day in bed, and solved the problem of my constant hunger by establishing my authority in the kitchen. Bobbity had no interest in food, except soup, which she believed could be made out of anything.

I peeled off paper money for the girl who did the ordering and Angelica obtained recipes from the Bagehots' cook, and before long cake was making daily appearances.

During the season she hunted, but in the summer Angelica and I would play tennis, and when we were rained off, or 'orf' as I learned to say, we'd play checkers instead or dance to records. She had led a very sequestered life and I was able to teach her all kinds of things, from the wild, darkie dances I'd learned from Badgirl Duprée to the best way to avoid babies.

'But why would one want to?' she asked. 'I can't wait to have babies.'

Social life at Kneilthorpe was feast or famine. Between April and the end of the summer nothing much happened, but in September the pace started to quicken. Once or twice a week Bobbity would go cub-hunting, riding off wearing what she called 'ret cetcher' and I would call a good tweed jacket. I believe the point of cub-hunting was to teach the fox cubs what was expected of them when the true hunting season began. Then the season opened and Bobbity changed into a much more flattering costume. Some of the ladies wore skirts and veiled hats, but Bobbity rode astride and looked a picture. She had a black frock coat and a canary vest. I would have taken up fox-hunting myself if I could have dispensed with the horse.

People came to stay during the season, to hunt and sometimes to shoot pheasant, which was Reggie's preferred sport. House guests were put up in the many bedrooms we had at Kneilthorpe, all as cold as the grave, and after dinner they played billiards or cards. We never played Truth or drank champagne wine or had any kind of *scandale*. They were dull types, and I especially disliked the way they ran off all the hot water. The only time I ever recall being cross with Reggie was when I was unable, because of this selfish behavior, to bathe before dinner. I asked for a tray in my rum.

'I don't know, old thing,' he said. 'It'd be pretty bad form. And it doesn't matter if you haven't bathed, you know? Bobbity hasn't, and she's been in the saddle all day.'

Then he discussed it with his brother, quite within earshot of our door.

'I think you'll find,' said Sir Neville, 'she'll come nicely to the bridle when she's hungry.'

Humpy did come to Kneilthorpe, just once. He said he'd come to see me, but I believe the truth centered around a rather handsome johnny called Gordie.

A party came down for shooting, and the small select group included Gordie, who actually owned a castle, and the P of W, who stood to inherit the whole country.

Then Humpy arrived looking altogether too debonair for shooting.

'Look at you!' he said. 'You've gone native!'

I hadn't at all gone native, but when you have slow circulation woolen socks are a great comfort.

I said, 'Are you really going to shoot?'

'No,' he said. 'But I may ride out with the lunch wagon and catch up on old times. Gordie and I go back a long way.'

I said, 'What about the P of W? I'd hoped to get acquainted with him but he hasn't paid me the least attention. None of them have. All they do is count dead birds.'

But Humpy said he had absolutely no pull with the royals. He asked whether I missed Paris.

'Not a bit,' I lied. I said, 'I'm so happy with Reggie.' That much was the truth.

Humpy reported that Gil had disappeared from rue Vavin, Hannelore Ettl was living in my house with a Dutch hermaphrodite, and Stassy's neckties were on sale in Samaritaine.

'And I suppose your babies will be joining you any moment?' he said.

That was the big unanswered question.

Reggie wanted us to do the right thing. But 'the right thing' could be viewed in different lights. Though Bobbity and Sir Neville had given their full approval to the introduction of children, I feared they would find, as I had, that the reality was more inconvenient than the prospect. Then, perhaps Sapphire and Emerald liked growing up in New York and would react badly to being transplanted. And perhaps my sister wouldn't bear to be parted from them. A photograph had arrived, the two girls posed on cushions side by side, not babies anymore, and Honey behind them, with an arm around each child, and a challenging light in her eye.

'Come and get them,' she seemed to be saying, 'if you dare.'

'The thing is,' I had explained to Reggie, 'my sister will need time to get used to the idea.'

'Oh, quite so,' he said. 'Absolutely. But sometimes what seems cruel is actually kind. I've seen it with bitches. No matter how devoted they are, there comes a time when they're actually pretty relieved to see the back of the whelps.'

I said, 'Perhaps we should go to New York? Kind of ease ourselves in?'

'I'd have to put it to Merrick,' he said. 'See when I can be spared.'

But another summer came and went. Sir Neville grew more and more gaunt, Bobbity had the girl turn great quantities of sour plums into great quantities of a condiment called chutney, and Bullyboy Beluga was stung by wasps. Then one fall morning, as I looked out of the morning-room windows, I saw a boy riding a pedal cycle up the gravel sweep. He disappeared and reappeared on the gentle wind of the road and it must have been fully five minutes before he reached the door and handed in a telegram.

'It'll be bad news,' the girl said. 'Telegrams are always bad news.'

The first bad news was the way the telegram was addressed. 'To Her Highness Poppy Minton Merrick.'

'RETURN NY IMMEDIATELY,' it said. 'FATHER DEAD.' It was signed 'GRACE'.

'Will there be an answer?' the girl wanted to know. 'Walter always waits in case there's an answer.'

'Yes,' I said. 'No. I'll let you know.'

The fact was, I didn't quite know what to make of it.

'The Mrs can't make her mind up,' I heard the girl say. 'Why don't you come round to the kitchen for a cup of tea, Walter, while she's pondering.'

The signature was GRACE, which was Harry. But whose father's death was he reporting? Not mine. Not his. And what had possessed him to address me in such a way? I saw Ma's hand in that.

For the rest of the morning the telegram lay on the table, defying interpretation. Bobbity was out, hecking over to the Bagehot place to look at a hunter that was lame. And Reggie was in Meltun Merbrey with Neville, seeing the feed merchant. I was alone except for the servants. Eventually I saw the delivery boy ride away, full of tea and my sultana cake, no doubt.

When Reggie and Neville returned from town they brought with them newspapers with gloomy reports about the United States.

'Things sound to be pretty rocky over there,' Reggie said. 'The stock market took a fearful dive.'

He suggested I send my own telegram to Harry, asking for clarification.

'I'll rush it over to the telegraphic office, drectly after luncheon,' he said.

I wanted to ride in the sidecar but he wouldn't allow it.

'Better not, old bean,' he said. 'I'm going to go like the clappers.'

It was 11 p.m., an extraordinarily late hour for Kneilthorpe House, especially on the eve of a meet, when another telegram arrived.

'HARRY DEAD,' it said. 'RETURN IMMEDIATELY. SHERMAN.'

And so the facts began to emerge. A tragedy had befallen my brother-in-law, and my nephew, who in my mind's eye still wore diapers, was suddenly old enough to send telegrams and give orders.

'Well,' said Reggie. 'There we have it. Emerald and Sapphire must certainly be brought home now. How often things work out this way. One wonders and wonders what to do for the best, and eventually the answer becomes clear.'

Bobbity said, 'Will they be here before the end of the season?'

Hunting took up an enormous amount of her time and I could understand she wouldn't want children around, getting beneath horses' hooves.

But Reggie said, 'I hope so. I hope they'll be here absolutely as soon as possible. I think it's going to be rather fun. Don't worry about getting their quarters up to scratch. I'll see to it. I'll have the girl bring in a spare sister, to do some scrubbing and so forth. And I suppose we'd better alert Nanny Faulds.'

There was then some discussion as to whether Nanny Faulds was merely old or desperately old. In any event, she had nannied at least two generations of Merricks and I was quite prepared to give her a chance with the next.

How Reggie clung to me in the week before I set off.

'Do hurry back, old sausage,' he said, curving round me till we were like spoons in a box. 'And while you're gone I'm going to look into ponies. One can't get them started too soon, and it'll help to get Bobbity on side.'

I said, 'Isn't she on side already?'

'Of course,' he said. 'But she and Neville aren't accustomed to small fry. I'm sure it's been a disappointment to them. Bobbity would have adored to have children.'

I said, 'How do you know?'

'It's obvious,' he said. 'Everyone loves tiddlers.'

That was what Angelica said, too.

'How many more shall we have, old turnip top?' he said. 'Let's have a hyce full.' 'Hyce' was the Merrick way of saying 'house'.

I douched three times that night, to make sure he didn't make an immediate start on his project to sire a dynasty. Reggie could be very impractical at times.

It was a melancholy scene, the day I left for Liverpool.

Angelica came over, blowing her nose a great deal, Neville delayed going out so he could shake my hand, and Bobbity feigned busyness, coaxing a worm pill into Bullyboy Beluga, in order to maintain her stiff upper lip. Even the girl put on a clean apron and came and stood with the general outdoors man and the stable boy, all looking most affected. When I first arrived, the story that I was a widow, left with two small children, had been allowed to spread by natural means, and so I suppose they felt I had already had more than my share of tragedy.

There was a freezing mist, right up to the window panes, and when I turned to take a last look at Kneilthorpe, it had disappeared already.

Reggie went with me as far as Leicester.

'Damn and blast it, I should be coming with you,' he said, kissing me over and over through the train window, until I wished he had stayed on the gravel sweep and said his goodbyes with the rest. I knew my mission was to go to New York and return as soon as possible, but I hadn't the faintest expectation of being able to do it. I hoped, or believed, that by the time I reached her side, Honey would be through her darkest hour.

She would refuse to be parted from her angel lambkins, Ma would beg me to reconsider before I dragged them to a foreign land, and we would reach some kind of mutually satisfactory arrangement whereby she brought them to Kneilthorpe for a holiday each year. I wondered why I hadn't thought of it before.

THIRTY-SIX

I sailed on my old friend the *Aquitania*, and all the talk was of who was ruined. I even began to wonder whether I was myself. I couldn't understand how people could have money one minute and nothing the next, unless someone broke into the bank and carried it all off. As I trusted, Uncle Israel's complicated precautions had kept my fortune out of harm's way. It was Harry who had come a cropper, cashing in Honey's treasury bonds, mortgaging everything they had, doing something called 'buying on margin'. He had driven out to one of his empty Bay Shore properties and shot himself.

Murray was waiting for me with this bleak story. He had come down to the pier to watch the old four-stacker come in to her berth. Whether he'd offered or whether he'd been sent, I don't know. He was very formal with me.

'I'm sorry you've come home to such sadness, Poppy,' he said.

I said, 'Thank God Harry had the decency not to do it at home.'

'Well,' he said, 'I see being an English lady hasn't softened you any. I'm instructed to take you straight to Honey. Then onto 69th Street. Your Ma has the girls there, and I know how eager you'll be to get reacquainted with them.'

I said, 'Why are you still mad at me for loaning them to Honey? If you only knew how she begged me to leave them behind.'

He said, 'You make them sound like a pair of gloves.'

There was no way of telling, from the outside, that my sister's house had been visited by tragedy. Everything looked the same as usual. As I climbed to the front stoop I could remember feeling just as affronted when Pa had been lost at sea but the milk still got delivered on time.

'Anyhow,' I said to Murray, 'why did Sherman Ulysses wire me? Wasn't that your job?'

'Not at all,' he said. 'Sherman is head of this house now.'

And I soon discovered what he meant. The stocky red-faced child who had seen off more nursemaids and governesses than I could count, had grown into a man. He had thin coppery hair and an earnest face. Sixteen years old. He was down in the kitchen carefully following a receipt from his Boy Scout Campfire Cookbook.

'Aunt Poppy,' he said, shaking my hand. 'Mother's resting so I'm going to speak to you plainly while I can.'

Then he turned to Murray.

'Did you tell her?' he asked.

Murray shrugged his shoulders.

'We haven't had time for much,' he said.

'The thing is,' Sherman said, wiping his hands on a kitchen cloth, 'Mother has lost everything. She can't be expected to support you a moment longer . . .'

I saw red.

I said, 'I have never asked *anyone* to support me. And I'm here to tell her not to worry. I still have my fortune. I'll buy her another house or whatever she needs.'

'You're missing my point,' he said. 'You have to take your children and raise them yourself. You've been helling around and pleasing yourself for long enough. It's time those girls know who they belong to, and Murray agrees with me, don't you?'

'I do,' Murray said. 'But Poppy knows that. There's been bad feeling between us since the day she ran out on Emerald.'

Those two pipsqueaks talking about me like that.

I said, 'Save your breath. I have a husband and a home waiting for them in England. I was about to collect them anyway.'

Sherman said, 'You make them sound like a pair of repaired boots.'

I saw a little something pass between him and Murray. How they must have rehearsed the way they were going to persecute me. I believed I'd grown accustomed to the world's disapproval but the hurt of their criticism took me quite by surprise. I began to cry. And neither of them rushed to comfort me.

Sherman returned to browning sausages in a pan, and Murray began to arrange a tray for tea.

'Have your cry, Poppy,' he said, 'and then we'll take this up to Honey. She's asked for you every day.'

My poor sister. She looked like she had had a quantity of stuffing removed from her. Her hair hadn't been combed. Her wrap was crumpled. She reminded me of Ma during the ups and downs of 1912.

I sat with her a while and seemingly managed to say every wrong thing in the book.

'Don't fret about money,' I said. 'I have plenty.'

'I don't care about money,' she said. 'I want Harry back.'

'Why?' I said. 'He was nothing but a fool and a thief. I'll bet you never saw your rose pearls again. And all those show-girls.'

'It doesn't matter,' she said. 'I still want him back.'

I said, 'And don't worry about Sapphire and Emerald. I'll take them to England and raise them as Merricks.'

'No!' she said, and she grabbed my arm. 'There's no need to do anything hasty. In a day or two I'll be feeling well enough to have them back here, and you can have Aunt Fish's room and gradually the girls will grow to understand who you are. You have to give them time, Poppy. Lots of time.'

I said, 'Have you been preparing them for this? You knew they'd have to come to me eventually. You have been showing them my picture regularly?'

She sank back against the day bed. Her silence confirmed my fears that she had not been following my instructions. I have often found in life that the only way to ensure a job is done properly is to do it yourself.

'Has Sherman told you to take them away?' she asked eventually. 'He thinks I can't continue but he's wrong. I shall soon be well enough. Shermy is taking good care of me. It's just that it's been such a terrible shock, Poppy. I didn't know things like this could happen, did you?'

I sat with her till Sherman carried in a plate of potato and sausage. Then Murray drove me across the park and down Fifth Avenue.

I said, 'Does she really stand to lose her house? There's no need for that, you know?'

He said, 'No. She can stay in the house, if she chooses to. My father and Dorabel are taking care of that. But some things can't be replaced.'

Honey's rose pearls were very lovely.

Murray said, 'Are you happy in England?'

'Very happy,' I told him.

'Good,' he said.

I said, 'And how's the bookkeeping and business and everything?'

'Oh, you know,' he said. 'Crazy. Wild, crazy fun, fun, fun.'

I said, 'And you must have a sweetheart by now?'

'Hundreds,' he said.

He was still holding out on me.

We pulled up outside the Jacoby house and I felt something gray and suffocating coil itself around me. Ma was in there waiting for me, and Aunt Fish, and no matter that I was thirty-two years old, no matter that I was second in command at Kneilthorpe and had poured tea for the P of W, I was about to be stripped of my rank. I would simply be Poppy and therefore in the wrong. I had kept my looks and my fortune, while my sister had lost both. I was bad for sharing the joys of my children with her and now, no doubt, would be bad whether I wrenched them from her or not. I also had some explaining to do with my mother *vis-à-vis* Queen Mary.

How I wished I were back in England, waiting for the dinner gong.

Emerald and Sapphire had been kept up to meet me. Judah was out of his seat, in a hurry to greet me and then disappear. My mother's husband recognized women's business when he saw it. Ranged on a couch were Ma and Aunt Fish, and between them, in nightgowns, candlewick wraps and Dora Minkel Ear Correcting Bandages were my babies. They fairly hurled themselves at Murray and he allowed himself to be brought down, and covered in kisses and tickled to death. Ma offered me a dry, papery cheek.

'Murray undoes all my good work,' she whispered. 'How was Honey when you left her?'

I said, 'Resting. Sherman was making sausages for dinner.'

I was ravenous myself, but it didn't seem the right thing to ask whether I'd missed dinner.

'Murray!' Ma rapped out. 'No more stimulation, please.'

Emerald's ear bandages had come adrift. Sapphire had hiccups. Gradually Murray restored calm.

'See here,' he said quietly, hauling them onto his lap. 'Do you know who this special visitor is?'

They shook their heads solemnly. Sapphire's hair, formerly Catchings blonde, had darkened to a full brown Minkel frizz. Emerald's hung straight and fine, just like Reggie's. Apart from that they passed for full sisters.

I said, 'I'm your Mommy.'

Emerald laughed.

'Oh no you're not!' she said. 'We already have a mommy.'

'Well,' Murray said, 'now you have two mommies. A Mommy Honey and a Mommy Poppy. And this is your Mommy Poppy. Two mommies. Aren't you lucky?'

Emerald said, 'That's stupid.'

She turned her back on me and tried to revive the tickling

223

game. Sapphire clung to Murray, watching me, and eventually she spoke.

'Did you bring us candy?' she asked.

I dropped down on the rug beside her.

'No,' I said. 'But tomorrow we can buy candy and dollies and anything else you'd like.'

'Just candy,' she said. 'I don't like dollies. Why do you have a mess on your face?'

Spending so much time around women like Ma and my sister who never did a thing to improve themselves, I suppose she wasn't accustomed to lipstick and powder.

I said, 'Would you like a tickle fight with me?'

But she did no more than spit in my eye and run from the room. Aunt Fish was after her like a shot.

'Well,' Murray said, 'it was never going to be easy.'

He got to his feet and swung Emerald onto his shoulders.

'I guess I'll carry this one up to her bed,' he said. 'You can start over in the morning.'

As he ducked through the door with her, I heard her say, 'Where's Mommy Honey?'

I was left alone with my mother.

I said, 'How are you, Ma?'

'Bearing up,' she said. 'I hope Harry Grace is satisfied, bringing inconvenience to us all. Judah has faced very difficult questions, you know?'

I asked where Harry had been buried.

'We don't need to know,' she said. 'We'll just pretend he never happened.'

I said, 'I remember you thought very highly of him. As I recall, he was always the first person you called for, after Pa was gone.'

'I don't remember any such thing,' she said. 'He could never be depended on. And now he's brought us shame and ruin.'

I said, 'Murray tells me Judah is saving Honey's house. But I'd have done that. I'd have liked to do something to help.'

'Well, I'm sure there's something for everyone,' she said. 'You can pay the school fees, so Abe can return to his studies.'

I said, 'Does Sherman answer you when you call him Abe?'

'Sherman!' Ma snorted. 'That was another of Harry's silly schemes. Well, now we can use the name God intended for him. Your skin is showing signs of age, Poppy. Are you using the Vinolia every night?'

Dinner was served the instant the nursery fell silent.

Aunt Fish said, 'Now tell us, Poppy, does Her Majesty sound . . . German, when she speaks?'

'Poppy and I already discussed this,' Ma leapt in. 'The Queen is so satisfied by Poppy's credentials she hasn't needed to send for her.'

I said, 'One doesn't simply *meet* the Queen, you see Aunt? Reggie has never met her. Even Sir Neville hasn't, and he's a baronet.'

'What a very odd family,' she said, helping herself to another slice of chicken.

'Is it a good life, Poppy?' Judah asked me. 'Are they good people?'

I said, 'They're very good. They visit their tenants and ride around in the fresh air a great deal. And they don't waste money on jewels or anything.'

I threw this in, wanting my stepfather to approve of the Merricks. I suddenly felt an indebtedness to him. When all around were rewriting history, consigning Harry to an unmarked grave, and renaming his son, Judah had faced the difficult questions and dug into his pockets. He must have loved my mother very much indeed.

'What? No jewels at all?' Ma asked, most alarmed. 'Then be sure they don't get their hands on yours. This family has suffered enough losses.'

Murray said, 'I think we should get to the point. Are Sapphy and Em going to England?'

I said, 'They have to.'

'No they don't,' Aunt Fish said. 'Mr Merrick can come here.'

'Could he?' Judah asked me. 'What's his situation?'

'Judah!' Ma said. 'I must have explained Mr Merrick's situation to you a hundred times.'

'Yes, but never satisfactorily,' he said. 'When a man is in business he can't just follow his wife, like a lapdog. Is your husband in business, Poppy?'

I wished I had come better prepared. Sitting in New York it was difficult to explain Kneilthorpe.

I said, 'Well, there's the estate. Sir Neville had a bad war, so Reggie has to assist him . . .'

'And correspondence.' Ma was eager to help. 'I expect he has a great amount of correspondence.'

'He does,' I said. 'Then there's tennis. And hunting. And shooting.'

'Poppy!' my aunt squealed. 'Never use that word again.'

'It sounds to me,' Judah said, 'as though Mr Merrick could easily be spared. Let him come here. If he's any kind of a man he can make a success of himself in New York. Then those children won't have to be uprooted and Dorabel will be happy. She won't have to sail that great ocean, fretting over her grandchildren.'

'There!' Ma said. 'I knew Judah would puzzle it out for us.'

'I wonder,' Murray said, carefully peeling an apple, 'whether Poppy's husband is going to fall in with your plans so easily? What do you say, Poppy? Didn't you tell me Reggie was counting the days till your return? Didn't you tell me ponies were being purchased?'

'Why does that boy have to spoil everything?' Ma cried.

'Of course . . .' Murray wasn't finished. 'Of course, if Poppy doesn't want to raise her own children she can always make them over to Honey, with a legally binding instrument, and then we'll never need to discuss the matter again. Reggie can stay where he is, doing whatever it is he does, and there'll be no more confusion, on any score. Because I do feel,' he said, looking directly at his father, 'that a child is entitled to know where it stands. Don't you?'

He stabbed a quarter of apple and ate it from his knife. Then the door swung open and Sapphire appeared, urged from behind by Emerald. They seemed to be carrying empty jam pots.

'Uncle Murray,' Emerald said, 'we forgot to measure our beans.'

Judah chuckled, and encouraged by this my two girls stepped right up to the table. Each jam pot contained a roll of blotting paper, and sandwiched between the paper and the glass, what looked like a squashed beetle, with blotchy broken wings and pale fleshy legs.

'So we did!' Murray cried, and he brought out a folding wooden rule from his inside pocket.

'See, Mommy Poppy?' he said. 'I'll bet you didn't know these girls are gardeners.'

I looked closer and he explained it all to me. How there's more to a bean than meets the eye. It can just sit in a canister for years, being a bean, until the help turn it into soup. But if you give it water and sunlight it'll grow roots and shoots and God knows what else.

'And today's winner is,' Murray announced, 'the bean belonging to Sapphire Catchings. Take a bow Miss Catchings!'

And everybody applauded. Even Aunt Fish.

'Don't be sad, Em,' I heard Sapphire say as they processed back to the nursery with their bean pots. 'Yours'll probably catch up to mine by tomorrow.'

Murray winked at me. I believe he was trying to effect a reconciliation.

THIRTY-SEVEN

Reggie was impatient to have me back by his side. 'The nursery is freshly distempered,' he wrote.

Bobbity dragged our old rocking horse out of the attic and has polished him up beautifully. I believe she's rather excited about being an aunt. It transpires that Nanny Faulds moved to Cleethorpes to live with a niece, so we're getting a person from the village. By the by, Angelica has had napkin rings engraved with S and E. So do hurry home old thing. Kneilthorpe seems terribly dull without you.

But getting away from New York wasn't so simple. Emerald had a quinsy of the throat, Sapphire developed sticky eyes, and Honey made my task of establishing myself as their rightful mother all the harder by appearing at unexpected moments with candy. I bought them candy, too, but they always preferred hers. I bought them adorable poke hats, too, and sateen bloomers and took them to Stouffer's for chocolate egg creams, but sometimes looking at their wary little faces you'd have thought I had grown horns. Sometimes I thought it still might be easier to leave them behind and let them be a project for my widowed sister, but I kept the thought to myself. Murray's approval of my efforts as a mother meant more to me than I can explain. He and I were friends again.

I lunched with Bernie Kearney one day. She was now Mrs Wendell Tite, looking pretty soignée in plover gray jersey trimmed with *lapin*. Her mother had passed away. Her sister Ursula had left Macy's and gone for a nun in Guatemala. And she and Wendell had lost two little babies, never even saw the light of day.

It seemed that no one had anything light or amusing to report.

'I have my womb in back to front,' she said. 'So you count your blessings.'

I only made the offer I did out of sympathy for her situation. Some people long for babies and never get them, some people seem just to catch them off tram seats and then wonder what to do with them. Bernie had lost two infants, I had two and I wasn't at all sure I was cut out for raising them. I was only trying to help.

She leapt up, grabbing her pocketbook.

'You are disgusting!' she yelled. 'How did you turn out so unnatural? I've a mind to report you. There's a law against selling people.'

Bernie could be so excitable. I wasn't suggesting *selling* her my girls. I was offering to loan them to her. I hated to quarrel with an old friend, but I'm sure it wasn't me who flew off the handle. It wasn't me who ran out of the restaurant and left a Waldorf salad untouched.

I remained where I was and finished my meal and smoked two cigarettes, to demonstrate to all those rubbernecks at the neighboring tables that I was perfectly calm. Then I went looking for Murray, in the little cupboard he occupied at Jacoby Furriers.

I said, 'Am I unnatural? Tell me the truth.'

'Yes,' he said. 'But I have every hope for you.'

The pressure was mounting. Reggie was waiting. Bobbity had polished the rocking horse. And Murray was looking to me to do the right thing. Then Ma informed me that both girls had started powdering their noses in their beds and the help were complaining about the extra laundry.

I said, 'What are help for if not for extra laundry?' and she replied that times had changed.

I booked three berths on the next sailing of the *Berengaria*.

'So,' Honey said, crestfallen, 'it's decided.'

'Now, Mother,' Sherman said. 'I'll come home every weekend. We'll go for walks and I'll cook.'

Walks. Sausages. Sherman was nothing like his father.

I was standing gazing at our waiting, empty steamer trunks when Murray came looking for me.

'I've been wondering,' he said, scratching his chin, 'whether you couldn't use some help?'

I said, 'Don't worry. Ma's Irish is going to do it.'

'No,' he said. 'Not the packing. I mean the journey, and England and . . . everything.'

I looked at him.

'How would it be,' he said, 'if I came with you?'

'Please do,' I begged. 'Oh please, please do.'

But I had no expectation that Judah would agree to it. As long as Oscar stayed resolutely in the country, mending broken chairs and suffering from nerves, all business hopes were pinned on Murray. He had learned how to add up and carry forward, and he did it from Monday to Friday without fail, even when there were much nicer things he might have done, like skating or taking a sweetie to lunch.

'Give me an hour,' he said, running out with his coat collar tucked in.

He was gone for three.

'It's done!' he said. 'I've been to Thomas Cook. I'm coming with you, Pops.'

'Well,' said Ma. 'Yet again Judah has been too soft-hearted for his own good. I hope you'll reflect on that, Murray, while you are gallivanting. That your father isn't getting any younger.'

'And neither are you, Dora,' added Aunt Fish. 'For if Judah is overworked and falls sick, whose shoulders will it fall upon? Yours.'

'Ma,' I said, 'I promise to send him back to you just as soon I've done with him.'

'Like a library book,' he whispered.

We drank a nightcap together after we'd measured the beans and settled the girls and the ancients had gone to their canasta.

'At Kneilthorpe,' he said.

'Niltrup,' I reminded him.

'At Niltrup, I suppose I might do a little gardening?'

I said, 'Murray, it's an awfully big garden.'

'Yippee!' he cried. And he stood on his head, criss-crossing his feet like an inverted ballerina, until he got a taste of second-hand scotch and thought better of it.

I said, 'We'll probably put you in the Pomegranate Rum, unless the P of W is expected, in which case you'll get bumped to the Willow Rum. And Bobbity will be determined to find you a congenial horse, but you must stand up to her, because no such animal exists. Tell her you have an allergy. I'll tell her. Also, she makes unspeakable soup so be prepared to fill up on bread. And when we have people staying to hunt, be sure to take your bath early. If you don't there'll be nothing left but a miserable trickle of lukewarm water.'

'Phew!' he said. 'I think I'd better take notes.'

All at once I was looking forward to taking Sapphy and Em home to England.

THIRTY-EIGHT

The day of our sailing Aunt Fish escorted Honey to the matinée of a light musical comedy, to keep her from melancholy thoughts. Judah didn't come to our farewell either. 'Times are hard, Poppy,' he said. 'Your Pa was a businessman, so I know you'll understand. I know you'll excuse me.'

We had never advanced to kissing terms. Neither of us would have wanted that. He just shook my hand, and then Murray's.

'Remember,' he said. 'Use your time profitably. And don't remain there longer than you have to.'

It was the last time either of us saw him. I have often wished his last words to Murray hadn't amounted to a lecture.

I had had the girls' hair cut in Dutch boy bangs and created smock dresses for them in satin charmeuse, shamrock green for Em and Stars and Stripes blue for Sapphy. They raced up and down the promenade deck and Ma wept a little, but not too much, wondering whether she would ever see them again. They rang 'All ashore' and I watched my mother retreat down the gangway, a stout little body on the arm of Judah's driver. She was going home to her husband, and I was going home to mine.

Murray turned out to be no sailor. He lay in his cabin with his head beneath his pillow and even Emerald's singing, of little songs she made up as she went along, failed to cure him of his wish to die. By the time we berthed at Liverpool he had slenderized by several pounds, Emerald had ceased asking for Mommy Honey, and Sapphire had drawn and colored a great quantity of boat pictures.

'These are for Aunt Bobbity,' she told me, dumping one pile into the trunk. 'And the others are for the daddies.'

Accustomed to the idea of two mommies, she had decided that Reggie and Sir Neville came as the same kind of package.

Murray hung back while Reggie and I embraced.

'I hope it's all going to be all right,' I said.

'Of course it will, old sausage,' he said. 'Welcome home!'

He had brought photographs of two Shetland ponies that hardly stood higher than Bullyboy Beluga.

'They don't have names yet,' he said, 'so you'd better put your thinking caps on.'

He was most fascinated by the girls, studying their ways, asking them about the *Berengaria*.

'Uncle Murray missed dinner,' Emerald told him, '*every* night.'

It was neat seeing them together, father and child.

Murray was sitting up front beside Reggie. They had slipped right into an easy, friendly manner.

'Did you really?' Reggie said. 'You must be famished! We could stop at a hostelry? We might be able to find you some cheese and pickles. Or we can just press on for home? I believe Bobbity has one of her soups on the go.'

The smile on Murray's face as he turned to look at me suggested he was on the mend.

Weary after days of motherhood, I fell asleep, with a daughter either side of me and Beluga curled on my lap, and when I opened my eyes we were just turning onto the gravel sweep.

'See what I mean about the size of the yard?' I said to Murray.

He gazed around him.

I said, 'Reggie honey, I do believe my stepbrother is lorst for words!'

Emerald took immediately to her pony, which she elected to name Brown, after its color. She sat aboard it without hesitating and would have led it into the house and upstairs to the nursery given half a chance. Sapphire named hers Coffee Milk, but she preferred the wooden type of horse, a sign to me that she had

233

inherited some of my good sense, even if later in life she didn't always show it.

They were awestruck by Bobbity, possibly because they thought she spoke a foreign language, and they kept a respectful distance from Sir Neville.

He never troubled them by speaking to them, but there was the horrid magnetism of his empty sleeve. The girl who had been drafted in place of Nanny Faulds told me they often discussed it before they fell asleep. Whether there was a tiny hand up inside his shirt, or a nice smooth shoulder. And whether an arm could just disappear.

They very much liked their girl. They allowed her to brush their hair, they swallowed down their cod liver oil, and they never tinkled in their beds again.

Above all though, they loved Angelica Bagehot and the highlight of their week was the day she came to play. Sometimes they played in the kitchen, making peppermint candy. Sometimes they played Hide and Seek. Once, after I had told her about my war work and Cousin Addie and all, they played at hospitals. Even Brown and Coffee Milk had their tails bandaged that day.

Murray spent a great deal of time pacing about outside, writing in a notebook.

I said, 'Are you writing haiku verses by any chance?'

'No,' he said. 'I'm designing a paradise garden.'

There was an outdoors man who kept tidy what could be seen from the house, and the rest was coppices and pasture.

I said, 'Does Bobbity know?'

'Sort of,' he said. 'Why?'

That was the dreamer in Murray. He didn't understand one couldn't go around just designing paradises.

But Bobbity said, 'If Murray chooses to make himself useful with a pair of secateurs I'm not going to stand in his way. He's staying on, then?'

This was a question I didn't care to ask. Sapphy and Em had made the tricky transition, his job was done and Judah's generosity was probably more than used up, but I didn't want him to leave.

I said, 'Do you mind? If he stays on a bit longer?'

'Not at all,' she said. 'I think we're all rubbing along rather well, don't you? Even the small fry. I think they show signs of promise, and I'm a pretty exacting judge, you know? If a puppy's not right I draft him immeejutly.'

I said, 'Bobbity, I'm so glad I brought them here. This is the nicest house and the nicest family I ever knew.'

'Is it?' she said. 'How extraordinary.'

I believe I had embarrassed her.

'Well,' she said, pushing butcher's scraps vigorously through her Spong mincer, 'you're not the only one heppy with the new arrangements. Angelica seems smitten, don't you think?'

Angelica Bagehot was signaling her romantic interest in Murray by visiting Kneilthorpe at every opportunity and then ignoring him.

'Should I say anything?' I asked Bobbity. 'To Murray?'

'I think not,' she said. 'When I decided to marry Merrick, I found it better to keep the blinkers on until I'd led him into the box.'

And so began Angelica's stealthy five-year courtship of my stepbrother.

Murray was earning his keep by totting up figures in the estate ledgers, renovating the gardens and generally lending Sir Neville, as Bobbity put it, a very necessary hand. Only Murray and I ever seemed to find this turn of phrase comical.

The old rose beds were grubbed up, and a quantity of privet hedges. A tree house was built, and an arbor. A white garden was planted and a perfumed grove, and a wild meadow where there had once been a very serviceable lawn. Sapphire began to study the pianoforte, Emerald rode out with her first hunt, and eventually the letters of inquiry about the date of Murray's return changed to monthly digests of life as seen from East 69th Street.

'Oscar is helping with the Civilian Conservation Corps,' Ma wrote, 'teaching the unfortunates forest-craft. And Little Abe has found a very good position with the Title Guarantee and Trust Company. What a comfort he is to us, kept at such a distance from our loved ones.'

I called her bluff.

'Dear Ma,' I wrote. 'No one is keeping you from your loved ones. You can set sail next week. God knows we must have a hundred bedrooms here. And stop calling Sherman Abe. It must drive him crazy.'

'How sad it makes me,' she replied,

to be corrected by my own daughter. I am unable to set sail, as you so gaily suggest. I am sixty-two years of age and the tragedies of my life have taken their toll. Your sister is under the care of a new doctor, for irrigation of her system. I pray that this will help her to reduce, where all else has failed.

I hope you are persevering with the ear bandages, in particular for Emerald. She will thank you for it some day.

Your loving mother
PS: Mrs Schwab passed over.

THIRTY-NINE

ngelica's experience with horses persuaded her she must never do anything to startle Murray. When there were point-to-point races to be attended, she was careful always to travel in the other brake. When Reggie's chums came for the shooting, she laughed in an especially bell-like way whenever Archie Vigo expressed any kind of opinion.

Murray noticed none of this. He was absorbed in ever larger plans for the garden, and he was uneasy in himself, too, about staying on.

'I suppose I should go back,' he'd say from time to time. 'I expect I've worn out my welcome.'

'No,' I always said.

'Well, if you're sure,' he'd say. 'And if my Pa really needed me, I think he'd have sent for me, don't you?'

Judah Jacoby was having trouble with communists.

I said, 'What if someone here very specially wanted you to stay?'

'Yes,' he said, 'I suppose the girls would miss me.'

'Not just the girls,' I said. 'A little bird told me there's someone here who thinks you're rather a dish?'

He flushed scarlet.

'Yipes!' he said, scraping mud off his gardening boots. 'Look at the time! I'm late for Neville.'

I did everything I could to promote the match. I liked the idea of having Angelica at Kneilthorpe and began grooming her for romance. I created a set of dinner gowns in silk acetate, with squared shoulders and gored skirts that fell gently to ankle length and drew the eye away from her rather solid prow.

I had once heard Archie Vigo remark to Reggie that a well-rounded chest was something to look for in a bitch, and I believe he may have been opening the bidding for Angelica's hand. But it never went any further.

It was during the course of one of Angelica's gown fittings that certain confusions came to the fore, creating bad feeling between myself and my daughters, just when we had grown quite affectionate.

'Look at those two noddles,' Angelica said. 'Could two sisters have hair more different? Em's is exactly like Reggie's.'

Sapphire was handing me pins. Emerald was making a pony rosette out of scraps.

'Yes,' I said. 'I guess it is.'

'Sapphy's papa . . .' Angelica said. 'Was he handsome?'

I was aware of the pricking of two pairs of small ears.

'Fairly,' I said. 'Sapphire, please go to the kitchen and say we need more tea.'

She said, 'But I'm helping with the pins. Why not ring the bell?'

'No more tea for me thanks, Poppy,' Angelica said. 'What was his name?'

'Gilbert,' I murmured, jabbing her with a pin.

'Hmm,' she said, noticing nothing. 'There are Gilberts in Harborough. Any connection, I wonder?'

Angelica knew everyone.

'No,' I said. 'Now wouldn't you like to run upstairs and see yourself in my mirror?'

'No thanks,' she said. 'I absolutely trust your judgment. And did he come to a tragic end?'

'Who's Gilbert?' Sapphire asked.

'Oops!' Angelica whispered. 'Have I put my hoof in it?'

'Gilbert was your daddy,' I said. 'Now I've finished pinning, so will you please carry the tea tray to the scullery before we have a mishap.'

'What kind of mishap?' Emerald asked.

'But the girl always fetches the tray,' Sapphire said. 'Where is Gilbert now?'

Angelica groaned. 'Sorry Poppy,' she said. She jumped down off the stool, still pinned into the rust-brown, and put her arms around Sapphire.

'I'm not sure,' I said. The time had come. Otherwise I foresaw a long list of unanswerable questions about gravestones and dates and other tricky details.

'Poppy,' Angelica said, 'I think the truth is best. Small fry can be awfully brave about these things.'

I guess I chewed my lips a moment too long. I guess Angelica believed she was helping.

'You remember how my cocker grew terribly old and smelly?' she said, gathering Sapphire to her ample front. 'You remember how Aunt Bobbity's Hector broke a leg out with the Belvoir?'

'Did they shoot Gilbert?' Sapphire said, leaping to a reasonable conclusion.

'No,' Angelica soothed her. 'But he did die. Didn't he Poppy?'

'Well,' I said, and I suddenly thought of Humpy Choate who was always armed with a vague reply. 'Not as such.'

The room was quiet except for the ticking of a grandmother clock and Emerald's busy tuneless humming.

'Gilbert went away,' I said, eventually.

Sapphire said, 'Where? I want to see him.'

'I don't,' Emerald piped up. 'Reggie is my daddy.'

I watched Sapphire and Angelica sifting their thoughts, allowing new possibilities to settle. Angelica began to look amused.

'Do you mean,' she said, 'you are d-i-v-o-r-c-e-d?'

'I know what that means,' Sapphire said. 'I can spell. It means you had Gilbert sent away. It means I'm an orphan. You beast. You hateful beast.'

'Sapphy!' Emerald called to her. 'Never mind. Reggie can be

your daddy. And then if Gilbert comes back, you'll have two daddies.'

But Sapphire always preferred to strike a tragic pose. She was ten, and this opened hostilities between us that never were resolved. Whatever happened in her life, when men left her, when friends grew tired of her, when she lost her looks, it would be laid at my door.

'You sent my father away,' she'd cry. 'I never knew my father.'

Angelica was completely decent about it all. She never let onto Bobbity or Neville.

'Divorced!' she whispered to me. 'How completely modern!'

I finished her gowns and showed her how to shape her eyebrows and rinse her hair in dark beer. I even made a gift to her of a pair of divine amber earrings but like all Englishwomen she was wedded to her cardigan, a garment I never persuaded her to leave off. Even when I loaned her my chinchilla wrap, so Murray might glimpse her powdered shoulders and find his appetite for the hunt ball unexpectedly whetted, she sabotaged the whole effect by wearing the wrap *over* the cardigan. Kneilthorpe was bone-chillingly cold, of course. But I was never so unprincipled as to dine in knitwear.

On Christmas Day 1934, Angelica proposed marriage to Murray and he accepted.

I took him to one side.

'Not that I'm not delighted,' I said, 'but are you quite sure?'

'Yes,' he said.

I said, 'You never told me you were in love with her.'

'Well, I am,' he said. 'And now I can stay here and finish the garden.'

I said, 'No, you'll live in the dower house at Lower Bagehots. You'll have responsibilities to your own land.'

'Will I?' he said. 'What do you think my father's going to say? About my marrying out.'

I said, 'He's never criticized me for marrying an English.'

'No,' he said, 'not *that* kind of marrying out.'

I said, 'No one bothers with that Jewish business anymore. This is the modern era. Anyone can marry anyone.'

'I bother with Jewish stuff,' he said.

I said, 'You do not. You go to church, same as I do.'

'That's because I'm a guest,' he said. 'But I don't actually listen to any of it.'

That was neither here nor there. No one listened to any of it.

I said, 'You eat lobster.'

'We never have lobster!' he countered, and it sounded suspiciously like a veiled complaint.

'But if we did, you would,' I said.

He said, 'Perhaps Angelica will be Jewish with me. I'll put it to her. It would make things easier on Pa.'

I said, 'Don't you dare.'

I've never been afraid of creating a *scandale* but in Meltun Merbrey it was considered boringly bad form to harp on about God.

The wedding date was fixed for June, and we ran into a small obstacle immediately. Sapphire refused to be a bridesmaid. This was part of her larger plan to thwart me in any way she could and to punish Murray for his complicity, as she saw it, in keeping her from her father. Even when she saw the divine blush satin I had purchased in Leicester, Leicestershire, and my witty design, with three layers and a yoked skirt, echoing the line of Angelica's gown, she would not thaw.

'Never mind, Mommy,' Emerald said. 'I'll wear two dresses.'

Then Ma wrote.

'Your Aunt and I have obtained a stateroom on the April fifteenth sailing. Sadly Judah is unable to accompany us because of the communists.'

Jacoby Furriers was still troubled by organized labor.

'You see,' Murray said gloomily. 'He won't come because I'm marrying out. Maybe I should call it off.'

I said, 'Are you getting cold feet?'

'No,' he said. 'Just wondering if I'm going to be disinherited.'

I'm sure it would have been no great loss if he were. The Jacoby boys had never had fortunes.

Angelica said she didn't care a hoot. She stuck by his side through all weathers, helping to prepare a new asparagus bed and her diamond ring, a rather old, used diamond ring, grew very grubby. She was an altogether cheerful girl.

She obtained a book called *Married Hygiene* and studied it closely.

Ma and Aunt Fish docked at the end of April. Reggie and I drove down to Southampton to meet their boat and by the time we arrived back at Kneilthorpe we had heard particulars of every luncheon, dinner and glass of seltzer they had enjoyed.

'There are musical diversions, and bouillon,' my aunt informed me, as though I had never crossed the Atlantic. 'And they change the linen every day.'

I believe she had been bracing herself for a hammock.

'Are the invitations sent out?' Ma asked.

For nine years I had tried to impress upon my mother the remoteness of the royal family from even well-attested kin, and I had been especially discouraging when she wrote of including a tiara in her luggage.

'Angelica and Murray are not known to Queen Mary, Ma,' I sighed. 'They are barely even known to the Prince of Wales.'

'Does it occur to you, Poppy,' said Aunt Fish, 'that if everyone were so reticent Queen Mary would sit at home and never be invited anywhere?'

'See what I mean?' I growled to Reggie. But Reggie couldn't see. He was always notionally on my side because I was his wife, but he never joined battle.

I felt let down by the way he got along so amiably with my old enemies, having an extra table set up in the Drawing Rum so they could enjoy their jigsaw puzzles without straining their backs, driving them across to Archie Vigo's so they could examine a bed slept in by some earlier monarch. But that was nothing to the betrayal I suffered when, toward the end of their first week at Kneilthorpe, Neville announced that Their Majesties were coming to Melton, as part of their Silver Jubilee journey.

'You see!' Ma said, growing pink in spite of the cold of the dining room. 'I knew it must be easier than you pretended. Thank goodness we brought our tiaras, Zillah.'

'Yes,' said my aunt, 'thank goodness we knew better than to depend on Poppy's word.'

I wasn't going to be seen as incompetent in my own house.

I said, 'They never came before, did they Reggie? And they'll probably never come again. It's a fluke.'

But Reggie was still honeymooning with my relations and good manners ruled everything he did, even in his dealings with preposterous old ladies. He would never come right out and say what he thought. Over the years I have never been persuaded that the American way isn't healthier.

'Well,' he said, taking each of them by the hand, 'we must make sure you're not disappointed. We must make sure you have a good vantage point. I'll have a word with Bagehot.'

One of the many Bagehots was a lord lieutenant. The kind of person who could make the difference between glimpsing the top of a passing coronet and getting a front row seat.

I tackled Reggie later.

I said, 'Couldn't you have backed me up, just a little? All they ever want to do is triumph over me.'

'Old sausage!' he said. 'Don't allow silly things to bother you. They both seem perfectly agreeable to me.'

Ma spent the next week displaying her encyclopedic knowledge of the King and Queen, and quizzing anyone foolish enough to loiter in the Morning Rum.

'Full names,' she'd warble, longing for you to admit you'd forgotten them again.

'Victoria Mary Augusta Louise Olga Pauline Claudine Agnes!'

This was the greatest feat of memory ever achieved by my mother.

'First betrothed to Albert Victor, Duke of Clarence, who sadly died . . .'

'From sleeping between damp sheets,' interrupted Aunt Fish, who only remembered causes of death and who had herself developed a chesty sniffle.

'Married George Frederick Ernest Albert . . .'

On and on Ma went, sorting through a selection of photographs she had brought with her.

'Her Majesty will be interested to see her new American relations,' she said, basking under Reggie's protection, daring me to contradict her, or pick her up and shake her and say, 'You're not going to get within a hundred yards of the Queen, you deluded, annoying old woman', which I longed to do.

Murray was no help to me, inventing urgent duties in the garden whenever the photographs were brought out.

'Time to lift a few carrots, Em,' he'd say, and off they'd run. Emerald and Sapphire each had been given a patch of garden. Like me, Sapphire found Nature worked too slowly and whimsically for her taste, so she soon abandoned hers, but Emerald took it over, allowing her own chaotic plot to spread, flowers and vegetables jumbled together.

Sapphire was more interested in Ma's collection of photographs.

'Do you have one of Gilbert?' she asked.

'Who?' Ma said. 'Certainly not. I hope you are practicing your curtsies, Sapphire. I hope you and Emerald are remembering to bandage your ears.'

The King and Queen were marking their twenty-fifth anniversary, not by taking a bronzing vacation at Cap Ferrat, which they must certainly have earned, but by visiting as many English towns as possible. That Meltun Merbrey was one of the chosen said much, I suppose, about the ones that had failed the selection process.

A light rain fell all night, petering out at breakfast but never quite going away. At eleven o'clock Reggie and I set off by motorcycle and sidecar. Bobbity followed with the others packed into the shooting brake. A large tent had been erected and filled with long tables for the service of a Jubilee tea. A second tent was being laid with assorted rugs and a small number of chairs. That was where I found Angelica.

'Just been organizing a potty,' she said. 'In case HM needs a tinkle. And when your mater arrives and your aunt, one of Bagehot's people will want to talk to them. They have to know when to curtsy and so forth.'

Strings had been pulled by a Bagehot in high places. Ma and Aunt Fish had been wheedled onto a receiving line.

I emerged from the tent to see them trudging toward me across the field. Murray was holding Ma's mink out of the mud, Emerald and Sapphire were doing the same for Aunt Fish, and they cut such figures, from their borrowed rubber boots to their Tiffany tiaras, that several small children began running toward them, cheering and waving Union flags, in the mistaken belief that they Were Somebody.

Ma swept past me. I believe it was the happiest moment of her life, bar one. And that was the moment when Their Majesties paused in front of her as they moved along the line.

'I always recall what our dear cousin the Queen said . . .,' became Ma's trump card, to be played in any conversational lull. And although Reggie told me it was unlikely Her Majesty had asked anything more than whether she had traveled far to be there, according to Ma they had enjoyed a wide-ranging discussion and parted on the most cordial terms.

FORTY

Murray and Angelica were married in the Bagehots' own chapel, at Wrotherby, pronounced Robey. I had taken apart an ancient Bagehot wedding gown of ivory Brussels lace and reassembled it in a line more flattering and *au courant*, and the large shield-shaped arrangement of crimson carnations and maidenhair fern helped complete the slenderizing illusion. Emerald assisted with six yards of veil, beaming proudly at anyone who's eye she could catch, and Sapphire, coaxed into her bridesmaid's dress with the promise of being taken to Leicester, Leicestershire, to see a moving picture show, slumped alongside her wearing a scowl.

It was a day of mixed fortunes.

The evening before Murray had been in a very good humor, allowing Reggie to get him tight on gin and even presenting me with a wedding haiku.

RELATIVE
If my wife's sister is
Your husband's brother's wife am
I one step removed?

At breakfast a congratulatory wire arrived from Judah, and another from Yetta Landau and Oscar.

'See?' I said. 'You're not disinherited.' But he didn't seem to take much pleasure in the news.

I said, 'Are you nervous?'

'Somewhat,' he admitted.

Reggie took him off to help him tie his necktie, and I went in search of Bullyboy Beluga, to dress him in his Hermès collar. He hardly greeted me. He lay on the floor of the Boot Rum looking up at me dully, and when I began to undo his everyday collar he turned, rather slowly, and bit me on the hand. Bobbity came and examined him, while the girl wrapped my thumb in a clean pudding cloth.

'He seems out of sorts, poor old chap,' she said. 'I'll bundle him up. Put him in the motor. We can get Phillips to take a look at him on our way to Wrotherby.'

Phillips was our veterinarian.

But Bullyboy Beluga wouldn't be bundled. He resisted, demonstrating a defiance animals usually didn't risk with Bobbity, and put an end to all talk of being driven anywhere or being ministered to by biting her on the ankle.

She ushered me outside. 'Leave him to consider the error of his ways,' she said.

Another clean pudding cloth was sent for.

I had created a very special origination for Bobbity to wear to the marrying: a calf-length dress in the darkest blue wool, worn with a Scotch plaid gilet and a matching glengarry. Bobbity was very fond of Scotch plaid and even fonder of darkest blue in spite of the unforgiving way it showed up dog hair.

For Murray, and for Reggie who was to be his groom's man, I had made amusing suit vests in figured silk, and I would have done the same for Neville, but he had recently taken up knitted vests and I suppose didn't wish to be seen as a man who was too susceptible to fashion.

The day had dawned bright and sunny. I had gambled on being able to wear silk day pajamas without having to ruin the effect with waterproofs. Hot pink has always been my color, and my matching pixie cap was undoubtedly the wittiest hat at the whole affair. Even the way I had hung my bandaged hand in a silk sling drew admiring remarks.

'How inventive you are,' people said.

'We always gave her every encouragement,' Ma told them. 'It was obvious from the start that Poppy had her Grandma Plotz's way with fabrics.'

It was the first I knew of it.

Aunt Fish was most impressed by the Bagehots having their very own church.

'What a pity you don't run to one at Kneilthorpe,' she said.

I said, 'We don't need one. We don't go in for that kind of thing.'

'Besides,' Ma said, 'Reggie could certainly have one if he chose to, Zillah. There are any number of rooms he might use. And you know, Judah has given such quantities of money to the temple, to all intents and purposes we must practically own that.'

Murray made his wedding vows in a rather small voice, encouraged by Angelica's loving smiles, and then we all processed to a wedding breakfast of Meltun Merbrey pie and sherry wine served in the library.

A Bagehot aunt had questioned whether dishes made from pig should be served, in light of there being what she called 'a Hebrew contingent', but pie was always served at Bagehot weddings, and funerals, too. No one knew of an alternative, and Murray's suggestion of shrimp was overruled. Shrimp was only served on buttered toast, before dinner, by people like Flicky Manners, who had houses near the sea and shrimp nets. In the Vale of Belvoir one ate pig.

I had supervised the baking of the cakes in the kitchens at Kneilthorpe. There were three tiers; one to be taken back to New York, for those who had been kept from the wedding by communists, one to be brushed with brandy, wrapped in muslin and preserved for the christening of Angelica and Murray's firstborn, and the largest for immediate consumption.

Observing how the upper tiers were sinking into the lower cake, and anxious to press ahead with the cutting ceremony before any more subsidence occurred, I was hovering by the cake table, gazing out of the long library windows, when I noticed someone approaching the house at as great a speed as a pedal bicycle permitted. It was our outdoors man.

By the time he had reached the kitchen door and I had been asked for, he was in a state of near collapse, purple faced, chest heaving.

'I'm sorry to trouble you, Mrs Reggie,' he wheezed, 'on this happy day. But your little dog has passed away and the girl won't stay in the house till he's been seen to.'

My darling Beluga. Just when I had decided to be kinder to him and pay him more attention. If only he could have become ill a day or two later. Murray's wedding had taken up such a very great deal of my time.

I said, 'Had you better bury him then?'

'Yes Mrs,' he said, 'I think I'd better. But I thought you'd want to pick out the spot where he's to lay. Lady Merrick's very particular where her boys lay.'

I said, 'Where do you suggest?'

The serving classes have to be told everything. This is why they never progress.

'Well,' he said, 'I don't know. I could find him a nice little corner by the lilac walk. That should dig nice and easy.'

Murray appeared at the kitchen door. 'Who's digging in my lilac walk?' he said.

And so it all came out. I would never have bothered him with Beluga's passing, on his wedding day of all days, but the outdoors man blurted out the whole story, about him howling a little in the Boot Rum and then falling into the sleep from which there's no waking, and the girl saying he had to be buried, wedding or no wedding, before there was a smell.

Murray did no more than run out of Bagehots' kitchen in his figured silk vest, snatch up the bicycle and hurtle away toward Kneilthorpe, leaving me to deal with a stranded outdoors man and a bride who was waiting to cut the cake.

The English are a very sensible people. They just quietly do whatever has to be done. They never flap. And so it was decided that the cake and the wedding party would transfer to Kneilthorpe. In fact it was decided that to do so would be the greatest fun and should have been thought of in the first place.

Reggie and I went ahead on the Flying Banana, with the outdoors man in the sidecar, and we didn't overtake Murray until the beginning of the gravel sweep. He was in a terrible sweat.

'Cavalry's on the way,' Reggie shouted to him over the noise of our engine.

Beluga Bullyboy was wrapped in a feed sack on the cool scullery floor.

'Would you like to see him one last time?' the outdoors man asked me. On balance I thought not. But when Murray pedaled into the yard, he insisted on paying his respects. I had never realized he was so fond of the old beast.

By the time Angelica arrived, and the rest of the party, he was down at the lilac walk, stripped to his shirt sleeves, giving unsought assistance at the digging of the grave.

The cake hadn't traveled well. The supporting pillars of the second tier had sunk without trace into the body of the principal cake, the cause being too much opening and closing of oven doors by foolish kitchen girls.

'I do hope this isn't an omen,' said Aunt Fish.

I believe my aunt always secretly hoped for the excitement of tragedy.

More sherry was served, the cake was admired for its moistness, and no one talked about the bridegroom turning grave digger, except to condole with me and observe that twelve was a good age for a bulldog.

But when the moment came for Murray to drive Angelica away to Lower Bagehot, to the dower house that was to be their new home, he froze.

'Poppy,' he whispered. 'Could I have a word?'

We closeted ourselves in the Morning Rum.

I said, 'Are you in a funk, Murray Jacoby?'

'Not exactly,' he said. 'It's just that I'd rather stay here.'

I said, 'Then why didn't you say so? I'm sure Angelica would be just as happy here. It can be arranged after your honeymoon.'

'No,' he said. 'That's not what I mean. I think Angelica had better go to the new place and I'll stay here with you.'

I said, 'But that won't do at all. Aren't you raring to be alone with her? Do you understand what I mean? *Married* alone.'

'Yes,' he said. He looked like a man preparing to walk to the gallows.

I said, 'You do know what you have to do?'

I had in mind to call Reggie in, to give him a short lesson on the birds and the bees, but he insisted that he knew perfectly well what was required of him. It was just that he didn't feel quite ready.

'Perhaps it's because I'm upset about Beluga?' he ventured. But I wasn't having any of that. No one had asked him to go grave-digging on his wedding day.

I said, 'Well, that's something you'll have to discuss with your wife. All I can tell you is, you have to drive away with her right now. Everyone is waiting to throw rose petals. Sapphire has tied old boots to your fender. And Angelica is eager for the spooning to commence. I know because she told me so.'

FORTY-ONE

No bride was ever more forgiving than Angelica. When my innocent words about honeymooning sent Murray running for a bathroom, where he bolted the door and refused to come out, she held her head high.

'Change of plan,' she told the waiting guests. 'Murray's got a queasy tum, so we probably won't be making a move today. Probably bunk down here tonight.'

'Poppy!' Ma hissed. 'What have you done with him?'

I might have guessed I would be blamed.

Bobbity took me to one side. 'Is he refusing at the first jump?' she asked.

I said, 'Well yes, he is. Isn't it extraordinary?'

'Not at all,' she said. 'Merrick was the same.'

Angelica was bearing up very well.

'Do you know what?' she said. 'I'll start up the motor anyway. It'd be a pity if the old rose petals went to waste. Em and Sapphy can ride with me. We'll just do a turn.'

And they did. Petals and rice and bird seed were thrown, and Sapphire and Emerald squealed with delight as Angelica gunned the motor down the drive, for a ceremonial circuit of the house, and a brief detour so the bridal flowers could be left on the fresh earth of Beluga's grave.

I asked Bobbity how long it had taken her to coax Sir Neville.

'Not long,' she said. 'A night or two. I just allowed him full rein and eventually he trotted up nicely of his own accord. It's to do with their school days, you know? Life in the dorm. Even now I'm absolutely not allowed in Merrick's night table. He only has a biscuit box in there and a torch, but it's strictly orf limits.'

But Murray had never known life in the dorm.

'Don't worry,' Bobbity said. 'Gelica is marvelous with nervy types.'

But even Angelica's wealth of patience and kindness wasn't enough to persuade Murray into the marriage bed. All he would say on the subject was, 'I'd just rather not at the moment.'

They gardened together, they dined together and they uncled and aunted together, but there was never the least little bit of spooning.

Ma remarked, on the eve of her departure for New York, that Murray was almost as considerate a husband as Judah Jacoby himself.

'And Israel,' said my aunt. 'Israel rarely troubled me.'

But word got round, and others were not so forgiving. The girl kept fetching out the wedding cake earmarked for the christening, brushing it with more brandy and sighing theatrically. When Murray happened to cross the stable yard while Bobbity's hunters were being shoed, the farrier stopped what he was doing and stared at him as though he had two heads. Eventually even Bobbity became impatient.

'I should really hate for this to turn out badly,' she said. 'I should hate Gelica to become egg-bound.'

I said, 'They do seem pretty happy.'

'Nevertheless,' she said, 'I think Murray should be made aware Edgar Boodle-Neary was always rather keen. If this should continue . . . If Edgar should decide the plum is still for the picking . . .'

Then, one morning early in the spring of 1936, Murray and I found ourselves alone together over our oatmeal.

'I seem to have made a hash of things,' he said gloomily.

I said, 'You do know it can all be undone? There not having been any romping, all you have to do is report back to the priest and it can all be canceled.'

'Yes,' he said. 'All the gifts would have to be returned, of course.'

I said, 'Well, Angelica might offer them, but Bobbity told me it would be very bad form for anyone to accept. Is that what you want to do? Call it a day?'

'I do like her, you know?' was all he said.

I didn't miss him at luncheon. I was obliged to go to Leicester, Leicestershire, whenever I wanted to buy scent or get my hair styled and I always went to Marshall and Snelgrove for tea and dainties before I motored home.

When the gong was struck for dinner I found Angelica waiting for me at the foot of the stairs. Her nose was red and swollen.

'He's god away, Poppy,' she sobbed. 'He took his thigs ad I don't even know where he's god.'

The temperature at dinner was even lower than usual.

Bobbity was cross with Sir Neville for having driven Murray to the railroad station without finding out his destination, Neville was annoyed by Angelica's sniffing, and when the girl came in to clear and found everyone's soup unsupped, a further degree of frost set in.

I had no appetite for anything. I kept combing through recent conversations with Murray, looking for hints, but I found none. He had no friends in England. He had no friends anywhere, except for me. He was twenty-eight years old and yet he was such an innocent.

I couldn't sleep.

'Tossing and turning, old thing?' Reggie said, wrapping his arms around me.

'It's Murray,' I said. 'Where on earth can he be spending the night?'

'At his club?' he said.

I said, 'Darling, Murray doesn't have a club. He only has Kneilthorpe and East 69th Street.'

Reggie thought about this for a while.

'High time he had a club, then,' he said, 'for precisely these occasions. Should I propose him for the Ramrod?'

It was difficult to quarrel with Reggie because he never really recognized a quarrel when he met one. He always saw things in the best possible light. Still, I sat up in bed and put on the light, so that at least he would understand we were having a serious discussion.

I said, 'Reggie, you must know how unhappy he's been since the wedding. You must know how he feels he's let everyone down.'

'Does he?' he said. He was genuinely astonished. 'But he's a completely decent sort. I couldn't like him more.'

I said, 'Yes, but what about Angelica? He gave her expectations and he hasn't fulfilled them.'

'I see,' he said.

I said, 'As a matter of fact, I don't believe he's even tried. And now there'll probably have to be an annulment or something.'

'Gracious,' Reggie said. 'What a pickle.'

I said, 'But he shouldn't have run away. He should have stayed and faced it, like a man.'

We sat side by side in silence for a while, leaning against our pillows.

I said, 'Do you think it possible Murray is inclined *the other way*? Like Humpy?'

'Possibly,' he said, 'quite possibly. But even so, that would be no excuse for disappointing Angelica. A great many husbands might prefer to linger over a game of billiards, for example, but they know where their duty lies. Perhaps it's because he's an American. I dare say his upbringing was very different over there.'

I said, 'He was raised by his aunt, you know? He never knew his mother.'

Reggie slapped the counterpane.

'There you have it,' he said. 'Raised by an aunt. Well, the very moment he returns I shall talk to him, man to man. And in the meanwhile I'll certainly put his name up for the Ramrod.'

But Murray never returned to Kneilthorpe. He vanished into that misty Melton morning and all we could do was watch for letters and hope for wires. If I could have known then how long it would be until I saw him again, I shouldn't have been able to face each new day and shop for amusing fabrics and attend Emerald's gymkhanas. And if I could have known how soon I would have to endure the sight of another empty seat at the table, I might have swallowed a whole bottle of Honey's Elixir of Hemp and never woken up. I have never wished to see the future.

FORTY-TWO

Just a few weeks after Murray's departure, while spring was still holding out on us and even the bedside rug felt damp beneath my feet, Reggie set off for Archie Vigo's to view a litter of retrievers. He climbed astride the Flying Banana and roared away into yet another misty morning. The alarm wasn't raised until he failed to appear at dinner. Archie himself had already gone out to dine by the time we telephoned, but his butler, reluctant at first to give out what he called 'private informations', eventually revealed that Reggie had never kept his appointment. The pick of the litter had gone to one of the Burton girls.

A party of nine set off to search for Reggie. Our outdoors man, and Walter the telegram boy, who unaccountably turned out to be sitting in our kitchen drinking tea with the girl, even though there had been no telegrams to deliver, and sundry peasants rustled up from our nearest tenant farms. Emerald begged to go too, excited by the sight of the rush torches, and when she was forbidden fell into a sulk, refusing either to go to bed or to play spillikins pleasantly.

It was a clear night, for a change, but with only a little cheese rind of moon. It was after midnight before they found where the motorcycle had left the muddy track and flung Reggie against a horse-chestnut tree.

They carried him back to Kneilthorpe on a stretcher kept for hunting misfortunes, and laid him on the billiard table. Doctor Liversedge was sent for, and a certain woman who did whatever it is such people do.

'They'll want to lift him off that nice baize,' I heard her say to the doctor, 'before there's any leaking.'

I stood in the hall, waiting for someone to tell me something.

'They've tidied him up,' Bobbity said. 'Are you ready to go in?'

'Going in' was what one was expected to do. Bobbity accompanied me and Angelica intended to as well, until she noticed Sapphire and Emerald were halfway up the stairs, watching, white-faced, and ran to bundle them away. In the billiard room an assortment of glass-eyed stag heads stared into the gloom.

It took only a second for me to see there was nothing could be done for Reggie. The man who had chatted to me so gaily over his oatmeal that morning had somehow gone away and left behind an understuffed manikin which bore a fair resemblance. There was a purple line across his brow.

I said, 'Why did he have to go and do this?'

'Too beastly for words.' That was all Bobbity could say.

We joined Neville and the doctor for large whiskeys in the drawing room, and I noticed, before I had taken even the smallest sip, that everyone was talking in strangely hollow voices. They all denied doing it, but I know what I know, and they persisted in it for several weeks.

Angelica came down from the nursery.

'I think,' she said, 'the tiddlers won't settle until you've been up and had a word.'

How I wished for Murray to be there. He would have found a way to soften Sapphire's hard little eyes.

'You spoil everything,' she spat at me. 'Everybody goes away because of you.'

I said, 'There was mud on the track.'

'You sent my Daddy Gilbert away, and Mommy Honey and Uncle Murray, and Gray . . .'

Gray had been a very disagreeable pet rabbit.

'I didn't,' I said. 'I really didn't.'

'And now Reggie's gone,' she said. 'I hate you.'

'Maybe he'll come back,' Emerald suggested.

'You goose,' Sapphire sneered. 'You're such a baby. Deads don't come back.'

She pulled the covers over her head and didn't say another word that night.

Emerald stood in front of me. Though she was blessed with silky Merrick hair, her ears protruded with the unmistakable hallmark of Minkel blood. Whatever other wrongs I did my children, I spared them the torture of nightly correction bandages.

'I don't hate you,' she said solemnly.

The girl had been hovering, with cups of hot milk that had grown wrinkly skins. Em shuddered when the skin touched her lip.

'Do I have to?' she said. She climbed into bed and I tucked her in tightly.

'Mommy,' she said, 'is Uncle Murray a dead too?'

I'm sure he might as well have been.

'No,' I said. 'He'll come back.'

'Yes,' she said, seeming quite satisfied. 'And maybe all our daddies will come back, too. One for me and one for Sapphy.'

The girl couldn't even wait for me to leave the nursery before she began undoing all my tucking in.

'This won't do, will it?' she said to Emerald. 'The Mrs doesn't know how we like room to kick about.'

FORTY-THREE

The day Reggie was to be buried the Vale of Belvoir paid their respects by canceling a meet, and the girls were excused their lessons to be taken by Angelica to Leicester, Leicestershire, to see a real stuffed giraffe. I watched out of the window all morning, until it was time to go to Buckby churchyard. I had a notion Murray might come driving up the gravel sweep, but he never did. Only Walter, with a wire of condolence from Ma and Judah.

'SUCH SADNESS,' it said. 'NO WORD MURRAY.'

My stepfather had become rather careful. He didn't approve of costly messages when so many people were ruined and having to make do and only get their old furs remodeled instead of buying nice new ones.

Bobbity brought the wire in to me, and a glass of sherry wine.

'Fortification,' she said. 'I'm afraid Merrick finished the scotch.'

I said, 'I wish Murray were here. I've been trying to remember what we say for the dead. We have our own words, you know? Hebrew words.'

'Oh, don't trouble about that,' Bobbity said. 'Our parson's an Oxford man. If any languages were needed he'd know them. But I'm quite sure they won't be. We always bury in English.'

Of course I knew that. But my mind kept casting around for the sound of those Hebrew words. Judah Jacoby had said them for my Uncle Israel. I could almost hear them, but not quite. They dangled like an annoying little thread that I could see out of the corner of my eye but couldn't quite catch.

A great crowd of the lower orders were waiting to see Reggie brought into the church, and some of them were weeping. He had been loved for the way he tirelessly rode around from hovel to hovel, inquiring about their milk yields and taking them gifts of cake at Christmas. That was the kind of man he was.

Gordie came, from his castle, but not Humpy nor the P of W who had become the King of England. Archie Vigo was a pall bearer. And Flicky Manners drove over wearing poorly aimed lip rouge.

'Darling,' she said, taking me in her arms, 'the good always die young.'

This was precisely what was troubling me most. I was only thirty-eight years old. Ahead of me stretched a long empty road, a theme my mother wasn't slow to take up.

'I sometimes feel,' she wrote,

that I have lived too long. To see both my daughters poor lonely widows and both stepsons hiding away when they might be here at dear Judah's side, helping him through such difficult times. Oscar says we are sure to have another war and Yetta says we must all be prepared for harder times yet and sacrifice, but we have already let go the driver and one of our help so I don't see what more can be asked of us.

Now Poppy, it is certainly time for you to bring Sapphire and Emerald home to New York instead of lingering amongst strangers. I didn't wish to be ungracious when we visited you at Kneilthorpe Castle, but your aunt and I noticed a worrying lack of attention to feminine grooming. Before you know it Sapphire will be a young woman, and valuable time is being lost. Neck whitener must be applied regularly if it is to have any noticeable effect, as you should not need reminding.

On your return Honey will be only too happy to help you with the great task that lies ahead of you. She has been in low spirits and it will be so beneficial to her to have something to do. Little Abe is a comfort to her, of course, and is very highly thought of at the bank, but a son is not a daughter.

Which brings me to the main point of my letter. Before you sail, you MUST ascertain the whereabouts of Murray and bring him home with you. Picture postcards from foreign parts are a poor substitute for the comfort and gratitude I'm sure Judah is owed.

We know he has been in a place called the Low Countries, but I fear he also has the intention of visiting Paris, France, and we all know what can happen to a person there. You must make it your job to find him. You will find as I did that duties and industry are a great balm after the loss of a loved one, and, of course, you will restore people's good opinion of you by retrieving what you have carelessly mislaid.

By the by, your aunt now has ulcerated veins.

Please give our fondest regards to Her Majesty. We are following with interest the young King's friendship with a fallen woman.

Your loving mother

I had no intention of returning to New York. I was lost and lonesome without Reggie, crying into my pillow for him every night, and I missed Murray, too, but it didn't seem like it was my place to go running after him, dragging him back to his father's account ledgers. His leaving wasn't my doing. He had mislaid himself. I had never said a cross word to him in my life, and besides, I had no idea where the Low Countries were.

I hung on at Kneilthorpe, watching Sapphy sprout bosoms and Sir Neville grow more sallow and silent. Bobbity became joint master of the Belvoir, Angelica moved back to Bagehots, and Mr Hitler annexed Czechoslovakia. The roof leaked but no one came to repair it. Each rainy day required another pot or bucket to be found to catch the drips, Murray's white garden turned brown, and suddenly, in the fall of 1938, I could endure no more.

'I think I'll take Em and Sapphy to Paris for a while,' I told Bobbity, quite prepared for her to argue against it. But all she said was, 'Probably for the best. Then Merrick can close up the leaky quarters. One spends such amounts keeping the old place heated to American standards.'

Kneilthorpe had never been heated to American standards.

I said, 'Does that mean we shan't have a home here anymore?'

It wasn't myself I was concerned for. I have always had the ability to create a home wherever I find myself, with whatever few sticks I can beg or borrow. But Emerald had her ponies, and Sapphire was rather attached to Angelica. Bobbity never really answered me.

'Well,' she said, 'if it comes to another war I suppose we shall be requisitioned, same as in the last lot.'

FORTY-FOUR

Everyone seemed to be talking up a war, but in Paris we found no sign of it. We stayed at the Athenée and had such fun buying witty hats and getting our portraits photographed. Humpy was still in rue Vavin, though looking rather old, Nancy and Orville Lord had fled to California, Coquelicot was a *boulangerie*, and Ava Hornblower was wearing a trilby hat and affecting to be a war correspondent. Of Cousin Addie, whom I thought my girls might be amused to meet, and Russian Stassy, whom I intended to snub, there was no trace.

I said, 'Humpy, did you happen to run across my stepbrother?' But Humpy didn't recall him.

'Jack Barty's in Tangier,' he said, 'and I believe Gil Catchings went to Buenos Aires. Or was that Oca? So many people on the move, Poppy.'

I said, 'The other possibility is the Low Countries. Any idea how I get there?'

'To Brussels and then bear left,' he said, 'but you mustn't go now. It's far too dangerous. And, anyway, I need your help. I need some money.'

People like the Choates and the Merricks and the Bagehots, they had large houses, and unfortunates to farm their land, but none of them had proper money. They wore the same old jewels every year and had the elbows of their jackets patched.

'Of course,' I said. 'How much?'

'Well . . . ,' he said.

I said, 'Have you been losing at cards?'

'Oh no,' he said, 'nothing like that. There are people who need to go to America, you see. They have to have tickets and papers and it all takes money.'

I had always paid my own way when I got the urge to travel.

I said, 'What kind of people?'

'Your kind,' he said. 'Things are getting pretty ugly, you know? For anyone . . . *juif* . . .'

I said, 'Are they? We've found things rather agreeable here.'

'Please take my word for it,' he said. 'You should think of going home yourself.'

I said, 'But we only just left. And I can't tell you how melancholy the place makes me feel, without Reggie.'

'I didn't mean Kneilthorpe,' he said. 'If it comes to a showdown, I'm not sure even England will be a safe haven. You should go home to America. Put as many miles as you can between yourself and the Hun.'

Humpy made the forthcoming war sound very thrilling. I wrote out a check immediately.

'Will this do it?' I asked.

'It's a start,' he said.

Rescuing people would turn out to be a good deal more costly than I had expected. Little by little I detected signs of war fever. Stores put up their shutters and left them there. Sandbags appeared in the streets. Sometimes, at night, I heard scuffles beneath the windows of our suite, but in the morning there was never any sign of anything amiss.

Emerald's letters to her ponies dwindled from daily to weekly, and she learned to love riding in the Bois de Vincennes. And Sapphire, for the first time in her life, seemed happy. She liked Paris.

Humpy had an endless supply of poor artists and writers who needed help in getting to America, and I believe Sapphy enjoyed the idea that we were engaged in dangerous, mysterious work.

'It's like catching the smugglers,' she said, 'in *Spring Term At Tiverton Towers.*'

I still was not entirely convinced by all the whispering and sad faces and wondered sometimes whether Humpy was being taken for a ride and me along with him. I walked around the city all the time and never saw a single Hun.

I said, 'I do hope you'll keep track of these people, so they can pay back their fare.' I could tell by his face he was doing no such thing. He didn't even have a list of their names.

'If it's bothering you, Poppy,' he said, a little testily, considering how many of his friends I was sending on vacation, 'why don't you have some of their work, as collateral. Paintings and so forth. I'm getting quite a collection myself. Frankl. Mellin. I've some interesting pastels by Vblescu. They'll probably be worth something if one waits long enough. Why don't you pick out a few pieces for yourself?'

This at least added a little interest to the project, but quite often I didn't like what was being offered.

'Heaven's sakes, Mom,' Sapphy said to me one day, 'you don't have to like it.'

We were looking at some small gloomy oils by Rinkelmann. I hated them.

'No,' I said. 'I'm sorry. No sale. Mr Rinkelmann will have to find someone else to pay for his jaunt.'

'A jaunt!' she said. 'It's not a jaunt. He has to escape from oppression.'

I said, 'Sapphire, *I* had to escape from oppression. I had to go to the Cunard office and buy our tickets and arrange for our trunks and all the while your grandma Jacoby and your great-aunt Fish were oppressing me, oppressing me, oppressing me. You are too young to understand.'

'Mom,' she said. 'I do understand. And if you won't buy Rinkelmann a ticket, I will.'

Of course, Sapphire was nowhere near coming into her money. But she threatened to sell her silver vanity set and her jade egg and whatever else it might take, so I relented and wrote another check. Rinkelmann then promptly disappeared. I don't believe we ever heard of him again, but Humpy was right about one thing. Those little oils fetched quite a decent price eventually.

FORTY-FIVE

They said we were at war but nothing happened. We heard from Angelica that she was going for a driver in the army and I thought of dashing back to do the same myself, but Emerald cried and said she didn't want to be an orphan. We stayed on.

One of the dividends of war was that Ma's letters stopped appearing on my breakfast tray, reproaching me for staying away, giving me weekly reminders that Murray was still unaccounted for and probably lay dead and unmourned in some foreign hell-hole. Another was that everyone became rather gay while they still had the chance. Some of the *juifs* had their windows broken and were called unkind names, so I began the precaution of frequently making the sign of the cross whenever I was out and about. I had learned how to do it in England and I found it a very useful habit.

One day in the spring of 1940 Humpy took me to one side.

'Poppy,' he said, 'I rather think it's time you made a move. I think I'm going to insist.'

I said, 'To New York?'

'Of course to New York,' he said, 'while the going is good. It could be pretty bloody awful for you, if the Germans arrive.'

I'd never seen him look so worried.

I said, 'I'll leave if you do.'

'But it's rather different for me,' he said.

I said, 'How is it different? I've been in a war before, you know? I worked for the Red Cross. I can fly a bi-plane.'

'Well,' he said, 'you have children. You must think of them.

You're also too old for war work, *real* war work. And well, to be perfectly blunt Poppy, you're very obviously Jewish.'

Humpy was famously inexpert on the subject of female looks. I had once heard him praise Nancy Lord's legs. Still, I knew he cared for me, and for my girls, and I began to wish we'd made a run for Kneilthorpe. He shook his head.

'England's done for,' he said. 'America's the only hope. I may even join you there myself, if I can finish what I've started here. I must get papers for Lionel and René.'

Lionel was another of Humpy's special young friends and René was Lionel's brother. He played the cello and Sapphire had a crush on him.

I broke the news to Em and Sapphy.

I said, 'We have to go to New York for the duration.'

They both kicked up. Emerald said she had to return to Kneilthorpe and rescue her ponies before the Germans ate them. Sapphire said it wasn't decent for us to run away when so many other people couldn't. This was an argument I never could follow.

I said, 'We have to go on a train and then a flying boat, and it'll be a great adventure because we may get bombed or shot down. And when we get to New York, who knows, Uncle Murray may be there.'

Every night I sent out thought waves to him. 'Be there, you fool. Please be there.' We drank a very good champagne that final evening, but Humpy was in a bad humor. He had decided to come with us as far as Lisbon, to see us safely aboard a clipper.

He said, 'I feel it's what Reggie would have wanted.' But even after it was all agreed, he seemed to be arguing within himself. I believe it was about 'unfinished business' as he called it, but as I told him many many times, he had been as generous with his time as I had with my money and one could not be expected to solve all the problems of the world and his wife.

He was carrying just one small bag, and grew quite impatient when I told him I'd had our trunks sent ahead to the railroad station.

'Trunks!' he cried. 'Didn't I say most particularly to travel light?'

But we were traveling light. Eight pieces between us didn't even begin to accommodate our needs. I had had to leave a full-length leopard and two foxes in the care of the Athenée, and photo frames and shoe trees and a thousand other useful things.

I said, 'I'll be back next year.'

The concierge said, 'Bien sûr, madame', but I dare say I was no sooner out of the door than he was dipping his grubby hands into my boxes. I never saw any of those things again.

The Gare d'Austerlitz was hell. The whole city seemed to be there and it was impossible to find anyone who could be sent for luggage or information. We were pushed and squeezed by every class of person and if we had not had Humpy with us I doubt we ever would have found our train. The great glass vault was filled with steam and a thousand echoes of uncouth voices and doors slamming and whistles blowing. Humpy and I were forced to shout at each other.

I said, 'Where are our seats?'

'Better climb aboard,' he yelled.

I said, 'We do have seats?'

'Not as such,' he yelled back. 'Just climb aboard.'

I said, 'But who can we send to find our trunks?'

He began to climb down out of the doorway.

'Poppy!' he said. 'Bugger the trunks. Get onto the bloody train.'

Then something happened.

The train began to move. Humpy grasped my arm and I turned to grasp Sapphire's, but she wasn't there. She had been right by my side, but suddenly she was gone and where she should have been there were only crude types determined to push me to one side.

'Sapphy!' I yelled at Humpy. He was preparing to jump down. Then we both heard Em. She was behind him, trapped in the corridor with strangers and unfortunates.

'Mommy!' she cried. 'Don't leave me!'

I don't know who pulled Humpy back inside. I only know there was nothing I could do. I watched the train slide away with Humpy looking for me, open-mouthed, and Emerald, hidden from view. They were gone without me. Our luggage was lost. And so was Sapphire.

I wept, but no one came to my assistance. People thought only of themselves that night, and I have made it a rule to avoid railroad stations ever since.

I waited beneath the clock. It seemed to me Sapphire might know that's where people meet at railroad stations. But I grew fatigued from peering into the crowds searching for her face and then, from one moment to the next, the champagne cleared away from my mind and I had a series of alarming thoughts. First, that she might not be in the station. She might have climbed aboard that train by a different door and found her way safely to Humpy and Em. Or, that she had not found her way to them. That she had been lured into a couchette by some villain and robbed of her citrine necklace. In either case I was the one left behind to face the Germans.

Alternatively, she might have run away deliberately. It might be her plan to disobey me and cause inconvenience. If I ever found her, I decided, I would send her directly to Buenos Aires. It was high time Gilbert Catchings experienced the burdens of parenthood.

There were no taxis to be had. I began to walk, but by the time I reached Pantheon I had to take off my shoes and carry them. No one gave me a second look, a lone woman in a good suit, walking in her stocking feet. That was when I knew something crazy was happening to Paris. And every painful step I took reminded me of another night when I had walked till my stockings were full of holes. The night my Pa didn't come home on the *Carpathia*.

Every house in rue Vavin had its eyes closed. No one answered at Humpy's door though I knew he was allowing people to stay there, and the old place, where Gil and I had once enjoyed happy times, was dark and shuttered, too.

I huddled on the step, too tired to walk any further, and yet wide awake. I was homeless. I suppose the sky began to lighten at about four.

At seven I limped to Lilas for coffee and there I received several great kindnesses from Nub the Armenian waiter. He gave me a pair of sturdy English laced shoes intended for a man, an omelette, and a suggestion where I might find Sapphire.

'The boy,' he said, 'the one she likes. He lives up in Rosiers with the rest of his kind.'

I had never heard of such a place. Nub drew me a map on a napkin.

'Better get her back quick,' he said. And he made a gesture, cutting across his throat with the edge of his hand.

I made slow progress, with my poor sore feet slipping about inside Nub's shoes, and I feared I was too late anyway. My baby, whom I had never really gotten to know, was probably lying in some thieves' den with her throat cut. Then, on the Pont Marie, I saw her coming toward me. It was the almond green of her dress I recognized first. She was walking fast, not looking where she was going. I had to call out her name three times before she heard me, then saw me, then came running into my arms.

'I couldn't find him, Mom,' was all she would say. 'I couldn't find him anywhere.'

I took her to a little place in Saint-Germain and fed her on bread and *café au lait* until she seemed more disposed to listen to me.

I said, 'Do you realize what trouble you've caused? Humpy and Emerald have gone without us and I've spent the night on some stranger's front stoop, and our luggage is entirely lost.'

'I didn't ask you to come looking for me,' she said. 'You could have gone. You could have taken care of your luggage and left me to take care of myself.'

'Some day,' I said, 'you will have a daughter of your own. Then you'll know why I came looking for you.'

That stopped her in her self-pitying tracks.

'And thank goodness for Humpy,' I said. 'Otherwise poor Em

would have been all alone on that train. Did you ever think of that? And who is this boy? Do we know his people?'

'Listen to yourself,' she said. 'You sound like Grandma Jacoby.'

I said, 'Nub at the Lilas says they're dangerous types.'

'What!' she said. 'Nub said that? He did not. He knows René.'

She was in love with René, Humpy's boy who played the cello. Sixteen years old, and she believed she had met the love of her life.

I said, 'But Sapphy . . .'

I thought René was probably one of Humpy's funny crowd. The kind that never fell in love with girls.

'I know what you're going to say,' she said. 'He's a Jew. But I don't care. I love him. I'm going to stay with him till this beastly war's finished. I'll be a Jew too.'

I always found that word oddly shocking in English. In French it just rustled silkily off the tongue.

I looked at her, my wilder skinnier junior. She had nothing of Gil about her, except her height. Even her eyes had darkened to match mine. I judged this was not the moment to do anything but persuade her onto a train.

I said, 'You know, Humpy may have got them papers, for America. For René and for Lionel. I know he was determined to do it. And wouldn't it be a terrible thing if René got to New York and you were stuck here with the Hun?'

She said, 'But I don't think Humpy did get them papers. I think they've been taken away somewhere.'

'Well then,' I said, 'you'll have to wait for him until we've won the war. You'll have to take your love somewhere safe and guard it patiently. If it's true love, it'll endure.'

I had read a number of novelettes recommended by Angelica, so I knew the gist of what to say.

Sapphy said, 'It is true love. And you don't mind about the Jewish side of things?'

'How could I?' I said.

Not telling the truth is not at all the same as lying.

On rue Monge I managed to obtain a taxi by stepping into its path.

'I want to look one more time,' Sapphy said. 'It won't take long.'

'Sapphire,' I said, 'you're grown-up now, and grown-ups have duties. We have to rescue your little sister.'

'Half-sister,' she said quietly, as we neared the Gare d'Austerlitz.

FORTY-SIX

We caught up with Humpy and Emerald nearly three weeks later at the Plaza Hotel in Lisbon.

'I was almost resigned to fatherhood,' Humpy said. 'With a bereft waif in a foreign land.'

There had never been anything waif-like about Em. She eyed me warily.

'What took you so long?' she said. 'Why didn't you get on the train? I could have been left all alone and not known where to get off or anything.'

The good news was that there was an agreeably gay crowd staying in town. The bad news was that they were all there for the same reason we were. Waiting for seats on a clipper. I sent Humpy to the ticket office with a bribe immediately, but he said it made no difference. For a man who promised to open doors for escaping artists he had surprisingly little spine in such situations. I believe this came of his never having had proper money. It has been my experience that money always makes the difference.

We ordered rum cocktails and waited for the girls to come down to dinner.

I said, 'It was about the boy René. She believes she's in love.'

'Oh God!' he said.

I said, 'She's only a baby. And now she's quite obsessed with the idea that Germans are going to shoot him and he has to be rescued. She's quite determined to play the heroine. I can't tell you what a strain it's been, Humpy, watching her every minute. I still wouldn't put it beyond her to jump on a train back to Paris.'

'She certainly mustn't do that,' he said. 'I don't think there's anything to be done for René and Lionel now.'

I said, 'Well, don't tell Sapphire that. I only succeeded in bringing her here by telling her those people were certain to turn up in New York. I told her you'd arranged papers for them.'

He groaned.

'God, Poppy,' he said. 'It's bad enough I've run out on things there. I hope you're not asking me to fib as well.'

I said, 'Damn and blast it, Humpy, why did you allow her to get so attached to this person? She doesn't just have a pash on him. She's decided she's going to be Jewish too, like René.'

He raised an eyebrow.

I said, 'She doesn't know. We just don't really bother with that kind of thing. Gil wasn't Jewish. But if she knew, if she thought for one moment . . . I'd have lost her completely. I'd never have dragged her away from Paris.'

'Gracious,' he said. 'What a muddle.'

I said, 'It's not a muddle at all, Humpy. It's very simple. You mustn't say anything. When all this has blown over I'll explain things to her, but right now she mustn't suspect a thing.'

We allowed the girls one cocktail each before we went out for a fine seafood dinner and I forced the conversation along at a furious pace so as not to allow Sapphire any opportunity for questions or reproaches. I talked until I was exhausted, and then Humpy failed to notice my signals that he should take over, and a dangerous silence occurred.

'Uncle Humpy,' she began, 'when do you suppose René will get to America? We're going to be married, you know?'

Humpy choked a little.

'Hard to say,' he said. 'Hard to know even when we'll be there.'

'I was so afraid he'd been taken away,' she said. 'The whole building was empty.'

She turned to Emerald.

'René's Jewish,' she said, 'but Mom doesn't mind. So when we get married, I shall become Jewish, too. It won't affect you, though.'

She gazed down at the debris of her lobster and Emerald looked at her, at first with the blandest of expressions. Then she began to shake. First she shook silently, then tears spilled down her cheeks and she began to make ugly whooping noises. Finally she fell sideways off her chair. All this on one rum cocktail. Her voice floated up while she was still on the floor.

'I shall become Jewish, too.' She had Sapphire's expression exactly.

'You twit, Sapph. You're already Jewish. You ninny. You utter, utter ninny.'

I spoke sharply to Emerald. Better, I felt, to focus on the disgrace of her falling down drunk than to allow her any kind of victory over poor Sapphy. Humpy was no help. I believe he found something amusing in the scene himself.

Em climbed back into her seat, watching Sapphire, looking for more trouble.

'Aren't we, Mommy?' she challenged me. 'Aren't we Jewish as can be?'

'Jewish, Jewish, Jewish,' she chanted to herself. I had a mind to slap her, right there and then, but Humpy placed a restraining hand on mine and called for the check.

'Perhaps you and Sapphy should head back,' he said. 'You must be tired. Em and I might go for cake.'

Emerald said, 'Sapphy's not tired, are you Sapphy? She wants to go for cake, too, and hear all about being Jewish.'

Sapphire said nothing. She refused cake or soda and when I tried to link arms with her, hers felt like stone. So we just walked, and I talked. For the longest time that night it seemed like I was talking to myself.

I said, 'You see, there's Jewish and there's *Jewish*. Like some people go to the opera if they're specially asked and some people go every week, even if they know they're not going to enjoy the show. Like some people will take a whiskey with you if you offer it, but they'd never think of keeping a bottle on their own sideboard. Then, actually, there are hundreds of different kinds of Jewish. Your Uncle Harry was only Jewish in business. Hardly even that. Whereas some people are Jewish every minute of the day, like . . . well, we don't really know any of that kind. Grandpa Jacoby is kind of medium Jewish. Anyhow, it's not a major thing. It's just about who your people were. You can be Jewish if you want to be. Grandma Jacoby'll probably like that. When I was a little girl we didn't act Jewish because my Aunt Fish thought it might . . . hold us back. But these days your Grandma goes in for it in quite a big way. It can be nice. I'd probably have been more Jewish myself but I've always been so busy. I always thought I might learn the Hebrew words. But you know how it is. Well, perhaps you'll do it. You're young. You have all the time in the world. And especially if you marry a Jewish person. Any Jewish person.'

'How can I?' she whispered. 'How can I even face him again? You've made me look such a fool.'

Without even trying I had managed to change her mind. She had gone from searching for his face in every place we passed, to dreading that they'd ever meet again, and all because of a silly misunderstanding.

I said, 'No one thinks you're a fool, Sapphy.'

'I do,' she said. 'I'm a fool ever to have trusted you. You told Em. Why didn't you tell me?'

But I had told Emerald nothing.

She said, 'I bet Reggie told her. He never liked me. Why didn't you just send me to my real daddy? He'd never have done this to me.'

She was shouting by the end.

'I hate you,' she yelled. 'I always hated you. And now you've completely ruined my life.'

It wasn't me who ruined her life, of course. She always had that

Catchings tendency. And then, eventually, there was the drink.

We finally boarded the *Dixie* clipper in October 1940. I wore a pair of wide-legged slacks in taupe, a kidskin jacket with a lightning fastener, and a black bandeau. Those were the kind of colors we were wearing in war-torn Europe.

We made Horta, our first stop, in five and a half hours and the wind was blowing so hard across that God-forsaken rock I remained on board and played red dog with an amusing boy from Chicago. He had found himself almost cut off in Marseilles and was disinclined to venture outside again until we were safely on American soil.

The next stage of the journey was the worst. Sixteen hours to Bermuda, with nothing to do but eat and drink and try to keep Emerald from tormenting Sapphire.

After Bermuda the whole tone of the party was quite changed. Many new passengers came on board, making it so much less comfortable for us, and causing long delays at the bar. Humpy was morose. My little card-playing friend attached himself to one of the new horde. And Sapphire, having chewed all her finger nails to the quick, developed the very irritating habit of nibbling at the ends of her hair.

I was relieved to hear we were nearing Jones Beach, and even more relieved to find no one had been sent to meet us. I had already decided to enjoy a decent night's sleep at the Brevoort before I faced family.

In the event, I found I needed two nights and a trip to Bonwit Teller to replace some of our lost treasures. Never one to be defeated by adversity, I had improvised interesting skirts out of Portuguese tablecloths, but they were jarringly unsuitable for a New York fall.

On the third day I called East 69th Street.

'Poppy,' Ma sobbed. 'Oh Poppy, where have you been? Such dreadful times. How I've needed you, and you weren't to be found. Lady Bumpety said you were gone to Paris, and the hotel said you were gone to Spain, and Honey is too delicate to be of much help although, of course, she's been angelic. And Murray is still gone. Oh Poppy. Please come immediately. I have new help, and she just doesn't understand our ways.'

My poor Ma. Judah had died, but the news had failed to reach either me, or Murray. There had been no warning. One moment he was enjoying corned beef and pickles with Ma and Aunt Fish, the next he was complaining of dyspepsia and then gone.

'A broken heart,' my aunt diagnosed, alluding to two sons and not a business head between them.

Oscar and Dear Yetta had hurried to town for the burying and hurried away again.

'He still suffers so, with his nerves,' Ma explained, 'or they'd have stayed longer and been a comfort to me. The noise of the city brings it on, you see.'

Aunt Fish had a different story.

'Yetta has never forgiven your mother for stealing Judah's affection,' she opined. 'She ruled the roost, you see, until Dora came along. And now she has ruined that boy Oscar, out of spite. It's my opinion she encourages his nerves.'

I said, 'Yetta Landau was your greatest friend.'

'She was an acquaintance,' she corrected me, 'and, anyway, that was when we were fighting a war.'

I said, 'Well, now we're fighting another. Shan't you be serving on any of her committees this time?'

'Poppy,' she said, 'as far as I'm aware we're not fighting a war. Let those it concerns fight and let the rest of us mind our own businesses. Besides, I'm far too old for heavy committee work.

Now, I know you'll be expecting to move in, to be at your Ma's side, but I have been here in your stead while you were gallivanting and not receiving your mail, so you must be patient until I find a place to go. I shall find a little room somewhere, with a cooking corner. Just enough for a widow.'

I said, 'I'm a widow, too, you know?'

'Yes,' she said. 'We're all widows now. By the by ...' She dropped her voice. 'On the subject of husbands. A certain person has been seen. On Fifth Avenue. By your sister.'

I said, 'Do you mean Gil? Well, whatever you do, don't let Sapphire hear you mention his name.'

'Poppy,' she said. 'I have *never* mentioned his name.'

I was able to put my aunt's mind at rest on one point. I had no intention of moving into the Jacoby house with Ma.

I took an apartment on 49th Street at Turtle Bay and enrolled Emerald at the Levison School. Sapphire refused to go to any kind of school. She had learned, she said, that nothing was ever as it seemed and no one was ever to be trusted, and that was all she needed to know.

Honey became rather self-important at this point.

'Let me have a word,' she said, as though she had some special understanding of the case.

I said, 'Have all the words you like. She's determined to be wretched. And she's determined to be Jewish.'

'Why doesn't she come to school then?' Emerald asked. She had already learned how to read a whole line of Hebrew words and was top of her class, of course, in French.

'I am surprised,' said Aunt Fish, 'to see Poppy allowing this. Emerald would profit from classes in deportment. I would never say this to your mother, but it's just as well Judah is no longer with us. Learning old-fashioned languages is the kind of thing he would have encouraged. But the Plotzes didn't come to America to be old-fashioned, and neither did the Minkels, so you'd best get to work on these girls, Honey. Especially Sapphire. Time is short. Encourage her in good grooming. Talk to her about gowns and making her debut. You always had a special way with her.'

And so began a battle for Sapphire's heart and mind. Honey, with Aunt Fish firmly in her camp, hoped to lighten her hair, teach her to waltz and guide her into the arms of a husband with good silver. Ma though reopened the case for adding Dora to Sapphy's list of names and teaching her the Sabbath *berukas* she had struggled to learn herself.

'I haven't found them to be disadvantageous, Zillah,' she said.

'That,' said my aunt, 'is because you studied them to *oblige* your husband, and not in order to acquire him.'

Sapphire submitted to all of this like a sleepwalker. She neither protested nor entered into the spirit of things, and nothing would stop her from chewing her hair and her nails. She read the newspapers avidly, an activity Ma and my aunt were unanimous in discouraging because of the way it deepened the furrow of her scowl and risked ugly deformities of her mind. Sometimes she remained in her room and drew sad faces with black ink.

'That child is melancholy,' Ma said. 'As soon as Judah's anniversary has passed I shall make a soirée. Leopold Adler's boy is just the right age for her.'

I said, 'Not Leopold Adler! Does he have his father's lips?'

'How easy it is to find fault,' Ma said. 'How much easier to mock another's efforts than to take action oneself. And how different your life would be, Poppy, if you had had the wisdom to choose a Leopold Adler.'

'We'll both make soirées for her, Ma,' Honey said. 'Mine will be a lighter, more modern affair. And perhaps Poppy will design one of her originations for Sapphy, if she can spare us one moment of her time.'

I was busy, it was true. I had made Humpy a monthly allowance, as he'd found himself strapped for cash, and I was helping him with the décor of the little place we'd found on Tenth Street. At street level we planned to show interesting works of art. Some by unfortunates we had rescued, some by artists who had sought our help too late. Humpy himself was to live over the shop and so reduce the expense of hotel bills.

It was to be called Art from the Edge, and was sure to be written up in the newspapers. One of my tasks was to reacquaint myself with *le tout* New York and discover who were the most fabulous and intriguing people to invite to the opening.

It was many months before my path crossed Gil's. I had gone to the Zanzibar Club with an amusing crowd from Humpy's new set, and I was on my way to powder my nose when I ran right into him. He had a good deal more forehead than I remembered. I was disappointed to find myself blushing.

'Yeah,' he said, 'I heard the great mustard heiress was back in town. I heard we had some trash in the city no one else wanted.'

I said, 'I'm a widow now', thinking to lessen his spleen a little.

'Is that so?' he said. 'Then I guess you're looking for the next poor sucker. You here shopping for Number 3, Poppy? Or is it Number 4? You here getting up your next wedding list?'

I said, 'I'm here with our daughters. Trying to keep them safe from the war.'

'*Your* daughters,' he said. 'One by that English sap, and God knows where the other one came from.'

I said, 'Sapphire's yours, Gil, as sure as night follows day. She looks like you. She acts like you. As a matter of fact I believe she'd be on your doorstep tomorrow if she knew you were in town.'

'I don't have a doorstep,' he said. 'I stay with friends, since my wife robbed me of my home and my health and my livelihood.'

He never had managed to write that book.

'I see you're still congregating with faggots,' he said.

Those were the last words Gil Catchings ever said to me, though not the last he said about me, I'm sure. I insisted Humpy take me home immediately.

In December 1941, just before we were to launch Art from the Edge, the Japs bombed our boys at Pearl Harbor. Around Times Square all the niteries put out their lights, and the harbor filled with gray ships. We really were at war.

Emerald brought her school atlas on our weekly visit to East 69th Street and we all studied the Pacific Ocean.

'Perhaps it will come to nothing,' Ma said. 'Perhaps the President will smooth things over.'

Aunt Fish said that she for one would not be relying on Mr Roosevelt.

'We must lay in a good store cupboard, Dora,' she said. 'And sleep with a weapon by the bed. I still have the stick Harry gave me when the Hun were at the door. Do you still have yours?'

Em flicked through the pages of her atlas and sighed.

'I wonder where Uncle Murray is?' she said. 'I wonder if he's somewhere with the goodies or somewhere with the baddies?'

'He's hiding out,' Honey snapped. 'Instead of stepping forward and doing his duty.'

She was anxious about Sherman Ulysses and this was making her unusually harsh. As for myself, I didn't care to be reminded about Murray. He had never returned to Kneilthorpe, nor had I heard from any of the people who had been asked to watch out for him. Flicky Manners. Ava Hornblower. The concierge at the Lisbon Plaza.

I had had every expectation he would just turn up one day or write a letter at least, but war changed all that. Frontiers closed, letters never arrived and wires brought nothing but heartbreaking news. The only good news was Murray's belongings had not been returned to any of us in a sad brown parcel.

I did feel for my sister, with her son liable to be drafted.

'There's no need for him to go,' Ma said, grasping at reasons why Abe, as she still called him, might be allowed to sit the war out.

'He always had a weakness of the ankles. And colic. Don't you remember how liable he was to colic?'

But Sherman didn't plead weak ankles or even wait for the draft. He enlisted for the navy, went to midshipman school and sailed away. Honey got a postcard, mailed from the Panama Canal. After that, things went quiet.

'Our only protector,' Ma wailed. 'Why didn't you tell them, Honey? Why didn't you tell them he was needed at home?'

'Ma,' I said, 'I'd rather have Sherman protecting us in the Pacific Ocean than from behind his desk at Title Guarantee and Trust.'

'Yes,' Honey said. 'If we're so in need of protection you had better send for Oscar Jacoby. If he can be spared from mending chair rungs. He's family, too.' This was unusually spirited for Honey.

'This war,' Ma said, to my aunt, 'isn't at all like the last one. In the last war people didn't become disagreeable and contradict their mother.'

Emerald said, 'What kind of family is Oscar, Grandma? I never met him.'

Ma said, 'He is your elder step-uncle, who fought in the Great War and now makes very lovely things. Sewing tables. And pretty applewood boxes. Not chair rungs at all, Honey.'

He did sometimes mend chairs. Murray had told me.

Aunt Fish said, 'And, of course, you're very glad of him to take charge of Yetta, aren't you Dora? Now she has grown so odd.'

Yetta Landau, once the brightest light in the Jacoby firmament, had become forgetful and difficult. I wished her no harm, but I was relieved to know she wouldn't be marching into town at the head of a column of sock knitters. By an accident of birth I had been too young for the Great War and I was too old for this new one. I was forty-four and nothing had quite gone my way. My first husband had turned out a beast. My second husband was a fading photograph. My originations hadn't brought me lasting fame, my Parisian soirées were forgotten, and I had never had the opportunity to be a heroine. My aunt still soured the air I breathed. My mother still defied me to do anything to her satisfaction. And when I walked into the Hawaiian Room no one turned to look at me anymore.

FORTY-EIGHT

War be damned. We opened the gallery anyway. I believe the rush to have the exhibition ready was what saved Humpy from a tendency to mope.

'I should never have left Paris,' he'd say, and I'd send him out immediately to pursue Tedeschi for the paintings he owed us.

'I dream about them, Poppy,' he'd say. 'The ones we didn't help. I can't quite see them, but they keep grabbing at my clothes, and then I wake in a frightful sweat.'

I'd just put the telephone into his hand and a list of calls that had to be made. As far as I was concerned we had done more than our share of helping and, besides, experience had shown me how quickly gratitude can turn to truculence. A person may be meek and mild until he's through Ellis Island. After that he's liable to start expressing opinions and declining to get out of bed before noon and apply a brush to a canvas.

Humpy also wondered whether it was appropriate to throw a party, but I insisted. No one can be expected to look at difficult art without a glass in their hand and we were showing recent work by Molinard and Straus, which is certainly my idea of difficult, as well as Tedeschi's monochrome stripes and Bella Yaff's stick people.

I said, 'We'll pass around a bucket, if it'll make you feel better, in aid of the unfortunates.'

Which we did. By the time the liquor ran out it was filled to overflowing with dollar bills and someone mistook it for an exhibit and demanded to buy it. We got written up in *The New York Times*, although Humpy's name appeared seven times and mine only once, and in just the first week we sold all our Tedeschi's, two Yaff's and a Straus to Tungsten Consolidated.

Everyone was most excited by our rescuees. Tragedy was suddenly in vogue, though quite what was so tragic about a person who had had his passage to America bought and paid for, I failed to see.

My sister found herself a wartime diversion too. She became a paid-up Dutch Reformed and a believer in the power of positive thought. She had begun to recognize though that even this had its limits with Sapphire, who was developing a taste for White Spider cocktails and boogie-woogie music.

'I don't know what more I can do for her,' Honey said, 'until she finds the kingdom of God within. I never saw a child so set on self-destruction.'

I said, 'Do you think she'd like a new nose?'

Honey said, 'Good governor, no! She cares nothing about her looks. She told me she considers herself a widow. A widow of the heart. She says she'll never marry, and if she continues helling around and acting fast she's guaranteed not to get asked. The Leopold Adlers certainly won't want her.'

So I bought her a Duesenberg automobile instead of a trip to the beauty doctor and advised her against drinking on an empty stomach.

I said to Emerald, 'What about you? It's only cartilage, you know? It's easily done. Or how about a permanent wave?'

'A permanent wave?' she said. 'Didn't you just spend money getting rid of your permanent wave?'

There was a procedure I had tried out, supposed to remove the kink out of darkie hair.

Emerald said, 'Either this family's crazy or I am and I know which way the evidence points.'

Em ran in a groove. She attended to her studies, rode horseback in Central Park on Sundays, whistled in the bathroom. Nothing ever seemed to get her down. Fridays she'd even volunteer to eat dinner with Ma and help her do the business with the candles.

'Why don't you come?' she'd say. But Fridays weren't good for me. I had the gallery.

'And why don't you come?' she'd ask Sapphy. 'Whatever happened to being Jewish?'

Sapphire said, 'I can be Jewish without lighting candles.'

'Oh no you can't,' Em said. But Sapphy had already left the room.

Emerald finished at the Levison in the summer of 1943 and carried off just about every prize going. I was in Pittsburgh at the time, tracking down an interesting Lithuanian we had heard about. He painted large oils of factories and we knew the Jebb Corporation were becoming interested in industrial collectibles.

So Honey went to Em's commencement in my stead, but the very next date I had free, I gave her lunch at the Astor and a check for her first mink.

I said, 'Go to Jacoby's. You'll get it at cost.'

'Mom,' she said, 'it's high summer. I don't want a mink.'

That's the younger generation for you. They never think ahead.

I said, 'And what are you planning to do with your life? I could use a *vendeuse* at the gallery.'

'No thanks,' she said. 'I don't think I'd know how to sell that stuff you have there.'

I said, 'I'll teach you. We have explanations for every piece. All you have to do is tell people what the artist is saying. As soon as you do that they buy. People worry about the silliest things. Whether it's worth the money. How they can be sure they've hung it the right way up. They just need reassurance.'

'Well, still no thanks,' she said. 'I'd like to work in a flower store.'

I said, 'I'll buy you a flower store.'

'No,' she said. 'I'd just like to work in a store and go to the lunch counter with nice friendly people.'

I said, 'You realize your life won't be your own? I tried it myself many years ago. You realize you'll never have time to get your hair styled or meet a beau for cocktails.'

'A beau!' she said. 'You sound like Grandma. Well, the kind of . . . *beau* I'd be looking for probably won't get off early either. I'll be fine Mom. I don't need my own store.'

In her own way Emerald could be as uncooperative as Sapphire.

She said, 'Were you really a shop girl?'

I said, 'I worked in neckties in Macy's. But then I met Gil and I found the hours didn't suit.'

I had said it before I thought.

'Gil?' she said. 'Do you mean Gilbert? Was he really Sapphy's pa?'

I said, 'I have to get back to the gallery.'

She clamped her hand over mine.

'Don't you dare,' she said. 'You missed me winning General Excellence so you can darned well order me Peaches Flambé and tell me about Gilbert.'

I said, 'He was a mistake, that's all.'

She wanted to know what kind of mistake.

I said, 'I don't know. He was a kind of revolutionary intellectual . . .'

She whistled.

I said, 'I suppose it was my fortune came between us.'

Em said, 'Why? Wouldn't Grandma let him have any of it?'

I said, 'No, I gave him as much of it as he needed, but he just didn't seem to enjoy it. He preferred sitting in cafés, drinking with paupers.'

She said, 'Do you have a picture?'

I said, 'No. There was a wedding portrait but as I recall your Grandma cut it in half.'

'No wonder Sapphire's such a misery,' she said. 'She hardly knows who she is. I'm sure glad Gilbert wasn't my daddy.'

I realized she was gazing at me through my cigarette smoke.

'Gilbert definitely wasn't my daddy, was he?' she said.

So I told her the whole thing, about flying down to Cap Ferrat with Humpy and meeting Reggie. Well, practically the whole thing. Between a mother and daughter there are certain details best kept veiled.

'Scandalous,' she said. But she was laughing. 'And did you know about sexual intercourse and everything?'

This was what happened when you allowed a girl a modern education.

I said, 'I knew enough not to use words like that in the Astor dining room.'

'Well, la-di-dah,' she said. 'And where is Gilbert now?'

'Buenos Aires,' I said, quick as a flash. 'I believe that's what I heard. Of course, he could be anywhere by now.'

'Mmm,' she said, scraping the pattern off her dessert dish. 'Like Uncle Murray. I hate it that the world is so big. Don't you?'

FORTY-NINE

So Emerald went as a junior at Fleischmann's Fresh Flowers. You could set your watch by her, swinging out of the apartment every morning in one of her adorable little suits. Of course, I made sure Artie Fleischmann knew who she was. I made sure he understood he couldn't make her life a misery, like she was any ordinary shop girl.

Not long after we won the war in Europe a letter arrived for me at the Jacoby house. It was from England, so Ma had felt justified in having the help steam open the envelope. But it wasn't from Murray. 'Thank goodness this beastly war is over,' Angelica wrote.

I've had a rather fabulous time myself, driving top brass, but many have had a perfectly horrid time. The Burtons lost two sons, we lost a distant Bagehot, and the Belvoir is looking generally depleted. Bobbity hoped Kneilthorpe would revert because Merrick's far from well, but it's being retained for convalescents so the poor things are going to be cooped up in the leaky wing for the foreseeable.

Now I must get to the point. Edgar Boodle-Neary has asked me to marry him and I rather think I might. I still think fondly of Murray but it seems unlikely he's going to return to me now. I hope you've all had a decent war.

Ma waited until I'd finished reading before she presented her case against mixed marriages.

'A cat may as well marry a horse,' she declared.

I said, 'Reggie and I were mixed and we had a blissful marriage. I believe Murray's problem may have been that he didn't realize he was a fairy.'

Aunt Fish said, 'This is what comes of art galleries, Dora. As I always warned it would.'

'Well,' Ma said, 'God is good. He spared Judah having to hear such a thing.'

I placed a transatlantic phone call immediately.

I said, 'Are you having him declared dead?'

'How extraordinary,' Angelica kept saying. 'How absolutely extraordinary to hear your voice.'

I said, 'I wish you well, Gelica, I really do. But I don't want Murray to be dead.'

'I'm applying for an annulment,' she said. 'It's quite easily done. Is this costing you a mint, chatting on the blower like this?'

I said, 'I'm going to have him looked for, you see? I'm going to hire a sleuth and track him to the ends of the earth.'

'How are Em and Sapphy?' she asked.

I said, 'He was very fond of you, you know? Whatever happened . . .'

'Yes,' she said, our conversation finally getting into step. 'I know. But, of course, you were the one he adored.'

That night I dreamt I was in my little orange Oriole, but Nancy Lord was at the controls. I was squashed so tightly between Gil and Reggie I couldn't prevent Nancy from doing crazy maneuvers and Murray was out on the nose of the plane, wearing a top hat.

Next day I visited the offices of a private detective called Pink and placed before him the few facts I had.

'Well,' he said. 'When a person chooses to disappear he can ask for no better cover than a war. The chances are not good.'

Nevertheless he pocketed my check.

I wrote to Angelica suggesting she try romping with this Edgar before any gowns were created or cakes frosted. They say lightning never strikes the same place twice but they say a lot of things I have found not to be the case.

I enclosed a picture of Emerald, and I promised one of Sapphire just as soon as she returned from her rest-cure at Cedarhurst. I had driven her out there and it had been the saddest journey. We saw so many little houses with gold stars posted in their windows for their lost loved ones.

July of 1945 was an unsettling month. It may all have been over for the likes of Angelica but the war dragged on for us. Gasoline was sometimes short and we couldn't get ice cream, and then, when the stories started, about what Mr Hitler had done to the Hebrews, I couldn't do a thing with Humpy.

'Now do you see?' he kept saying. 'I could have stayed. I should have.'

He seemed to be heaping everything upon himself, even things Mr Roosevelt and Mr Truman hadn't been able to prevent, and I hated to see a man cry, even if he was a pansy.

Emerald said, 'That would have been us too.'

In Paris they had driven all the *juifs* to the velodrome and after that something terrible had befallen them.

I said, 'It wouldn't have been us. I'd have made sure those people knew who we were. I'd have given them money.'

Still, I was glad we'd come home.

Just before VJ day I ran into two figures from the past. Mrs Wendell Tite née Bernie Kearney who blanked me on Madison Avenue, and Ethel Yeo who was seated behind the reception desk of the new nail parlor I'd begun patronizing. It was she who claimed me. She was wearing her eyebrows in a different style so I would never have known her.

'You ever roll bandages at the Red Cross?' she asked.

I didn't make too much of remembering her.

'Well, I sure remember you,' she said. 'Weren't your folk in pickles?'

I said, 'Were you the one that caught for a baby?'

'No,' she said. 'I never caught for a baby. That was Junie. Are you rolling bandages this time around?'

I told her about escaping from Paris, France, by a squeak.

I said, 'I suppose you just started here? I didn't see you before.'

'I own the place,' she said. 'This one and three more. Soon as peace comes I intend expanding into facials. You should look out for me. I'll give you the works, for old times' sake. You look like you've been doing a lot of living.'

I tore up her card into the tiniest pieces the moment I was outside. I couldn't forget her remark, though, and immediately after Labor Day weekend I took myself off to the Mayo Clinic and had my face neatened.

Honey attributed my rejuvenated appearance to the uplifting effect of Pastor Norman Peale's addresses which she had been passing along to me in pamphlet form.

'Unless, of course,' she said, 'you have a secret beau.'

But it was Emerald who had the secret beau. His name was Mortie Boon and he bought flowers in Fleischmann's every Friday for weeks before he got up the courage to pick out a dozen long-stemmed roses and hand them right back to her.

His people had started out in corsetry.

'Well, Emerald,' Ma said, 'people will always need corsets. Corsets and mustard. You will never go hungry.'

Fortunately Mortie's father was a forward-looking person. He had begun diversifying into swimming costumes.

Mortie was no oil painting but Em had eyes for no one else and in the early days he was always civil to me. Ma and Aunt Fish he had eating out of his hand. So much so, he was able to override Ma's wish to have the wedding at East 69th Street. The Boons lived in Lenox Road, which was as good an address as you could hope for in Brooklyn, and they always did their marrying at Union Temple.

'It's a family tradition, Mom,' Emerald explained to me. 'And seeing as how we don't seem to have any of our own I think I'd like to go along with Mortie's.'

Then Sherman Ulysses arrived home from the war with a piece of Japanese shrapnel and a fiancée. Ma placed the shrapnel in the vitrine alongside Pa's old treasures. It was harder to know what to do with the fiancée.

Her name was Vera Farber and she had served in the WAVES at Guantanamo Bay. This had given her a high and mighty opinion of herself over those of us who had kept the home fires burning, an opinion quite out of proportion for a person who had been a mere yeoman in the Fleet Post Office. Her people were in gloves.

Ma immediately suggested a double wedding but Vera was an agnostic atheist so that idea was strangled at birth.

Nineteen forty-six was a two-wedding year for us, three if you counted Angelica who became Lady Boodle-Neary far away in Melton Mowbray, England. She wrote me how she had placed her flowers on my darling Reggie's grave and I was touched beyond words. From Mr Pink the detective I received nothing but accounts due.

We still had wartime yardage restrictions but I have always regarded restrictions as something to be circumvented. I created for Emerald a full-skirted gown in ice-white duchesse satin, and I would have done my best for Vera, too. Perhaps something with a butterfly peplum or some other back interest, to draw the eye away from her solid shoulders and her heavy jaw. But I was not asked. She and Sherman Ulysses tied the knot at City Hall in wool suits and felt hats with never a feather nor a diamond pin in sight. Then, five days later, we all crossed the East River to see Emerald and Mortie joined as one.

As Ma observed, that was a *real* wedding.

We had had only one moment of discord, when Em realized she was expected to have a Hebrew name and demanded to know why I hadn't given her one.

She said, 'I have to have one for the marrying contract.'

I had never heard of such a thing.

I said, 'Does Mortie have one?'

'Of course he does,' she said. 'It's Mordecai, but don't you dare tell him I told you. It's not a name you use. It's just a name you have. So now what am I going to do?'

I took the problem to Ma.

I said, 'Do you know anything about this?'

'It's probably something they do in Brooklyn,' she said. 'But don't fuss so. Let her take "Dora". Dora is a good name and it saddens me that neither of my granddaughters were given it.'

Aunt Fish said, 'Dora isn't a Hebrew name. Zillah is, though. Let her take that.'

But Em wasn't satisfied. She rummaged through our family history, prodding us with questions until Ma remembered that Sarah had been the name of my grandma Plotz and my grandma Minkel. No one had ever troubled to tell me.

So, Sarah it was. Sarah Emerald Minkel Merrick married Mordecai Mortie Boon and then we all adjourned to the ballroom for roast sirloin of beef and dancing.

Mortie's father waltzed with me in an alarmingly warm clinch, but given Mrs Boon's lack of physical charms I could understand how exciting he found me. I allowed him his moment of pleasure. The whole affair went off in a very good humored way until Sapphire collapsed into the fresh fruit platter.

'She is far far too fatigued,' Ma explained, to anyone who would listen.

'She's had too much rye,' said some judgmental Boon.

I said, 'I'm sorry if Sapphy spoiled your day.' I was buttoning Em into her going-away dress.

'Nothing spoiled my day,' she said. 'I just wish she didn't have to be so contrary and miserable. If only she could find a Mortie.'

But since the war ended Sapphire had done nothing but date a series of Displaced Persons. Thin, broken people who had no money and didn't speak. She even omitted to catch the bouquet of perfect Fleischmann gardenias Em tossed in her direction. Some people will never be helped.

FIFTY

In 1951, one of our artists, Orfie Sokoloff, became discovered. Many of our unfortunates had chosen to remain unfortunate, refusing to attend parties and talk pleasantly to people from National Benzene or DeWitt. But Orfie understood what he had to do. His murals were large anyway, and he was always amenable to making them larger. Between six and nine he was willing to put on one of the fabulous silk vests I'd designed for him and engage buyers with his beautiful tawny eyes. Best of all, he turned those eyes on a most influential commentator, Jerome Sacks. Sacks fell quite in love with him and wrote him up in *Art Now* and *Trends* and every important magazine.

I hadn't cared very much for Sokoloff's work myself. I found it too brown and messy. But after I had studied on it a while I began to see there was something energetic and fearless about it, so I commissioned him to paint me a mural of my own and I had him come over to Turtle Bay to see the color of my dining-room drapes.

By 1952 everyone had heard of Orfie Sokoloff, and anyone who took the trouble to be *au courant* had heard of Poppy Minkel Merrick. I had saved the future of art from the smoking ruins of Europe and I was photographed for *People* magazine. 'Grandmother in the Vanguard' the caption said. I had Humpy to thank for divulging that piece of information. My mother might have looked like a grandmother, but I certainly didn't.

Emerald and Mortie's firstborn had arrived in August 1951.

They named him Alan Mordecai and he was subjected to the full Hebrew procedure in a private room at Mount Sinai Hospital. Mortie's brother was chosen to be *kvatter* and his sister-in-law for *kvatterin*, owing to Sapphire's being too indisposed to accept the position. As far as I was concerned a hospital was no place for a party. Still, I did provide a very good champagne, and I might well have stayed longer and admired the child more if Mortie's mother hadn't so monopolized the scene. I looked at it this way: Mrs Boon wasn't leading the full and exciting life I was so who was I to begrudge her her silly triumphs.

Sherman Ulysses and Vera had also expected what my sister referred to as 'a happy addition' but in the event it came to nothing. Vera had a complication and was fated always to be brought to childbed prematurely. I must say this for Vera, though I found her dull and homely, she at least wasn't the kind of woman who grew bitter about her childlessness. She took herself off to Barnard College and read books and became even more homely.

If 1951 was the year of arrivals, 1952 turned out to be a year of departures.

Aunt Fish was the first to go, slipping on a patch of ice on her way to a canasta afternoon and striking her head against a curbstone. Ma reacted to this tragedy with a mixture of perplexity and annoyance. There had hardly been a day of her life when her sister hadn't been at her side with a ready opinion and I believe she felt that absence more keenly than any other she had had to bear.

'I never cared for Mrs Weiss' canastas,' she said. And then later, 'gallivanting in February always was a perilous thing'.

I felt my aunt's death profoundly. My breathing was easier. I had a sensation of well-being, of floating, almost. This was marred only by a momentary pang of guilt as we stood in horizontal sleet and saw her lowered down on top of Uncle Israel. He must have endured at least as much as I had, and yet I had never heard him say a truly disloyal word. But by the time we drove away from Pinelawns, I was floating again.

Then Bobbity, out with the Belvoir, misjudged a ditch and took a fatal tumble.

'Merrick is pretty cut up,' Angelica wrote.

The padre at Buckby wouldn't allow us to bury Fearless alongside her, which is what she would have wished. Ordinarily we would simply have taken her home to Bagehots, but the new people there don't hunt and so wouldn't have understood, and Kneilthorpe is almost certain to be sold to a frightful little builder, so one daren't have left Bobbity there. She might end up entombed under something called 'affordable housing'. As Edgar says, 'one dreads to think'.

Anyway, I regret to say we had to cave into the Buckby man. If we could have fitted Fearless into a casket we would have done so and had the last laugh on the little upstart.

We knew Oscar and Yetta were living in rustic simplicity in Bethel, near the Pennsylvania state line. We knew Oscar played with wood and Yetta had become odd. I suppose we also knew the day would come when something had to be done about her, but it had never seemed pressing enough to identify what that 'something' might be. A letter addressed to 'The family of Miss Yetta and Mr Oscar' changed that. A Lutheran pastor, who described himself as a friend and neighbor, informed Ma that Miss Landau was in a state of 'high derangement' and had been living for an unknown period of time with the decomposing remains of her nephew.

'Little Abe will see to things,' said Ma. 'And Poppy will go with him.'

But I had an opening. I couldn't just drop everything.

Sherman said, 'That's OK, Grandma. Mother has offered. We don't need Aunt Poppy.'

'It's the least I can do,' Honey said. 'They're family, near enough. What must people think?'

I said, 'Don't concern yourself with what people think. For

a friend and neighbor this pastor can't have been visiting them too often.'

Ma said, 'All Yetta had to do was telephone. If she had telephoned I would have had someone go up there right away.'

But Yetta and Oscar had never bothered with a telephone.

'Nor with help,' Honey reported back. 'You can't imagine the squalor. I don't believe they ever threw away a newspaper. And the stench, Poppy!'

Yetta Landau had been taken to a rest home in Monticello and what remained of Oscar was returned to New York. The only thing Sherman managed to salvage was a little side table with inlays of holly wood dyed pink and purple.

'I thought Grandma'd like to have something,' he said.

'Or Murray,' I said. 'If he should return.'

'Aunt Poppy,' Sherman said, 'I hope you're not still throwing away money on detective agencies?'

That was my business, I'm sure. I knew Ma had never cared for either of her stepsons and if anyone should have had the inlaid table it was me. But, of course, I couldn't say so. My reasons for remembering Oscar were secret ones. I was glad anyway that our marrying had never come off.

And the year still hadn't taken its full toll. One November afternoon, as Humpy and I were hanging some new Molinard abstracts, Emerald telephoned in a flap.

'Mom!' she said. 'You'd better get up to Grandma's fast. She says she has police on her stoop peering through the glass and the help's out buying nova.'

I said, 'Have you tried your Aunt Honey? I can't go running errands right now. We have Jerome Sacks coming for a preview.'

'To hell with your preview,' she yelled. 'Just get up there. I'm on my way as soon as Alan's had his bottle, but there's traffic.'

Emerald took way too much upon herself with regard to giving orders.

'But, of course, you must go,' Humpy said.

I sometimes felt he was too eager to have me off the scene as well.

There was an empty patrol car parked just down from the Jacoby house. In the time it had taken me to find a cab, Officers O'Halloran and Fitzpatrick had talked their way into Ma's upstairs parlor.

Ma said, 'Poppy, I don't know what I've done. They're looking for someone called Mary, but I haven't seen her.'

'Marie Nooge Catchings,' the red-haired one said, and he brought out a baby picture of Sapphire.

'See?' he said, turning it over. 'It has this address on the back.'

I believe I asked if she was hurt. Then I had to be helped to a chair and brought a glass of water. The next thing I recall, Mortie had arrived, sent uptown by Emerald, and Ma was asking over and over, 'What did I do? What did I do?'

Officer Fitzpatrick said as far as they knew no harm had befallen Marie Nooge Catchings. He apologized for any misunderstanding. The casualty was a white male, aged approximately sixty, who had partially cremated himself smoking in bed in a rooming house.

'They just knew him as The Writer,' Officer O'Halloran said. 'And we did find a few scribblings. A few scribblings, a number of empty bottles and the baby picture.'

I said, 'I guess it's Gilbert Catchings you're talking about. He was once my husband and Marie Nuage Sapphire is our daughter, but I never knew he kept a picture of her. That is the darndest thing.'

Officer Fitzpatrick said the body was in the Elizabeth Street morgue.

Mortie said, 'Do we have any obligations here? Shall I arrange for a mortician or do you think Sapphire'll want to do that herself?'

I said, 'Well, it's too late in the drinking day to ask her now, and I don't expect her to have any strong opinions about it. She really never knew him.'

Mortie was trying to explain to Ma why a mortician was required when Emerald arrived.

She said, 'Whoa there, Mortie! Are we expected to bury a person just because he was found with a picture of Sapphy in his room? Mom, shouldn't you ride downtown with the officers? Make sure it is Gilbert Catchings? Wasn't he meant to be in Buenos Aires?'

'Oh no,' Ma said, becoming lucid at the most inconvenient moment. 'Honey saw him on Fifth Avenue on several occasions. And we decided not to notice it, didn't we Poppy? We decided to pretend Mr Catchings had never happened.'

Emerald was in a testy mood anyway. She hated anything that disturbed her domestic routine and driving in from Brooklyn when she would normally be preparing Mortie's dinner counted as a major upheaval.

'Mortie,' she said, nice as pie, 'why don't you turn on *Amateur Hour* for Grandma while I show the officers to the door?'

Those two boys picked up their caps and rolled out of the parlor like a pair of nice friendly bears. They left me to her mercies. I guess they had no idea how she was planning to turn on me the instant they were gone.

'Why?' she kept yelling at me. 'Why couldn't you just tell her where her daddy was? What was it to you anymore? She could have met him, or not. How old did she have to be before you quit interfering? Well, it's too late now. But you're for it. She's going to pitch into you when she finds out about this, and for once I'm going to be right behind her. Don't you think it's eaten her heart out ever since she realized I had my daddy right there where I could see him and she didn't even have a picture?'

I said, 'Gil Catchings was no Reggie.'

'That's nothing to do with anything,' she said. 'A person needs to know where they came from. Doesn't matter if it's a bad address.'

Em had become interested in the workings of the human mind since the arrival of baby Alan, reasoning everything out with him, talking to him all the day long as though he understood. She wouldn't even have a night nurse for him. She was full of theories.

'Did it ever occur to you,' she said, 'he might have been good for Sapphire even if he wasn't good for you? Even if he was lousy . . . he'd have been *somebody*.'

I said, 'It was that experience in Paris that turned her to drink.'

'I don't know about that,' she said. 'But she certainly made a fool of herself and all because she didn't know who she was. And if Uncle Murray hadn't told me a few things, I wouldn't have known either. We were like little blobs of jello, only no particular flavor. Heck Mom, first I thought I was Aunt Honey's little girl, then I thought I was some kind of English princess. I was all of nine years old before I started working things out. And Sapphy just never did. She's kind of limited, you know? I do love her, but she's kind of limited.'

I said, 'I did the best I could.'

'Yes,' she said.

I said, 'I had a pretty raw deal myself, you know? I lost my Pa. I had Grandma and Aunt Fish flattening me out and strapping me down and disapproving of every move I made. Then we had a war . . .'

'You loved the war,' she said. 'Well, OK, someday we can talk about that. We can see how far back cruelty to children runs in this family. That'd be fun. But right now you have things to explain to Sapphire. Such as how her daddy was living just a cab ride away, with her picture on his night table. And by the way, do you realize how much benzedrine she's taking these days?'

I said, 'Lots of people take benzedrine. Anyway, I'll tell her in the morning. There's nothing more to be done now. I may as well get back down to the gallery.'

'Yes Mom,' she said, 'why don't you just do that.'

Her voice was unpleasantly tight.

'Em,' Mortie said quietly. 'Don't upset yourself.'

No one seemed to consider how I might be feeling. Questioned by police. Dragged back into Gil Catchings' sordid affairs. Obliged to stand up Jerome Sacks.

FIFTY-ONE

So the very Minkel money Gil had turned against paid for his admission to a cemetery in Flushing, and as soon as that was done Sapphire commenced to make a life's project of building him into a giant and a hero. She gathered up a few paltry things from his room on the Bowery and took a low-rent apartment on Second Avenue, to be nearer Ukrainians and bohemians and others she described as 'my daddy's kind of people'. After that she only ventured north of Gramercy Park to see her mind doctor, and her regular coolness with me turned into an arctic freeze.

Baby Alan learned to walk and talk, Vera graduated *cum laude* and immediately began another course of study, and Ma gave up all pretense of a social life. She adored the television, once Mortie had convinced her that the people on the screen could not see her the way she could see them, and the acquisition of a new help named Coretta completed her happiness. Coretta loved television, too, and was most willing to serve Ma's evening slop on a tray and then sit with her through *Hopalong Cassidy* and the *Colgate Comedy Hour*. I believe Coretta became a kind of friend to her. She was certainly the person who introduced Ma to Shirley Temple cocktails.

Then the time came around for the setting of Oscar's headstone, and the marking of his anniversary. His name was to be added to his mother's on a bronze plaque in Temple Emanu-El.

I said, 'How come Judah's name isn't up there yet?'

Ma said, 'Because he'll share a plaque with me. And if my aching bones are anything to go by, he won't have long to wait.'

Emerald said, 'I don't suppose you'll be gracing us with your presence on Saturday morning?' But I did go. Once in a while I liked to hear those squiggly back-to-front words.

The Landau cousin came up from St Louis, wearing old-fashioned eyeglasses, probably the same ones he'd worn to the Seder, and Judah Jacoby's friends from the Men's Club and the Temple Youth Committee. You can't just say Kaddish. You have to have a certain number present, otherwise I guess God can't hear you, and for a person who had chosen to live like a hermit Oscar managed to pull in quite a crowd.

Ma came with Emerald and Mortie, leaning unnecessarily on Mortie's arm I thought, and Coretta came, too, although she was a Baptist Total Abstainer, and I stood slightly apart, needing to get away punctually for lunch with Humpy and an important collector from London, England.

I was wearing a divine boxy jacket and long-line pencil skirt in cranberry silk with a witty velour toreador hat.

Someone came in late, when the ordinary praying was almost finished, and stood behind me, quite close. I could smell the breath of a person whose mouth is too dry.

Mortie was to be chief mourner. He had never met Oscar in his life, but it had to be a man, and Sherman Ulysses didn't go to temples and think irrational thoughts. If there was one thing we were short of in our family it was Jewish men.

'Yisgadal va yiskadash,' Mortie began, and when it came to the 'y'hay shm'ay', where everyone joins in, I heard a voice I thought I knew.

'Y'hay shm'ay raboh m'vorah . . .' May His great name be blessed.

I turned around. It was my stepbrother Murray. But changed into an old man, with sunken cheeks and no teeth and thin, colorless hair.

He didn't look at me, though, until after he'd said, 'Omayn'. That's how you know the praying is finished. 'Omayn.'

Then he just took one look at my hat and said, 'Olé.'

We went right out, before anyone else made a move, and stood under the temple awning till an empty cab came along. My head felt like one of those little shake-and-view snowstorms.

I said, 'I have a lunch.'

'OK,' he said.

I said, 'Ride with me, while I think.'

'OK,' he said.

I pushed him into the cab.

I said, 'I thought you were dead, of course.' And he grabbed my arm with his bony old hand.

'I'm sorry.' That was all he'd say. 'I'm sorry.'

I didn't know what the hell to do. I couldn't take a refugee to lunch with James Foliat. Murray wasn't even wearing a collar and tie. Besides which, I wasn't sure I'd be able to master my emotions if I had him sitting there before me. He was a sorry sight indeed.

He said, 'You can drop me at 44th Street.'

I said, 'Are you staying at the Algonquin?'

'Not exactly,' he said. 'But I could see you there, later.'

The cab pulled over.

I said, 'Swear to me you'll be there.'

'I swear,' he said.

I said, 'Swear properly. Put your hand on your heart.'

'Lady,' the driver said. 'This is a cab not a court of law. You want Dominique's Grill or don't you?'

Humpy and James Foliat were late. Bella Yaff had been told to expect them but Bella Yaff had failed to remember and they had had to wait for her to roll out of her bed and throw on her stinking coveralls. I had once given her a tablet of Roger et Gallet Muguet soap but the hint had passed her by, and I instructed Humpy to retrieve it next time he was in her neighborhood, which he did. She made slovenliness her trademark, and it worked very well. Better to be famous for one's unwashed hair than to be an unknown.

Foliat, though, turned out to be a fastidious little man. Yaff's domestic arrangements were making him think twice about buying, so Humpy was in a bad humor.

'Take over, would you?' he whispered. 'I'd rather like to skip lunch.'

'Me too,' I whispered back. 'My stepbrother just rose from the dead and I don't know whether I'm coming or going.'

'Murray?' he said. 'How extraordinary! Well then. Let's order a little something and press on, shall we? I think I might have an egg salad? I never eat much at this time of day.'

But James Foliat had a very serious attitude to lunch. Shrimp Appetizers were required, followed by Broiled Squab, Nesselrode Pudding, and after a bottle of Beaujolais wine the damage done by Bella Yaff was repaired. It was three-thirty before I raced into the Algonquin, searching for Murray's face.

He was in the back lobby, sipping a glass of milk and pretending to read a book. I sat opposite him, the better to look at him.

'I suppose I've been very, very bad,' he observed.

I said, 'Where have you been?'

'Is Auntsie dead?' he asked. And that was how it was. Every question was answered with another question.

'Did you know Angelica's not your wife anymore?'

'Have you been back from England long?'

'I searched for you in Paris.'

'How are Sapphy and Em?'

'You look terrible. What happened to your teeth?'

'Would you care for a cocktail? Or we could go to Hegeman's for old times' sake.'

We stayed put.

I said, 'You saw Emerald this morning. In the Prince of Wales check? She has a baby now, and Sabbath candles and a husband. The whole thing. She's old before her time. Sherman Ulysses the same. He's gone gray. Your pa's gone. But if you know about Oscar, I guess you know that. Do you know all this already? Have you been hiding out down here spying on us all these years? Do you intend showing your face at 69th Street?'

'Well,' he said, 'I think I'll visit Auntsie first.'

But that required no great courage. Yetta Landau wouldn't

have known if President Eisenhower himself had paid her a call.

I said, 'Is there anything you'd like me to say to Ma? Anything to prepare the way?'

'Yes. No,' he said. 'Well, no hurry. There's no one left who'll have missed me very much.'

I said, 'I've missed you very much.'

'Tinkety Tonk,' he said, and a teardrop rolled down his cheek and into his fresh glass of milk.

'Tonkety Tink,' I replied. Manhattans always did make me cry.

He wouldn't entertain coming home with me to 49th Street. Hotels suited him, he said, when he was between gardens, and he was between gardens just then. The best I could manage was to remove him from the Tenth Avenue fleapit he was staying in to the Algonquin. I went to the desk and arranged it right away.

'I'm really quite all right where I am,' he said. 'Isn't this place a bit steep?'

I said, 'You're worth it. Shall we call up Em? We could drive across to Brooklyn, then get a late supper. I have to look in at the Blue Angel for five minutes. Pookie Callan's giving a party for one of our unfortunates. But no more than five minutes, I promise. And then we can talk. Oh boy!'

'Poppy,' he said, 'I take my evening meal early these days. I hope you'll understand. A light supper and early to bed.'

I said, 'Are you sick?'

'No,' he said. 'Just old.'

But I was older. He would never catch up to me.

I saw Murray installed into his suite. He looked like he just hatched from an egg, sitting on the edge of the bed gazing around him.

I said, 'And don't try running away again. I'm having you watched.'

I felt on top of the world. After the Blue Angel I went onto the Stork Club with Orfie and Jerome and stayed up till three. It was when I put my hand in my pocket to pay the coat-check girl that I found the scrap of paper Murray had written on.

MISSING
Missed you. Wished I were
Nearer. Now I am does that
Make me a near miss?

FIFTY-TWO

Ma received the news about Murray calmly. Old age and the watching of amusing television programs had brought her a new serenity.

'It the calm before the storm,' Coretta predicted. 'You see. She be having a breathing hattack any minute now.'

Sapphire wept. She said Murray had to be hiding some terrible tragedy that had kept him from us and robbed him of his health. The family curse had struck again.

I said, 'What family curse? Murray's not blood.'

'Any family connected with you,' she said.

Honey said he'd feel better the moment he found the kingdom of heaven within, and sent him some pamphlets.

Emerald just screamed for joy.

'I knew it!' she kept saying. 'I knew he'd turn up. Mortie, you're going to love him. Bring him today. Bring him here right now.'

But he wasn't quite fit for company.

I said, 'Murray, about your appearance. We're going to have to get you some dentures. And a shirt that fits. You look like a death's head on a stick.'

'I have dentures,' he said. 'I just can't get along with them.'

I said, 'Well, you can't go visiting looking like that. You'll terrify Baby Alan.'

So he put in his dentures, but they seemed like they didn't really belong to him. They crowded out his mouth and shone unnaturally and because they pinched you were lucky to get a civil word out of him while he was wearing them. In the end he developed the habit of commencing a visit with his teeth in his mouth and ending it with them in his pocket.

I said, 'As long as you only do it in front of family. If you ever do that in the Zanzibar Club, I'll kill you.'

'Don't worry,' he said. 'If I ever find myself in the Zanzibar Club I'll save you the trouble.'

Murray's removable teeth seemed to endear him to Baby Alan, who smiled at him incessantly whereas he only ever peeped at me anxiously.

I said, 'Why does that child always look so worried?'

Em said, 'Because you make the room spin. Plus, your hair's a different color every time he sees you.'

It was most annoying to see how she fussed over Murray. Apparently a person can go away and leave his responsibilities for others to shoulder and then return, as cool as you like, and be found fascinating and adorable. I always took fabulous gifts when I visited my grandson, and yet when Murray turned up with nothing but a package of sunflower seeds and one of his stupid haiku verses you'd have thought he had bought every goddamned toy in Schwartz's window.

PROGRESS, he had written.

> It seems like only
> Yesterday I was a mere
> Uncle. Now I'm great.

Ma came right to the point.

'You realize you killed your father?' was how she greeted him, but that was as bad as things got.

Sapphire broke her rule about never crossing my threshold and came to visit him at 49th Street, where I was endeavoring to wean him off milk dinners and persuade him to move in.

'I'm only here on account of Uncle Murray,' she said. 'So don't get any big ideas.'

Sapphire was never one to let go of a grudge.

I suppose Murray had grown accustomed to people being shocked by the change in his appearance. Now it was his turn to be surprised. Sapphire had the tired, gray look of a person who attracts misfortune and never gets a facial.

'Uncle Murray, Uncle Murray!' she said, squeezing his hands. 'I want you to tell me everything. Absolutely everything.'

'Everything?' he said, most alarmed.

'About the camps,' she said. 'You'll feel better if you talk.'

He looked to me for help.

I said, 'Murray, were you in camps?'

'No,' he said. 'No.'

'It's OK,' Sapphy said, starting the hand-squeezing routine again. 'It doesn't have to be now. Whenever you feel strong enough. I lost someone, you see. That's why it's so important you tell your story. You're our witness.'

'Sapphy,' he said, 'I'm so sorry you lost someone. That's a terrible thing. But I don't have a story, you know? I've just been . . . roaming around. That's all. But why don't you tell me your story? I'd like that.'

'He's very sick, you know?' she whispered to me over the drinks tray. 'It could take years.'

'She's crazy, of course,' he said to me, after she had gone.

I said, 'You're both crazy. She has roaches. You own one pair of pants. As far as I can see neither of you has done a damned thing with your lives except ruin your looks and live like unfortunates.'

He was quiet.

I said, 'And just give me one good reason why you won't move in here. It's the best address in town. It's the best view in town. Or let me buy you the Pearlsteins' duplex, then at least we'll be neighbors.'

He said, 'I'm going to live somewhere I can make a garden. That's what I'd like. A garden by the sea.'

I said, 'If you live here I can introduce you to people who'd adore to have one of your gardens. The best people. I know everyone who's anyone in this town. You'll be the talk of the Hamptons.'

'I don't want to be the talk of anywhere,' he said. 'I want to live quietly and not have to wear my dentures.'

I was so frustrated with him. I said, 'Why won't people be helped?'

'Poppy,' he said, 'it's the funniest thing. As far as I can see, Sapphire's the one needing your help but you don't seem interested in attending to that. I watched you, and you never even kissed her goodbye.'

I said, 'We don't kiss. And anyway, she's a hopeless case. She's a Catchings through and through. She'll never amount to anything.'

'I see,' he said. 'And what's your big success story?'

I said, 'My galleries are in the absolute vanguard. I helped Humpy Choate when he didn't have a pot to piss in, and Sokoloff and Yaff and all those other dreary little daubers. Who brought them here? Who fed and clothed them?'

'Yes,' he said. 'I'm sorry.'

I said, 'I do my duty. I found Coretta for Ma. I found a mind doctor for Sapphire. I made a trust fund for Alan Mordecai and what thanks do I get? Emerald treats me like a stranger.'

'She does not,' he said. 'You are ridiculous.'

He didn't know the half of it. How they insisted on living in the suburbs and having dinner with Mortie's people all the time. How they never came to my openings.

'I just think,' he said, 'Sapphire still needs you to be a mommy. That's all.'

I said, 'She's twenty-nine. I've been a mommy, now I'm a phenomenon.'

'You certainly are,' he said.

I said, 'And don't preach to me. I get enough of that from Honey. I did a whole lot better than any of them said I would. How do you think I got where I am today?'

'I'm sure it's an interesting story,' he said, 'but not tonight, please. I want to go back to my hotel and sleep. I'm tired and I have gas pains.'

I said, 'You need a digestion doctor.'

He said, 'And you need to take a look at yourself.'

I have often noticed how hard people find it to be gracious about one's success.

FIFTY-THREE

By November of 1953 Emerald and Mortie had another child on the way and Murray was well advanced in his plans to run out on me for the second time.

'I can't take New York winters anymore,' he said. 'I'm going to Florida.'

But he stayed on long enough to participate in a falling-out I had with my son-in-law. Mortie didn't like it that I had ordered a Hornby train set for Baby Alan's Christmas.

'We don't do Christmas,' he said. 'You know we don't.'

I said, 'I don't see why not.'

He said, 'Because we do Hanukkah.'

I said, 'Heaven's sakes Mortie, the child's two years old. He doesn't care about all that.'

'Well, he's going to,' he said, 'if I have anything to do with it.'

Murray said, 'Maybe he could have the train set for Hanukkah?'

'No,' Mortie said. 'It's too much. You should just give him a little something at Hanukkah. A little candy. A little *gelt*. He can get the train for his birthday.'

A little candy. A little *gelt*. This was the way Emerald lived since the Boons got her into their clutches. Always volunteering at the Temple Sisterhood and shining up her candlesticks and following Mrs Boon's recipe for chopped liver. I hardly recognized my own child.

I said to Murray, 'Personally, I'm an open-minded kind of person.'

'You are,' he said. 'Minds probably don't come any opener.'

So I had the train wrapped in reindeer paper anyway, plus an electric menorah for Mortie and Em, since they were so set on being Jewish. I'm sure I don't know what the pair of them found so amusing about my gift.

Early in the New Year Murray bought himself an ancient Buick and packed it with everything he owned in the world. He was going to Florida to live in a hovel. He had only ever had a small fortune compared to mine, and somewhere along the way he seemed to have lost even that.

I said, 'I suppose that was the communists' doing.'

Judah Jacoby had often said they'd be the death of him. There was the house though, with Ma and Coretta rattling around in it, barely using more than one room.

I said, 'Why don't I tell Ma to sell 69th Street? She can go live with Honey. I'm sure that house ought to be yours by rights.'

'No,' he said. 'It belongs to the bank. And, I wouldn't dream of it. It's Dorabel's home. And you can't just move people around like they're pieces on a chess board. Honey has had a hard enough life.'

My sister was born with the ability to attract sympathy. She was pitied because Harry bankrupted her. She was pitied because her glands prevented her from reducing and keeping an attractive line. She was pitied because Sherman Ulysses had married such an uncongenial person.

'I believe Vera thinks me rather silly,' Honey confided in me one time, and Sherman himself confirmed it.

'Vera finds Mother a little . . . light,' he told me. 'It makes me very sad.'

The longer I lived the closer I came to agreeing with Ma and Aunt Fish on this point at least: education is a greatly overrated thing.

I would have bought Murray a place myself. A nice apartment in a good building in Miami Beach, but he wouldn't have it. He wanted to live on some kind of salt marsh and get tormented by bugs and murdered by the neighbors or blown out into the ocean and I was too tired and too busy to argue with him anymore. I was about to open Art As Gesture, with a Yugoslav unfortunate named Dragomar who ripped posters off walls. It was called Décollage and Jerome Sacks was predicting it would be very big indeed.

I waved Murray off. He had put in his dentures, just to please me I suppose. I guarantee they were in his pocket before he was through the Holland Tunnel. His Roadmaster was a dingy shade of ivory and its radiator grille looked for all the world like a mouthful of nightmare teeth. They say dogs grow to look like their owners, and I believe the same may be true for automobiles.

Baby Maxine Miriam was born in June. She had the Minkel ears but I saw a definite look of my darling Reggie flicker across her face which caused me a moment of sadness.

I took Ma and Coretta and Honey to visit while Em was still lying-in at Mount Sinai.

'You have all the luck,' Honey said to me. She was monopolizing the cradling of her great-niece, burrowing her nose into the folds of Baby Maxine's neck.

I said, 'Let me give her to Ma to hold.'

'Now sit nice and steady, Miss Dora,' Coretta said. 'And I'll stand with my arms at the ready in case you have an hattack and drap the child.'

For help Coretta had grown very self-important.

I placed Maxine Miriam in my mother's arms.

I said, 'Don't you think she favors her Grandpa Merrick a little, around the mouth?'

'Grandpa Merrick?' Ma said, playing at being old and forgetful.

'Are they giving you milk puddings, Emerald? Are they feeding you well? Your Grandpa Jacoby did so much for this place, you know? He paupered us with his good works. You make sure they know that. And you'd best start binding her ears, too. Start it directly you get her home. Coretta will make you some bandages. We all know what happens if that gets neglected, don't we Poppy?'

Mortie came in with Baby Alan and Mrs Boon, followed by a

nurse who said we were too many around the bed, too tiring for the mother.

Em said she wasn't a bit tired and Ma sat tight until Coretta whispered something in her ear, reminding her about one of the shows they liked to watch.

'Poppy,' Ma said. 'I believe we have an appointment to keep.'

Em said, 'Mom, did you see what Uncle Murray sent?'

MAXINE MIRIAM
Hai can't write haikus
Hany more. Here's an Israel
Savings Bond hinstead.

'Of course,' Ma announced, as she swept past Mrs Boon, 'we are able to visit at any hour we choose. My late husband practically *built* this hospital.'

FIFTY-FOUR

Ma passed away the day after Baby Maxine's first birthday. If she ever suffered any of those hattacks Coretta alluded to I never witnessed them. She simply fell asleep in front of *The Perry Como Show* and never woke up.

Emerald went with me to view her in the chapel of rest, and seeing her that way, so dwarfed by the casket Mortie had picked out, I felt regretful that the only time we had gotten along was when the Great War had given us common cause. In death she looked like quite an agreeable person, and her skin was still good. This was a consequence of her easy life, I suppose. She had been doted on by two good husbands, and two good children, then grandchildren and great-grandchildren. She had started off a Plotz, become a Minkel, sidestepped to Minton and ended up a Jacoby. She had braved out two widowings, two wars and the financial ruin of Harry Glaser. She had learned to answer the telephone and overcome her fear of crossing Central Park. And the only other thing I might have wished for her was that she could have been born late enough to enjoy more fully that important dividend of television, the extinction of conversation.

Murray had been correct about one thing. The house was mortgaged. Either the bank had to be paid or the house emptied and the vultures allowed to take possession. So I presided over the breaking up of the Jacoby home, but not before I had saved Ma's bone amber pendant for Sapphy, a step-cut peridot ring for Em and the lavender pearls for Baby Maxine.

Emerald said, 'What about Uncle Murray? It was his home.'

I said, 'Help me go through Judah's old stuff.'

Em suggested sending him his pa's prayer shawl, but what would a person want with that, living like a wild man on Merritt Island? I had in mind something I would like to find for him but it took us days, sifting through drawers and closets.

Then Em said, 'I think I found her.' She had opened a package of brown photographs tied with string, and there she was, with Murray in her arms and Oscar kneeling beside her, and a young mustachioed Judah standing behind them all, with his hand on her shoulder. Rosa Jacoby. She had a little heart-shaped face and a fuzz of hair, not unlike my own, and a mouth I liked, wide but firm.

I said, 'Shall I send it? Do you think he'd like to have it?'

She said, 'I think anyone would like to own a picture of their parents. Don't you, Mom?'

She was using a tone of voice.

I said, 'Don't start on that again. It's been hard for me to keep pictures. I've moved around a lot in my life. I've been too busy for making up albums. If Sapphire's so grieved about not having pictures let her go to Scranton, Pennsylvania, and plague the Catchings family. And if it's yourself you're hinting at, write to your Uncle Merrick. Or your Aunt Angelica. She'd be sure to have photographs.'

Em said, 'I want to take something for Alan, too.'

I'd already decided about that. Whenever Emerald took him visiting at 69th Street Alan had loved to look in Pa's old vitrine, marking the glass with his little fingers, asking what things were.

I said, 'I'm going to keep all these treasures safe for him. When he's old enough he can have them. Everything except the piece of shrapnel. I'll give that back to Sherman, if he'd like it.'

But Sherman wasn't allowed it.

'Keep it for the boy,' he said. 'Vera doesn't care for clutter.'

I didn't hear from Murray for the longest time and I feared the one and only picture of his ma must have gone astray, which is no more than you might expect when a person doesn't even have a proper address. But then one day his letter came.

'Dearest Poppy,' he wrote.

I've been very hard on you, I think, and now I come to consider, you deserve only thanks from me. I got a sister in you, which I never expected to have. You gave me haiku by way of Gil Catchings and my English garden by way of Reggie, and Angelica, who was more than I deserved. Then you gave me a second chance when I walked back into your life and you didn't press me with questions. And now you've given me my mother. When I add it all up, you've done a lot of giving and I've done a lot of taking, so it seems to me the very least I can do is refrain from criticizing your way of life.

I am hard at work in my new garden. There's no fence around it so it's as big or as small as I want it to be, according to how the mood takes me. The main thing that grows here is Bermuda grass, but I have scrub papaya clinging on pretty well and a kind of rosemary, which is for remembrance you know, and after the hurricane season I'm going to try poppies again. You need long roots to survive here.

I drive into Titusville once a week, or oftener if I get a craving for candy, and sometimes I give a ride to my nearest neighbor. Her name is Xenia. She tells me she was brought here by star travelers and that she can communicate with pelicans. I have asked her to communicate to them that they should stay away from my garden.

I have an indigo snake living outside my door. He doesn't bother me and I don't bother him. I really hope you'll come and see all this for yourself when you can be spared from the front line of art. I'll give up my bed for you.

I send you love which you must pass along to Sapphy and Em and the babies, and may peace be upon Step-Ma Dora.

Yours
Murray

I had no intention of visiting with him until he quit living in a cabin with snakes and star travelers for company.

So Pa's treasures finally came home with me. The fool's gold, and the silk cap, and the beaver skull, and the Ojibway Indian necklace, and a book I had loved to look at on those lamp-lit evenings before he went out for a cigar and a blintz. *The Story of Our Wonderful World*. It had pictures of how you get maple syrup from a tree, and people who shoot fish with a bow and arrow and don't wear drawers.

The final thing to dispose of was Coretta, whom I gave to Honey. I already had satisfactory help and Emerald declined to have anyone who wasn't family living in her house. Two babies and all she had was a person to rake leaves and keep the yard tidy and a sitter when it was Young Marrieds evening at temple.

She was always busy with something. Table decorations, alphabet friezes for the nursery.

I said, 'You never come to any of my openings. I'm setting the art world alight and the whole business is passing you by. You need to get out more. Have some kind of life.'

'Mom,' she said, 'I have a life. The best kind.'

FIFTY-FIVE

I didn't see Murray again until the winter of 1958 when he came home to bury his Aunt Yetta.

He said, 'I get the feeling you're never going to visit with me. Was it my mentioning the snake?'

I said, 'It's my firm belief you've taken leave of your senses and sharing a shack with a madman is not my idea of a vacation. My idea of a vacation, if I ever had the time to take such a thing, which I don't, is a place where they iron your sheets and you can get a Bloody Mary any hour of the day. Besides, you can get used to not seeing a person. When they've been written off for dead it makes a pleasant change to know they're only in Florida wasting their lives.'

'I see,' he said.

While Murray was in town it was my intention to get some answers from him, so I instructed Humpy to take him to lunch and quiz him on the following points. Was he a secret pansy? And where precisely had he been all those years, doing what he called roaming?'

'Just roaming, Poppy', was as far as I ever got with him.

Humpy said, 'Why me? Ask him yourself.'

But I no longer did lunch. One reaches a certain stage in life where one pays for every calorie and I had no wish to go the way of my sister, in the direction of ever-increasing circumference.

I said, 'He may confide in you, man to man.'

Humpy took him to an amusing Oriental place on Mott Street but the occasion failed to amuse either of them.

Humpy said, 'He's not a natural conversationalist, is he?'

I said, 'He requires practice. Did you ask about the missing years?'

'Not as such,' he said. 'It seemed rather an intrusion.'

I said, 'And what about the other thing?'

'No,' he said, 'nor that. Not as such.'

I said, 'Then what did you talk about?'

'Integrity,' he said. 'He questioned the integrity of our galleries.'

Our galleries! They were *my* galleries. And my stepbrother wasn't meant to be questioning anything. He was meant to be providing answers in exchange for lunch.

Murray said, 'I never ate a thing. They had chicken parts that belong in a trash can not in an eatery. Also, I suspect that sodomite was making love to me.'

'By the way,' I said, 'I'd hate for you to have the wrong idea. Humpy is my employee. Those galleries are all mine.'

'So much the worse for you,' he said. 'They're not the kind of thing I'd brag about, personally.'

I said, 'How short your memory is. Didn't you promise to cease criticizing my life?'

'I did,' he said. 'But I find it's deteriorated further in my absence so I'm releasing myself from my promise. I don't understand why you do it. It's not as though you need the money. And you're not exhibiting a damned thing that isn't an insult to intelligence. You've got a list full of hoaxers, Poppy.'

I said, 'You're behind the times. My galleries have redefined the avant-garde.'

'Bunch of phoneys,' he said. 'Bella Yaff! I was getting paintings better than that from Alan Mordecai when he was no more than four years old!'

It was hard to be good-humored in the face of such ignorance. I had heard it all a hundred times before and I wasn't sure I had the patience to explain, yet again, how Yaff's work liberated us from the fallacy of perspective.

He said, 'Well, I see you're set on being famous. I know I'm not going to persuade you against that. But couldn't you be celebrated for something decent? What about those fine originations you used to create? Or at least sell paintings that would grace a person's home.'

I said, 'Murray, you have been too long out of circulation to understand any of this. Gracing homes is old hat. The frontiers of art are on the move and wherever they're heading I arrive first.'

But Murray returned to his shingle garden without ever seeing the point of Brunnenbaum's grids or Wagy's rubber extrusions.

By 1960 I had reorganized my galleries and dispensed with Humphrey Choate. As so often happens, he grew resentful of his subordinate position. We had cross words once too often and he returned to England and set up on his own, in a very small way, of course.

He opened with a charmingly passé little stable. Hoche, who did portraits in oil, Lamb, who did small bronzes, and that fool Oca, still flogging his pianola roll jokes after all those years. I suppose it was the only idea he ever had. Choate and Oca were welcome to each other.

I moved a few doors along Leonard Street to a larger building and turned Tenth Street over to Sapphire. The whole world had opinions about what should be done about Sapphire. Murray said she needed motherly love. Em said she needed a good shaking. Honey said she needed Jesus. But I was the one who threw her the life-saver.

She renamed my old gallery Witness, had the walls covered with black felt, and showed a permanent collection of gloomy photographs with occasional special exhibits. Pictures of dejected types traveling with bundles. Grimy street vendors. Whole families of unfortunates huddled under greasy coverlets. There was never anything gay or witty. It was no wonder to me that some days she simply couldn't face opening up.

Leonard Street couldn't have been more different. I named it The

Place and I was there all the time. I loved to see people stopped in their tracks by the vastness of it. In my first year I showed a divine set of ballpoint drawings by Rommer, an installation of basalt *trouvé* by Erik Boe, and Kenny Porter's painted absences. I could sell Kenny Porters faster than he could paint them and he could paint them fast.

I must also confess, Humphrey Choate wasn't the only one to try his hand with a has-been. Hannelore Ettl walked into The Place one morning, as cool as you like and asked me for a show.

I said, 'I don't do macaroni.'

'Neither do I,' she said. 'Haven't done in more than thirty years. I do hair.'

First thing she showed me was a noose woven out of horsehair. The next thing she showed me was a collage of human hair. The private kind.

I said, 'I'm surprised you have any to spare at your time of life.'

'Poppy,' she said, 'does this have to be personal? Are you still sore about Gil leaving you for me?'

I said, 'As I recall, it was me who left him. And you must have nearly fallen over my luggage, on your way in. I'll bet you never even bothered having the sheets changed.'

'You are still sore,' she said. 'How infantile.'

And she would have been on her way, only Jerry Sacks arrived. He had quit being Jerome sometime before.

I saw his eyes light up when he saw Ettl's stuff, and Sacks' eyes were always worth watching. I recognized in an instant that hair was going to be big. Especially private hair. By the spring of 1961 there can't have been a dinner table in the world where the audacity of my gallery wasn't being discussed.

Emerald took up a position, of course.

'And you wonder why we never drop by?' she said.

I said, 'Emerald, it's only hair.'

'It is only hair,' she agreed. 'It certainly doesn't belong in an art gallery. But I'm not going to debate it with you. I'm just glad I changed my name to Boon. If you want to see us you'll have to come to Brooklyn. Do you remember where that is?'

Of course, I was always compared unfavorably with Miriam Boon, no matter that I did go to Brooklyn, as often as my schedule allowed. I sat with those kids a whole afternoon one time, stringing cranberries for their Sukkot party. Some party. Drafts and insects. Dinner in a home-made shed.

I said, 'At least let me buy them a top quality playhouse.'

Em said, 'It's not a playhouse, Mom. It's a tabernacle. And home-made is the point of it.'

Nothing I did was right. I was a household name, I had kept an amazingly youthful line through self-control and submission to the beauty doctor's knife, and I was fun.

But it was Mrs Boon who picked up the bouquets, baking cookies, churning out her shapeless handknits, driving them home from Talmud Torah.

As I remarked to Murray, a less fulfilled and resourceful person than myself would have become embittered.

'And thank goodness too for your humility,' he wrote.

But enough of your problems. I am being compulsorily purchased by the government. They're expanding the Banana River Proving Grounds so they can send a man into outer space and they say they need my backyard.

Xenia claims she already knew. She might have told me before I made my asparagus bed.

Yours

Murray

PS: What is private hair?

330

FIFTY-SIX

I n 1962 a most annoying thing occurred. Irish Nellie became a television star.

I was in Daytona Beach, Florida, supervising the convalescence of my stepbrother Murray from a compound fracture of the thigh bone, sustained while he was resisting eviction from his hovel, and so had time to watch the shows ordinary people depended on to bring excitement and variety into their lives.

A special program had been got up to mark the fiftieth anniversary of the loss of the *Titanic*, and certain parties had been invited to tell their version of things. No one had thought to invite me.

They gave her name as Helen Gorman and her face was as wrinkled as an old paper bag, but I knew who she was even before she'd opened her mouth and started her bunch of lies.

'I lost my fiancé,' she said. 'We were coming home to be married.'

I telephoned Honey from Murray's bedside.

I said, 'Just look at her! I'm writing it all down. Every lying word. I'm going to sue.'

'Good governor, Poppy!' Honey said. 'What does it matter? She's an old woman. We're old women.'

I said, 'I'm not an old woman. And that Irish is besmirching our Pa's name. We shouldn't take that lying down. You were always way too meek.'

My sister had grown to resemble one of those pale milch cows with the dark eyes and upturned nose. She rarely moved, except to amble between the couch and the feeding trough. Mainly she just sat around, reaching for candies and chewing over her scriptural pamphlets.

She was well cared for. When Coretta had commenced having visions of six-winged many-eyed seraphs and had had to go home to Jamaica, a niece was sent in her place. Coretta II. Emerald always called by on Wednesdays, which was Coretta II's day off. And Sherman Ulysses was a most attentive son. He had had a handrail fitted alongside her bath, for the prevention of falls, and devised a special box for her medicaments, with a compartment for each day of the week, which he refilled on Sundays, doling out the next seven doses and reviewing the past week's improvements and reversals. He had become an avid reader of those small-print advisory notes that come with a jar of pills. I sometimes feel he has been a loss to the medical profession.

Irish Nellie was saying, 'I never did marry. After Abe, there could never be another for me . . . I still dream about him. I still see him disappearing into the crowd. He went to fetch my muff, you see. It was so cold that night.'

I heard Murray sniff.

I said, 'I hope that's me you're weeping for? That's my father's good reputation she's sullying.'

He said, 'I didn't hear any sullying. She makes him sound kind and considerate.'

I said, 'It's not her place to make him sound anything. She was just an Irish. He was my Pa. They should have asked me.'

'Well,' he said, 'how about if I ask you? You never told me about your Pa.'

I said, 'You're not the television.'

He said, 'What's so important about television? It's only a noise in the corner of the room.'

I said, 'It's important because everybody sees it.'

'Oh, stop whining,' he said, 'and tell me about your Pa.'

It's very easy for a person to say 'Tell me.' I didn't know quite where to begin.

Murray said, 'When you think of him, what do you remember?'

I remembered a dark gray three-button suit. And cigars he smoked somewhere else. And cologne.

Murray wanted to know what kind.

I said, 'I don't know. I was only fourteen. And gradually it faded away.'

'Poland water probably,' he said. 'Do you look like him? You don't look like your Ma.'

Sometimes Murray knew the right thing to say.

I said, 'Pa was so handsome. He could have had any showgirl. Why would he choose a stupid Irish? She had crooked teeth.'

'She looks all right to me,' he said. 'Anyway. If it was love . . . If it was passion.'

Then again, sometimes he could just open his mouth and ruin everything.

I said, 'Pa was forty-nine. That's what Sherman Ulysses is now. Forty-nines don't do passion.'

'You're mistaken, Poppy,' he said. 'Passion is like being able to waggle your ears. Either you can or you can't, and if you can, you never lose it. Doesn't matter how old you get.'

Murray had always been oddly proud of this party trick.

Nellie had disappeared from the television screen. They were showing a photograph of two old marrieds who had perished. She was offered a seat in a boat, they said, but she wouldn't leave her husband's side. Not like some. Running to save their lying Irish neck.

I said, 'That would have been me. I'd have stayed with Reggie and drowned, if we'd been there.'

Murray was quiet for a while, gazing at those jerky old pictures. Men moving about like clockwork soldiers, milling outside the White Star offices. If I had paid closer attention maybe I'd have spotted my Uncle Israel or that fool Harry

Glaser. But I was still trying to conjure up the smell of Pa's cologne.

'Of course,' he said eventually, 'a person never knows, until it's asked of them. They might imagine they have a fund of courage, till they come to draw on it. Then they find they'll do pretty much anything to save their own miserable hide. Best not to make too many noble plans.'

I said, 'Nothing would have parted me from Reggie. I don't expect you to understand.'

He patted my hand. I hated it when he did that.

I said, 'You don't know anything about passion. You wouldn't even romp with your own wife.'

He blushed.

'No,' he said. 'But I can waggle my ears.'

The doctors at Brewer Memorial said Murray was a man who had neglected himself. They said it was a pity he didn't have family to watch over him.

I said, 'I'm putting him in a brand new, ocean view apartment, windows floor to ceiling, entrance security, real air conditioning, not just one of those old ceiling fans. What more I can do? Strictly speaking he isn't even family.'

They said he had the body of an older man.

I said to Emerald, 'I'll never understand why. He's never done much to wear it out.'

'Would he come to us do you think?' she said. 'We have room. Let me talk to him.'

But Murray wouldn't hear of leaving Florida. I took him to see the apartment and he shuffled around on his stick, looking for a latch to open the window, complaining about the smell of the rug.

I said, 'I've arranged for a help, to keep you clean and tidy and bring in food.'

'What kind of food?' he said.

I believe he'd have turned it all down if it hadn't been for the terrace.

'I could have a lemon tree up here,' he said. 'And hibiscus.'
Emerald said, 'I shall still worry about him.'
I said, 'Well, don't. A creaking door hangs long.'

FIFTY-SEVEN

Alan was a cute kid. Being around him sometimes made me wish I'd had a boy myself. I believe I'd have taken better to a boy. Maxine was OK. She was never going to win any beauty contests, having inherited the oriental features of the Boons, but she was a southpaw, like me, and she loved to sew. She was full of divine ideas for originations for her dolls.

Em always said, 'I can't help you Maxine. I never saw anyone so awkward looking with a pair of scissors. You'll have to ask Grandma Poppy.'

I always warmed to another southpaw. The way people squawked and mocked us you'd have thought we sewed with our feet.

A few months before Alan was bar mitzvahed he had his adenoids fixed and then they all went to Florida for his recuperation.

'Uncle Murray has a parrot,' Maxine told me. 'Her name's Grizel and she can say nearly a whole *beruka*. She poops *everywhere*.'

I said, 'Emerald, is he becoming a health hazard?'

'No,' she said. 'He cleans up. He's all right. He uses a separate cloth.'

I said, 'And is he making the big trek north? Is he coming to the party?'

'How many times do I have to tell you?' she said. 'It's not a party. Alan's being called to the Torah.'

As far as I'm concerned a seated rib roast for forty and a cake with a marzipan *tallit* amount to a party.

I said, 'Whatever. Is your Uncle Murray coming?'

336

Sometimes I missed the old nuisance.

'No,' she said. 'It's too far. His leg pains him where they pinned the bone.'

I said, 'Did he give you a check for the boy? How much did he give you?'

'Mom!' she said. 'He's having trees planted for Alan. In Israel. Isn't that nice?'

Trees for Israel. Parrots pooping on the rug. There was a crazy streak in those Jacoby boys, and in their father, too. Judah may have looked like a rock, but he did foolish things. Gave away his money. Married Ma.

I instructed Sapphire and Honey not to be cheap with their bar-mitzvah gifts.

I said, 'Those Boons give Timex wristwatches and to hear them talk you'd think they bought out Tiffany's. You'll see what I mean.'

For once Sapphy listened to me. She bought Alan a good camera, which is how he started on the path to fame and fortune. Honey gave him a stamp collector's album, but she never did pay attention to a word I said. Sherman and Vera gave a book on first aid, proving that the Boons weren't the only ones who were cheap and the Jacobys weren't the only ones who were crazy.

Sherman always asked if Alan had joined the Boy Scouts and he always got the same answer. 'Not yet.'

'You should join,' he said to Alan. 'Every boy should learn to take care of himself. Every boy should know how to mend his own pants and be a good American.'

Vera had a prior engagement that Saturday.

'It's a symposium,' I heard Sherman telling Honey. 'On the oppression of women.'

'Oh dear,' she said.

Oh dear, indeed.

The approach to the Williamsburg Bridge was so backed up, Alan Mordecai had already started his chanting by the time we reached Union Temple. I don't know what he was chanting about, but he sounded word perfect to me, and he hardly missed a beat when he saw me wheeling his new bicycle up to the front.

Mortie stared at me and then commenced burying his head in his hands. Em made a big frowning face, gesturing to me to take the bike away.

I said, 'Leave it outside? In this neighborhood? Are you nuts?'

Then I took out Grandpa Minkel's little silk cap and handed it up to Alan.

I said, 'Put it on.'

He shot a look across to his father, checking it was all right to change hats halfway through, but Mortie was still studying the floor.

I said, 'This was your great-great-grandpa's, on the Minkel side. And now it's yours.'

Em nodded at him. Gave him the go-ahead. I left the bike propped up near the *bimah*. I wasn't going to wheel it away again and make an exhibition of myself.

As it was I could hear a good deal of gasping and tsking.

Sherman whispered, 'I guess it's the first time they saw a bike in here.'

The first time any of those Boons had seen an eight-speed Schwinn with chrome fenders, that's for sure.

'Aunt Poppy,' Sherman said, 'I hope you got a free puncture repair kit with that?'

'Mom,' Emerald said to me, while everyone was scrumming for the cold hors d'oeuvres, 'the only thing saved you from death was that old *kippah*. Mortie was ready to murder you, I swear, temple or no.'

Alan wanted to know how many Minkels had worn it.

I said, 'How should I know? What about the bike? Do you like it?'

'Yes, thank you,' he said. He always was a polite boy. His voice was just on the turn, too. He was shooting up and filling out, turning into a real young man. He wanted to know where my Grandpa Minkel came from.

I said, 'I don't know. Did you see it has a real shift stick?'

'Germany,' Honey said. 'The Minkels came from Germany.' She was on her second plate of herring, like she hadn't eaten in a year.

'Same as the Boons,' he said. 'So we're German all round.'

I said, 'Oh no you're not. You're one quarter Merrick and don't you ever forget it. Your Great-Uncle Neville is an English Sir. Your Great-Grandma Jacoby met the Queen of England.'

'And first and foremost,' Sherman chipped in, 'you're American. It doesn't get any better than that.'

Maxine had just learned how to whistle in wonderment.

'Wow!' she said. 'I always knew we were pretty fancy.'

FIFTY-EIGHT

There was a new gallery opening every minute. You'd blink and there was another one. You'd blink again and there was a good chance it'd be gone. I was the big name. I'd thrown down the marker and set the standard when half of those newcomers were still in diapers. Sapphire's place did OK, too. She opened late and closed early and, of course, photographers are never difficult. I found her openings rather dull and always made sure I had some other event to rush away to.

Emerald never understood how exciting and entertaining my life was.

'Mom,' she'd say, 'don't you ever get tired of people blowing smoke in your eyes? Don't you ever get tired of listening to phoneys?'

When a person lives in a rut they may not even realize it, and Emerald and Mortie ran in a very deep rut indeed. Mondays they helped with Temple Youth, Tuesdays Em had Temple Sisterhood. Wednesdays she visited Honey and sometimes Sapphire, depending on Sapphire's mood, and sometimes me, depending on my schedule. Thursdays she took Maxine horse riding at Jamaica Bay and Mortie had Men's Club. Fridays she played house all day, Saturdays they visited with the Boons, Sundays the Boons visited with them. Vacations they mainly went to a small house they had bought in the Catskills. I would have shot myself.

One day she said to me, 'You know you're going to be seventy . . .'

I said, 'I'd like to know who's spreading a filthy lie like that.'

She said, 'We'd like to do something to mark it.'

There appeared before me a horrible vision of a catered buffet. There wouldn't be enough liquor and none of my amusing artists would turn out to Eastern Parkway and the Boons would all be there because Emerald couldn't open a cookie jar without them attending.

I said, 'No thank you.'

'Why don't you wait,' she said, 'till I've told you what we thought? We're going to England. I want to show Mortie and the kids where I did my growing up.'

Angelica wrote that we were all welcome to stay at Stoke Glapthorne.

'We're quite cosy "en famille",' she wrote.

During the summer we do cream teas and tractor rides so Edgar and I just hunker down in the West Wing as far away as poss from the rubbernecks. We have ourselves roped off but occasionally one finds oneself being gazed at by a tripper who's jumped the fence.

We're no great distance from Bagehots but you'll find the old place very much altered. Kneilthorpe is gone. They built something called a housing estate. Em, I do hope you won't be terribly disappointed. There are still a few of our old rides you may remember, and Merrick is still with us. He's writing a memoir of his time in Mesopotamia but is otherwise rather forgetful. He's very keen to buy something called a 'mobile home'. It's a kind of van with a bed and a potty and no wheels. He visualizes it installed alongside the summer kitchen and I suppose it would be rather fun to have one's own little billet, but Edgar won't hear of it. The rubbernecks would be sure to discover it and then one would have inspectors inspecting. Everything is inspected these days. The town hall is full of little Hitlers. One sometimes wonders why we bothered going to war.

Now I have a nice little chestnut Maxine can ride whilst you're here, but what about the boy? Edgar has a grey he might try out but she is inclined to take advantage of inexperience so we may have to find him something a little steadier. Are you absolutely sure you can't stay on for some cubbing?

I said to Emerald, 'What about Paris? You grew up there, too.'

'I don't want to go back to Paris,' she said. 'I was always waiting for something bad to happen there. You go if you want.'

So it was arranged that after Leicestershire I would take Alan and Maxine to Paris while Mortie and Em motored around scenic England.

'But only if you're up to it,' Em kept saying. 'Kids can be a handful.'

I was up to anything. I still am.

Before we flew to London I kept my annual appointment with Dr Newton and he tidied me up a little around the neck and eyelids.

I said to Em, 'Why don't you let me take Maxine with me this time?'

My granddaughter had a very racial nose.

Emerald said, 'She's twelve years old.'

I said, 'She has a deviated septum.'

I never did get my way over that. But Dr Newton made me look fabulous and refreshed, as usual, and I had my *styliste* give me a soft blush tint.

Honey said, 'Ma always told me I was the pretty one, but you're the pretty one now. I wouldn't be surprised if you don't come back with another English beau. And don't worry about Sapphy. While you're gone I'm going to plead loneliness and have her eat dinner with me twice a week at least.'

Sapphire was going through one of her episodes.

Air travel was not what it used to be. One couldn't circulate. All kinds of dreary people were crammed in together. And I had to tell the stewardess several times that I was a former aviatrix myself and the pilot would certainly wish to meet me, before she invited me forward to the cockpit.

I said to Mortie, 'We should have sailed.'

'Who has that kind of time?' he said. Mortie was always in a hurry. If he was at home he needed to run to the factory for an hour. If he was at the factory he was trying to get away and eat dinner with his wife.

I believe it took us longer to drive from London Airport to the Boodle-Nearys than it did to cross the Atlantic Ocean. Emerald would drive and Mortie would keep grabbing the wheel and yelling, 'Watch out!' and I was altogether nauseated by the twisting and turning of those English roads.

As we approached the house we spotted a figure, bent over, weeding in a most inelegant posture. It was Angelica. Em began banging on the horn, and by the time we pulled up our vehicle was entirely surrounded by excited hounds, smearing the windows with their snouts and sliding down the bodywork with their big muddy claws.

Mortie said, 'There goes my insurance deductible. Holy smoke. Em, I have to take an antihistamine before I open this door.'

I needn't have worried about comparing unfavorably with Angelica. Even after flying in an airborne slum and being flung from side to side in a tinny British station wagon, I still could have given her ten years at least. Her cheeks had that dull redness of broken veins, her permanent wave had all but grown out, and her considerable bosom had moved south.

'Oh, how marvelous to see you!' she cried. 'How simply marvelous! Edgar will be out drectly. He's in the Smoke Rum reminding Merrick who you are.'

Stoke Glapthorne was a wide, shallow, gray stone house. It had terraced lawns and yew hedges and portraits of Boodles or Nearys who had been there since 1682. Had Ma ever seen it she would have found even more reason to feel discontented with Kneilthorpe.

Angelica had four gardeners and an under-gardener, two persons serving tea and cake in the old dairy, a manager, a seller of entrance tickets and souvenir brochures, and an elderly woman who cycled up twice a week to dust, but no one to carry in our luggage.

'Edgar!' she roared. 'The Americans have landed. All hands to the pump.'

Edgar Boodle-Neary had been present at Angelica and Murray's wedding but I had no clear memory of him. He had just been one of that set of colorless, shapeless young men, given to neighing helplessly at the most unamusing things and clinging to each other for company. I don't believe they were intentionally unfriendly. But they all seemed to have known each other every minute of their lives and couldn't conceive of how to converse with anyone from another land, let alone a person who hadn't attended their school. Reggie had been the only one among them to be a friend to Murray and not disregard him just because he chose not to hunt or shoot.

The years and perhaps the influence of Angelica had improved Edgar's sociability, if not his physique. He had turned into a sphere, though how this had happened still perplexes me. Food was a minor concern at Stoke Glapthorne and while we were guests there I was often reduced to going into the Tea Rums, after the day trippers had left, and taking some of the small, dry muffins.

I can only think that Edgar had another feeding station, perhaps in London where he belonged to a great number of clubs and was sometimes obliged to go to a place called The Hyce in order to register his vote. He apparently had a very important role in the passing of laws, though I never saw him engaged in it. Somehow, in spite of short rations at home, he was able to maintain an enormous waistline and very good spirits.

He greeted us all warmly on our arrival and assisted Alan and Mortie in bringing up our bags while Angelica made soup from a yellow powder.

'One of the great benefits of going into tourism,' she said, 'is that one can get a special card and buy in bulk. It's extraordinarily cheap and one only needs to shop once a month. You must come with me whilst you're here. There might be something you'd care to take back with you. This coffee frinstance. You simply add hot water, and this canister has lasted us months. How adorable Emerald is, and her little family. Quite adorable.'

Gelica never once commented on my youthful appearance. She petted Emerald incessantly and Mortie and Alan and Maxine, but beyond that her mind was filled with horses and discount cards. Edgar did whisper to me one evening, 'Still got a good pair of pins on you', but I believe I may have paid in advance for the compliment with the very fine single malt that had been my gift to him, and, anyhow, his persistently calling me 'Polly' diluted the satisfaction.

As for Sir Neville, he rarely left his writing desk and when he did he seemed not to notice there were five extra people in the house.

'Merrick!' Angelica goaded him. 'You remember Poppy. Reggie's bride?'

'No,' he said.

'Of course he does,' she said, as though he weren't there. 'He pretends, so as not to have to talk. He even pretends not to remember Bobbity, and then he scribbles orf reams and reams. He recalls the name of every man who was in his regiment.'

The only time Sir Neville voluntarily broke his silence was to laugh, suddenly and heartily, at some secret regimental joke I suppose.

We drove in convoy across to the old places, Edgar with Mortie and Em, Alan and Maxine with me and Angelica. Past Bagehots first, with its smart new gates.

'Wrecked cars,' Angelica told me. 'Those people have made millions of pounds out of wrecked cars. Extraordinary.'

Then onto Buckby, to the churchyard, where poor Reggie's grave stood neglected, and two places along lay my sister-in-law, Marigold Alice Bagehot Merrick, parted in death from her hunter.

'Not only would the parson not allow Fearless to be interred here,' Angelica explained, 'neither would he permit "Bobbity" on the inscription. I said to him, "Who's paying for the bloody hole to be dug? Who's paying for the inscription?" But he's one of this new breed. They come from secondary modern schools and they don't at all understand country ways. Poppy! Here I am chatting on. Perhaps you'd like to be alone for a moment? With Reggie?'

But I didn't need to be alone. I had Reggie in my heart, and this was Emerald's moment. She had brought flowers to lay on her father's grave.

'Daddy,' I heard her say, 'I brought Mortie to see you. I wish you could have known him. And Alan and Maxine. I wish you could have known them all. It doesn't seem fair.'

I hadn't planned on doing any weeping, but when you hear your child making introductions to a cracked headstone it's impossible to resist. I held her in my arms.

'Mom,' she said.

'Em,' I said.

Even the kids had ceased goofing around.

'Kleenex anyone?' Angelica asked.

As we left, Em plucked off one of the flowers she'd brought for Reggie and left it on Bobbity's grave.

Somehow, seeing what had become of Kneilthorpe was the worst. The old house and its gardens were gone, and in their place was something called The Thorpes. Little houses as far as the eye could see, with carports and patches of lawn and women in synthetics pushing bassinets. There was a Kneilthorpe Drive and a Merrick Avenue and a Batey Parade with a post office and food store and a hair salon.

I said, 'Who was Batey?'

Edgar said, 'Need you ask? The dreadful individual who built all this.'

I said, 'I wish Merrick had asked for my help. I'd have sent money.'

Angelica shook her head. 'Poppy,' she said, 'you have no idea. It would have taken a fortune.'

I said, 'I have a fortune. And I'd have liked to keep the place going, for Emerald and future generations.'

'One of these days,' I heard Mortie say to Edgar, 'she's going to dip into the well and the bucket's going to come up empty.'

'Well, I wouldn't have wanted it,' Em said. 'I have a home. Uncle Neville got some money and the land got used. Those people got to live in nice new houses. There's nothing wrong with that.'

I said, 'This land was your heritage. Now look at it. A heap for the ants. No wonder Neville is a broken man.'

We looked in on Melton Mowbray, too, all quite ruined with self-service stores. You even had to pump your own gas.

I said, 'Gelica, tell me to mind my own business, but is your place liable to be sold for an ant heap, too?'

'We've taken advice,' she said. 'And if we expand the day-tripper side of things. Perhaps an aviary, or an orchid house, or a shop selling fudge. But then, one has to be flexible. We did receive an offer. Someone had the idea of turning the place into a sort of hotel. Health and beauty. Turkish baths and salad for dinner. Apparently there's money to be made doing that. But Edgar says "over my dead bod!" So we'll probably go for the fudge.'

I said, 'You and Edgar seem like a match.'

'He's a very agreeable sort,' she said. 'And, of course, I completely depend on him for dealing with Merrick.'

I said, 'Strange how we both ended up with another family's problems. You really had no obligation to take on Neville, any more than I did to . . .'

I hadn't raised the other business, but it seemed like the moment.

I said, 'Murray's in Florida, you know? He sends his best wishes.'

'Oh, yes,' she said. 'Florida. Grapefruit segments.'

I said, 'He never did marry. And now he has a pin in his thigh and he doesn't much care for company. I shouldn't complain, I guess. All I have to do is pay his rent.'

'Do you really?' she said. 'Is he bankers?'

I said, 'No. Just . . . eccentric.'

'No,' she said, '*bankers*. Is he bankrupt?'

I said, 'Well, his father never made wise investments. Apart from marrying Ma. And anyway he gave money away like there was no tomorrow. That was his mentality. Give till it hurts. So there's nothing left. It doesn't seem to bother Murray, though. He just potters around in his own little world.'

Angelica said, 'I'm glad you're taking care of things. I should hate to think of him being alone. I was awfully fond of him. Awfully. Susie Manners ran across him, you know? Flicky's sister? Nineteen forty-seven, I think. It was certainly after I'd had us annulled. He turned up in a Displaced Person camp in Epping Forest, searching for a friend. Susie was with the Red Cross.'

I said, 'What friend?'

'No idea,' she said.

I said, 'Gelica, do you think Murray is *that* way? Was it *that* kind of friend?'

I heard a little snigger from my grandson in the rear seat.

'Possibly,' she said.

I said, 'Well, let's call up Susie and ask her.'

'Can't be done,' she said. 'She married a South African. Durban, I think. Drowned swimming after a heavy luncheon. Sorry.'

I felt so frustrated.

I said, 'Didn't you think to ask? I would have.'

'Poppy,' she said. 'One moves on. You did. Even Merrick did. One can't sit around in the doldrums, wondering what might have been.'

I said, 'If that's what you call moving on. I can't believe he didn't fight harder to keep Kneilthorpe. All that land, gone for hovels. Little boxes for unfortunates.'

Maxine said, 'Grandma? What is an unfortunate?'

Alan said, 'You are, sap head.'

He loved to torment her.

'An unfortunate,' I said, 'is a person who doesn't come from a good family.'

Maxine said, 'You mean the kind that dump their grands in hospitals when they get old and never visit them?'

Alan said, 'She doesn't mean that kind of "good". Good families are where the kids go to college and nobody gets into trouble.'

I said, 'No. Unfortunates are people who have nothing. They live

348

in tiny rooms and all share one bed and have fleas. And they can never go to Sardi's for a *filet mignon* or anything like that because they have absolutely no money.'

'Absolutely none?' Maxine said.

'Absolutely none,' I said. 'They have to wear rags and eat dry crusts and mop their own floors because they can't afford help.'

'Those people weren't wearing rags,' she said. 'They were wearing nice things.'

Angelica said, 'Well, in England a good family is a family you can place. Because your people have known their people forever.'

Alan said, 'But what if they've done bad things?'

She said, 'Frinstance?'

'If your parents knew their parents and everything,' he said, 'but one of them murdered somebody or cheated.'

'Ah!' she said. 'Like the Vigos. Well, they're still a good family. Archie turned out a bad lot, but they're a very good family. George is eighth baronet, and his mother was a Conyngham. Do you see?'

Neither Alan nor Maxine did see, besides which they were all overlooking my point that the sign of an unfortunate was that he had nothing.

Maxine said, 'Angelica, I'm going to be bat mitzvahed next year.'

'Are you darling?' Angelica said. 'What fun.'

The modern way Emerald had raised her children, they expected to have their opinions listened to, and Maxine was like a dog with a bone on the subject of The Thorpes.

'Grandma says those people have fleas,' she harped on at dinner, 'but they looked OK to me. I liked those little houses.'

I said, 'You wouldn't say so if you had to live in one of them.'

'Did you ever live in one, Grandma?' she said. And everyone waited on my reply though they were all perfectly well acquainted with the story of my life.

I said, 'I don't have to have lived in one. I visited enough of them, when I was helping the Misses Stone. When I was doing good works.'

'Did you Mom?' Em said. 'I never knew that.'

'Stanton Street,' I said, 'Orchard Street, Eldridge Street. We worked for The Daughters of Jacob, teaching them hygiene and reading.'

'So they could stop being unfortunates,' Maxine piped up.

Mortie was sharp with her. 'Maxine,' he said, 'I don't ever want to hear you use that word again. If people need help, help them. If they deserve respect, respect them. And if they don't, just stay away from them. But don't call them names.'

'Grandma does,' she said, but her face was burning, being corrected like that in front of company.

'Grandma . . .' Mortie began, but he pressed his lips together and went no further. He was in a sullen mood anyhow because it was Friday and Em said it wouldn't be appropriate to do the Kiddush and the Motzi and all that business in another person's house.

'What Daddy means is,' Em tried to soothe her, 'anybody can have misfortunes. Some people can pick themselves up, and some need a hand, but misfortunes can come to anybody out of a clear blue sky.'

'Very true,' Edgar said. 'Herd gets brucellosis. Bank goes belly up. One can be ruined. That's why one should diversify.'

Maxine commenced to glare at me, as though I was to blame for her receiving a telling off.

Alan said, 'I think there are people you could call unfortunates. I don't think they're the people Grandma means though. People who don't have anyone are unfortunate. People who don't have family.'

Mortie liked that.

'Well said, son,' he said. 'It's nothing to do with money in the bank, or fancy houses. If you have a place to go on Friday nights, see the candles lit, share a blessing with your loved ones, you have everything you need.'

He cast that particular fly for Emerald but she wasn't biting. I had raised her to know politeness is more important than discommoding other people with your prayers.

'And another point is this,' Mortie pressed on. 'A great misfortune is for a person not to know who he is.'

'True, true,' Edgar nodded. 'Like that whipper-in from the Asfordby. Remember, Gelica? He was in a fearful collision with a milk tanker. Unconscious for days and when he did come to he had no idea who he was. Not a clue. Hunter had to be destroyed as well, of course. Terrible business.'

Angelica said, 'But he did remember, eventually.'

'Yes,' Edgar said. 'He did. Although he was always rather odd afterwards.'

Maxine had ceased her glowering. She and Alan had found something amusing.

'A person who knows where he came from,' Mortie said solemnly, 'need never feel lost. Roots are a blessing. If you know where you came from, you know where you are and you can decide where you're going.'

'True, true, true,' Edgar agreed. And Sir Neville let out one of his inexplicable hoots of laughter, recalling some gay remark from Mesopotamia I suppose.

'We're from the Boons,' Maxine announced.

'And from the Minkels,' Alan reminded her. 'And from the Merricks, and the Waxmans.'

Miriam Boon had been a Waxman.

'So we know who we are, and we always have Friday night dinner, and we have money,' Maxine said. 'We're real fortunates. Where exactly does our money come from?'

'From hard work and thrift,' Mortie said. 'From corsets made on a kitchen table. And a factory built up from nothing. And a premier range of swimwear.'

'And mustard,' I said. 'Don't forget Minkel's Mighty Fine Mustard.'

'Grandma,' she said. That child asked way too many questions. 'How does the mustard get made?'

'In factories,' I said.

'Yes, but how?'

I said, 'I don't know. I'm a collector and discoverer of important art.'

'Don't you ever go to see your factories?' she said. 'Where are they? Do they just make the mustard and send you the money?'

'Maxine!' Em warned her.

'I'd like to see your factories,' she said. 'I've seen Daddy's and Grampy Boon's. I'd like to see how mustard gets made, so I know where I came from and where I'm going . . .'

'To bed, if you don't watch your step,' Alan muttered.

'Because if I don't know that, I'll be nothing but an unfortunate. Isn't that right, Daddy?'

'Seconds anyone?' Angelica asked. The twenty-servings beef pie had been all afternoon in the coal oven, but I had found an icy lump at the center of my slice.

FIFTY-NINE

Maxine didn't want to come to Paris. She wanted to remain at Stoke Glapthorne and go horseback riding every day, but Emerald and Mortie insisted. They said it was part of her education and I believe she would now agree with them. During that week she learned a great many things, including the story of my life. I took her out beyond Charonne and showed her where I used to keep my Curtiss Oriole.

I said, 'I used to fly Humphrey Choate to the racetrack. I flew him all the way to the Mediterranean Ocean, too, and that's where I met your Grandpa Merrick.'

'You did not,' she said, and I hadn't expected to be able to prove it to her, the St-Blaise airdrome now being a flying school run by a foreign person, but in the front office they had a fine display of old photographs, and there I was, parked outside the sheds. It was difficult to make out my features, and there was no sign of Choate or Beluga, but it was clearly labeled. 'Mrs Poppy Catchings, *circa* 1923.'

Maxine did her wonderment whistle.

She said, 'Could you fly us home?'

'I could,' I said, 'but I choose not to. There's no style to being an aviator anymore.' We also went looking for Coquelicot which, as near as I could say, had become a *chocolaterie*, and to the Athenée to inquire about my lost property. A leopard and two foxes. The concierge had an inflated opinion of himself for a man who stands behind a desk all day handing out keys.

'Madame?' he said. 'Since 1940? This a joke?'

I said, 'It certainly is not. And what about my shoe trees?'

There was something about the words 'shoe trees' that caused Maxine to dissolve into a silent, shaking type of laughter that reminded me greatly of Emerald. The concierge did no more than turn his back on us and start paying lavish attention to a pair of darkies in bright orange robes.

I said, 'Now see what you did? How d'you expect this important monkey to treat me seriously when you're sniggering at my side?'

I called to the darkies. I said, 'Your robes are adorable. I've a mind to get something like that myself.'

They smiled most vivaciously.

I said, 'Never mind, Maxine. The Athenée Hotel is welcome to my old furs. There are plenty more where they came from.'

'Grandma!' she said. 'You're shouting.'

Sometimes she was a real goody-two-shoes. When I was buying her a faux pony skin jacket she said, 'I don't know if I'm allowed. Maybe we should ask Mommy?'

I told her, 'Of course you're allowed. Give people the opportunity, they'll start prohibiting things. Make the least move and there'll always be a line halfway round the block waiting to catch you out. This has been my experience in life.'

Meanwhile Alan roamed the city with his bar-mitzvah camera. Maxine didn't think that was allowed either but I figured sixteen was old enough. The way I looked at it, he might even meet a pretty girl and open his account. Then we'd be spared having another Murray in the family.

Alan usually came and found us when it was time for dinner. Chartier was their favorite. I tried showing them a fancier side of Paris, but they liked the way waiters wrote your order on the tablecloth. They liked the way dinner arrived fast.

'Know something, Grandma?' he said one evening. 'Nobody in this town talks about our people. About what happened to them.'

I said, 'What do you mean?'

I knew what he meant, but I didn't want him turning tragic on me, like Sapphire.

'Before the war,' he said, 'there were Jews here. And after the war there weren't. There are Jews here now. I've seen three temples today. But they're not the old Jews come back. They're a new lot. And nobody talks about where the old ones went.'

I said, 'People don't care to dwell on those things.'

'So I see,' he said.

I said, 'Hitler sent them away.'

'I know that,' he said. 'We learned all about that in school. I've seen pictures.'

'What pictures?' Maxine wanted to know.

I shot him a warning look. I didn't want to be up all night with questions and nightmares.

'Camps,' he said.

She said, 'Like Seneca Lake Summer Camp?'

He was a sensible boy.

'Not exactly,' he said. 'Yeah. Kind of.'

I dreamed I was eating dinner in Chartier. Aunt Fish was there, and Ma. They were trying to erase the writing off the tablecloth. And Neville Merrick was there, too, laughing at regimental jokes. Then a telephone began ringing but I couldn't pick up because my arms were tied to my side. It rang and rang until suddenly it wasn't a dream anymore and my arms were free and I answered.

'Mom?' Emerald said.

They were staying at the Lygon Arms Hotel in Cotswoldshire, at my expense. There was a cheap side to Mortie and I wanted my girl to have the best.

I said, 'Did you get a bed with drapes?'

'Mom,' she said. 'We have to go home. Something terrible happened.'

Then Mortie came on.

'Poppy,' he said, 'I don't know an easy way to do a thing like this, so I'll just come right out with it. Sapphire has passed away.'

How few are the moments we remember precisely, long after they are past. I recall perfectly the color of the sky as the *Carpathia* came home without my Pa. But I can't remember his going away. I recall exactly how it felt to have to go to the ballet wearing black day shoes with a borrowed Directoire gown. And the feel of Gilbert Catchings' fist against my jaw. I don't at all remember the moment when Sapphire was first placed in my arms. But I remember when she was taken from me.

Our room had a marble mantelpiece and a complimentary bowl of fruit and Maxine's clothes left in a heap where she had stepped out of them. I listened into the telephone and saw an old lady's hand on the celadon coverlet, plucking at the machine embroidery with a fleshy finger. Maxine was still sleeping and Mortie was talking about airplane tickets, and someone had slipped in unseen and placed the heaviest weight around my heart.

SIXTY

We were met by Sherman and Murray.
I said to Murray, 'I thought you couldn't travel anymore.'

'I gave myself a talking to,' he said.

Mortie drove Alan and Maxine home. Sherman took us directly to see Honey.

'She's beside herself,' he said. 'She's having tranquilizing pills, one three times a day, to be taken with food, but she's still beside herself. It doesn't matter what anybody says, she's determined to blame herself.'

Sapphy was meant to have been going to dinner. But when she didn't show up Honey didn't think too much of it. Sapphire was partial to the cocktail hour and sometimes it drifted on and she never got as far as dinner. Neither was she a person you'd call up with a little reminder, not unless you were willing to get your head bitten off. So some time passed before the neighbors complained that the television had been playing against their bedroom wall for two full days without a break and the police were sent for.

Like her predecessor, for hired help Coretta II had a lot to say for herself.

'Miss Honey brought very low by this,' she said. 'She bin passed the bitter cup, no mistake.'

But I found my sister quite composed.

'Poppy,' she said. 'I let you down.'

'Mother!' Sherman said. 'No one let anyone down. Sapphire was a grown woman.'

'No!' she said. 'I should never have handed her back. She was a darling happy child until she went to Europe and came back all crazy and mixed up. Poppy's life was no life for a child.'

Em said, 'Well, hang on there, Aunt Honey. I turned out OK.'

'That was sheer luck,' Honey said. 'Sapphy was never right from the day I let her go and now I'm judged. Do you think it's just chance I was the one she went and died on? It isn't. She paid me back.'

Sherman said, 'It was a simple case of erroneous self-medication. Pills and rye. It's easily done.'

Em said, 'Did she leave a letter?'

'No,' he said. 'No letter. Ask me, she just neglected to read the accompanying leaflet.'

'Ask me,' Murray said, 'she just lost count.'

'Well,' Em said, 'that's something. I was afraid we wouldn't be able to give her a proper burial.'

We all looked at her.

'You know what I mean,' she said. 'S-u-i-c-i-d-e.'

'Don't!' Honey cried. 'Oh please, don't!'

I said, 'Was that what was bugging that husband of yours all the way back here? You'd have thought he was the one had lost a child.'

'It's a serious thing, Mom,' she said. 'A person's soul isn't theirs to extinguish. Mortie and I discussed this. But, anyway, there wasn't a letter, so we're in the clear.'

I was thinking I would have liked a letter. I'd have liked something.

Honey said, 'It's of no significance anyway, Emerald. West End Collegiate will be happy to have her. We'll take her over to New Jersey and give her a good Christian burial.'

Em said, 'Are you crazy? We're Jewish.'

Sherman said, 'I don't see why you two are arguing over this. Aunt Poppy's next of kin after all.'

'On paper, perhaps,' Honey spat out. 'But I was the only

real mother that child ever knew and I haven't been Jewish in years.'

I caught Murray trying to slip away.

I said, 'Where do you think you're going?'

'To find a glass of milk,' he said.

I said, 'Take me with you. I think I'm liable to faint.'

He took my arm and we walked slowly to the Broadway Yum-Yum.

I said, 'I meant to be a better mother. I'd been thinking a great deal about her. Seeing Kneilthorpe again and Paris, she'd been on my mind and I'd decided I'd come back and be a better mother to her. She never forgave me over Gil, you know? She was always waiting for Gil Catchings to walk into her life and make up for lost time. And she never forgave me over that French boy. There's truth in what Honey said. I could have given her up, let Honey raise her. Then none of this might have come to pass.'

'I think,' Murray said, 'Sapphy was just Sapphy. She'd have ended up miscounting her pills whoever raised her.'

I said, 'I did love her.'

'Of course you did,' he said. 'I loved her, too. But she was a pain in the neck. Never happier than when she was miserable. There was something at the heart of her . . . maybe it came from her father's side. Do you know, I wrote her a page or two most weeks but I never heard back from her, not once in fifteen years. Do you want to go to the viewing chapel? I'll go with you if you like.'

I said, 'Do I have to?'

'It's recommended,' he said, 'but not compulsory. Leave it another half hour and Em and Honey'll have decided for you.'

I said, 'Do you think she should be buried Jewish or buried Church?'

'Church,' he said. 'But that's because I like the flowers. How was England?'

'Pointless,' I said. 'Never go back.'

He had a mustache of milk. Murray never did learn to drink tidily.

359

I said, 'Neville Merrick has a screw loose. They built houses over Kneilthorpe. Angelica's old.'

'We're all old,' he said. He drained his glass, started to make a move. 'Better be getting back,' he said, 'unless we want a multiple funeral on our hands.'

I said, 'Angelica told me something. A person called Susie Manners saw you in England in 1947. Flicky Manners' sister.'

'Don't remember,' he said.

I said, 'You were in Epping Forest looking for someone. She was Red Cross and she told Angelica it definitely was you.'

'Well, then,' he said, 'if Susie Manners said it I suppose it must be true.'

He was quiet for a moment.

'If I tell you something,' he said eventually, 'will you promise never to repeat it?'

I promised.

'And no questions. No coming back for more.'

I promised again.

'I had a friend,' he said, 'after I went away. I went to the Netherlands and I had a friend. We grew things. Scillas and hyacinths, dwarf tulips, paper narcissus, and then potatoes, after the war came. It was pretty quiet, considering. Just sky and good earth. It's called the polder. We didn't bother anyone and nobody bothered us. But you never know. You might think you have good neighbors, but . . . who's to say what a person will do when it's his door they're knocking on? We were sent to a place called Vught. And then one day I had a choice, to go with my friend to Westerbork or stay where I was. I had a job at Vught, making soup. I had somebody watching out for me. People didn't usually get choices in Vught, so I grabbed at mine with both hands. And my friend went to Westerbork without me. Did you ever hear of Westerbork? Nobody ever heard of Westerbork. They had a restaurant there and a hairdresser and a train that left every Tuesday at eleven. But, anyhow, I never got to see it for myself. I saved my own scrawny neck, Poppy, ducking and diving till the Canadians came and set us all free and then I went looking for my friend. Hoping for the chance to explain. Or something. There were a lot of places to look. I don't remember any Susie Manners, but if she said she saw me, I'm sure she did. I just went looking in too many places to recall them all. And that's that.'

I said, 'Where did the train go? Every Tuesday at eleven?'

'No questions,' he said. 'You promised. We have to go, Pops. We have to go and arrange a burying.'

SIXTY-ONE

U nited in grief, Honey and Emerald reached an accommodation. Em and Mortie burned a *shiva* candle for Sapphire and made a donation in her memory to the United Jewish Appeal. A reverend minister of the Dutch Reform Church conducted her funeral service, and she was laid to rest in Flushing not so very far from her daddy Gilbert.

I stayed away from the burying. It was more than I could bear. Honey and Murray kindly represented me at the graveside, and I was comforted to hear that Alan had been his own man. He had attended, bringing flowers for his Aunt Sapphy and wearing Grandpa Minkel's old *kippah*. There had been pink roses, too, from Humpy Choate in London, England. Births, deaths, Humpy always sent roses.

I said to Murray, 'And now what will you do?'

'Go back to Florida,' he said. 'And if you have any sense you'll join me there.'

I said, 'And get pooped on by a giant bird and have to look at you with a milk mustache?'

'Please yourself,' he said.

Which I tried to do, but there's not much pleasure to be had once you've buried a child. I sold my galleries and tried to be kinder and more attentive to my kith and kin, though it wasn't always appreciated. I visited with Honey every day after she became too obese to leave the house. It was by sitting reading the *Riverside News* to her I learned that one of the Misses Stone had attained her hundredth birthday. It was by watching television shows with her that I learned about women burning their brassieres and marching for rights and hanging on the words of a sour-faced woman called Lily Lelchuck.

I said, 'Do you know, I believe I may have met that person. She was an unfortunate. There was a whole tribe called Lelchucks down there.'

'Vera has all her books,' Honey said.

Imagine. People like that writing books and getting onto television shows.

I said, 'What do these women want?'

'Just . . . everything,' Honey said. 'How fortunate we've been, Poppy. We never had to burn our bust bodices and we've had absolutely everything.'

I said, 'Well, I know *I've* had everything, but I wouldn't have said it was true in your case.'

'Oh yes, I have!' she said. 'I've had everything, with extra whipped cream and chopped nuts.'

But Vera hadn't had everything. She left Sherman Ulysses and went looking for whatever it was she'd missed. According to Lily Lelchuck marriage was nothing but codified rape and oppression, although I found it hard to look at my nephew and believe him capable of either of those things. I would have left him because of the way he always looked in his handkerchief after he blew his nose. The only thing I can say in Vera's defense is, she waited until after Honey had passed over.

There was standing room only in the West End Collegiate for Honey's obsequies.

I said to Emerald, 'I hope you won't be cutting your aunt's funeral just because she's resting in the arms of Jesus.'

'Mom,' she said, 'I'm not an unreasonable person. Of course I'll attend. I'll just close my eyes and *daven* in my own way. Alan, by the way, is seeing the Strauss girl.'

Then, just when Honey's place was almost cleared and ready to be closed up, Vera left Sherman. I suggested he might like to take Coretta II, but he wouldn't have her. He said he had his Boy Scout

Campfire Cookbook. So Coretta II had to be let go. As far as I know she went to California to seek her fortune.

With Honey gone I felt myself move up a place in line.

I said to Em, 'You realize I'll be next.'

She said, 'Not if Mortie doesn't ease up, you won't. Sunday he was there till midnight doing inventory.'

I said, 'No. My time's coming. I can see it when I look in the mirror.'

'Sounds like you're due a trip to the beauty doctor,' she said. But I had lost the inclination for all that.

I said, 'I'll go if I can take Maxine. If she doesn't get her nose done soon it'll be too late.'

Of course, a person called Barbra Streisand had made Maxine's type of nose fashionable.

I said, 'Let me treat you. Just get the bump smoothed out. Call it a little vacation.'

'No thanks, Grandma,' she said. 'But when I get my driver's license, let's go and see your mustard factories. Let's go and see where we came from.'

That child has a pretty good sense of humor for which I believe she has me to thank. Nothing to do with the Boons, that's for sure.

SIXTY-TWO

We did take a trip, as soon as she finished Senior High, to Blue Grass, Iowa, where we failed to find any installations bearing the name Minkel, but a man in a diner lectured us at length on the importance of Grade I Yellow mustard flour in barbecue relish, all the while perusing down the front of my granddaughter's décolleté.

I said, 'You had better get dressed. This is rough territory.'

'What I don't understand, Grandma,' she said, 'is how come you still get money when you don't have the factories anymore?'

It was a mystery to me, too, but I believe it had something to do with diversification and wise investment by my Uncle Israel. Everything else I left to Mr Brooks at the bank.

In Duluth, Minnesota, the only place we could find carrying the name of Minkel was an apparel store for men who fish and trap.

I said, 'I'm a descendant of Jesse Minkel. Is he anything to do with this outfit?'

The man said, 'No. And we don't give credit neither.'

I was about to explain how many times over I could buy and sell his miserable establishment when Maxine jumped in and told him she was writing up a college paper on her Minkel forebears.

She said, 'There was a Meyer Minkel. And an Addie Minkel. Did you ever hear of them?'

'Addie Minkel!' he said. 'Mad Addie! You only just missed her.'

I said, 'Which way?'

'No,' he said. 'She went to her rest. Last year. Maybe two years. Mad Addie. She was as wide as she stood high.'

Maxine said, 'Maybe there's family. Can we look in your phone book?'

'Addie didn't have family,' he said. 'She was the end of the line. They say she had medals, from French France. I don't know. She always looked an unnatural type of woman to me.'

'Grandma,' Maxine said, as we were leaving the wader store, 'it seems to me the Minkels have died out.'

The man called us back. 'There was talk,' he said, 'of naming a scenic picnic area after her, but nothing ever came of it.'

I said, 'Let this be a lesson to you, Maxine. In life you have to look ahead not behind.'

In 1976 Mortie and Em celebrated their thirtieth anniversary in the ballroom at Union Temple, and less than a year later we were back there eating an identical buffet for Alan's marriage to Ruthie Strauss.

I said, 'Shall I buy you an apartment?'

'No thank you,' he said. 'A washer-dryer would be good though. As long as you promise not to wheel it into the temple.'

Angelica and Edgar sent a gift certificate from Harrods department store.

'You'll be able to choose something if ever you're in London,' Angelica wrote.

I said to Em, 'A gift certificate! How long is that good for? Those things expire, you know?'

'It doesn't matter,' she said. 'It's the thought that counts.'

That's another adage I have never understood.

Ruthie was a cute kid. She had pretty hair, curly without being troublesome. The only thing about her was, she was so Jewish. She wouldn't even serve Boston Crème Pie after a roast chicken.

Em said, 'That girl will run herself into the ground.'

Ruthie had a position teaching kindergarten as well as keeping kosher at home and taking a turn once a week at a night shelter for unfortunates. That was the way things were since Lily Lelchuck's books were all the rage. Before a person decides she wants everything I'd recommend her to find out just how big this 'everything' is.

I had moved to a smaller apartment after I had had three robberies and claudication of the arteries, but I never settled. Smaller didn't suit me, somehow.

Then Sherman announced he was taking early retirement from the bank.

I said, 'Is it that time already?'

'Not quite,' he said, 'but I'm ready. I'm tired of this city. Tired of looking over my shoulder all the time and getting grit in my eyes and hearing the F word. I'm taking a leaf out of Murray's book. Going to Florida.'

I said, 'I see.'

'Now what?' he said. 'You look like you lost a dollar and found a dime.'

It was just that I had always been given to understand that I had first refusal on Murray's spare room.

I said, 'I didn't think you two got along so well.'

'We don't need to,' he said. 'I'm not moving in. I may drive over once in a while. Play checkers. No, I'm going to the Pelican Bay Retirement Home. You get assisted living and amenities.'

I said, 'What amenities?'

'Shuffleboard,' he said. 'And round the clock medical attendance. Why don't you come with me?'

I said, 'Shuffleboard? I used to fly my own plane to the Bois de Vincennes.'

Besides, I had to stay in New York and comfort Emerald while Mortie had coronary bypass surgery. Then Ruthie and Alan presented me with my first great-grandchild.

I said, 'Flower names are coming back into vogue.'

We got a boy though, as things turned out, and they named him Abraham. Abraham Strauss Boon. He arrived at five o'clock in the morning and Alan was so excited he phoned me there and then.

'I saw him born, Grandma,' he said. 'I took pictures and everything.'

I said, 'I'll pass on those.'

I was thrilled, though. It was still dark outside but I called Murray right away and roused him out of his haiku retirement. Here is what he wrote.

> GREAT GREAT NEPHEW
> Welcome Baby Abe
> Abhorrible Dorabel is
> Happy now. Maybe.

We talked on the phone once a week, unless something came up.

He said, 'You called me yesterday. Are you getting forgetful?'

I said, 'My mind is razor sharp. But it occurred to me to ask you something. Angelica Bagehot once told me you adored me. Is that true?'

'Does that mean you'll move to Florida?' he said.

That was Murray. Always answers a question with another question. Well, two can play that game.

I said, 'Did you get diapers yet for the parakeet?'

'Parrot,' he said. 'No. When I start wearing them she'll start wearing them. That's the deal.'

SIXTY-THREE

We like to get the Early Bird Special, half past four to six, Monday through Friday. Fixed price soup, entree, dessert and choice of beverage. Weekends Sherman drives over and we try different places. Sophie's Place is OK. The salad bar, the bathrooms, everything's on the level and the parking lot is at the rear. I can drop those two old fools out front and then proceed to park without Sherman Ulysses waving his arms, giving me directions.

Murray said, 'Why don't you just drive over his foot.'

I said, 'Get thee behind me, Satan.'

Murray asked the girl if she was Sophie.

'Hunh?' she said.

'Poppy's would be a good name for an eatery,' he remarked.

'Or an opium den,' Sherman said.

'I'd like to have had something named after me,' Murray said. 'I guess it's too late now.'

I said, 'Such as? A mall?'

'Probably not a whole mall,' he said. 'Maybe a medium size shopping opportunity with a food court. I think I swallowed a fish bone.'

'Suck on a lemon,' Sherman said. 'That'll move it.'

They were out of lemons.

I said, 'Then bring him the key lime pie. Limes are nearly the same as lemons.' I'd warned him not to have the seafood bake. I'd told him to order the eggplant roulade.

Sherman said, 'I'd like to be a medical center. The Sherman Grace Medical Center.'

Murray said, 'I don't want key lime pie. The fish bone's cured so I'll get the ice cream medley. I think I'd rather be a causeway. The Murray Jacoby Causeway.'

I said, 'Cousin Addie Minkel got war medals and they couldn't even get around to naming a scenic picnic venue for her.'

Murray said, 'Or, The Murray Jacoby Wildlife Refuge. That'd be fine. I need another glass of milk.'

Sherman said, 'I don't know how you can drink that stuff. Medical research shows that many human beings lack the enzyme for digesting cows' milk. So the stock I told you to buy and you ignored me? I bought it. And it went up. Still going up as a matter of fact. Aunt Poppy, loan me your specs. I'm going to read the contraindications on your medication.'

I said, 'Well, of course, my name is already known.'

Murray said, 'I'll bet Sophie here never heard of you. Pass me your serviette. I'm going to take some of this foliage home for Grizel. May as well. We've paid for it. So what happens to the milk?'

'Turns to rubber,' Sherman said, 'and just lies there, giving you gas pains for the rest of your life.'

'Rubbish,' Murray said. 'Now pipe down while I read you my latest haiku. And don't tell me you can't understand it.'

Sherman never got the hang of haiku.

'QUESTION,' Murray began,

> Jew suppose we'd still
> Be wandering if we hadn't
> Found Daytona Beach?

'No. Didn't understand it,' Sherman said. 'Poppy, have you been experiencing dizziness, breathlessness or muscular cramps? If so, you should consult your physician immediately.'

If you loved *The Unfortunates,* why don't you try . . .

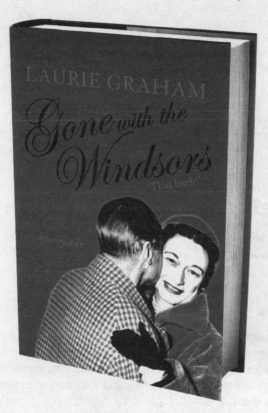

Out in hardback this July for only £9.99!

Get closer to the authors you love

Which authors are you passionate about? And how would you like to be kept up to date with their latest releases before they're even out? Author Tracker is a unique service that sends you exclusive news, previews and offers on forthcoming and previous titles from your favourite authors.

Register for Author Tracker today